The Royal Mob

Theresa Sherman

PublishAmerica
Baltimore

ISBN: 1-60441-774-9
PUBLISHED BY PUBLISHAMERICA, LLLP
www.publishamerica.com
Baltimore

Printed in the United States of America

To my dear parents and wonderful family

ACKNOWLEDGMENTS

The letter from Prince Louis Battenberg to his parents on p. 164 and 165 quoted from: *Louis and Victoria* by Richard Hough, Hutchinson & Co (Publishers) Ltd., (London: 1974), p.122.

Letter from Victoria to her lady-in-waiting Nona Kerr on (ms) p.537 quoted from: *Ibid.* p.327.

I am grateful to Lord Brabourne and the Broadlands Archives for permitting me to read and quote from documents there. Dr. Christopher Woolgar and his staff at the Hartley Library Archive & Special Collection, Southampton University, were unfailingly courteous and helpful.

LIST OF CHARACTERS AND THEIR RELATIONSHIP TO:
Princess Victoria, Princess Louis of Battenberg, the Marchioness of Milford Haven

Albert, Prince Consort. ("Grandpapa"). Married to Queen Victoria (QV). **Victoria's** maternal grandfather.

Albert Victor, Prince of Great Britain and Ireland, Duke of Clarence and Avondale. ("Cousin Eddy"). Oldest son of "Uncle Bertie" and "Aunt Alix", brother of Maudie, Toria, and Louise, **Victoria's** first cousin.

Alexander II, Tsar of Russia. ("Uncle Alexander"). Married to "Aunt Marie" who was **Victoria's** paternal aunt and Ella's father-in-law.

Alexander III, Tsar of Russia. ("Cousin Sasha"). Married to Dagmar who took the name Marie. **Victoria's** first cousin once removed and Alix's father-in-law.

Alexander, Prince of Hesse and by Rhine. ("Uncle Alexander"). Married to "Aunt Julie", father of Louis, "Sandro", "Liko", "Franzjos" and Marie. **Victoria's** Uncle and father-in-law.

Alexander, Prince of Battenberg. ("Sandro"). Prince of Bulgaria, Louis' brother, and **Victoria's** brother-in-law.

Alexandra, Queen of Great Britain and Ireland, Empress of India. ("Aunt Alix"). Married to "Uncle Bertie", who was **Victoria's** maternal uncle.

Alexandra, Tsarina of Russia. ("Alicky, Alix"). Wife of "Cousin Nicky", **Victoria's** sister.

Alfred, Prince of Great Britain and Ireland. ("Uncle Affie"). Duke of Edinburgh, who was married to "Aunt Marie" and **Victoria's** maternal uncle.

Alexis, Tsarevich of Russia. Son of "Alix" and "Nicky". Brother of Olga, Tatiana, Marie and Anastasia, **Victoria's** nephew and nieces.

Alice, Princess of Great Britain and Ireland, Grand Duchess of Hesse and by Rhine. ("Mama"). Daughter of QV. **Victoria's** mother.

Alice, Princess of Battenberg, Princess of Greece and Denmark. Daughter of **Victoria** and Louis, wife of Prince Andrew of Greece and mother of Prince Philip, Duke of Edinburgh.

Andrew, Prince of Greece and Denmark. Son of King George I of Greece, and husband of Alice of Battenberg. **Victoria's** son-in-law.

Augusta Viktoria, Empress of Germany. Princess of Schleswig-Holstein-Sonderburg-Augustenburg. Wife of "Cousin Willy". **Victoria's** first cousin and Irène's sister-in-law.

Beatrice, Princess of Great Britain and Ireland. ("Auntie"). Youngest daughter of QV, married to Prince Henry ("Liko") of Battenberg. **Victoria's** maternal Aunt and sister-in-law.

Charles, Prince of Hesse and by Rhine. Married to Princess Elisabeth of Hesse and by Rhine. **Victoria's** paternal grandfather.

Constantine I, King of Greece. Son of George I, King of Greece, brother of **Victoria's** son-in-law, Andrew, husband of **Victoria's** first cousin Sophie of Prussia.

Dimitri, Grand Duke of Russia. Son of Grand Duke Paul Alexandrovich, and ward of Ella and Serge.

Edward VII, King of Great Britain and Ireland, Emperor of India. ("Uncle Bertie"). Married to "Aunt Alix". First son of QV, and **Victoria's** maternal Uncle.

Elisabeth, Princess of Hesse and by Rhine. Married to Prince Charles of Hesse and by Rhine, **Victoria's** paternal grandmother.

Elisabeth, Princess of Hesse and by Rhine. ("Ella"). Married to Grand Duke Serge of Russia, younger brother of "Cousin Sasha". **Victoria's** sister.

Ernst Ludwig, Grand Duke of Hesse and by Rhine. ("Ernie"). Married to Princess Victoria Melita of Edinburgh ("Ducky"), then to Eleonore of Solms-Hohensolm-Lich ("Onor"). **Victoria's** brother.

Frederick William, Emperor of Germany ("Uncle Fritz"). Married to "Aunt Vicky", Uncle to **Victoria** and father-in-law to Irène.

George V, King of Great Britain and Ireland, Emperor of India. ("Cousin George"). Married to Victoria Mary of Teck ("May"). **Victoria's** first cousin.

George I, King of Greece. Father of Andrew of Greece, and father-in-law of Alice of Battenberg, **Victoria's** daughter.

George, Prince of Battenberg, later Second Marquess of Milford Haven. ("Georgie"). Eldest son of Louis and **Victoria.**

Heinrich, Prince of Prussia. ("Henry"). Second son of Empress Victoria of Prussia ("Aunt Vicky"), brother of "Cousin Willy", **Victoria's** brother-in-law and husband of Irène.

Helena, Princess of England. Daughter of QV, mother of "Thora", "Marie Louise", and **Victoria's** maternal Aunt.

Henry, Prince of Battenberg. ("Liko"). Married to Beatrice ("Auntie"), Princess of Great Britain and Ireland. Brother of Louis, **Victoria's** cousin and brother-in-law.

Irène, Princess of Hesse and by Rhine. Married to Prince Heinrich of Prussia, **Victoria's** sister.

Julia, Countess von Hauke, and later Princess of Battenberg. ("Aunt Julie"). Mother of Louis, Prince of Battenberg, **Victoria's** Aunt and mother-in-law.

Leopold, Prince of Great Britain and Ireland, Duke of Albany. ("Uncle Leopold"). Son of QV, **Victoria's** maternal Uncle.

Louis, Prince of Battenberg, later First Marquess of Milford Haven. Son of "Uncle Alexander" and "Aunt Julie". Brother of "Sandro", "Liko", "Franzjos" and Marie. **Victoria's** husband and cousin.

Louis, Prince of Battenberg, later Lord Mountbatten of Burma. ("Dickie"). Louis and **Victoria's** son.

Louise, Princess of Battenberg, later Lady Louise Mountbatten and then Queen of Sweden. Second daughter of Louis and **Victoria**.

Louise, Princess of Great Britain and Ireland, Marchioness of Lorne, Duchess of Argyll. ("Aunt Louise"). Married to the Marquess of Lorne, later the Duke of Argyll, QV's daughter and **Victoria's** maternal Aunt.

Ludwig IV, Grand Duke of Hesse and by Rhine. ("Papa"). Husband of Alice, Princess of England, and **Victoria's** father.

Marie, Princess of Battenberg. Married to Gustav of Erbach-Schönberg, sister of Prince Louis of Battenberg, **Victoria's** sister-in-law and cousin.

Marie, Queen of Romania. ("Missy"), daughter of "Uncle Affie" and "Aunt Marie" of Edinburgh. **Victoria's** first cousin.

Marie, Princess of Great Britain and Ireland, Grand Duchess of Russia. ("Aunt Marie"). Married to "Uncle Affie", **Victoria's** maternal Aunt.

Marie, Tsarina of Russia. ("Aunt Marie"). Born a Princess of Hesse and by Rhine, married to "Uncle Sasha" and **Victoria's** great-aunt and Ella**'s** mother-in-law.

Marie, Tsarina of Russia. ("Cousin Minnie"). Princess of Denmark. Originally Dagmar, Princess of Denmark, was the sister of Queen Alexandra ("Aunt Alix") of England and mother of Tsar Nicholas II.

Marie, Grand Duchess of Russia. Daughter of Grand Duke Paul Alexandrovich, and ward of Ella and Serge.

Marie Louise of Schleswig-Holstein, Princess Aribert of Anhalt. Daughter of Princess Helena and **Victoria's** cousin.

Nicholas II, Tsar of Russia. ("Cousin Nicky"). Son of "Cousin Sasha", **Victoria's** cousin married to Alix.

Serge, Grand Duke of Russia. ("Cousin Serge"). Son of "Uncle Sasha" and "Aunt Marie or Minnie", husband of Ella and **Victoria's** brother-in-law.

Victoria, Queen of Great Britain and Ireland, Empress of India. (QV) ("Grandmama"). **Victoria's** maternal grandmother.

Victoria, Empress of Germany. ("Aunt Vicky"). QV's daughter. **Victoria's** aunt and Irène's mother-in-law.

Victoria Melita, Princess of England. ("Ducky"). Grand Duchess of Hesse and by Rhine, later Grand Duchess of Russia. Married first to "Ernie", then to Grand Duke Kyrill of Russia, her first cousin. **Victoria's** first cousin.

Victoria, Princess of Hesse and by Rhine, later Princess Louis Battenberg, Marchioness of Milford Haven and finally Dowager Marchioness. Married to Prince Louis of Battenberg, **main character.**

Wilhelm II, Emperor of Germany. ("Cousin Willy"). Son of "Aunt Vicky", grandson of QV. **Victoria's** first cousin.

PROLOGUE

Kensington Palace, September 1947

The afternoon fire burns low.

Pye always laughs at me, but I've needed the warmth, even in August...these palaces can be terribly drafty, and my circulation has always been dreadful.

"Here's the afternoon post, Your Highness."

Pye, my stalwart lady's maid of fifty years, makes no pretense of not having perused the contents of the tray before setting it down. There are several envelopes in the tray...perhaps letters from Dickie and Edwina in India, or Alice from Athens.

Underneath the pile is a large, thick, creamy vellum envelope. The other pieces are forgotten as I take the large one in my hand. Turning it 'round and 'round, I relish the luxurious feel of the paper with my fingertips and my heart beats just a little bit faster. The pleasure I receive from this vellum envelope is almost indecent. Oh, I've received plenty of heavy vellum envelopes with engraved announcements of births, marriages, balls, parties, and even naval promotions, but, this one is different...special. This is something that will validate Louis', and indeed, his entire family's lifetime quest for acceptance. This would have had Willy and Sasha on their ears. I smile a little, my grin of pleasure, tinged with mischief, then turning wistful. I profoundly wish that Louis could be here.

Slowly and painfully, I rise from my chair, and walk out of my sitting room. Pye protests as I close the door of my bedroom.

"Aren't you going to open it?" she calls after the shut door.

I go over to my jewelry case, turning on a small lamp at my bedside. My daughter Louise says that I own more old-fashioned jewelry than all the antique shops in London. It's even funnier when you consider the jewelry I lost in St. Petersburg. Ah, well, I don't care. I love each of my Mama's jewels and all the fine old settings that Grandmama and Louis gave me. There's nothing to compare to them today, even considering what I lost in Russia.... I open up my secret compartment and take out the pearl. I smile, as I always have and my heart beats almost painfully. The pearl glows pink and incandescent—I almost imagine that in its luminescence, it lights up the room.

I roll it between my fingers for a moment—just enjoying the feel of it on my skin. I gently replace the pearl, wondering how many more times I will look at it. I close the box carefully, and go back into the sitting room, really needing the warmth of the fire; I am already feeling very stiff. Pye is standing, her arms akimbo, clucking at me.

"I'm opening it," I say, querulously.

Carefully, my trembling fingers slit the seal. The envelope is lined with heavy, dark paper. I lean over and turn on the lamp...the late afternoon is grey. I take a ragged breath and remove the stiff card.

It is here...the invitation I'd been waiting for...for so many years—

"The Lord Chamberlain..."

Yes, yes, yes...

"...is commanded by Their Majesties..."

Blah, blah...

"...the Ceremony of the Marriage of...The Princess Elizabeth..."

Ah...

"Lieutenant Philip Mountbatten, Royal Navy...."

My grandson....

PART I

CHAPTER ONE
1868-1884

I
Heiligenberg, 1868

I have been often told I talked too much. Even Grandmama, who always gave me such excellent counsel, felt I was too garrulous and, in fact, called me a gasbag— though it was lovingly said. That is why to say that I was struck dumb the first time I saw him in his naval uniform, may be a bit of an exaggeration. However, at five, I was, at least, momentarily tongue-tied.

Louis had joined the Royal Navy two years before at the age of twelve. Since it was necessary that he have a profession, his family wanted him to join the Austrian army, and his Aunt thought it would be a wonderful idea if he joined the Russian military. However, though this caused conflict with both sides later on, Louis preferred

England and the Royal Navy. He was strongly influenced in this decision by my Uncle Affie, Alfred, Duke of Edinburgh, and my Mama, Alice, Princess of Hesse and by Rhine.

We were all at the Heiligenberg for one of our annual summer get-together. Heiligenberg was Uncle Alexander and Aunt Julie of Battenberg's summer palace. It was a beautiful idyllic place, rich with courtyards in which to play and woodlands in which to stroll. There was Aunt Marie, Empress of Russia, and Uncle Alexander's sister, who came with her boys, we, Hesses, and, naturally, the Battenberg cousins.

My sisters and I were called the Three Graces. I suppose that meant that we were beauties. I couldn't see it, not that I cared much at five...but Ella—even at that young age, I could see that my sister Ella was a vision. Ella's name of Elisabeth was uncommon in a family full of Victoria's and Albert's. She'd been named for Papa's Mama. I cannot write as well as Cousin Missy, Queen Marie of Romania, who described her as one of the most exquisite creatures she had ever beheld. Missy wrote that she had wanted to dip her pen in rich colors to describe her, for words never could.

But my Ella, the sister nearest to me in age, was as sweet and kind, as she was beautiful. She cared about everyone, from the lowliest servant, to the animals in the barn, and was even careful of the feelings of our bombastic Cousin Willy, Crown Prince of Prussia. I could never understand that any more than I could understand her attraction to Cousin Serge of Russia, but these things came much later.

For now, it was I, Victoria (yes, common, everyday Victoria), my dearest Ella, about four years old at the time, and the baby, Irène—sweet, amiable Irène, named for the Greek word for peace because she had been born around the conclusion of the Austro-Prussian War. We sisters were lodged in the back house of the Heiligenberg with the rest of the young cousins, and managed to drive our nannies and various minders utterly insane with games of hide and go seek, blind man's bluff, and other pursuits. Most of the time, however, Ella followed eleven-year-old Serge around like a puppy, and I fought with my Cousin Liko, Louis' little brother, Henry of Battenberg, who was five years older than I.

That day, the day I was nearly struck dumb by the splendor of Louis, I had managed to elude my nanny and was outside looking for a suitable tree to climb.

Liko trotted over and shouted, "Victoria, come and look! Louis's in uniform."

"Why should I want to look at him?" I asked haughtily. "I've seen him before."

Liko shrugged.

"I just thought you would. He's quite splendid. I'm going to look just like that when I grow up," he declared and thumped his chest proudly.

Considering his love for uniforms in later years, I

should have seen that as a prediction. At that time, however, I was completely unimpressed with male posturing. I was more interested in the tree I had spotted on the top of a small grassy mound, and ran to it. Disregarding my white dress with its sky-blue satin sash, I easily gained the lowest branch and took a seat, swinging my white-stockinged legs. I noticed a grass stain on my knee and shrugged fatalistically—Mama would be angry that I'd got them dirty so soon.

Liko was following me up the mound and I could see a figure emerging from the house. I hoped it wasn't Orchie, the nanny, Mrs. Mary Anne Orchard. She'd tell me to get down and I had no intention of doing so.

"Louis is coming now to show us, and you look stupid sitting up there."

"Looking stupid is better than being stupid, you beast," I replied, smugly, I could always get the better of Liko in a verbal duel.

"Shut up," he whined.

"You shut up," I answered, charmingly, as he began to clamber up to the branch. "There's no room, you can't come up here."

"Yes, I can," he replied, and tried to get next to me on the branch. We began tussling, and I made the fatal error of using two hands to push him off. Instead, I was the one who tumbled unceremoniously to the ground. It was a wonder I didn't break my neck, but my concern was for the new rip in my dress. Orchie and Mama were going to roast me alive.

24

I was busy contemplating my unhappy fate, punctuated by Liko's crows of triumph, and trying to brush the dirt off my frock, when a low voice said, "Cousin Victoria, what are you doing on the ground?"

I looked up and was momentarily robbed of speech. Louis, in his naval cadet's uniform, was a sight to behold. He was tall, slim, though, as yet, no naval style beard, but terribly elegant, as he would always be—while I was, as I would always be...disheveled, untidy....

"He pushed me."

Louis smiled and held out his hand.

"Orchie will have something to say about that," he grinned, eyeing the rip.

"He pushed me," I repeated, holding back tears.

"So he did," his voice gentle as he looked up at his younger brother.

"Liko," he called, "Come down, we have a lady in distress."

"That donkey...?"

I began scrambling up, ignoring the gentlemanly hand.

"I'll show him, he can't push me around..."

I tried to climb up the tree again, but, without access to the lower branch that Liko now occupied, I couldn't. Tears of frustration rolled down my cheeks.

"Victoria," a gentle adult voice broke through the fracas...firm, resolute, and above all, quiet. "Victoria, come here at once."

I continued the struggle, but Louis grabbed me, once again, gently, by the scruff of my dress. I resisted briefly then stood still, head hanging, defeated.

"Here, Orchie, is your little offender." Louis took me by the shoulders and navigated me over to where Orchie was waiting. She looked stern and unhappy.

"Thank you, Prince Louis," she said graciously, and to me, "what have you done to your dress?"

She took my hand and began to cart me off.

"See you later," Louis murmured to my retreating figure.

Covered with humiliation, I said nothing, nor did I look back. He was so grown up, and I such a baby. It was strange for me, even then, to feel humiliated about anything. I had the kind of spirit that charged in and waited for the consequences to fall where they may. Later, I was more intelligent about rushing to action, but then, at five, I was fearless and heedless.

"I don't know what your Mama will say. What kind of hoydenish behavior is this, miss?"

"Oh, Orchie," I began, recovering my considerable verbal abilities. "I was only climbing a tree. If that stupid Liko hadn't pushed me off…"

"It looked a very equal struggle to me."

"Hmm, if it looked the least equal, it was because he cheated."

I saw a peep of a smile as she led me into the house, up the stairs to our bedrooms on the second floor. As usual,

I was sharing with Irène and Ella. They, little angels, were playing with Marie of Battenberg's old dollhouse. Marie, being all of sixteen, was no longer interested in such things.

"Let's get you changed, and if this dress doesn't survive, your Mama will have to be told."

I wrapped my arms about her and gave her a big, wet kiss. She wasn't going to tell Mama. I stood happily while she pulled the dress off. Now, my thoughts were free to concentrate on Louis.

I can't say that it was love at first sight that day, though seeds of confusing feelings began to foment. Rather, it was envy, as I thought it would be very fine idea to run away and join the English Navy. I could get into all the scrapes I wanted, and never worry about getting my clothes dirty or torn.

I wriggled into another white dress, hardly hearing Orchie's admonitions, instead thinking how much fun it was to come to the Heiligenberg and have Mama with us. She was usually so busy that other than saying good morning or good evening, we never saw much of her. I realized later on, that we saw far more of her than our cousins saw of their parents. In fact, she and Papa had actually taken quite an interest in our upbringing—far more than was usual for aristocratic parents. At the time, however, like any child, I wanted all my Mama's attention and, naturally, I didn't get it.

She was here now, however, with our aunts, uncles,

and cousins, and having a good time. She looked happy, which, in itself, was unusual because Mama rarely looked happy. I had always thought it was because I was not a good girl. I was always getting into scrapes, climbing roofs and trees, tearing my clothes, and talking too much.

I asked Orchie one day, while she was combing my hair.

"Your Mama has a lot on her mind, and works very hard."

I thought about this for a few moments.

"But, she is a princess, Orchie. She doesn't need to work hard. She has servants to do all the work for her." I couldn't understand why no one else thought of that.

"Listen, miss," Orchie tugged at my unruly braids, "it's true that princesses don't have to cook and clean, however, many feel very strongly about working hard to improve the countries in which they live. Your mother does a great deal of work organizing care for sick people, and helping the lot of the deserving poor...she's what the Hessians call a true *Landsmütter*."

That had me just about nodding off. She was beginning to sound like our Pastor Bender and church always had me squirming. The first part, however, set me thinking. Princesses did work. It was a concept I had never considered.

Orchie saw that I wasn't listening, and turned me around to face her.

"Another reason she might be sad is that she misses

your Grandpapa. The ceremony of marriage between your Mama and Papa was a very sad affair. Your Grandpapa Albert had died six months before, and your Grandmama Victoria wore black and cried throughout the service. People there said it was more like a funeral than a wedding," she trailed off, tsk-tsking about what a shame it was for a young girl to be married in such an atmosphere.

That did, however, explain much to me. How could anyone be happy if people had been crying buckets throughout their marriage ceremony? With great satisfaction that I understood one of the mysteries of life, I was back in the present getting my hair combed, yet again. I thought about how much I would like to cut it all off and join the navy like Cousin Louis.

"There," Orchie said. It was the best she could do, as she squinted at me from all angles. I didn't care. I just wanted to be on the move again.

"Come play with us, Victoria." Ella came over clutching her doll. I remember many years later reading that someone had written that she was the most beautiful child they had ever looked upon. This, I could not know then, but I sensed, even in my childlike ignorance, that there was some special quality to her, something like a Christmas angel.

Ella had many times, even as a child expressed the desire to be a nun. We didn't pay much attention to such talk—after all, I had wanted to be a teacher, and naturally that was thought to be absurd enough. Certainly in Ella's case, a princess, and such an incredibly beautiful one, had no business choosing the chaste life. No—Ella would marry and have a great many children. I didn't understand it then, and I wouldn't always remember, though, much later it was to haunt me. Usually, however, as children, Ella and I fought like any sisters close in age.

I went to play with my sisters, though dolls usually bored me. I decided Orchie needed a break from my shenanigans.

That afternoon, we children took an excursion into the little village of Jugenheim. The village lay just below the Schloss and was a favorite place. This was our activity while the adults took their siestas. I thought it was very comical that they ate luncheon in full evening dress and was always going to the window to make sure it was still daytime. Poor things, they had so many courses, no wonder they were all tired out.

The party consisted of my sisters and me, with Serge and Paul of Russia. Our young hosts were Louis, Sandro, another of Louis' younger brothers, Liko, and Franzjos, a year older than I, who was the youngest of the Battenberg clan. I thought it was a pretty rotten deal that there were no other girls besides my sisters and me.

The nannies took the other carriage, relying on the older boys to watch us. Since I was in awe of Louis and Ella would have jumped off a cliff for Serge, we were a fairly orderly group.

We loved to look in the tiny shops and have our nannies buy us wonderful pastries called *schneeballen,* or in English, snowballs. These were strips of noodle-like dough that were formed into a ball, deep fried, and sprinkled with lots of powdered sugar—surely food for the gods.

That day as we walked down the narrow cobbled streets of the town, I especially remember Louis saying, "Come, Victoria, I've still some money from my navy pay, I'll buy you a *schneeball.*"

It was nice of him, I suppose, but since I'd never had to buy anything on my own, I wasn't that impressed.

We went into Frau Morgenstern's bakery for the pastries. Frau Morgenstern was a jolly and robust woman with a red face and a loud booming voice, just the sort of woman you'd expect to run a bakery. She, like most of the shopkeepers in the village, knew my cousins and me. We were frequent visitors over the summer, and always in town to buys sweets. I remembered specially a time when Frau Morgenstern showed me how to make *schneeballen.* It was an epoch in my small life.

Louis bought this delicious treat for everyone including our nannies and nursery maids. That, I decided was exceedingly generous of him and looked at him quite admiringly, as I chomped on my *schneeball.* I must have been quite a sight with powered sugar all over my face, hands, and dress. Poor Orchie, once again, she would be required to admonish me.

I slipped my sticky hand in Louis' and looked up at him. I had to reward him for his generosity and tried to think of something suitable. As we left the shop, and distributed the treats to the others, I thought of something.

"I have a secret," I began, in a dark, confiding tone.

To his everlasting credit, Louis manfully suppressed a smile at the thought of my childish confidences.

"Really," he replied, seriously. "Perhaps we should walk over to the square so that the others won't hear."

I nodded my agreement, and off we went just a few steps away. Like most German villages, Jugenheim had a square with a splashing fountain. This fountain was a little odd, even to a small child like me. I never liked the statue of the poor martyred saint, I forget which one, out of whose wounds, sprang the waters of the fountain. It was something frightening and grotesque.

At any rate, Louis and I sat down on the edge of the pool and finished our pastries. When he was finished, Louis put his hands in the water, to wash them and I followed suit, managing, of course, to get myself and my dress wet.

"Now, Victoria, for your secret," he urged, his deep brown eyes looking at me with admirable concentration.

"Well, I happen to know..." I paused, looking around, and lowering my voice, as I leaned forward, "that Mama is going to have a visit from the stork."

That he didn't burst out laughing, he told me much later on, was just a sign of the tremendous self-control he was beginning to learn in the Royal Navy.

"You don't say," he began quietly, "and how do you know this?"

"Well," I said, delighted to impart such juicy news. "I asked Orchie why Mama was getting so fat, and she said that she was expecting a visit from the stork, and I know what that means, too."

"You do?" he replied, maintaining his serious demeanor.

"Yes, of course, I do. It means the stork is going to bring me another brother or sister. However, I happen to know that it will be a brother."

"And, how do you know that?"

"Because Orchie said a boy was what Mama wished for, so naturally..."

"Yes, naturally."

"However, he won't be born in the Tapestry Room in Windsor."

"He won't?" He looked slightly puzzled at this turn in the conversation.

"No," I replied in triumph. "I was, though...in the Tapestry Room, in the Lancaster Tower, at Windsor Castle," I recited proudly. I was the only one of my sisters that had actually been born in England.

"So, you are an English girl?"

"Well, I'm half-and-half, aren't I," I replied proudly. I liked, even then, anything that connected me intimately with Grandmama.

"Certainly."

So, although Mama was six months pregnant at the time, I thought that I was the only one who had noticed. Typical of the insularity of children, I suppose.

That night, as we did every night at Heiligenberg, we children fell asleep to the music of the dance orchestra below. I imagined my Mama, looking beautiful in one of her exquisite ball gowns, and Papa, handsome in his uniform, waltzing away those warm summer nights. I dreamed about the times when I would also be dancing. That night, Louis was the partner in my waltzing dream. He took up residence there, and never seemed to leave.

Later that year, my little brother Ernst Ludwig, whom we called Ernie, was born, not, as I had told Louis, at Windsor, but at the New Palace at Darmstadt. I remembered being disgusted that he was in precedence before me, as the heredity Prince of Hesse, but, as time went on, he listened as attentively and slavishly to my orders as the rest of the children.

II
Windsor, 1871

Sometimes I think I am a time traveler. I close my eyes to remember something, and by some mysterious alchemy, like the traveler in Mr. Wells' story, I'm there. I lose myself in the sounds, feelings and sights of eighty years ago, within, metaphorically, the blink of an eye.

The Franco-Prussian war had robbed my Papa of

sovereignty over his little Grand Duchy. From then, until the end of the Great War, we were just another part of the German Empire with two measly votes in the Imperial Council. It had, altogether, been a difficult year for us. Not only had my mother worn herself out nursing, but as new members of the German Empire, we were required to pay indemnities to that Empire. Not yet being the Grand Duke and having completed the building of a New Palace in Darmstadt with my mother's dowry, we were, at least relatively speaking, poor. Therefore, a long visit to England, living under my Grandmama's largesse was not only welcome, but necessary.

I was, of course, blissfully ignorant of all of this, while my Mama was gone during that awful time during the summer of 1870. She worked hard at nursing—being a devoted advocate of Florence Nightingale's *Notes on Nursing*, and a personal friend of that worthy lady. Mama, herself, went into the hospitals, supervised the cleaning and disinfecting of each ward. She cared for wounded soldiers, and came home exhausted every night. To make matters worse, my Papa was away nearly the entire time, fighting on the side of Prussia. There was constant worry about his well being and safety. Princesses surely did do work.

Again, during this inopportune time, Mama was expecting another visit from the stork—or so I persisted in thinking of it at the time. I always wondered about the relationship between my Mama and Papa. She struck me as the tireless intellectual, always questioning the world around her, to the extent that she even thought that Royalty was an anachronism. She was a progressive liberal who thought continually of the best way to help people without that help resulting in the loss of their dignity.

She read voraciously, something I inherited from her; she listened to and played music—even extending to playing duets with the composer Johannes Brahms; she loved the theater, opera and so many other pursuits. Yet, she had a spiritual side that was sometimes melancholy— I think that my sister Ella and certainly, Alix inherited this from her. My Papa, however, sweet and loving man that he was—well—I can't honestly claim that he was a shining star of brilliance.

They seemed to have a loving partnership and I believe that Mama truly missed him when they had to be parted. However, I had felt for a long time that they were indeed a mismatch.

That fall, Frittie was born. Dear precious little boy, who, by the time we joined Grandmama in England, was beginning to show ominous signs of bruises. Mama had this new sorrow to add to all her others—just like her dear brother Leopold, she would murmur around the palace— just like poor Leopold....

She naturally thought of Uncle Leopold. He was, of all the uncles and aunts (and there were many), our favorite, and was a very close friend of my Papa's. Cursed as he was with hemophilia, he, nevertheless, was determined to live as normal a life as possible, even though Grandmama was so determined otherwise. He was our most intellectual and artistic uncle, and Mama and he had many a lively discussion on those topics. He lived until adulthood, and even married, producing two children. Unfortunately, he slipped on the stairs while on holiday in France, and did not recover from the incident.

There was, however, nothing ominous about our visit to Grandmama at Balmoral and Windsor, the following year. It had been a marvelous summer. Traditionally, my Grandmama spent much of her summer at Balmoral so when we came over from Hesse we made our first destination that Scottish Castle. I loved Balmoral, though I think I was one of the few that did. It was always fashionable to wince at the dullness of the place, the awfulness of the tartan wallpaper with thistle designs, and the inedible, traditional Scottish fare.

Never mind the naysayers, though, we always had a wonderful time.

My sisters and I played with our Wales cousins, Eddy, Georgie, and Louise, the first of Aunt Alix's girls. We would tramp about the misty, grey, countryside playing games, singing, and generally eluding adult supervision. We usually ended up in the small village near the castle to buy sweets. Like Jugenheim, everyone in the village knew us and was always so nice to us.

Poor Eddy was the leader of the children in our walks.

He never had much to say, and was leader only by virtue of his seniority; there wasn't the least bit of forcefulness or even personality in his character. I never said it out loud, not even to my sisters, but I frankly thought there was something essentially wrong with his brain. How could someone so slow and stupid be the heir presumptive to the British throne?

I didn't worry about that too much, after all, my cousin Willy, a terrible bully, was heir presumptive to the German throne, and everyone thought that was normal. Ella and I agreed, however, that playing with Georgie and Eddy wasn't nearly as much fun as being with Louis and Serge. I had never considered Serge fun, but I did agree with the sentiment.

In the fall, instead of going back to Darmstadt, we went to Windsor. I believe that Grandmama missed my mother and her Hessian grandchildren, and this year seemed to be one that we spent almost entirely with her. Mama told me that she and Grandmama had a slight falling-out after she had married. Grandmama had expected Mama and Papa, since they weren't yet ruling the Duchy, to spend most of their time in England and do the drawing rooms and other functions that Grandmama refused to do because of her perpetual mourning.

When my Mama refused to spend nearly all her time in England, Grandmama became angry and thought of her as undutiful and disloyal. However, when Uncle Bertie married Aunt Alix, the duty of drawing rooms fell to her, and Grandmama's feelings of resentment dissipated somewhat. After that, they slowly began to retrace some of their old and close relationship.

While at Windsor, however, several calamities, in the form of serious illnesses, occurred. We had lingered quite a while in England and by November, we were at Buckingham Palace having tea with Grandmama, playing with the Wales's and having our lessons. That month all of us, the Wales's and the Hesse children, came down with whooping cough and had to stay at Buckingham Palace, while the rest of the party moved on to Sandringham. More important, my Uncle Bertie of Wales came down with a nearly fatal case of typhoid. Since Uncle Bertie was my mother's favorite brother, there was absolutely no way that she could or would leave during such a critical time.

Mama knew about typhoid since she had been Grandpapa's principal nurse during his fatal bout with the relentless disease. She left us at Buckingham Palace and joined Aunt Alix, who was wringing her hands nearly worried to death about the whole thing. Sick as we were, I remember that we had a good time playing with Mama's and all the aunts and uncles' toys at the nurseries. It was particularly ironic that one of our favorite toys was a large stuffed lion, meant to represent the British Empire, who, when you cranked his tail, would swallow a Russian soldier whole. Perhaps we should have all taken that as a warning. Certainly, Grandmama would have thought so.

Naturally, even when we got over the cough, it was

decided that we children should not join Mama and Papa at Sandringham. It was considered prudent that the Queen, and her youngest daughter, my Auntie Beatrice, who was only six years older than I, stay away from the residence as well.

We did, however, remove to Windsor when we were all feeling better. That left my Aunt, my sisters and me, with Ernie and baby Frittie, in the care of Grandmama. I always loved being with Grandmama. When I was very little I thought of her as a being quite apart from the rest of the human race. She had auras and powers that we mere mortals could never understand. She could also inspire loyalty, love and obedience that the rest of us could only aspire to, but never attain.

Our governess, Madgie, Miss Margaret Hardcastle Jackson, didn't tax us too much with lessons when we were ill, but she did her best to instruct us about our deportment in the presence of the Queen. I don't suppose we learned too badly, because the Queen did not complain to my parents, except at certain times, about the noise.

I remember vividly the times when Ella, Irène and I were combed, cleaned and dressed within an inch of our lives in white lawn dresses with innumerable flounces, eyelet edging, and satin sashes, and marched over to the Queen's apartments in, appropriately enough, the Queen's tower. We didn't normally take any meals or teas with the Queen, being too young, so these little teas were all quite momentous.

When we were ready and inspected by Madgie, she, and several of our nurses, would take us to the Queen's apartments. As we came ever closer, the instructions, the scoldings and the admonishments would come in more and more hushed tones. The carpets seemed thicker, so that our heels made not a sound as we trod closer and closer to the rooms.

Madgie would knock, ever so discretely, while I would fidget and Irène would ask a question in a normal tone and would be frantically shushed. The door would open and in, quietly and reverently, we would go. Once we entered Grandmama's drawing room, no further admonishments were necessary. Just being there was inspiration for good behavior. As we walked in slowly, we would quietly look about us, taking in all the decorations and photographs that Grandmama kept. Mostly, they were of Grandpapa—family groups and Grandpapa, Grandpapa in kilts, and Grandpapa with Grandmama gazing lovingly at him. These were all there, along with portraits and photos of innumerable cousins, aunts, uncles, and the like.

We were bid to sit down, which we did solemnly and would look upon Grandmama, who, as ever, was clothed in black silk. She must have been in her late forties or early fifties then, but she looked positively ancient to us.

The cakes and tea always had a very special taste in Grandmama's drawing room. She would talk mostly to Madgie, questioning her about our deportment, our health, and all that we had been doing and looking terribly sad when some transgression was reported. Sometimes, she would address a few remarks to us and we would answer slowly and carefully, as we had been taught. Then, I would notice a twinkle in her eye, and she would look at us and give a shy little laugh. Grandmama's smile, though a rarity was so sweet...especially since she must have been worried sick about Uncle Bertie. Her anxieties at that particular time were, no doubt, magnified by the fact that we were nearing the sacred date—December 14, the day Grandpapa died.

But nevertheless, Grandmama did smile, and it was then that I really loved her that I had a glimpse of the person under the plumpish figure in severe mourning clothes; the person of whom I would forever be reminded when I smelled the scent of orange blossoms.

It was ironic, or, as Grandmama would say, mysterious, that when we received word that Uncle Bertie was out of the wood, it was on that very date. My Mama and Aunt Alix had been nursing him tirelessly and he had finally passed the crises.

I didn't see much of Louis that year. I heard from Aunt Julie that he had been appointed Midshipmen and was sailing around on a ship called the *Royal Albert*. I was growing up in an eight-year-old sort of way and thought I was getting rather good-looking with my red-gold hair and blue eyes. Perhaps he wouldn't think I was such a baby next time he came home.

III
New Palace, Darmstadt 1878

When you're browsing through time and memory, you can't be as selective as you'd like. You're faced with the imps and demons of your life wherever you look. It's unfair, but your brain works that way—it refuses to skip the bad bits.

I was reading *Alice In Wonderland* to my brother and sisters one very cold and gloomy November evening. We were home in Darmstadt, and had done all our lessons, and had our supper, so Mama permitted us to spend some time in the drawing room with her and Papa. It was a treat and family time of which many others in our positions never took advantage.

I was just getting to the part about the Mad Hatter's tea party when I started to cough.

"You continue, Ella," I said between gasps. "My throat is getting quite sore."

"Come sit with me, darling," Mama said, her nursing instincts coming into action. She felt my head, and shook hers. "You're a little warm, Victoria, perhaps you ought to go to bed."

She gently took six year old Alicky off her lap, and I shook my head.

"Mama, may I listen to the story a bit longer?"

"All right, but then, right to bed," she said tenderly,

and put her arm around me as I rested my head on her shoulder.

As we continued to listen to Ella reading in her low, sweet voice, I looked about me. Two more additions had come since that harrowing winter at Grandmama's: Victoria Alix, whom we called Alicky, and dear little May, who was now about four and a half. We also had tragedy. Little Frittie had died of a hemorrhage after falling out of a window in Mama's bedroom. He'd been playing hide and seek with Ernie, and had run, arms outstretched, toward a window, that he thought was closed. It wasn't, poor lamb, and he tumbled out, falling on the concrete below. For a few moments, we had actually thought he would be all right, but, unbeknownst to us, he was hemorrhaging internally, and fiercely. He died that evening.

Mama, who was playing Chopin's Funeral March, during the morning game, never stopped blaming herself and became extremely morbid. It had a similar effect on little Ernie. I'll never forget what he said at the time, "Why can't we all die together? I don't want to die alone like Frittie."

I'm afraid that from then on, Ernie inherited not just a little of Mama's morbidity.

I sighed, hoarsely, and Mama looked at me sharply. I nestled into her arms, enjoying being her baby again for a few minutes.

We also had come into good fortune. My strange old

Uncle Hesse died, and Papa became the Grand Duke. Though it made Mama even busier than ever, there was no doubt that it made things a lot easier on our family.

I shivered; it was getting cold.

"That's it, Victoria, you're going to bed with a cup of hot milk and a hot water bottle."

I was beginning to feel positively dreadful and made very little protest as Mama and Orchie led me away to my room. That was the evening of November 5 and I never forgot it because it was the last peaceful time I spent with Mama.

I ran a high fever that night, and later, I was told that everyone else in the family, excepting Ella, came down with diphtheria. As I was the first down with it, I was the first to mend. Ella was sent away, and I helped Mama with Papa and the others, as best as a weak convalescent could. Grandmama sent her special physician, Sir William Jenner, and we had a whole host of nurses and doctors attending us—but that didn't save my poor little sister, May, who developed a membrane over her throat and went quickly.

The famous story goes that Mama, heartbroken at the death of May, eventually told Ernie, who had been asking incessantly about his little sister, that she had died, and put her arms around him for comfort, kissing his brow. The disease, insidious and contagious, struck her. She, being worn out from all the nursing and melancholy from all the tragedy, could not, or would not fight the illness.

She sank fast and died on the 14th of December. Dearest, sweetest, Mama—with so much to give to the people of her Grand Duchy and her family—was gone in an instant—and none of us would ever be the same.

Mysterious, Grandmama pondered.

CHAPTER TWO

I
New Palace, Darmstadt, 1878–80

I became, for all intents and purposes, the head of my family. That part wasn't difficult, as I had always thrived on being in charge and since I was always rather independent, this calamity nurtured that. It also helped that I was one of those people, unlike dear Grandmama, who refused to dwell on mourning. Naturally, I mourned for my Mama, and have missed her every day of my life however, I also believe that the constant mourning in which my Grandmama indulged was wrong. We were a young family, and we needed to get on with our lives.

When Mama died, Grandmama wrote all of us a terribly sweet letter expressing her own pain and sympathy.

"...think of me as your mama..." she had exhorted, and, indeed, commenced a correspondence with me that was full of mothering and excellent advice. This went on until a few months before her death, and hers were the most precious group of letters I have received.

Everyone was involved in the process of taking care of the poor orphaned Hesses. The funny thing was that Papa seemed to be included in the group of orphans. He was lost and unhappy without Mama. He wandered around the New Palace, and everywhere he looked, he was reminded of Mama. On the outside, the New Palace, which had been completed in 1866, was built in the Italian Renaissance style, but on the inside, it was pure bourgeois British. Mother loved the substantial wood furniture she had ordered from Maples in London, and the mauve chintz, which was later to become such a favorite of my sister Alicky's.

Papa seemed as confused and as baffled as my little brother Ernie and poor little Alicky. It was no wonder that he easily let me bully and lead—which was what I did best. The English aunts, uncles, and cousins, who could, also traveled here every summer to be with us, doing their share of mothering and pestering. I remember that Auntie Beatrice, Aunt Helena and Aunt Louise, came the most often, but that our favorite, Uncle Leopold, made the effort as often as he could, considering his health problems. And, when they weren't there at the New Palace or at our new summer place, Wolfsgarten, we were at Osborne or Balmoral or Windsor.

Louis was a lieutenant in the navy by then, but we

seldom saw him, since he was appointed from one ship to another in quick succession. He seemed to be always taking long and fascinating cruises with Uncle Affie, who was first sea lord, or with Uncle Bertie, who had nothing else to do, as Grandmama would never let him even read a state paper.

Uncle Bertie's cruise to India was the most exotic and Louis joined the expedition just before he received his promotion. How I envied him all that adventure. He came home and showed us the most extraordinary drawings of his experiences. The official illustrator of the Prince of Wales' cruise became ill and Louis, who was actually quite a talented illustrator, acquitted himself quite well in taking over those duties. One drawing of his that particularly made us laugh was a picture of several men doing their best to load an ostrich on board the HMS *Serapis*, the cruise ship.

Louis told us, too, of the darker side of his adventures. At the time, the British Navy had an anti-intellectual and anti-foreigner streak that made his life difficult. As a result, Louis was often misunderstood by his fellow officers. They couldn't comprehend why he would rather read or draw than spend time in the mess halls drinking with them. Perhaps Louis was unwise in that regard and probably should have choked down his protests and done as the others did. However, it was simply not in his character and he suffered for it; then—with all the bullying that he endured, and, later, with far more serious consequences.

Ella continued to be preoccupied with Serge, although Grandmama most strenuously disapproved. She thought Russia dreadful, autocratic, and much too exotic for girls who were practically English. She used to say quite often and emphatically in her letters to me that I should do my best not to let Ella or any of my sisters go there—it would be too horrible. I knew that I would have no influence on my sister in that respect, any more than she would have any over me.

So, Ella and I continued to think and talk about Serge and Louis though our immediate concern was our family. Little Ernie was a worry since he seemed unable to shake his morbidity, and Alicky, who had been so bright and cheerful that we all called her "Sunny", had become shy and introverted, with a perpetually unhappy look on her face. After a while I had the impression that she enjoyed wallowing in her sadness—something that struck me quite forcibly in later years.

In time, however, as in all things, our family slowly recovered. We began to talk about the good memories we had together, and no longer dwelled on the tragedies of lost siblings and our darling lost mother. Ella and I particularly enjoyed recalling that last golden summer in 1878, when Mama was alive and well, and we were all in England.

We stayed at Buckingham Palace, and Ella and I were terribly excited about the highlight of our stay: we were going to be permitted to attend a Garden Party at Uncle Bertie's Marlborough House.

It was a gorgeous summer day, the kind of clear blue sky of which only England can boast. Ella and I had, as was our custom when we were set loose in a large group, given poor Madgie the slip, and were wandering around staring rudely at everyone. Eventually, as was also our custom, we began to feel very gauche and mousey amongst all the smart people.

Ella grabbed my hand.

"Come on, Victoria; let's get out of this crowd. I have a good place where we can hide and watch."

I had a glass of punch in the other hand, was living in pure dread that I would get my dress dirty. Ella had an excellent idea, though, and I sighed with relief. I was not good at these kinds of social gatherings. It wasn't that I couldn't talk—far from it—I just disliked meaningless social chitchat, even then.

We arrived at a spot near the edge of the huge tea tent. It was actually next to one of the large tent spikes that was holding up the entire thing, and next to the rope, were several chairs.

"If you hold the chairs, I'll go get us some cakes." She left me sitting as she made her way back through the crowds.

My eyes were glazing over at the sight of so much gorgeousness, and I was beginning to count the feathers in Lady Randolph Churchill's hat. Then, I had the wicked thought of how funny it would be to somehow unfasten the rope from the spike next to me, and watch the confusion as the tent collapsed. Then, to my surprise, I saw Louis. I gasped…having not seen him in ages. He was quite grown up. Tall and slim, over six feet, wavy dark brown hair, liquid brown eyes, and a full navy-style beard. The beard made him look older and more authoritative, though he was in his early twenties. As usual, he looked effortlessly elegant and fastidious in his morning clothes. Cousin Louis always had the effect of making me feel unkempt.

I was going to call to him, but suddenly, I felt shy. He looked my way and gave me a quick nod and a smile. I looked away, concentrating hard on the rope and burning with an unfamiliar blush. I had just about figured out how to untie the knot, all the while puzzling over this new feeling of shyness, when Ella came back laden with cakes and, even better, miraculously had retrieved Louis for me.

"Look who I found, Victoria," Ella cried in genuine pleasure, "an ally!"

I got up thanking heaven I hadn't spilt any punch on my dress, and shuffled a bit.

"Hello, Cousin Louis," I muttered and stuck out my hand, which he gracefully bowed over.

"You look like you're plotting over here, Cousin Victoria," he smiled.

"Just how I could possibly collapse the tent," I said without thinking, then blushed. How unbecoming…

Louis laughed and Ella, who didn't approve of such anarchical tendencies said, "Louis has had the most wonderful idea."

"Really." My attention was off the rope, and on his face. His expression indicated he was amused and relieved to have found compatriots. I could also see that he was intently looking at me. This embarrassed me even more.

"Victoria, you have grown so tall," he remarked, smiling mischievously.

"Well, after all, I am fifteen," I replied, and could have sunk through the floor. It was humiliating to act so backward in front of my handsome cousin.

"Yes, you are and, you," turning and giving equal attention to Ella, "I believe, are just fourteen."

Ella nodded eagerly, evidently free from the humiliation that I was suffering.

"That's right. And, what do you think, Louis? Victoria and I are going to study together and be confirmed at the same time. Mama says so, doesn't she, Vicky?"

Ella was one of the few people allowed to call me Vicky. There were so many in our family. I nodded weakly, thinking how ludicrous it would be for anyone to think us grown up. Certainly Louis did not. He was about twenty-four and as far away from us as the moon.

"I'm glad to hear it, Ella.... Say," he looked around the tent, as if he were checking to make sure that no one was listening, "here's the idea...do you two want to get out of here?"

My eyes must have shown my delight as I nodded emphatically.

"I'm not sure..." Ella looked around, too. She was

worried about consequences, what Mama or Orchie or Madgie would think which, of course, I never was.

"No one will care, Ella. They're all too busy showing off for each other," I said, forcefully.

"Are you sure?"

"Yes," I replied emphatically, though I was not. I turned back to Louis, "What do you have in mind?"

In a very short time, Louis had us back to Buckingham Palace. We walked through the place quickly and went to the gardens in the rear of the building. There was an artificial lake there with several boats tied up on a tiny dock.

"Perhaps we ought to have told someone we were going." Ella had been harping on this theme throughout the carriage ride.

"Don't worry," I reiterated through clenched teeth. Ella was beginning to try my patience, and that rarely happened. I wondered, fleetingly, what was wrong with me.

"You girls have no idea how much I miss the sea." Louis remarked as he untied one of the boats, and we got in. Evidently, he was paying little attention to our furtive conversation, for which I was grateful.

Ella and I both put up our parasols, looking especially elegant (or so we thought), and Louis began rowing us about the lake. We laughed and talked and sang silly songs like, "...Row, row, row, your boat..." I must admit my heart beat faster as I watched Louis row. He had taken off his topcoat, rolled up his sleeves, and rowed with bare, tanned arms. I saw him with awkwardly grown-up eyes and I was completely smitten and irked. He made me shy and I had never been shy in my entire life.

I flushed and heard Ella giggle. She looked at me and giggled again. I realized I had been staring at Louis' biceps and he'd asked me a question.

"I said," he repeated, "have you heard the story of Sandro?" Sandro was, of course, Alexander, Louis' younger brother.

I shook my head, no.

"The Bulgarians are thinking of asking him to come over and be Prince of Bulgaria."

"Prince?" I exclaimed, forgetting my shyness in my interest. "What will Grandmama say?"

"I'm not sure Grandmama would be involved," he replied pensively. "Bulgaria borders on Russia and I believe the Tsar is far more concerned. A Prince of Bulgaria would have to consider Russia's interests as well as Bulgarian ones...."

"Dreadful Russians," I burst out, mimicking Grandmama. I didn't like the idea of another Empire's interests being considered more than Grandmama's. It seemed disloyal.

"Vicky!" Ella reprimanded.

"Well, Russia is dreadful. Grandmama says so all the time. The society is terrible, the government is backward..." I turned to look at Ella. "You mustn't think of going there, darling," I said, apropos of nothing in the conversation, "The climate isn't good for German Princesses. Mama feels the same way," though in actuality, my Mama had gotten along well with the Russians.

Ella blushed and looked at Louis, who appeared to be enjoying my outburst.

"I don't know what you mean, Victoria, although, I see no harm in visiting the court. After all, Aunt Marie is there." She looked angry and only called me "Victoria" like that when she was upset.

I had put my foot in it once again. I supposed Ella would tell Mama who would shake her head sadly at me. That always made me feel worse than outright anger.

"Well, we don't know if that's going to happen yet," Louis said, in the way of placating us both. I'm sure he regretted making his retreat with us two, a pair of termagants. A less amusing group..."Come on, you two, let's sing again..."

And as quickly as we erupted, it was over. We were having a marvelous time, again, with Louis rowing us up and down the lake until he was exhausted.

I remembered that day, and marked it as the beginning of my adult feelings for Louis.

Ella and I got into trouble for leaving the party without permission, but I hardly noticed. I was too busy trying to understand my feelings for Louis—not that he was around too much. As usual, he was busy being appointed from ship to ship, and, I was positive, thinking nothing about me. Besides, I was starting to get hints from Grandmama about postponing marriage for a while.

Not that I was thinking of marriage, because, among other things, as I said, I was sure that Louis didn't think of me one way or another. Grandmama, however, also wanted me to think that my whole goal in life didn't have to be early marriage, and that rather appealed to me. She said let others, who think about nothing else, get married early. Papa and the family, she reiterated, needed me.

Ella, on the other hand, seemed to have a surfeit of suitors. I knew that Serge continued to be her favorite, but I also knew that she liked to keep him on a string. One week, she would be writing him bright, cheerful letters, and other weeks, she'd tell me they weren't on speaking terms.

Frankly, I wished, during that spring of 1880, that she wasn't on speaking terms with Willy of Prussia. He was going to the University of Bonn, only a few miles away, and visiting us all the time. I couldn't bear him. He was unbelievably moody, one moment being a bright and cheerful companion, playing tennis and riding, and the next he was such a bully and usurping my place, which was even worse. When he came to the palace, we would all be expected to go on outings with him. We'd go in carriages to the edge of town, and then be expected to march up and down the countryside with him in the lead.

Then, when he became tired, we'd have to sit where we

were, and listen to him read the bible. Not that I had anything against the bible, though at the time, I did not see it as having any real entertainment value—I should have preferred Homer or King Arthur. But no, Cousin Willy rambled on bombastically, as though he were in charge of our religious education.

Even more annoying than this was the fact that Willy had conceived a tendresse for Ella. He wrote her love poetry, which can only be imagined, and insisted on her company whenever he traveled to Darmstadt. Naturally, Ella insisted that I be around as much as possible in order to deflect any romantic ardor. That was fine with me. But in the process, Willy taught me what I consider my one truly bad habit, well, besides sloppiness of dress—smoking. Yes, Willy was the culprit and from that spring on, I became an avid tobacco addict. I hated being addicted to anything because that made one dependent, but I enjoyed them too much to give them up.

The really dreadful part was that Grandmama detested smoking. Uncle Bertie had one tiny room in Windsor in which he was permitted to smoke. I remember constantly having my head out windows or blowing smoke up chimneys in the hopes that Grandmama would not find out. She knew, of course.

Several years later when I was at Windsor, Grandmama stunned me while we were sitting in the gardens, by asking me to light up a cigarette.

"It keeps the midges away," she explained, and asked

58

me for a puff. Needless to say, she made a horrible face and hated it. I certainly never thought of smoking again in her presence.

Willy did propose that summer and Ella turned him down. He never talked to her again during her life, and only admitted his feelings to an American journalist when he was quite an old man in exile. Perhaps, her considerable talents would have been put to better use improving Willy's disposition and stability, while preventing Willy's descent into war.

Another event occurred in that spring which I was not to learn about until much later. It was however, so much before my time that I try to think of it with some detachment. Louis was loitering in London, waiting for his next appointment. Uncle Bertie was tremendously fond of Louis. It was said that Louis was his favorite cousin, and had always encouraged him to go on half-pay and become an habitué of Marlborough House. Louis, however, had always been serious about his career and didn't want to cool his heels with Uncle Bertie going to endless parties and theaters…so he waited, chomping, as it were, at the bit.

It was also at this point that Uncle Bertie's affair with the notorious courtesan, Lillie Langtry, was cooling down. She'd thrown some ice down his back during a costume party, and far from being amused (though he was constantly given to pranks of such a nature himself), he cut the lady dead. She happened at that time, to catch

Louis' eye, and he fell, as a romantic young man will, passionately in love with her. I don't hesitate to say this because it was a passion that cooled nearly as quickly as it flamed, and was, from what I had subsequently heard from Louis and others, only one of many.

The permanent part of this relationship was that Mrs. Langtry had her only child by Louis—Jeanne Marie. Louis confessed all of this to me during our courtship, though I had heard rumblings of it from overheard conversations, and sentences left unfinished. He assured me that the affair was over before he was assigned to the *Inconstant,* in November of that year.

I had to be amused. Men, I thought, took themselves so seriously. Frankly, being pragmatic in nature, I chose not to think much about it. However, I do sometimes think about the half-sister of my children. I wonder if her life is good, if she is happy.

II
New Palace Darmstadt, 1881

Ella and I were confirmed together just as we had told Louis we would be. We wore lovely white dresses and had a coming out ball that was memorable. It was memorable because I finally decided that I liked dancing. Dancing had been an activity I had avoided most of my teenage years, preferring gymnastics or just running around outside for exercise. However, I now decided that it was an amusing activity, and it was far more tolerable than social chatter. In the end, I would have rather been upstairs hiding in the library with a book and a cigarette.

Ella, who had always enjoyed dancing, did so with Serge only as much as she danced with everyone else. That included Papa and the uncles, and even Ernie who was permitted down for dances with his elder sisters. Naturally, I was not the only one who was aware of Serge and Ella. As I said before, I received constant letters from ever-seeing Grandmama about keeping Ella away from Russia. Even when we spent summers with the Russian cousins at the Heiligenberg, I was exhorted by Grandmama not to go "all Russian" and to please make sure that my sisters didn't either.

Ella, however, continued to be enchanted by Serge, who had grown tall, slim, and was quite handsome in a stern and austere kind of way. He had a beard much like Louis' and penetrating gray-green eyes. But, for me, Serge had no warmth, and whenever he was around Ella, he would constantly and severely criticize her clothes, her deportment, and the things she said. All Ella would do is cast her eyes down and say, in the French that we spoke to our Russian cousins, "Mais, Serge...."

Then he would soften slightly, look at her like an indulgent schoolmaster and that would be the end of the issue, whatever it was. This kind of treatment would have gone exactly nowhere with me, but then, I was not as good and sweet as Ella. It bothered me more, however, that

Papa—dear, sweet, good natured, oblivious Papa, seemed not to notice any of this. At least Willy was an out and out bully. Serge had something else about him—a quiet, inner cruelty of which Ella seemed completely unaware. There was little use worrying about this, however, since he would in all probability be my brother-in-law.

I was looking especially lovely that evening. I say this without a trace of vanity—since I can count on one hand the times I think I looked pretty. I was wearing, as I mentioned, a white dress, which fit my slim figure wonderfully well. My red-gold hair was elaborately arranged, (not my usual fringe, brushed up and pinned back look) with flowers stuck in strategic and attractive places. I wore a simple strand of pearls around my neck (Grandmama had been sending me pearls for some time, and Papa had them strung).

We didn't expect Louis to be able to come though I knew that Liko and Franzjos would be there. Liko hadn't stopped teasing me, and we had a hilarious dance together, him pretending to step all over my feet, and me stepping right back. Liko looked glorious in uniform. His breeches were just about as tight as a human being could stand and his boots were polished, so I heard, with champagne (though why that should look good, I haven't a clue). His uniform was white, exquisite, and elaborate in what would be called today Ruritanical and his mustache was waxed within an inch of its life, causing it to stick out positively to there...

I was catching my breath after this adventurous round on the dance floor when I glanced over at the entrance. Liko and Franzjos had made their way over and were pumping his hand, and there was Louis, looking incredibly handsome in his naval uniform. My heart did a tiny little flip and my face began its slow hot flush. This was a sensation that I had only experienced when I was around Louis and I looked around to see if anyone was noticing. Ella was completely absorbed with her flirtation with Serge and Fritz, Prince Frederick of Baden. However, instinctively, I believe, she looked over at me and followed my eyes over to the cousins. She smiled and nodded knowingly, and as the hostess, I glided, gracefully, I hoped, over.

I curtsied, although, by rights, I had no reason to curtsey to a morganatic prince (or so Willy, that insufferable snob, would say), and Louis gallantly put his hand out raising me up.

"Cousin Victoria," he smiled with great pleasure. I think he enjoyed the fact that I had curtsied. He was so often reminded of his inferiority of connection by people like Cousin Willy. "Would it be too boring to tell you how beautiful you look this evening?"

The subject of my beauty was never boring to me, just a bit obscure.

"Thank you, I'm so glad you came, Cousin Louis, we weren't sure if you would be able to get away."

Was this soft spoken, well-mannered debutante me? I had to think about that—but later.

"I wouldn't have missed this—you and Ella both coming out at the same time. Remember that summer in England you told me about it, and I have had it noted in my engagements ever since."

I smiled and flushed with pleasure. I really did have no idea of social chatter, but if this was social, I was enjoying it immensely.

"May I put myself down for a dance on your card?"

"Please..." I said faintly, and I heard both Liko and Franzjos sniggering. They had never seen such a feminine and compliant Victoria. I felt like knocking their heads together, but thought it would ruin everything.

He had reserved the supper waltz which was, of course, just what I hoped. I bade him goodbye and went back to where Ella, Serge and Fritz were standing.

"Now Victoria is happy," Ella said, smiling.

"What is this?" Serge asked with some curiosity, but no smile.

"Louis is one of Victoria's favorites, isn't he, dear?" Ella was completely without guile, so I suppose she didn't realize how embarrassing this revelation was, especially in front of Serge and Fritz.

"He is a cousin I grew up with," I remarked, hoping to fend off any teasing or questions.

Serge, however, merely nodded curtly. I should have known since he really wasn't the teasing type at all. He rarely laughed and never ever made jokes. Furthermore, my preoccupations were of absolutely no interest to him.

He was constantly focused, nearly obsessively, on Ella. No one else counted or even mattered.

The supper waltz took ages coming, but finally, when I had nearly given up hope, Louis came up smilingly, to claim his dance.

He nodded to Ella and Serge, and waltzed me away.

"That couldn't have been very amusing," he remarked.

"What wasn't amusing?" I asked, dreamily, enjoying the sensation of his hand on my waist.

"The marble man, Serge...."

I immediately became defensive; after all, I had to defend my sister Ella, even if it were only her best beau and a dreaded Russian to boot.

"Serge is all right..." I began lamely, only to stop. I really couldn't think of much good to say about him. I think Grandmama's prejudices were really beginning to influence me. If they weren't, how else could I explain that my dearest sister, one of the best people I knew, could like such a man? He must have redeeming qualities of which I simply wasn't aware.

"Whatever you say—for tonight, my dear cousin."

For once in my life, I didn't want to talk. I just wanted to experience this dance...and dance, and dance...

A few minutes later, Louis remarked, "Sandro's in Bulgaria—did you know?"

Papa and I had discussed this at some length when Sandro was appointed Prince of that Balkan country. I had always been confused about the politics of that area that for so long had been under the suzerainty of the Ottoman Empire. It was all so perplexing.

"Yes, we heard that he was. It's been for quite a while, hasn't it? It must be very difficult...I personally, can't even understand what's going on there right now. There seems to be something with the Russians wanting Bulgaria to be a dependency and Sandro's desire for her to be independent and make her own decisions."

He smiled, evidently thinking, Victoria's found her tongue again.

"Yes, that's about it. Also, the Congress of Berlin has divided the country which has made no one happy."

"Sandro seems awfully young to cope with such a complicated situation."

"The Tsar is supposed to help him..." Louis left off, as though realizing how unlikely that was.

"Oh, dear," I said, not liking the look on his face. "I hope that things won't become dangerous—being there all by himself."

"Rest assured, Victoria, if there is a problem, there are always many willing to help."

"Franzjos, Liko, and you, I should think...?"

"I certainly hope that Sandro could look to more than his brothers if he really needed help."

"I'm sure Grandmama..."

"Grandmama will not wish to get entangled in the situation should it involve Russia and some other power..."

"Namely the German Empire," I added. "Certainly, Grandmama hates to get involved with anything to do with Russia."

"Yes," he smiled, ruefully. "You made it quite clear that day what you and your Grandmama thought of Russia."

I blushed.

"That was awful of me, Louis. I hope you'll forgive me."

"I shall, but," he glanced over at Ella, who was still talking to, or being lectured by Serge, "I wonder if Ella will."

"Oh," I replied confidently, "if Ella really does go to Russia, I shall just make the best of it."

He nodded absently, and we continued our waltzing around the floor. He was lost in thought, and I didn't think it was all just Bulgarian politics.

"So, you try to understand the politics of these countries?" he asked, after a few minutes.

"Indeed," I replied, eagerly. "I read the newspaper every day, and discuss it with Papa. Grandmama and I discuss the news in letters..." Louis chuckled at that. "She thinks that I read too much..."

"Do you really, Victoria?" That seemed to interest him.

"I don't think I do, but Grandmama doesn't approve of what I read."

"And, what do you read?"

"Just about anything I can lay my hands on," I answered looking around, unaware, Louis told me later, of the intense interest he was showing in me.

"I love to read, too."

I looked back at him. That was good. Papa was a man of action, he loved to drill with his troops and put on his very English Norfolk jacket to ride out with the hounds and shoot. He wasn't a man of books, and I had always wanted to be with more people who read.

"I love to shoot, too," I began to feel the need to be completely honest and not misrepresent myself in any way.

"You shoot as well?"

"Certainly, though you seem surprised," I said with a laugh, I was on sound territory here.

"No, and I'm not in the least surprised," he chuckled back. "It's just hard to reconcile the picture of you climbing masts, and roofs, with the lovely young lady I see before me this evening...," which naturally had me blushing all over again.

"Yes, Grandmama thinks that the shooting I do and the kind of rough horses I ride make me rather 'fast'—is the word I think she used to describe it," I reiterated, looking at my feet. For some reason, I repeated this assessment. I had hoped that he wouldn't agree.

"You, fast?" Louis burst out, and began laughing in earnest. Others in the ballroom were looking at him as he continued.

"Shh." I was uncomfortable with the attention. "They'll all wonder what we're talking about."

"Victoria, I can't believe that you would care," he said

rightly, with a huge grin, and so handsome, I thought my heart would burst.

I smiled slowly back at him.

"You're right, Louis, I don't care," and we continued to waltz madly to the music, and he became lost in thought again. I had a feeling that I was losing him, and I wasn't pleased.

It was all over much too quickly. When I reflected on that first dance, I wondered if Sandro and the vicissitudes of Bulgarian politics were the only things Louis was worried about. Surely, at that point, it looked well for his brother, and it was a tremendous step up for the family. Now there was a Battenberg as a ruling sovereign instead of morganatic rulers with an extinct title.

No, there was something else bothering Louis. Naturally, at the time I didn't know this, but, later on, he told me that this was period that Mrs. Langtry was with child. Louis was struggling between doing what he felt would be the right thing and ruining his naval career. As it turned out, he did do the right thing for that era, though I suppose the young today would protest about the lack of romance in it all. His family made sure that Mrs. Langtry was comfortable and provided for, and that was that.

We had supper together, with Serge, Ella, Irène, who had been allowed to come down for a bite and was now proceeding to stuff herself, and little Ernie, who was twelve. Papa had let him stay for the supper, only if he had promised to go to bed right afterwards, which he, obediently, did.

Dear, lonely Ernie, such a sensitive, artistic soul—and when he succeeded to Papa's dukedom—entirely too young. His attributes never struck me as the proper traits for a ruler. But, I think now of another young man, equally sensitive and lonely and, moreover, completely unfit. Nicky succeeded equally young and unfortunately, he paid for his mistakes with his life. Ernie only had to retire to Wolfsgarten. But those sad events are ahead. Now, I can continue to dwell on the more pleasant aspects of my life.

CHAPTER THREE

I
New Palace, Darmstadt, 1883

I remember reading somewhere, that when Grandmama was married and began having her nine children, someone commented that the Royal Court was nesting. I chuckled at the time, but I believe that for a period in the 1880s and into the '90s, the Hessian Court was doing much the same thing. In some cases it was blissful, but in other cases, it is not an understatement to say that it was fraught with peril.

It was summer of 1883, and we had heard that Louis was appointed to the *Duke of Wellington*. Papa was sure that it was time for the Royal Navy to promote him again, and I agreed. Naturally, I followed his career with interest. We hadn't seen much of each other since Ella and I had come out and interestingly enough, no marriages were talked about for me, though I was already twenty. In those days, princesses in their twenties were definitely on their way to being on the shelf. But, I suppose I followed Grandmama's dictum of not marrying early. In any case, I didn't worry about it for even a minute.

Ella continued to tease her suitors, though I should say right now that she never did it in a malicious way. She was such an extraordinary beauty with her dark blond hair and blue eyes, that men were drawn to her like moths to a flame. These men were always treated with sweetness and serenity—but never seemed to touch her.

Grandmama wanted Fritz of Baden thrown in her way as much as possible in order to deflect Serge, however, I believe there was never a chance for poor Fritz. This was confirmed to me, when Ella told me in the beginning of the spring, that Fritz had proposed, and she had rejected him. Grandmama was very sad when I wrote her about this. All, she lamented, for a Russian. Evidently, the Empress of Germany, Aunt Vicky's mother-in-law, let her annoyance at Ella's refusal make itself known to Grandmama. Ella was certainly in no doubt, since the Empress cut her dead at the next ball.

Irène, the third grace, was about to come out herself and had expressed a particular interest in a certain beau. She was a docile, domestic, unremarkable sort of girl, neither as beautiful as Ella was, nor as rebellious or eccentric as I. Irène was simply an attractive, sweet girl, who had enticed the interest of one of our first cousins.

The unbearable Willy of Prussia had a very nice young brother named Heinrich, whom we, like everyone in our family, called Henry. Henry was, like Irène, extremely tractable and amiable—in fact, as a couple, later on many called them the "very amiables."

As in Ella's case, Grandmama did not approve of this *tendresse*, but not for the same reasons. Grandmama didn't have anything against the Prussians, after all, these were all the children of her daughter, my Aunt Vicky. Grandmama actually liked Henry, who had joined the German Navy. She just didn't like the influence of his older brother and sister. She quite rightly thought that Willy and Charlotte, whom we called Charley, bullied him within an inch of his life. I can certainly believe it—as I've stated already, Willy was the most dreadful bully. Grandmama simply didn't like to think that their malevolent influences, which had hurt her daughter Aunt Vicky so much, would be good for one of her beloved Hessian granddaughters.

There was, however, something else going on, as well.

Aunt Vicky and Grandmama were in the middle of promoting another marriage, which was of far more interest than Aunt Vicky's uninteresting second son. I recall talking over the situation with Papa one morning during breakfast.

"Your Aunt Vicky has written that Moretta has fallen madly in love with Sandro," he remarked, mentioning Aunt Vicky's daughter, yet another Victoria, whom we called Moretta. He was reading a letter from the New Palace in Potsdam.

My ears perked up. I was fascinated about anything to do with the Battenbergs. Naturally, being a Battenberg, Sandro was of such interest...but Moretta?

"Papa, Moretta was just waiting to fall in love, and it would have hardly mattered with whom, though Sandro is very dashing and handsome," I said with superiority. I suppose that when events played themselves out, I regretted my smugness. Nevertheless, it has to be said that Moretta was a flibbertigibbet. She would have fallen in love with anything in trousers, and was said to be extremely wild and eccentric.

Yes, I am eccentric, too. However, I was blessed with several things that poor Moretta didn't have—a sense of proportion and, for some odd reason, even having lost my mother, a sense of stability.

"Your Aunt says that Bismarck and Uncle Fritz won't have it, though—nor the old Emperor, nor Willy..." Papa interjected.

"That's a powerhouse of opposition."

"Indeed, it seems that Sandro is not good enough for their family. A mere morganatic prince does not deserve to marry into the Royal Hohenzollerns—your Aunt Vicky is furious."

So was I.

"But, Sandro is a ruling prince," I began passionately, totally shaken out of my previous complaisance. "Just because he's not dancing to Sasha's tune in Bulgaria and just because Bismarck is afraid of offending the Russians..." I paused for breath. I could see that Papa was amused at my defense. "Well," I continued, trying to calm down, "he's not just some obscure morganatic prince. What utter nonsense. They are far too proud of their blood in Potsdam, Papa, and we know that it runs red like everyone else's."

"You sound just like your mother."

"Well, she was right, Papa. Royalty is simply going to become irrelevant. If Moretta is really so in love with Sandro, why doesn't she just marry him?"

"Well, for one, because everyone in her family, except Aunt Vicky and Grandmama, a ruler of another country who is not particularly friendly towards the Russians, are against it. That seems good enough for me."

"But how can we stand by and see members of our family being abused by Willy and his ilk. We've spent summer after summer with the Battenbergs and no one objected. Certainly Aunt Marie or Uncle Alexander of Russia, God rest their souls, stayed in the Heiligenberg as did we all. Just because Sasha hates Sandro..."

Sasha was my aunt and uncle's eldest son, our cousin, who had become Tsar Alexander the Third of Russia several years before. Sasha hated Sandro because he refused to be his puppet, and unlike his father, Sasha had no sympathy for Sandro. I always thought it was because Sandro was everything Sasha wasn't—tall, handsome, and slim. Sasha was a large Russian bear of a man, and towards many people, extremely good-hearted, but when it came to the Battenbergs, those princes of "inferior blood", he had no time.

"Wasn't Sandro in Moscow for the Coronation last year?" I asked.

"Yes, but evidently Sandro did something that angered Sasha, I think they might have even come to blows..." Papa replied, carefully.

"Sasha is just a big, blowhard..."

"Victoria, dear, that's no way to talk about the Tsar of all the Russias."

"I don't care what he's Tsar of, Papa, I hate this snobbery..."

Papa sighed. His background had not prepared him for outspoken women. First he had Mama and now me. I really don't think he knew how to cope. I went over to him and put my arms around his neck.

"Never mind, I'm sure it will all come out right in the end."

He nodded. I believe that's just the way he liked to end any sort of conflict or unpleasantness.

Grandmama was writing constantly to me about this aspect of the "Sandro" situation, just as I was explaining everything that Papa and I knew about the political aspects.

In all, I think that this was a particularly distressing year for poor Grandmama. It was not only Aunt Vicky's marital machinations for Moretta or Ella's preference for Serge, but also something far worse. Her faithful John Brown, the gillie that had lifted her out of the despair of her first mourning for dear Grandpapa, had died. She was bereft and began putting busts of him all over her residences (this to Uncle Bertie's disgust, who loathed the Scot). She even asked Lord Tennyson to write his epitaph. I understand Auntie Beatrice had to actually talk her out of writing a remembrance of Brown and having it published.

She poured out her grief in her letters to me, though I felt useless to try to assuage the onslaught. I had never understood the torrent of grief in which Grandmama gloried. It's not that I thought she really enjoyed it, but she seemed to think that this was the only way to mourn the death of a loved one. Nothing less would do.

I left Papa and went back to our bedrooms. Ella and I were supervising the packing for this summer's visit to the Heiligenberg. I wasn't sure which of the Russian cousins would be there. Happily, I was as sure that Sasha wouldn't be there, as I was that Serge would be.

We would spend some weeks there, and then probably go off to Grandmama at Balmoral or Osborne. As I have said, in the years after Mama's death, we spent a great deal of time in England. We children enjoyed being with our aunts, uncles and cousins, and my Papa, rabid Anglophile that he was, just enjoyed playing the English gentleman.

My favorite spot was Osborne House. Loving the island atmosphere, I enjoyed the fact that it was, naturally, built near the sea. I also loved the house itself. Grandmama and Grandpapa built it to be a family home. More than any other of the Royal Residences, it was a home to me. It wasn't as large as, say, Sandringham, and although it was an elegant Italianate building, it had a very homey atmosphere.

The residence itself was several stories with many, many small rooms. There were cozy sitting rooms with copious amounts of family photos and the usual clutter associated with the Victorian era.

I spent most of my time with my sisters and brother, playing in the Swiss Cottage or more recently, hiking, riding and bathing. Grandmama's bathing machine was a large elaborate affair drawn by two horses. It drew us down to the shore and out we'd emerge with our bathing costumes on. At first we would touch the water with our toes, very gingerly at first. Then with a couple of whoops, we would dash in, be shocked by the cold water and begin intense splashing. Grandmama, prodded by poor Brown, would sometimes come in with us. Then we'd, regretfully, have to moderate all our splashing and roughhousing.

Sometimes Auntie Beatrice would join us. I remember, at six years my senior, she should have been considered eligible for marriage. Grandmama, however, would have none of it. Her last child, her "Benjamina" as she called her, would stay at home and keep her Mama company.

Auntie Beatrice served as the Queen's secretary, companion, reader and general factotum. The words "marriage" or "engagement" were literally not allowed to be uttered in Beatrice's presence, and certainly, no eligible young men were allowed to be lurking about.

Louis later told me that he was never invited to Grandmama's while he was on leave those years of the late '70s and early '80s, because Grandmama was concerned that he just might take an unwelcome interest in Auntie. Not that Auntie would have thought it unwelcome. Louis would laugh and say that interest was never the right word—he was just intrigued by the mystery of the missing Princess.

I had heard that at one point, Auntie was unofficially engaged to the exiled Prince Imperial of France. Nothing ever came of that because the unfortunate young man was killed in West Africa. I never knew the truth, but I later had my suspicions when Auntie's daughter was called Victoria Eugenie after the Empress.

We were all looking forward to our time at the Heiligenberg. Grandmama had wanted me to go straight to Balmoral, but I preferred my Battenberg cousins that year. Ella later told me that she had written Grandmama that if I did not come to Balmoral, a certain event just might occur. It's amazing how everyone else seemed to know more of what was going on than I.

Shrouded in my unspoken desires, I merely looked forward to hiking around the beautiful woods, and hoped that Liko would be on leave from the Austrian Army so that he could accompany us. I dared not hope that Louis would be there. He, looking forward to an important promotion, would not have time for summer holidays.

Since the huge Romanov retinue no longer came on a regular basis, we could all be housed in the front house; no more relegation to the back with servants and couriers finding refuge at Jugenheim, or elsewhere. Now, no one had to be inconvenienced and I didn't have to tolerate Cousin Sasha, or most of his family, for which, at this point, I was grateful.

That summer, Ella and Irène were in their late teens and even Ernie was quite a grown up fifteen, so none of us really needed looking after. This gave Madgie and Orchie much needed rest. All of us, except, of course, Alicky. Alicky, at eleven, would mope around complaining that there were no children her age to play with. When I reminded her that Ernie was there, she wrinkled her nose and said, "Ernie's always here, I meant other children."

That response was ironic, when I thought about it much later on. Alicky would never let her children play with other children—only family and each other.

"Let me see...hmm, perhaps Sophie and Mossy will come," I said, naming Aunt Vicky's two youngest daughters, Sophie and Margarethe and knowing well enough that the Prussian contingent would not be coming.

"Oh, you know they won't be coming," Alicky burst out. "They don't think that the Battenbergs are good enough for them."

"Alicky!" I was shocked especially that she had read my own thoughts so accurately. "Where do you get such ideas?"

"Because, I listen when you and Papa talk at the breakfast table."

I made a note to myself to try to watch what I said in front of the younger ones. However, hard as I tried, that would always be a losing battle for me.

"Well, Aunt Lenchen's girls will no doubt be here."

Alicky sighed. Aunt Helena's daughters Thora and Marie Louise weren't very interesting, although, their papa most certainly was. My sisters and I got a thrill of horror whenever Uncle Chris, Prince Christian of Schleswig-Holstein, Aunt's husband, would take out his glass eye. He did this quite frequently and at the dining table. His eye had been put out due to a hunting accident, and I believe that he rather enjoyed the exhibition of his glass eyes.

"Why don't we try to see how many glass eyes Uncle Chris wears this visit," I proposed, putting my arm around my little sister. She smiled at me with her rare, delightful smile.

"That's a good idea. I want to see if he brings his bloodshot one."

I groaned and then we both laughed. Alicky, in a rare

comic mood, began to discuss all the various eyes that our Uncle owned, both giggling as we finished her packing.

It was a happy time for my family that year. The field was clear for Serge, if he wanted to take it and Irène and I were just biding our time.

II
Heiligenberg, June 1883

I always loved arriving at the Heiligenberg. It represented summer and happier times before the Great War and all the horrible deaths. It was a refuge on a mountaintop amongst the blooming trees and ivy-covered arches and gateways. The woods we played in as children, became the woods we explored as we grew older. There was serenity up there in that small compound, truly a world of its own, and I was sorry when Louis sold it after the War. Perhaps, it was a good idea. The world of the Heiligenberg had nothing to do with the world after the war. It was gone forever, along with all the phantoms of our younger selves.

Just for now, though, going back in memory is a pleasurable experience. I see ourselves laughing in the courtyards. There is Liko, as ever, looking splendid in his Austrian uniform. Serge has come without the other members of his family—the Battenbergs and the Romanovs are not mixing, as Alicky rightly says. There are my sisters and I in our summer whites—Alicky wears a matching frock though hers is shorter. Whenever I see pictures of our families, I notice that the girls seem to be dressed alike no matter how old they are—only the length of the hems denotes age. The Wales cousins, Toria, Maudie and Louise, under the auspices of their mother, certainly did, and later on, Alicky's girls, did as well, although the results there were far more felicitous.

Such was the scene that June when we gathered. I was more than pleased to know from Aunt Julie that Louis would, indeed, be arriving that day. I had, so obviously, what the young people call today, a great crush on Louis. I had recently decided that he was the man I wanted and was very grateful that no other candidates were danced before me. As with most girls of my age, who decided something like this, I had had very little encouragement from him other than his gallant cousinly attentions.

Ella, Irène and I shared a room on the second floor overlooking the courtyard. They were unpacking and I, chin resting on my hand, was daydreaming at the window. The valley and village below had no interest for me.

"Victoria's in love," Irène chanted in a singsong manner.

I decided not to dignify such a remark with an answer.

"Irène, leave Vicky alone," Ella said in a motherly tone.

"Well, so are you." Irène was sixteen years old, so this kind of teasing seemed to come naturally.

Ella shook her head and came over to me.

"Let me fix your hair, Vicky, it's untidy from the journey"

"Is it?" I replied absently.

Ella chuckled, "As usual."

She led me over to the dressing table, brush in hand, and took the pins out.

"Orchie used to have to comb my hair every five minutes," I smiled at Ella in the mirror.

"That's because you were forever getting into trees or on roofs...come to think of it, I believe you still do," which had my disorderly sisters laughing and giggling.

She continued brushing, twisting, pinning and putting it in a far more elegant chignon than I was accustomed to.

"Honestly, Vicky, you have the most beautiful red-gold hair, I don't know why you don't do more with it. I mean, you're always running down your looks, but you have wonderful blue eyes, a lovely straight nose—you should care about your appearance more."

"I don't know—I guess I just can't be bothered..." I trailed off, wondering if I had time for a cigarette before we went downstairs for our luncheon. It wasn't quite as formal as it had been in my mother's day, but we couldn't go down in our travel clothes.

"Let's go down. Victoria looks about as good as she's ever going to look," Irène teased.

"Thanks, urchin," I replied good-naturedly and started chasing Irène around the room.

"Irène, Victoria," Ella started laughing. "Stop now! You'll ruin your hair."

I stopped. I was supposed to be the eldest. We composed ourselves, and descended the broad staircase—I, trying to be sedate, and Ella and Irène, as far as I could determine, succeeding.

Everyone was already gathered in the large drawing room. Ella, I imagine, made sure that we were last to do so, so that we could make an elegant entrance. She thought of these things. I, naturally, didn't—but then, Ella could make elegant entrances and I couldn't. Papa was busy with Uncle Alexander and Aunt Julie, while Alicky was hovering around Uncle Chris. I caught her eye and we nodded at each other conspiratorially. It was good to see Alicky light-hearted.

Serge immediately attached himself to Ella and began, what was, for him, social chatter. It was only directed to Ella. The rest of us were pointedly excluded. Irène and I rolled our eyes at each other. We were handed a glass of sherry and began to scan the room.

"There's Aunt Lenchen," I said to Irène. Our Aunt Helena, whom we all called Lenchen, had motioned us to come over. "We have to go over and say hello."

"You go ahead," Irène replied. "I don't want to have to sit with Thora and Marie Louise all day.

"Irène," I said, trying to sound disapproving. It didn't work and I was left alone to make my way over to Aunt Lenchen.

I reached my aunt and we kissed and sat down.

"I suppose there's nothing for it..." she began.

"I beg your pardon?" I asked politely, having no idea about what she was talking.

She motioned over at Ella and Serge.

"No...I suppose not," I said noncommittally.

"A wedding at St. Petersburg—that should be quite an extravagant and opulent affair."

"Yes..."

"It looks like it's just you, us and the Battenbergs this year," she remarked, completely changing the subject, to my relief.

"Yes, but, perhaps, Uncle Leo and Aunt Helen will come."

"Yes, Leopold did mention something...I wonder if they'll bring the baby, or leave it with Mama."

"Grandmama is not very fond of little babies," I smiled.

"True, but I believe, as she gets older, they don't bother her quite as much. Besides, she's so happy that Leo's married and has children—well..." she left off delicately. I didn't pick up the thread. The last thing I wanted to talk about was Uncle Leopold's delicate health.

"Ah, more of the Battenbergs," Aunt Lenchen smiled, looking at the door. Like her mother, my Aunt Lenchen appreciated a handsome man. I too was watching appreciatively as Liko and Louis entered the room. Aunt Julie and Uncle Alexander rushed up to them both, kissing and patting them on the back with visible delight.

I was unaccountably delighted to see Louis, as Aunt Julie turned to the room, smiling, "I think we can go in now." She positively glowed when she had her sons about her.

She took Louis' arm and we all went into the dining room.

"We're not formal this afternoon," she announced, as everyone began milling around the large polished table, looking for place cards. "Everyone sit where you like."

I felt Ella take my arm putting me next to her and Serge. Liko and Louis sat across, grinning at us. The meal passed with my stealing glances at Louis and Liko, wondering what on earth they were grinning about—two grown men—as I listened to Aunt Lenchen, who had planted herself at my other side. She was in the mood for a good gossip, and I wasn't paying enough attention. Everything about Louis was fascinating to me, and I couldn't tear my eyes away from him. He and Liko were busy eating and talking. They laughed about something and he looked up at me. I flushed and looked away. Really, my reactions were more suited to a girl of fifteen. Irène could have handled this better.

Ella and Serge chattered happily and Aunt Lenchen was asking me if I thought Grandmama would ever get over the death of Brown. I was really the last person to ask about such things, as I had very little patience with long protracted periods of mourning.

"Honestly, Victoria," Auntie was confiding, as she chewed her roast beef, "Sometimes I don't know where to look. There's a bust of Brown in every corner."

"How odd," was my brilliant reply.

She was taken aback. I could always be counted on to hold forth for quite a few minutes, while the other person ate, and suddenly, I was only good for a two-word reply?

"Yes," she answered quickly, and followed my eyes to Louis and Liko. "How odd," and I looked back at her. She was looking across the table and then at me with a speculative look.

I put my fork down. Was I that transparent? Thankfully, before Aunt Lenchen could begin speculating on this new and far more interesting topic, dessert was being served.

"Victoria," Ella finally tore herself away from Serge, and spoke to me. "Serge has the most wonderful idea..."

Wonderful, I thought. Usually Serge's ideas were dull as tombs, but anything to get me out of this ridiculous situation.

"Serge is going to forego brandy and cigars and we'll all go out to the gardens and get away from this mob...what do you say?"

I nodded. Aunt Lenchen, whom I normally enjoyed, was most definitely getting on my nerves. I wanted some air and to get away—not to sort out my feelings—but just to get away from this talk. I was about to decide that I should die an old maid and give up my life to good works, when Aunt Julie rose and nodded to all of us.

We, women moved back to the drawing room and Aunt Julie took her place at the coffee urn and began pouring.

"Er...I have to get a shawl," I blurted out to Aunt

Lenchen. "I'm getting a little cold." It was actually quite warm.

"Cold?" she looked at me quizzically. "Are you sure you're feeling quite well, dear?"

Ella rolled her eyes.

"Perhaps it was the sherbet, Auntie, but I'll go with her just in case."

Ella grabbed my arm, and we fled out of the drawing room.

"That was a pretty silly excuse," she commented, as we went back upstairs to get wraps.

"I'm sorry, Ella, but I just had to get out of there."

"Poor Victoria, are you in the throes of unrequited love?"

"How should I know?" I replied sharply, and Ella giggled.

"Serge couldn't decide which one was interested in you, Louis or Liko."

"I'm amazed Serge gives anyone besides you a second thought."

"Well he does," she giggled again, "occasionally..."

"I wish I knew what you see in him, Ella...I mean, I know he's our cousin, and I love him as a family member, but he's so—contained and quiet."

Ella let me rattle on. Heaven knows I was probably offending her, but she let me finish.

"You just don't know him like I do."

"Of course not, but, Ella, that's such a standard reply. I really want to understand."

"He's very handsome..." she laughed. "That isn't it.

Maybe because he is hard to know. There's something lost and sad about him, and perhaps it's my compassionate or mothering instincts coming out...I really can't say...what attracts you about Louis?"

I should have thought that was completely evident.

"He's very handsome," and we both laughed, as we walked out of our rooms, and headed down to the gardens. "He's also extremely intelligent, cultured, well-read, and above all, charming..."

"Is that all?"

The day was really beautiful as we walked through the gardens.

"Serge is going to meet us by the courtyard," Ella told me, as we wandered past blossoming trees and shrubbery. "It's a wonderful day, isn't it?"

"Yes, but not cool," I replied bluntly.

"Poor Aunt Lenchen. She really wanted to chat...she's not going to be happy with either one of us."

We spotted Serge's tall, slim form next to the fountain. Ella brightened up even more than she normally did.

"Serge, here we are."

His smile, though I thought it grim, seemed enough to warm Ella's heart. He put his arms out and we both, on either side, took them.

"I believe there may be several other stragglers coming out into the fresh air," he said stiffly, though I know he was attempting to be sociable. No sooner had he said it than we spotted Louis, Liko, and Irène.

We were a happy group rambling into the woods, laughing, talking and gossiping about everyone we knew. There was nothing too juicy going on at the moment, which was rather unusual for such a large family. Sandro and Moretta's situation simply wasn't very funny, so we kept away from that subject.

We all stopped next to a group of trees and looked back at the Schloss. I especially loved the two towers in the building. As a girl, I had climbed them many times and knew them well.

"You like our Heiligenberg, don't you?" a deep voice said from behind me.

I walked a few steps forward. I didn't want anyone to overhear our conversation.

"Yes," I replied, slightly breathless, as my heartbeat elevated. "Heiligenberg has such wonderful memories for me. I see myself, as a child, climbing towers and roofs, and trees..."

He laughed and put out his hand...I slowly took it, enjoying the pressure of his warm fingers on mine.

"Victoria, you were an incorrigible tomboy. I used to laugh at the way you and Liko used to fight."

We began to wander slowly off, hand in hand.

"Yes, Liko was rather a pig," I smiled, beginning to relax in his company.

"You shouldn't be too hard on him...I think he's always had a rather special feeling for you."

I looked down.

"Really," I replied, quietly. "He certainly had a funny way of showing it.

The mountain was getting a little steep, as we progressed downward, towards Jugenheim.

"Yes, I remember the tree pushing incident quite well, but you know what they say—such incidents are just a precursor to...well, you know—the real thing."

"I can't imagine. Besides, Liko and I aren't...well, I'm not...he's not the one I'm..." and I broke off. I just couldn't be my usual articulate self.

"Not what?" he asked gently, stopping to look at me.

I didn't know what to answer. I certainly wasn't going to blurt out my feelings. It just wasn't the way we did things in those days. As outspoken as I've been all my life, I can't see it. I certainly had no such nerve that day. I took refuge in petulance.

"Not anything," I said and continued walking.

We reached the village and wandered through its narrow streets. He never let go of my hand.

"Papa and I were saying that you should be promoted soon."

He smiled.

"I'm afraid it depends on the navy, not on what should be."

"Do you really like it now? Or, are you sorry you chose it?"

He considered the question as we reached the village courtyard.

"In the beginning, I was miserable, the accommodations were terrible, the food was filled with maggots and lice—it was pretty grim. Worse than that, everyone treated me terribly..."

"Yes, but you were so young..."

"I know. I wanted to quit a dozen times, but my papa knew how to buck me up. He told me to stick to it, and give it my best."

"That's always excellent advice, but how about now?"

"Well," he paused. We had reached that grotesque fountain from our childhood, and sat on the edge. "I still don't drink away the night with the other officers; I still don't have many friends. They still look at me, at times, as though the only reason I'm there is because I'm a prince, and they still are scornful of my foreignness."

"Then why...?"

He looked at the fountain for a moment and gave the water a splash.

"It's hard to explain..."

"The standard reply," I said for the second time that day. "Try."

He smiled at me. Strangely, he seemed to enjoy my bluntness.

"I love the sea, for one thing. A man gets attached to it and that I really can't explain. For another, the British Navy is the greatest navy in the world—it's a privilege to belong to it." He stopped a moment, as though overcome by this thought. As for me, I was puzzled. "And, for another," he continued, finally, "I have the loyalty and obedience of the men under me. With such cooperation, the ship runs smoothly and we feel like there is no difficulty that we cannot overcome together."

Some of that mysterious brotherhood talk...it was something I did my utmost to fathom. I could understand it during wartime, but it stretched my credulity during peace.

"So those three points outweigh all the abuse?"

"Naturally, and knowing my family are there at the end of a voyage. Those things are also important."

I got up and started back.

"What about a *sneeball*?" he asked, as we passed Frau Morgenstern's.

"No, thank you."

"Think they'll make you waddle?"

"No," I blushed. I suppose that cousins are allowed certain leeway with regard to personal remarks. "They're just too sweet for me now. That's probably why they were my favorites when we were small."

Louis took my hand again, and tucked it under his arm. I felt quite the lady, strolling along on the arm of such a dashing figure. I saw the eyes of the women as we passed. They knew he was a prince, but I could see their appreciation for him went far beyond his title.

"You have admirers, Cousin Louis," I said primly.

"Oh, yes," he replied lightly, "and a girl in every port."

"You haven't!" I burst out.

"Would it bother you, Victoria? Would it make you jealous?"

It was another uncomfortable question, to which I refused an answer. Besides, better to be silent than to lie.

"Oh, Victoria," he murmured, as he tucked my arm closer, "you'll break my heart."

"Not from what I've heard," I remarked tartly, before I could stop myself.

"What do you know?" he asked seriously, the smile wiped from his face.

"Nothing really," I said in a meek, little voice. "Only Liko is always bragging about how you—well, how you most definitely have a girl in every port."

"And Liko most definitely has a big mouth," the grim look left his face.

"I told you he was a pig," I smiled, and we both chuckled.

"I'm twenty-nine years old. You wouldn't think I've just been spending my leisure time getting tattoos?"

"Tattoos?" I exclaimed—I had never thought of that.

Then he laughed in earnest.

"No, don't worry, I don't have a tattoo. Never could see the point...but back to what we were talking about..."

I was about to whine, do we have to, but thankfully kept my mouth shut for once. It was all so dangerously close to either my greatest fear, or my dearest hope, which would make me happier than anything in the world.

Louis and I reached the others with Ella smiling and

wagging her finger at me. I was actually relieved, as I really wasn't prepared for the direction of the conversation.

Louis and I sat down on the grass, laughing and talking with the others. The rest of the day and evening, I managed not to be alone with Louis. Ella looked at me with concern, and Irène stopped teasing me—Ella must have warned her.

We spent a few idyllic days, once again, managing to keep away from our elders. Sometimes, Marie Louise and Thora came along, and what the two of them lacked in looks, they made up for in personality. They were more of our family's great talkers. Irène and even Alicky had a marvelous time romping with them. It was watching them that made me realize that I really wasn't a child anymore. More importantly, I had to start making decisions about my life.

CHAPTER FOUR

I
Heiligenberg, June 1883

We were to leave by the end of the week. Ella was miserable because that would mean separation from Serge, and I...? I wasn't sure how miserable I was. Avoiding Louis hadn't worked any more than I thought it would. Louis, Liko and eventually, Franzjos appeared, all insisting on escorting their cousins around the entire valley. So, of necessity, we all became comfortable again, walking, talking, hiking and riding. All the wonderful things we always did.

I had gone off myself one very summery and warm morning. Somehow, being with that big gang, which was usually so pleasant and carefree, suddenly, had no appeal. Aunt Julie had an extensive collection of English novels, so I decided to spend the morning with *Pride and*

Prejudice—it was one of my favorites. Perhaps, it would cheer me up, since it could always be relied upon for a good laugh.

My English had always been good, Mama having spoken to us in that language. Nevertheless, I knew that I had a bit of a German accent and sometimes practiced alone, when no one was listening, to try to correct it. Louis and I always spoke English together, but he, too, had an accent, which I found strange since he'd spent nearly fifteen years in the British Navy. Perhaps that Germanic accent could never be gotten rid of.

I was giggling over the foolishness of Elizabeth Bennett's sisters and particularly her mother, thanking heaven that I didn't have such silly sisters, when I was interrupted.

"Victoria," Louis called, and I looked up. He was walking towards me. "Where have you been? Ella and Irène are bullying Liko mercilessly. Believe me, we've all been looking for you."

I smiled.

"I just wanted to catch up on some of my reading...," I said aimlessly, putting a hand to my hair, which, as usual, was a mess.

"Ah," he said, and settled himself on the stone bench next to me. "And, what are you reading?"

I slowly brought up the spine of the book and showed it to him.

"*Pride and Prejudice,* I've read it."

"Really?" I was surprised. It was not the kind of book I would have pictured a naval lieutenant reading.

"You'd be surprised what I've read."

"I can see that I would," I smiled.

"We have long sea voyages, sometimes, for months on end I'm cooped up in my cabin."

"Oh, I imagined you having to sleep with the crew on the decks in hammocks—gently swaying in the balmy sea breezes," I became carried away in the exotic image.

It was his turn to smile.

"I did that and it wasn't very pleasant, I can assure you—certainly no balmy sea breezes. Actually, that's when we would have the maggot derbies," I shuddered. "Oh yes, Victoria, we shook them out of our rations, and we trained them." I wondered if he was serious. "However, now that I'm a lieutenant, I get quarters of my own."

I nodded, trying to shake the image of those maggots.

"So, I've read many books that you probably wouldn't think I had...mainly because you'll read anything you can get your hands on if you've nothing else to do."

"I do that anyway," I said, unconsciously.

"So you've told me. Often, if a Captain's family takes a voyage with us, the wife or daughters invariably leave some of their novels behind..."

"I don't know why you think women are the only ones reading novels—I know lots of men that do." I didn't know any, but I was a little stung over his superiority.

There was silence. He didn't respond, and I didn't know

what to say. The carefully constructed camaraderie of the past few days seemed to fade, just like that. We were back at those awkward moments at the village at Jugenheim. I felt that intolerable blush, slowly spreading over my face.

"How should you like that?" he asked finally.

"What?" I practically jumped off of the bench.

"How should you like it if I were constantly on long sea voyages?"

It seemed an odd question. Certainly one to which I had never given much thought. Nor, could I imagine why he was asking me. When I look back, today, I can't understand why I was so obtuse. My only explanation was that I couldn't believe such an exceptional person could ever have any interest in hopeless me.

"I should miss you, I suppose," I said slowly. "I always do when you go on your voyages."

I'm not sure that was the answer he wanted, but I could feel a sense of purpose coming over him.

"That will, for some time, be part of my life," he murmured. "I'm afraid, that moving around is part of a naval officer's job."

I nodded dumbly. I was staring pointlessly at the book now resting on my lap.

"I hear you're a secret smoker, Victoria," apropos of nothing.

My hackles went up.

"Who told you? Ella?"

He chuckled, "I think so."

I wished that Ella had not told him about my habit. Even though I was completely addicted at that point, I realized it wasn't the most attractive of pastimes. I sighed.

"Willy taught me when he was at Bonn going to University. I can't seem to quit. I didn't realize that tobacco was such an addiction."

"I was just thinking of you and Grandmama."

A smile began on my face, despite myself.

"She really hates it. She won't even let Uncle Bertie smoke in her houses, except in one small room...and not after midnight," I trailed off and looked down again.

Suddenly, I felt my hand being taken.

"Victoria..."

I became breathless. I tried to take my hand back, but he was clutching it as though it was a life preserver.

"Yes, Louis...," I answered finally, my voice choking.

"I think you love me."

I looked up at him, speechless. My cheeks were burning, my breathing quickened and my heart beat painfully.

"Well...I...do you?" he persisted.

He really was the most handsome man. He had been quite a Lothario during those years, from all I heard. He even had one of the most sophisticated women in London Society for a mistress. It was amazing that he was now acting like an embarrassed schoolboy in front of a rather naive, sheltered, girl. When I think of it now, I get endless amusement as well as joy.

"Do I what?" I was stalling. Was he just toying with me? But Louis would never toy with me; he was far too decent a man—at least the cousin I knew was. This, however, was far from a cousinly conversation.

"Victoria, please don't play the fool with me…"

I sighed.

"I'm sorry. I've never had a serious conversation with you before, and I'm feeling extremely nervous." At least my accustomed honesty was still working. I drew myself up and said, "yes, I love you…you know it," I couldn't resist adding.

I looked at his face when I said it. Now, I thought, here comes the crashing blow. He loves someone else; he's going to marry someone else; a richer princess—heaven knows he needs the money—a prettier princess…

"Will you marry me?"

He was tense. He still had my hand. His brown eyes were bright with a pleading look. I could hardly take it all in. He was asking me. I felt a little less nervous, now.

"Tell me that you love me, first." I was prevaricating while I tried to get used to this new idea; the idea that he could be my husband and had actually proposed. So, I was acting like an aforementioned naive girl.

The pulse began beating at his temple. He was completely intent on what I would say.

"I do love you and I have wanted to marry you for a very long time. Even when we were children, it was you I liked best."

That was true for me, of course, but I didn't tell him. At the time, I was hoping to be a woman of mystery. He, naturally, had many other romances since our childhood. I believed him when he said he liked me best all along— but the road had been paved with many forks and detours.

"So, you will marry me?"

He still had that agonized look on his face, as though my answer was all that was between him and a burst blood vessel.

I nodded, yes, not trusting my crackling voice anymore. All of a sudden, he broke into a smile. I smiled back and we both, quickly looked away.

"I have something to tell you; so perhaps, I should wait for your answer until after I've done so."

His smile was replaced by that previous earnest, desperate look. I frowned. I thought this awkwardness was over. I was looking forward to, that is to say, I was hoping, he might kiss me. After all, we were now, with Grandmama's and Papa's permission, engaged.

Then he proceeded to tell me about his reputation with the ladies and about his liaison with Mrs. Langtry.

"I told you at twenty-nine I hadn't spent my time getting tattoos."

"Louis," I began, slowly, "I already know about you and Mrs. Langtry."

That left him speechless and he actually dropped my hand.

"You know?"

"Louis, you may not have spent your time getting tattoos, but I haven't spent my time painting screens, either."

I was satisfied. I imagine he was trying to puzzle out what I meant by that, which was rather fun.

Then, suddenly, Louis laughed and took my hand again, bringing it up to his lips.

"I'll never underestimate anyone who's a granddaughter of Victoria again."

I grinned.

"One thing, though," I began, and my faced flushed again. "What about the child?"

He looked away again, embarrassed, and I think, sad.

"You had to mention the one thing that really makes me feel like the biggest cad of all. The lady had the child," he started, looking me straight in the eye, "and she informed me that the little girl, Jeanne Marie, thinks Mrs. Langtry is her aunt."

"Jeanne Marie..." I whispered. "My children will always have a half-sister they won't know," and blushed again at the mention of children.

"I won't give you any excuses...I was weak, but, I hope I've done right by her...she was evidently not too heartbroken."

"Oh, Louis that's tremendously harsh. I believe that is something that you can never know."

He looked down at the hand he held, and seemed to

contemplate what I said. It was as though he was thinking something through, very seriously, then he looked at me again.

"You're right, of course, and I'm glad I asked you to marry me. Can you possibly accept, knowing what a bad specimen I am?"

"I don't think you're at all bad, Louis, just a typical man, with more than your share of good looks and charm. I should know—however, I hope that you won't be working them on anyone else after we're married."

"You don't even need to ask," he replied bluntly. I think that he was genuinely offended. Louis was nothing if not a man of complete honesty and decency. He always would be.

"Then, I accept you with all my heart."

He breathed a sigh of relief, smiled and then he kissed me. It was a curious, as well as wonderful sensation. I thought his beard would be itchy, but it was extremely soft. Louis told me later that he'd had a beard ever since he was able to grown one, so he'd never actually shaved.

"I love you, Victoria," he said again as our lips parted.

"I'm very happy," I whispered.

We looked at each other for a moment.

"You don't mind that I'm only a Serene Highness?" he asked, suddenly, harshly.

"You don't know me very well if you could possibly think that. I think I like the fact that you're only a Serene Highness, in fact, I love it," I answered positively.

"Well, then," he smiled, although I'm not sure he really understood how much I enjoyed not marrying anyone too royal. "I'd better go ask your father if it's all right."

We both got up.

"...And I'll write to Grandmama..."

II
The New Palace Darmstadt, 1884

It was more than all right with Grandmama. I think that she was happy that Auntie Beatrice was out of the way of Louis' unwelcome, though, imaginary, attentions. She was delighted and made sure that Louis received his promotion very quickly. I don't think he liked getting it that way, but it was inevitable if he married me. After we were married, Louis would get his appointment as Commander. For now, however, he considered himself rather frivolously engaged on the royal yacht, the *Victoria and Albert*. It wasn't a difficult assignment, but it gave us a lot of time to be together and get to know each other as intimates instead of cousins.

Louis seemed to approve of my bluestocking streak and we often read and discussed books. We loved opera, the theater, art, and music, and so had much to share together. He wasn't nearly as talkative as I was, but he never hesitated to silence me. My son, Dickie, used to say that only three people in the world could get his mother to shut up: Grandmama, his father, and himself. Louis was never so rude as to tell me to shut up, it was usually, please shut up—to see him, so politely telling me that was hugely funny. I often ended up laughing, but luckily, so did he.

Grandmama had me come and spend some time with her before my wedding. She carried on this custom for Ella, and later Irène and Alicky. These times, she used to say, she valued because we still belonged to ourselves.

Those weeks I spent with her in Osborne, in early 1884, were wonderful. Grandmama and I had lovely talks and nice long gossips about all our relations. She was amused to find out that that was what we younger ones did at the Heiligenberg to pass the time. It was also nice to spend time with Auntie Beatrice. She was tremendously intelligent, and when she was away from Grandmama, nearly as talkative as I was. But, she seemed doomed to be forever at her mother's side, as some sort of secretary, or companion, and never have her own life or family. We would never speak directly of Louis, but she was interested in Sandro's problems in Bulgaria.

"It's never been easy for him there," I remarked to her one day after breakfast, as we took a turn in the gardens behind the house. "Since he refuses to be a puppet of Russia, he's been in acute danger."

Auntie nodded.

"Poor man, for I understand that he wants to make all kinds of reforms for the people and education..."

"He is quite idealistic, though I believe less so since Sasha tried to have him kidnapped."

I referred to a scandalous, and in my opinion, reprehensible incident that had taken place several years before. Because of Sandro's support of the Bulgarian Parliament, the Russian Secret police made a botched attempt to kidnap him and remove him from the country. Sasha and his henchmen were unsuccessful, but, nevertheless, Sandro and his supporters had been on tenterhooks ever since. Come to think of it, all of them, including, Sandro's brothers had been on tenterhooks since Sandro took over this frustrating and precarious throne.

"Yes, I know," Auntie sighed. "But far lighter and more interesting is the problem of Sandro and little Moretta."

Not to me, I thought.

"Moretta, I understand, is wild about Sandro," I remarked, repeating what Louis had told me. "She's always writing to him. It seems they met when Sandro was in the Prussian army, before he was elected Prince of Bulgaria."

"Yes, I remember Aunty Vicky mentioned that in a letter."

"But, I'm told Bismarck does not approve. Not only does he not want to offend Sasha, but he, too, thinks very little of the Battenbergs...he thinks they're upstarts."

"I've always thought they were a nice family—the boys are so handsome," she sighed and turned away. For some reason, she blushed. Had she hoped that maybe Louis...?

"I don't know where it will all end," I continued, not

wanting her to see that I noticed. We walked on. I knew that Grandmama was very concerned about Sandro since she personally liked him very much. And politically, as well as personally, she was so anti-Russian.

When Louis actually came to Cowes to stay, Grandmama was extremely annoyed with me. She hated watching engaged couples. She said it annoyed her, but I believe it made her sad and heartsick for Grandpapa. Louis and I did our best not to bother her until I went back to Darmstadt to prepare for the wedding, which was scheduled for early spring.

It was not to be, however. My dear Uncle Leopold, our family favorite, died in the South of France, that March. The doctors said that he died of a hemorrhage due to a fall, but, as Uncle Leopold suffered from hemophilia, we cannot know exactly what caused his death.

This sorrow overshadowed the happiness that we felt when Papa finally announced Ella's engagement to Serge. Naturally, Grandmama was not euphoric about this turn of events, for her, I imagine, it was adding insult to injury. But she'd had plenty of time to get used to it, and she didn't have too much more to say on the subject.

My wedding had been moved back to the end of April, and Grandmama, who had prepared me all along for the fact that she would not be attending, suddenly notified Papa and me that, indeed, she would be. This gave my wedding a great deal more importance, in general, than I expected. Now it was being labeled as the Royal Wedding of the Decade. It was ironic, in view of the fact that the Berlin family, outside of Aunt Vicky, had such a negative reaction to my marriage plans. I could just see the curl of Willy's lip when he said that Battenberg wasn't "of the blood". When Grandmama heard they were making such comments, she drew herself up in fine form. She said that if she approved the marriage, what could other people possibly have to say?

I drew not only comfort, but also glee in that little show of snobbery by Willy and his ilk. I believe it rather showed him what I thought of him and all his rantings of bloodstock, as if he were talking about a prize pig or stallion. The only member of the Berlin family I felt any sympathy for was Moretta. When she was informed that I would marry Louis, she evidently retired to her bedroom and cried her eyes out.

III

The New Palace, Darmstadt, April, 1884

As the time for the wedding approached, something else, besides poor Uncle Leopold's death happened to take the focus off of the festivities. Papa, who had been a widower for nearly six years, took himself a mistress. Far from feeling resentment, we actually liked the lady. I, especially, felt that Papa's having a mistress, someone to keep him company, would make him miss me less when I left for England with Louis. Her name was Alexandrine de Kolemine. She was originally a Polish Countess, who for the past two years had lived in Darmstadt. The wife of the Russian Charge d'affaires, she had recently divorced him. She was extremely beautiful, and it was good to see Papa smiling and happy again.

I must admit that the preparations for the wedding were beginning to wear on me. For one thing, I was depressed about Uncle Leopold's death—I and all in my family had truly loved him, Papa, in particular, and for another, it seemed as though everyone in the family was attending the wedding. It was going to be one of those Royal mob scenes, as Grandmama called them, and trying to house all the visiting royalties and more importantly housing Grandmama properly, was a worry. I hated to have this thought, but I secretly wished she wasn't coming. It would have been a lot better to just spend part of our honeymoon at Osborne, or wherever the Queen was. Nevertheless, they were all coming—the Germans, the Romanovs, Uncle Bertie and Aunt Alix, the Hapsburgs, the Hohenlohes, and the list went on...and on.

"Honestly, I wish they would all stay home," I told my father in exasperation at breakfast, about a week before the wedding. Grandmama would be arriving the following day and it seems to me I'd spent days getting all the rooms ready.

"Victoria, don't talk that way. This is your wedding, and I think it's wonderful that everyone is going to be together and an honor for you. Besides, I really enjoy these family gatherings."

That's because you don't have to do all the work, I thought to myself, wickedly. I enjoyed them, too, but it was usually for getting a glimpse of Louis, or being with Grandmama. Out loud I said, "I suppose they're fun, it's just that I'm getting married, and I never seem to be able to see Louis."

"Oh, Vicky," Ella, who had been applying herself to her breakfast, said, "You'll see plenty of him when you're married."

"Not necessarily, since he's in the navy—and this coming from the person who's always upset if Serge isn't constantly in attendance."

"Hmm," is all she replied, as Alicky and Irène giggled.

"It will all be over too soon," Papa said, trying to soothe me. "And, believe me, Mama would be thrilled. She always liked Louis."

I nodded slowly. That was certainly true.

Papa looked around the table. He was thinking, I suppose that this was the last time we'd all be sitting together like this—unmarried, and eating breakfast as a family. He seemed to be struggling with something, when he said, "Victoria, would you please come into the library for a moment?"

I nodded and got up. I looked at Ella and Irène, who both looked back, perplexed. Ella shrugged her shoulders, as though saying, "I have no idea...." It was a surprising thing for Papa to ask anyone to the library, since he hardly ever spent any time there himself. This should be interesting.

He sat, and motioned me to sit down in one of the horsehair chairs that Mama bought in England. I waited for him to begin. Perhaps it was another wedding gift...

"Victoria," he began slowly, "I have to ask you to do something for me."

I nodded slowly, my brain working furiously trying to figure out what earth he might ask of me.

"Your Grandmama will be here tomorrow," he cleared his throat. For some reason, he seemed nervous and uncomfortable. "You must tell her...prepare her for me."

"Prepare for what?"

He hesitated. He came over to the chair next to me and sat down facing me, taking my two hands in his.

"You know I loved your Mama very much."

"Yes, of course," I answered impatiently, "but what is it?"

He paused, looking this way and that, avoiding my face. Finally, going slightly red-faced, as though he were struggling even to speak, he said, "I'm going to marry Madame de Kolemine."

It was as though he dropped a bomb. It was one of the few times in my life I was speechless. I wasn't even sure I heard him correctly—

"You're...what?" I replied finally, weakly, faintly.

"You heard me, my dear. I know this is a little

surprising, but well—you know how lonely I've been, and, well—I love her and she has consented to be my wife."

"But, Papa," I began, trying to gather what wits I had left about me, "uh...she's a divorced woman. Surely you don't plan on putting her in Mama's place...presenting her to Grandmama, to Hesse...?" I paused. He looked absolutely stricken, but he needed to hear sense. We tolerated la Kolemine because she made Papa happy, but marriage was quite a different issue.

"You must tell Grandmama for me."

"Me?" I spluttered. "Papa, there is so much for me to do—must it be now?" casting around for any excuse, "couldn't you wait for a few weeks after my wedding?"

It was odd timing to say the least. I had to presume that the lady was pushing him, and didn't want to give him too much time for reflection.

"You must tell Grandmama, Victoria, you're the only one who can make her see reason. You have a very special relationship with her."

"Reason?" I exclaimed. I was getting a little angry at the injustice of doing something like this to me a week before my wedding. "Papa, how can I get her to see reason when I don't see reason. I know it's unfair, but the lady simply isn't of your station...there's no getting around it. Grandmama will never accept her into the family, nor can you expect her to invite you to her homes as before. Don't you see, Papa, it's simply not the right thing to do."

Especially now, I added silently.

"All I see is that you won't stand up for your own father. I thought you and the others liked Alexandrine."

"I do, Papa...we do. But it isn't proper to make her your wife, and even if I and the rest accept her, you know very well that Grandmama won't, and let's be realistic—she's the final authority."

"...and all your protestations about royalty being outdated...you're as bad as any of them."

"Papa," I began, feeling my anger deflate, "I protest what ought to be. Unfortunately, in this situation, you and I live in the world of what is. No matter how either of us might feel or say, you know that I am right; the most important opinion is Grandmama's. Madame simply will not be accepted."

I sighed. I did feel like a hypocrite, but I was the last person who would try to persuade Grandmama to do something so utterly against everything in which she believed. I could never tell her how to react.

"I hardly need point out to you that Louis is the son of a Polish Countess and a Prince of Hesse—why is he more acceptable than Alexandrine?" His voice was cold, and I was floored.

"Aunt Julie wasn't a divorcee," was all I could think to say.

"I see that I shall get no help from your direction..."

I began to protest, but thought better of it all. I had no desire to get involved, and Papa was only getting angrier. I excused myself murmuring that there were more preparations to make for Grandmama's arrival, and quickly left the room. Papa said nothing, and I felt sorry that we were now angry with each other.

That evening, after supper, I was able to speak to Louis about the situation. We sat in the drawing room far enough away from Alicky and Irène for me to see them giggling and pointing. Honestly, having a twelve-year-old sibling was irritating at times. Ella, busy embroidering, was shushing them, and smiling faintly at me. I hadn't told her yet, although she knew and approved of Madame de Kolemine.

"It's damned unfair for him to do this to you now," he exploded, angrily.

"Shh," I said, looking over at the others. "They don't know, Louis, and I don't want them to..."

"If you want my advice, I say, let your father tell Grandmama, and be done with it. You've got other things to worry about..."

"Yes, like where everyone in our entire family is going to sleep, if Grandmama will be comfortable, if Willy is going to cut Ella and be nasty to you and your family...I've always loved having such a large and interesting connection—until now."

Louis smiled and took my hand. Giggles floated over.

"Don't worry, darling Victoria, you can handle it—I've always thought that you would probably make a better naval officer than I do."

I smiled.

"Don't think that I hadn't thought of it. When I first saw you in your cadet uniform, I had visions of cutting my hair and running away to the navy."

He chuckled.

"The Royal Navy is missing the best..."

And, we spoke no more about Papa's embarrassing position.

The following day, accompanied by appropriate fanfare, Auntie Beatrice and Grandmama arrived. Papa, who made sure the red carpet was rolled out, literally as well as figuratively, was at the station, all smiles and benevolence, to meet her. He and I hadn't spoken since the previous morning, and as I hadn't slept the entire night, I had a pounding headache and a white face. Thinking about what to do was wearing me out.

For the first time, I managed to get hold of some rouge, and lightly dabbed my cheeks. I refused to have Grandmama see me as anything but the serene bride-to-be. I met her as she came up the steps of the New Palace with a curtsey and a kiss, and showed her and Auntie to their suites. Grandmama looked beautiful in her black silks and inevitable bonnets, and Auntie, lovely with her hourglass figure, and fringe.

We drove back to the palace, Grandmama's entourage following behind with luggage and other necessities. We led her straight up to her apartments, and Papa excused himself, telling Grandmama that he would see her at dinner.

"My dear Victoria," she began, as Auntie settled her in one of chairs in the room. "You look happy, but also extremely tired. The rouge simply won't cover it up—heavens knows where you got it. It won't do—you've got to rest. You want to look your best for the ceremony."

Whoever thought Grandmama's eyesight was failing ought to have talked to me, I thought. I shrugged my shoulders slightly and looked at Auntie.

"Grandmama, there's just so much to do, and I have to do it. Please don't scold; Ella and Irène are being tremendous helps."

"Well, you can forget about Ella as soon as Serge arrives, all the girl does is follow him around," she said with disgust.

"She does do that," I smiled. "Almost as long as I can remember, she's been doing that, however, at least now there's a good reason. They are engaged."

"Hmm," was all Grandmama would say.

"Grandmama, you must give him a chance—now that he's to be your grandson."

"I don't have to do anything I don't want to do," she replied, petulantly.

"No, Grandmama."

The door opened.

"Look, here's tea," Auntie Beatrice remarked cheerfully.

"Yes, just in time," I smiled.

I went on my way, sending my siblings in one by one to

greet Grandmama, and as the day wore on, many others in our family arrived. The Battenbergs were all there, including the eldest, their sister Marie, with her husband Prince Gustav of Erbach-Schöenburg. The Prussians, including my Aunt Vicky and Uncle Fritz, had to be given special consideration when they arrived. Their suites had to be carefully chosen and their retinue given the greatest care along with their six children who included Willy, who, studiously avoided Ella, and, naturally, the unhappy Moretta, who mooned constantly after Sandro.

I know it sounds cruel when I describe it as such, but I had such a strong impression that Moretta was in love with the idea of being in love. She, it seemed to me, could have picked anyone, though, I can't question her choice of Sandro. He was nearly as handsome and elegant as his brother Louis.

Willy was there with the wife he had married in 1881. I thought that it was ironic that Princess Auguste Viktoria of Schleswig-Holstein-Sonderburg-Augustenburg, whom we all called Dona, was, despite the length of her title, about as insignificant a princess as one could find. She was a rather plain, dull, hausfrau-ish kind of person, and I later learned that Willy never had much to say to her. She was, however, excellent in her dynastic duties, as she had already given Willy two sons by the time of my wedding, and would go on to give him four more.

Uncle Bertie and Aunt Alix also arrived and had to be housed and given all the courtesies, so the day that they all arrived was an utterly exhausting whirlwind. Uncle Bertie, however, managed to take me aside for a little talk about the Kolemine Affair. I was appalled that he knew about the situation, and I was intimidated that he wanted to discuss such a matter with me.

He was able to waylay me, as we were both going down to dinner. Grandmama was doing me the great kindness of presiding over meals until after the wedding. It was a great relief, since I was going mad with worry about Papa and everything else.

"Victoria," he said in his slightly accented English. I could never understand why Uncle Bertie spoke English with a German accent—it seemed very odd to me. "What is your opinion of this affair of your father's?"

I was taken aback. I had tried unsuccessfully to shove the issue to the back of my mind.

"I really have tried not to think about it, I'm more interested in trying to get through this week."

He chuckled, softly.

"Poor little Victoria—this is supposed to be a happy time for you, and all your family is doing is giving you trouble."

"Yes, and Papa wants me to tell Grandmama, and I can't, Uncle Bertie. I simply can't do it right now."

"Well she knows something of it."

"She does," I was extremely surprised.

"Yes, she knows that your Papa has a mistress, which doesn't really bother her at all. She does understand about that," he paused, bitterness tingeing those last words. I suppose it was because there was very little about Uncle Bertie that Grandmama took the trouble to understand, and it was always a cause of distress to him. "She doesn't know, however, about this plan to get married. She said to me the other day, that she wouldn't mind Louis' marrying again if it were some nice, quiet, acceptable woman..."

"All the things that Madame la Kolemine is not," I said bluntly.

He gave me his arm, and we quietly walked down the stairs to the dining room.

"I just can't understand why he's doing this to me, now, before my wedding," I whispered.

Uncle Bertie leaned over, and gave me a kiss. "Never mind, my dear. Things have a way of working themselves out," which wasn't much comfort.

He opened the door, and didn't say anything more as we entered the room.

CHAPTER FIVE

I
The New Palace, Darmstadt, April, 1884

It was a beautiful April day, as I limped down the aisle. In one of my scrapbooks, I have a photograph of myself in my mother's wedding dress. It was another one of that handful of times that I looked rather splendid. I am standing there, appearing quite solemn and stiff, since it was impossible to look cheerful when the exposures took so long. I remember that even standing without expression was an act of deep concentration. My very serious look had many causes, not the least of which was a very tight corset, and the sensation that I was a trussed up goose.

The dress was unbelievably beautiful, made up of the Honiton point lace pattern with roses, orange blossoms and myrtle over a white satin skirt and bodice. Along with it came a full veil, a sapphire and diamond diadem and a wreath of more orange blossoms and myrtle. The limping came with the six-foot train, and the fact that I had hurt my ankle jumping over a coalscuttle the night before.

In this case, however, my grim expression had much more to do with all that had been happening the previous days. Not only was I worrying about Papa and about Madame, who, thankfully, was staying very properly in the background—but...

Several days before the ceremony, I had escaped into the gardens for a snatched cigarette. I really needed it since I was becoming more and more jumpy, and it wasn't about getting married. Marrying Louis seemed to be the sanest and most natural part of this entire week. I was comfortably ensconced on a stone bench hidden behind some elm trees, which was my thinking place and refuge since I was a little girl. Being well concealed here, I was privy to the comings and goings of those choosing to walk in the gardens. One couldn't help but eavesdrop, and I had always learned the most astounding things. It had made for endless hours of trying to puzzle out the adult psyche. Mostly, I might add, without success.

Today, however, I just wanted to hide. My sisters were busy with their various concerns, and Louis was at the Heiligenberg, spending some time alone with his father. I was wishing quite desperately that I could go off alone with Papa...no, not Papa in his state; perhaps, Grandmama, or, maybe, Aunt Vicky, who was so sweet and understanding. It made me grind my teeth when I thought of how appalling Willy and his sister Charley were to their mother, my dearest Aunt. I have, perhaps irrationally, thought that they were responsible for her death. Well, I suppose, if someone could die of a broken heart.

I was thinking of lighting another cigarette, when I saw an extremely interesting sight. There was my vain and handsome Liko, arm in arm with Auntie Beatrice. He looked to be all charm and attention, and Auntie seemed completely enthralled. She had the look of a starving puppy that sees a bowl of food—it knows it's out of reach, but that maybe, just possibly, with great effort, it will get it.

What's Liko playing at now? I thought, cynically.

Surely he'd have to be aware that this was an exercise in futility. Auntie was enjoying her state of single blessedness as the Queen's right hand. Even if he could persuade her otherwise, Grandmama would never, never allow it. Come to think of it, though, he looked as though he were being extremely persuasive. Auntie was blushing and looked quite sweet. Liko looked as though he were teasing her gently. He plucked a daffodil from the ground, and handed it to her. Her blush went even deeper, as I heard her thank him.

He saluted her gallantly and walked off. Auntie stood, transfixed, watching his retreating figure. When he'd been gone a good five minutes (and she was still standing there, motionless!), I called her.

"Auntie, I'm here," I said in a loud whisper.

I seemed to have jolted her awake.

"Victoria?"

"Just follow the smoke," I laughed, and saw her, picking her way through the trees to where I was sitting. Her cheeks were still rosy, and she looked like a young girl. She was clutching the flower in her hand, as though it were a precious jewel.

"Sit," I said, making room for her.

"So this is where you've been for the last hour. Mama's ready to send out a search party."

"So you must have been the advance sentries," I remarked smartly and giggled.

"Are you, perhaps, speaking about that fact that you saw me walking with Liko?"

"Certainly," I said, blithely. "But, don't worry, I won't tell. Besides, it's fine with me if you like him."

"I don't know what you mean."

"Standard reply," I said lightly.

"Victoria, don't be rude—I'm still your aunt."

I laughed at her reprimand and she began to chuckle.

"Do let me try one, dear. Mama would be absolutely horrified," she smiled, looking at my cigarette. I nodded and handed her one. After the usual coughing, she seemed to at least, master the art of blowing the smoke out nearly as quickly as she drew it in.

"You do like Liko, don't you?" she asked in a serious tone.

"Of course I do. He and I grew up together. He was an awful pig and bully...but then, of course, so was I," I finished, smiling at a host of memories.

"Do you think he still is?" she asked doubtfully.

"Oh, Auntie, of course not. Perhaps a bit full of himself, but that's all."

"I don't think so. I think he's nice. He can't help being so handsome. He reminds me of Lohengrin of the legends...especially in his white uniform last night," she trailed off, dreamily.

Truly, Liko had surpassed even himself at the banquet last night. He was positively dazzling.

Another gentler incident happened the previous evening. Before dinner, Grandmama and I, without attendants, or even Auntie, walked into Mama's rooms. As was the custom for our family, Papa had chosen to leave her rooms exactly as she had left them. Arm in arm, Grandmama and I looked at all her things: her night dress folded on the bed; her silver brushes and mirrors laid out just so on her dressing table; her piano in the sitting room, with a Spanish shawl spread on its body—all contributing to the strange affect of someone just being away for a few days, not gone forever.

We walked slowly around the dimly lit rooms, both of us trying, I think, to drink in Mama's spirit and essence. I, doing my best to remember the happiest times we had together. Grandmama, however, was not of that ilk.

"Do you come here often," she asked me quietly, tears

running down her cheeks. For Grandmama, Mama's death could have been yesterday.

"Not really, Grandmama," I replied softly. I didn't wish to tell her that I thought dwelling over the tangibles of the departed was nothing less than morbid. It would have hurt her.

"Dearest, Alice," she murmured, "she was such a gentle and decent soul."

And we both paused at the window out of which poor little Frittie had fallen. Mama had been playing the piano that morning—oddly enough, it was Chopin's Funeral March. I always shiver when I think of that.

"Such a sad family, the Hesses...," she remarked.

"I try not to think so, Grandmama," I hated to see her sad, though that was often enough. "I hope that my sisters and I will make it a happy and thriving family."

How I wish that had been so, but, as is often the case, youthful predictions have an annoying habit of not coming true.

I sighed as Auntie and I puffed on our cigarettes for a few moments. She was deep in thought, and I was wishing that Louis were here, or that he and I were rambling around the Heiligenberg instead of hosting this royal gang. I didn't see why he could escape and I had to stay with the whole crew.

"He wants to marry me," she said finally. It was like dropping a bomb, and my mouth fell open. I was genuinely unprepared for that particular line of conversation...hadn't another bomb just recently been dropped on me?

"He what...?" I said weakly, thinking about the very similar conversation with my father several days before. In this case, while Beatrice was entirely suitable for Liko, there would be a host of people who would say that Liko wasn't good enough for the youngest daughter of the Queen.

"I said, he's asked me to marry him."

I looked at her. There was her usual composed face, the rosiness completely gone. She was simply looking at me to gauge my reaction.

"Auntie, I couldn't be more pleased. I think you would enjoy having a family...but what on earth will Grandmama say?"

"I really don't know. I know that she has always hoped that I would stay with her always. But, Victoria, don't tell anyone I've said this, but I've always longed for a life of my own." She stubbed out the cigarette, and continued to look at me. "I think it began when Louis was in England...no, dear, I wasn't in love with him, but it was so pleasant to have such a handsome young man around— someone my age with whom to talk."

"I do understand, Auntie," I said quietly.

"But then, mama just decided that they should all be kept out of my way; that nothing of the sort was to be mentioned in my presence. Is it any wonder that I was awkward with men of my own age...that they thought I was cold? I didn't know how to act because I had absolutely no experience. Since I've been here, Liko and I have renewed our acquaintance...and, well—"

I had no idea that she had felt that way. With the typical myopia of youth, I thought she was perfectly content, and that the Louis incident was funny.

"I'm happy for you," I said as I put my arms around her and hugged her. "I wish you to be very, very happy. But, when are you going to ask Grandmama?" I was a little tense about this, as I moved away. I don't think anyone's nerves could have stood Liko and Beatrice along with my father's amorous difficulties—my wedding would have been an absolute circus.

"Don't worry, dear, I wouldn't dream of discussing it with her until we are back home. I have no intentions of ruining your wedding with a family upheaval..." I must have looked very relieved, because she took my hand.

"I hope that you don't think I'm being selfish, Auntie."

"Not at all, I think you have enough to think about right now. Mama and I are helping, but it's basically you who are taking care of an awful lot of visitors."

I smiled.

"I don't mind," I lied. I certainly wouldn't have minded if Papa hadn't...but there wasn't much to be done about that. He and I were at an impasse. I had said nothing to Grandmama. Not just because I couldn't find the right moment, but also, because I couldn't find the right words. After all, Papa was proposing to replace one of her dearest daughters with a common divorcee...I simply had no idea how to tell her. I just couldn't cause her the distress, and because of this, Papa didn't talk to me, except in public. It was too unfair and becoming more and more upsetting.

Then, I began to worry about Auntie Beatrice, too. Grandmama had been so firm, all along, about her staying home. I sincerely hoped that she wasn't bargaining for a broken heart. And poor Liko—I hated to think this—but this was such an excellent opportunity for him. This kind of thinking was also cynical, but I hadn't a clue about his feelings for Auntie. I hoped that he cared for her, but wouldn't know until I could discuss it with Louis. She was very sweet, and fragile, with no knowledge of these things.

"I have to go in to Mama," Auntie said absently, brushing off her dress as she rose. We were both so lost in thought that I said nothing, just watched her leave.

I slowly stood, also brushing off my dress. I supposed I had better go in and take tea with Grandmama. Perhaps, that would take some of the pressure off Auntie. Anyhow, maybe now was the time to beard the lioness in her den— no point putting it off any longer.

With this now or never attitude, I walked into the house and trudged up the stairs to check my appearance. Not too bad...anyhow, my hair was in place. I sent my maid to Grandmama's drawing room, and was told that she'd be happy to drink tea with me.

I walked through the corridors, thankfully, not

meeting any of the familial hordes, to Grandmama's suite. As I entered, I saw Auntie sipping her tea calmly, with a closed look on her face, as though her life hadn't been completely changed in one afternoon.

I wish I could be so cool, I thought, as Grandmama bade me sit.

"Dearest, you're looking all done in. I believe no more late nights until after the ceremony."

If only she really would take charge, I thought, wearily.

"Grandmama, it's difficult. There's still so much to do, what with getting the chapel ready, the wedding breakfast...my sisters' clothes..." I began ticking off items one by one.

"You must delegate, dear," she replied quietly. "Now that you're going to be running Louis' household, you must learn you can't wear yourself out doing everything."

Whom did she think had been running the Grand Ducal household for the last five years? Actually, I was looking forward to giving up my hostessing duties, first to Ella, who was getting married in June, then to eighteen year old Irène, who could certainly manage everything. Running the household of a Naval Officer was going to be easy by comparison.

"I shall, Grandmama," I replied meekly. "I'm fine, really. I've done large parties for Papa before."

"Yes, Mama, Victoria knows what she's doing," Auntie remarked absently, as she sipped her tea.

"I'm sure she does," Grandmama smiled, handing me a

cup. "Nevertheless, I believe that sometimes we need to be told to slow down."

I accepted the cup, resisting the impulse to roll my eyes.

"You're so right, Grandmama," I murmured meekly, once again.

She looked at me sharply. Meekness was not usually a quality associated with me. I took a few fortifying sips, clattered my cup down on the saucer, and looked straight back at her.

"Grandmama, I have some rather...delicate news..."

She put down her cup quietly, with a lot more composure than I would have had with such an announcement, and waited. Auntie looked at me, too. She looked as though she was frightened I would reveal her secret. Frankly, at that moment, I cannot say how much I would have rathered it was neither her secret nor Papa's. I also had the sense that a man that Grandmama admired, like Louis, might have been a better choice to break the news. No help for it, though, I was in for it...

"I have been charged, by Papa, to tell you that he is engaged to Madame de Kolemine." I had said it straight out, but I was glad she had put her cup down, or I believe she might have dropped it. Talk about dropping bombs...my heart was beating at an unpleasant rate.

"I believe Papa would not wish you to think ill of him, Grandmama, or turn away from him. He depends very heavily on your regard...as do we all."

Auntie had a faint look of relief on her face, and that annoyed me. I cannot think why she would believe that I would betray her confidences.

Grandmama remained silent for some moments. As she was forming her answer, I studied the emotions playing on her face—emotions that might not be discerned by one who knew her less. She was certainly upset and was trying to master herself. I was glad I'd got it all out.

"Firstly, I would never turn away from your Papa. I know how attached he is to me and to our entire family...and I know how much he loved dear Mama. However," now it comes, "it would make a great difference to me if he remarried."

I nodded...how well I could imagine...I had been holding my breath and let it out slowly—my heart would not stop its painful thumping.

"I want you to understand this so that you can explain it to dear Papa. I understand that he will be lonely without you and Ella and if he really wants company and solace, I think, after Irène marries, which won't be for some time, he could find a nice, quiet, amiable person...well, it would pain me, but..."

She was starting to get upset. I wished Papa had more sense than to do this. I hated to see her agitated. Beatrice looked at me and imperceptibly shook her head.

"If he brought this lady to England, she being a divorcee, and a Russian—well—I could not have him so near to me as before and I believe his brothers and sisters-in-law would be shocked—at least most of them..."

I had to bite the inside of my cheek to stifle a wild chuckle. I quickly looked down so that I would not catch Auntie's eye. She was obviously talking about Uncle Bertie, whose way of life she had always vastly disapproved. No doubt, in her mind, renegade would embrace renegade.

"I hope you will tell him, dear child, to pause and reflect. Such a course would hurt his nearest and best friends, not to mention, and most importantly, his subjects. He must think, Victoria—think..."

I sighed as I thought about the conversation later on. I don't think that Papa could stand to be distanced from Grandmama. She was, in so many ways, the center of our existence. If she rejected him, I believe he would be shattered.

After supper that evening, I told Papa everything Grandmama had said. Grandmama actually shook her head at me for attending the meal, but I had to speak with Papa. She, however, acted towards Papa, as though nothing untoward had happened. Having told her, I felt much less nervous, but I wondered what went on in Grandmama's head—whether she would relent, or if she would remain firm.

I was able to get Papa into the library for a little talk after the men had come in for coffee. He was grim-faced and tight-lipped, as I spelled out Grandmama's feelings on the subject. When I was finished, he said.

"Thank you, Victoria. You did your best, and I imagine the worst is over," and he patted my head and walked out. I was sorry Papa was unhappy, but even I could see that worst hadn't even begun. I was glad, however, that he was talking to me again.

Louis, Ella, Serge and I talked the whole thing out that evening.

"Well," I spoke up firmly, "Louis and I would receive them. The very idea of rejecting Papa—and besides, we liked Madame, Ella, Irène and I—she's been wonderful to Papa."

"There is no reason that Papa can't keep a mistress, if he does so discretely," Ella murmured softly. "Isn't that right, Serge?"

He looked at her fondly, and I thought, patronizingly.

"Ella, I hardly believe you comprehend the situation, and I really wonder if this is something that we should be discussing..." he said in a schoolmaster-ish voice. I rolled my eyes, and I saw that he was about to reprimand me, but then, thought better of it. Instead, he took up the thread of his thought, "A mistress is one thing, my dear, but, I believe that your Papa may indeed wish to present this lady as his Grand Duchess."

"That's hardly possible, Serge," Louis cut in. He of all people understood the ins and outs of unequal marriages.

"Ella and I could never receive them together. There could be no discussion on the subject."

Serge just looked at me coldly, and Ella looked unhappy. There was no help for it, the Romanovs could be such awful snobs. The arrogance of youth, I suppose should be forgiven, but, I later came to regret that Papa didn't take his happiness where he could.

Discussion with Serge effectively over, Louis and I went out into the gardens.

"What a thing to get you involved with," Louis opined as we walked slowly arm in arm. The spring evening was chilly, and crisp, but the flowers were fragrant.

"I've been a nervous wreck about the entire episode, I can tell you that."

Louis put his arms around me and held me close. I took a long ragged breath, and relaxed.

"Poor, darling, Victoria, it was courageous of you to brave Grandmama's wrath."

I sighed.

"Everyone thinks I'm the only one who can break bad news to her. I think it's most unfair," I sniveled unbecomingly.

He smiled and kissed me.

"So do I, darling, but, it has to be admitted, you are the favorite."

"I think it would have been better if a handsome young man like you or Liko broke it to her. You know how much she likes a good-looking man. Although," I started walking again, "maybe Liko's not a good idea, at this point."

He chuckled, "So, Beatrice has told you?"

"Yes, and I don't know what Grandmama is going to say."

"I should imagine tremendous shock might well describe it."

"My only concern is that Liko should genuinely care for Auntie. I'd hate for Liko to lure her away from a happy home into an unhappy one."

"If you're asking me if Liko genuinely loves Beatrice, I'll be honest, Victoria, I really don't know."

"Well, at least you're truthful," I growled, sounding very much like my six year old self. "He'd just better not hurt Auntie."

We walked along in silence for a few minutes, when a thought occurred to me.

"I hope Liko and Beatrice don't think I can smooth the way with Grandmama, I certainly don't plan on being in that position again..."

"Poor Victoria," he said once again, and put his arm around my shoulders. It was nice to be nestled next to him while we walked. It made everything else seem very unimportant.

"I'm not so poor," I replied. After all, a sense of proportion was one of my strongest points. I was getting married to the man I loved in a couple of days. We were moving to England, and I could leave everyone else's problems behind—or so I stupidly thought.

"Just remember," he was saying, "apropos of being poor, my naval pay will not allow too many frills."

I grinned.

"Surely I'm the last person you would think need worry about that."

"Yes, that's true—Victoria, ever tomboyish...I believe, if you could, you'd love nothing better than to romp around in trousers."

"It'd be a lot better than these insufferable corsets..." I said under my breath and blushed furiously, as Louis laughed. "I hate all this controversy at our wedding," I said over his laughter. "First Papa and Madame, then that donkey Liko with Aunt Beatrice..."

"...And there's more," he said between chuckles.

"No," I groaned.

"I'm afraid so. Haven't you noticed Moretta and Sandro spooning furiously behind the potted palms?"

Then I did roll my eyes.

"That girl—honestly..."

"Oh, Victoria, I believe they are truly devoted to each other and wish to marry. Sandro, I may add, has confided in me a lot more than Liko has."

"Well, as long as it makes Willy furious, I'm all for it. It must really gnaw at him that they are together here, and there's nothing he can do about it."

"Perhaps you oughtn't to feel quite so gleeful about it," he grinned. One thing I learned early about Louis, he was the voice of reason.

"Why ever not? I wish someone would take Willy down a peg or two."

"I couldn't argue with that, but people in the family listen to him."

"Hmm, I can't think why—though Charley and Henry always side with him—it makes me sick." I actually felt like growling like a dog. "I believe I'm feeling more sympathy for Moretta already."

We walked along a few minutes, and I decided it was best to change the subject.

"You can't imagine what Grandmama's given us as wedding presents."

I went on to enumerate the set of diamond stars, gilt fruit dishes, shawls and fabrics from all over Britain, and the Empire. I felt quite overwhelmed when they were shown to me. I'm afraid, however, such talk just about put Louis to sleep, and that's where we both went. I, with a tremendous relief in my heart, and Louis, I hoped with tremendous anticipation.

II
The New Palace, Darmstadt, April 30, 1884

I didn't come down to breakfast that morning. I felt quite unwell. Being extremely tired and drained from the week's controversies, I wanted to just laze around—something completely out of character. That, however, didn't stop Grandmama, my entire family, Aunt Alix, Uncle Bertie, and the Wales cousins from tucking into very substantial breakfasts and later, lunches. I tried to remind myself that I was starting my life with Louis, and that a whole new family would begin. However, very little seemed to cheer me up. Perhaps, I could only think, there was no way I would ever be rid of all this extended family. I would spend my life involved with them no matter where I went—unfortunately, marrying Louis would provide no escape.

I had just put my covers over my head, hoping to hide even my thoughts, when Ella and Orchie came into the room.

"Good gracious, Victoria, you're not up yet?"

"I'm not getting up, I'm sick of everyone," I whined underneath my impromptu fort, punctuating my words by pummeling the pillows.

"Oh, darling," Ella's voice was near. "Please, you're just nervous. Orchie's brought you some nice tea, and toast. Please get up—Louis will be so concerned if you don't."

That was true enough. What if the bride didn't show up for the Royal Wedding of the Decade? Who would care, besides, possibly the groom? Never mind, I thought hopelessly, Papa could always take this opportunity to marry Madame, instead.

"This whole thing's been a nightmare," I said frowning, as I lifted the blankets off. Swinging my legs out of the bed, I managed to get up, or, at least try to get up. I let out an involuntary yelp. I had forgotten. Last night, after leaving Louis, in a puerile fit of exuberance, I had jumped over a coalscuttle, and bruised my ankle. And devouring all that lobster on an empty stomach might not have been such a good idea....

"Oh, great heavens above," I exclaimed. "I can't even walk," and I burst into tears.

Ella, dear soul, put her arms around me and began crooning as though I were a child. I must admit, it was enormously comforting. I sobbed and sniffled for a good five minutes, and then felt better.

"There," she said, sweetly, "all better now?"

I nodded, like a little girl. Orchie was smiling broadly.

"Very typical, if I do say so myself, now try to hobble over here and drink your tea, it will settle your stomach. We're here to get you ready."

I did hobble over and began munching toast.

"Just think about how wonderful it will be to be married to Louis."

I nodded. My sister was a romantic, but she was right. All the other silly things that had gone on this week simply didn't matter. All that did matter was Louis, and my heart swelled as I thought of him.

"All the others have been having a fine time downstairs eating everything in sight," Ella commented.

"As usual," I chuckled.

"That's better, dear," Orchie said. "Now let's start combing your hair."

"Oh no, Orchie," Ella interrupted. "I'm to do Victoria's hair. I do it best."

I nodded. "I don't know what I'm going to do without you, Ella."

"Probably just your usual scruffy style," she grinned, and began brushing.

"No, I mean it. I shall be awfully lonely."

"Yes, but, darling, soon we'll all be off to St. Petersburg together."

"And, you'll be living there and I'll hardly ever see you."

"Nonsense, I'll be here in Hesse quite often, and naturally, I'll be in England to see Grandmama and you as often as I can."

Ella would be off straight after the wedding, to spend her last single days with Grandmama. I wouldn't be seeing her until June. That seemed ages away.

"No more gloomy thoughts now, missy," Orchie said briskly. "The bride should only have happy thoughts."

So, there I was hobbling down the aisle, as instructed by Orchie, with only happy thoughts. Grandmama was dressed in her black silk with pearls and diamonds. She looked so lovely as we rode in a carriage together for the civil ceremony, and then back to the palace for the religious one, right in the castle chapel. We all entered the chapel according to our rank, with me on the arm of my father, and Uncle Alexander. Thank heavens for them, as my ankle was beginning to really hurt.

Louis looked magnificent in his full dress naval uniform. Across the breath of his beautifully cut tailcoat, he wore the Star of the Hessian Order and the Grand Cross of the Order of Bath, awarded to him by Grandmama. The ceremony was quite loud and impressive. The choir was singing, there was a bone shattering gun salute, and all the appropriate prayers, sermons, and hymns.

I have always heard that brides usually don't remember their nuptials. They often say that the whole thing just flies by in some kind of blur. I, however, to this day, remember every minute of it. It is such a pleasure to remember how elegant and handsome Louis was, and how he looked at me. I didn't realize, until that very minute, that despite the fact that the chapel was crowded to the rafters, one could feel so much intimacy. I was overwhelmed by my love for Louis and by how much I was looking forward to our being together. All else was swept away, and the joy of that moment pervaded my entire day.

We had the traditional wedding breakfast, a meal that took place sometime in the very late afternoon. My appetite, which had been conspicuously absent, up to that point, returned with a vengeance. I was absolutely ravenous, and Louis teased me about this forever after. None of that blushing bride nonsense for me, he laughed, reminding me of how I had wolfed down the delicacies. I was concerned, however. Papa was not there to toast me, nor was he there to be the first to congratulate us, as was Grandmama. I looked hastily around, but he was nowhere to be seen. Eventually, I forgot all about it as I was enveloped in countless bosoms, and pinched on the cheeks by untold uniformed gentlemen.

I did have other concerns, however, as I scanned the reception room. Toasts were being thrown out at the speed of a train and everyone seemed to be trying to down as much champagne as possible. We all tended to give way to abandon at weddings. I think our subjects would have really been shocked. I suppose they thought that we were a quiet and dignified assembly, forever on our best and most royal behavior. How false that picture was!

Auntie Beatrice looked very happy, positively glowing while she chatted with Liko. I glanced around to see where Grandmama was sitting. Happily, she was ensconced with Aunt Vicky, having no idea that this would be the end of their solitary twosome. In another corner, Moretta and Sandro were likewise having a very close conversation, and I looked around apprehensively for Willy. I feared their ending might not be as happy...

"Victoria," I heard a deep voice at my side. "Stop worrying about all of them—their lives will have to work out without you. You're only to worry about me from now on," and he kissed me chastely on the cheek.

"That's a selfish thought," I smiled at him. I felt like a tourist looking at a particularly beautiful view. It was obvious that the beauty in our new family wasn't going to be me.

"Darling Louis, even though I shall devote myself almost entirely to you, there should be some room for me to worry about others as well..."

"I don't suppose I'll ever persuade you to get out of the habit, will I?"

"No, I don't think so, there's far too many of them, and, they're not going to go away. Besides, I've been mothering much of this group for far too long. But, most of what I'm worrying about now, will have an ending of some sort, for good or ill, fairly soon."

"So, I suppose I'll just have to be patient," he smiled and raised his glass. "You need more champagne." He motioned to the footman, who filled my glass.

"I'm only drinking this for medicinal purposes," I said primly, but the truth was my ankle was really beginning to throb unmercifully.

"A toast," he again raised his glass, and everyone quieted down, "to the most beautiful, sweet, and loving bride, a man would be privileged to have. I give you, Her Grand Ducal Highness, Princess Louis of Battenberg."

"Hear, hear!" everyone cried in unison—and I hoped in agreement. Dearest Louis...no one had ever described me in that way. I blushed at the use of my married title, and everyone laughed. I realized that I had just entered into a morganatic marriage, which delighted me tremendously.

I looked over at Ella, who was naturally with Serge. For once, he actually looked as though he was having a good time. They were sitting hand in hand. She looked up and smiled at me, I could just hear her saying, take the compliment, Victoria, don't think so much—just enjoy yourself. She was right, of course. Ella was a woman who understood the human heart better than most people I have ever known. Her empathetic nature followed her her entire life, through all the tragedies. But I can't bear to think of that now, that is for much later—much later. All I want to think about is my wedding and those wonderful days that followed.

That night we went to the Heiligenberg.

CHAPTER SIX

People today have a longing to reveal everything about their most private moments, and personal feelings. The memoirs of so many are peppered with their most "closely guarded secrets", and the most intimate details of their otherwise uninteresting lives. They leave no stone unturned whether you care or not. I have always felt that they wished to confide in the world because there was such a loss of friendship and intimacy as the world became more modern.

It was so different when I was young, and most that were young with me. We were far more circumspect. Though I imagine, if a reader was perceptive enough, he could easily read between the lines and learn our secrets, too.

I remember poor Moretta's memoirs. I have never read anything more insipid or dull in my life, not because she didn't reveal anything, but because there was nothing of herself in the book. Conversely, when Cousin Marie of Romania wrote three volumes, in which she carefully concealed much of the scandal and unhappiness, so much of Missy's heart and passion for life were revealed. I'm not really sure which category this all falls into, except that I love to remember—and sometimes, I have no choice but to remember.

After we'd drunk far too much champagne, I caught Grandmama's eye, and she, very discretely, motioned me to go and get ready. I whispered to Louis and went upstairs. Although, we were only traveling as far as the Heiligenberg, I had got a beautiful new traveling suit as part of my trousseau.

I remember closing the jacket with trembling fingers. I would no longer be at home with my father and my siblings. Louis was my family now. It was altogether a strange feeling. I took a deep breath, put on my hat, and walked out of what was now my former bedroom.

Everyone was still celebrating as I hobbled down the stairs. There were crowds of the family waiting at the foot of the stairs with rice and other paraphernalia, making a loud racket. Thankfully, Grandmama and Louis had positioned themselves to intercept me when I reached the bottom. I put my arms around Grandmama and kissed her. When, I moved away, I saw that there were tears in her eyes, as there were in mine.

Finally, we extricated ourselves from the boisterous crowd and left through the front doors of the palace.

There was a horde of well wishers, our subjects, cheering noisily as we walked out of the palace towards the carriage. It was sweet how many of the women, especially, wished me good luck. I always felt that they transferred their love for my mother onto my sisters and me. Mama had done so much to change social conditions in the Grand Duchy, and the women, in particular, had always appreciated this.

As Louis and I got into the carriage, we were again bombarded by rice and someone took aim at Louis and flung a slipper. It missed, thank heavens and hit the carriage door. Through the shouts of laughter from the celebrants, I looked again for Papa, but, again, did not see him. I was tremendously disappointed, but tried to forget about it as Ella, Irène and Alicky kissed me goodbye. Ernie hung back a little. I think he was wondering about whether he really wanted to kiss his sister in public. He finally moved closer and I could see there were tears in his eyes. I grabbed him and held him close. I realized anyone leaving the family circle would particularly hurt Ernie. After our embrace, I held him at shoulder length and smiled. Finally, he gave me a watery smile, and went off without a word.

I winced as I took the weight off my ankle, and sat in the carriage. I painted a smile on my face and got to the business of obligatory waving. It was still light and more and more crowds of people had gathered. I waved and smiled as we drove out of the city. The people were also laughing and shouting as we reached the outskirts of Darmstadt. Then, suddenly, there was silence. I was alone with Louis, and I was immediately shy again. It was annoying because I felt I should not feel shy with my husband. He was looking at me with half-shut eyes. I'm sure he was nearly as exhausted as I was.

"Louis, did you see Papa at all during the party?"

He opened his eyes, alert for a moment.

"Come to think of it, I didn't see him...I wonder where he got to?"

"I've been wondering most of the day...when I thought of it, and I'm very upset that he didn't say goodbye."

"Poor Victoria," he said gently. "Don't be angry, it's not as if we aren't going to see them all very soon. Just a few days at the Heiligenberg, then we have to find a house in England. By the time we're settled, we'll have to be off to St. Petersburg for Ella and Serge's wedding."

"Oh," I groaned. "The thought of another wedding..." and Louis burst out laughing. "Not that ours wasn't wonderful," I added quickly.

"It's all right," he chuckled, "I know what you mean. We're both just exhausted. I'm looking forward to a good rest the next few days," which had me blushing. I wasn't at all good with romance.

It wasn't long before we reached the Heiligenberg. With the exception of a few servants, the house had been completely vacated for our use. Louis helped me out of the carriage and we walked slowly, me limping, arm and arm, into the house.

"Victoria, what on earth did you do to your ankle?"

I was a little embarrassed to confess the coalscuttle incident, but I felt I ought to always be truthful. Louis laughed and hugged me.

"You really are irrepressible, do you know that?"

I giggled, I'm afraid I did know that.

"I've never known this place to be so quiet," he remarked, when we reached the entry hall. "Usually there are any amount of cousins and dogs running about."

We were shown to the suite of rooms that Aunt Julie had made ready for us. I had some difficulty going up the stairs, and Louis, in a fit of pure chivalry, picked me up and carried me up to the top.

"Now I really feel like a bride," I giggled.

Louis looked around and gave me a quick kiss when the butler wasn't looking.

When we reached the room, I was having a fit of giggles, caused, I am sure, by fatigue and possibly a surfeit of champagne. I believe that the butler thought that poor Prince Louis had made a really bad bargain, as he left the room rather sadly.

I limped around, taking in all the details of the suite in which I was to spend my honeymoon. It had the usual view of the courtyard, including that small fountain around which we often played. All the rooms in the castle's four sides faced the courtyard. It had always made that area a concentration of activity and of particular interest to me.

Louis came up behind me, as I was looking down.

"I've never been in these rooms before," I said.

"These were used by Uncle Alexander and Aunt Marie when they came here."

I nodded, wondering what else to say. There were too many awkward silences for my taste.

"Shall I have someone send your maid to you?" he asked, tactfully. "I thought we'd have supper up here instead of down in the dining room."

"Of course," I answered, grateful that he was a man of the world. "Since it's just us," and then looked down blushing again.

Louis went out of the suite, and sent Elsa to me. Elsa had been my mother's maid. When she died, Elsa attached herself to me. I was grateful for all her help and advice. I was, of course, usually hopeless in all those areas in which a ladies maid was most proficient.

"Let's get these traveling clothes off," she said briskly. Louis had withdrawn into what, I supposed, was his dressing room. Elsa began to lay out my negligee while I pulled the pins out of my hair.

There was a knock at the door, and I retreated behind the screen. Elsa opened to admit a footman who had brought what looked like a cold supper and another bottle of champagne.

"All clear," she called out as he left.

I quickly put on my negligee, made of candlelight silk trimmed with lace. Nuns in Belgium, I was told, made the garment. It seemed like all fine undergarments were made by French or Belgian nuns. I giggled at the thought and Elsa looked at me sharply. Heaven knows what she was thinking.

She began to comb my hair as I gazed into the mirror. I was looking at the heightened color of my cheeks and the shine of my eyes. I could feel my heart beating in anticipation.

"There, your highness," she said, spreading my hair around my shoulders. "You look beautiful."

"Thank you, Elsa."

"If your dear Mama..." she began, and her eyes filled with tears. She kissed me on the cheek quickly, curtsied and left. We were all thinking of dear Mama these last few days.

It was a sentimental time, I suppose, but, I thought, with a small dart of anger, my own father had not seen fit to be a part of it. I sighed and moved over to the fireplace. Someone had lit a small fire, just to take the chill off the spring evening. I heard a tiny knock from the Louis' dressing room door.

"Come in," I croaked, and cleared my throat with another giggle. I was beginning to think that all the champagne I drank at the banquet was having its affect. Louis walked in slowly, tall in his dressing gown and looking at me anxiously. I wanted to tell him there was nothing to worry about, but, oddly enough, I couldn't find the words.

"Victoria, you look beautiful," he said as he walked over to me. He put his arms around me and kissed my forehead and cheek. I turned, in his arms, to look at the fire.

"Even I can manage, once in a while," I tried to say, lightly.

He rested his chin on my head.

"I don't know why you keep saying that. I've always thought you were beautiful."

"Not like Ella or Alicky..."

"Stop fishing. I think you're the most beautiful of all your sisters."

I suppose I was fishing, but the answer was satisfactory, whether I believed it or not. I leaned against him, fatigued and excited at the same time. It was the most astonishing feeling.

"Shall we have something to eat?"

I nodded slowly. Strangely enough, I was hungry. We moved the small table with the tray of breads, cheeses, cold meats and fruit, in front of the fire. I filled a plate for Louis while he opened the champagne.

"Not more," I exclaimed, as I covered my goblet with my hand."Well, I'll have just a little, it is a very good year," he grinned as he poured some for himself.

We sat, and between us managed to finish most of the food.

"I don't know about you," he smiled, "but I didn't really eat very much at the banquet. I was too busy toasting or being toasted."

"Well, then it's a good thing you're eating something now," I said in my motherly voice. "I suppose I ate a great deal, though, I haven't any idea why. I suppose I was extremely hungry."

"You've been working hard, what with all the relatives, and all the family conflicts, besides, you've been forgetting to eat these last few days. It's enough to make anyone hungry."

"Actually, it's just enough to make anyone sick," I muttered in disgust.

He smiled and poured me a glass of champagne.

"Drink just a little," he coaxed. "It will relax you."

"I'll drink it, but I don't really need to relax."

"Well, I think I do," he smiled ruefully, and downed the rest of his glass. I took my glass and he removed the table. Taking some cushions from the chairs, he propped them up so that we could lie on the floor and look at the fire comfortably. We settled there, and I stared into the flames, sipping the champagne slowly. He put his arm around me and pulled me close, and I shivered, with the cold, I thought.

"How's the ankle?"

"It still hurts, but I think the champagne has been helping a little..." I giggled again...I was really feeling very giddy.

"Let me see," he said, and put his glass next to the andirons.

He moved to the end of my leg, and slipped off my

slipper gently. He began to softly massage my foot, which felt utterly wonderful. I never realized that a foot massage could be felt all over. He started to rub my arch with more enthusiasm. I must have winced because he became gentle again, as he lifted my foot and began to examine the ankle.

"Not sprained," he said succinctly, and began moving my foot slowly until I said, "Ouch!"

"Sorry, sorry." He leaned over and kissed my arch then, put it down gently. "All better," he murmured.

"How do you know it isn't sprained?" I asked blushing, a state that seemed perennial at this point.

"We learn all this in the navy. Things like how to take care of broken arms and legs, cuts, bruises, and the like."

"I can see that you'll be a good man to have around."

"I certainly hope so," he grinned, and caressed my ankle and calf once again, but much more gently.

"That feels much better," I said, wanting him to stop, and yet not wanting him ever to stop.

"Good," he said, and moved back next to me. He pulled me towards him again, and I took a long, ragged breath. We sat quietly for a while, and then he reached into his pocket and brought out a box.

"I should like to tell you a story, do you mind?"

"No," I said, and snuggled even closer.

"This all happened during my journey with Cousin Bertie."

"Oh yes, the famous *Serapis*. I can't tell you how much I envied you going on that cruise."

"Well, I shall admit to you, Victoria, that I was a little chagrined. It seemed to me at the time to be preferential treatment, and I couldn't afford to let the other fellows think that I was special."

"You are special," I replied, but quickly returned to the subject. "It was a little hard to avoid, I should imagine" I murmured.

"Yes, but I tried—I really tried.... It was an incredible trip—we must have traveled at least seven thousand miles by train, in addition to the voyage by sea...each Indian Prince tried to outdo the other in entertaining Cousin Bertie—tents were set up with thousands of servants at our disposal. They had sitting rooms, drawing rooms, and bathrooms, one Prince even insisted on Cousin Bertie keeping a solid gold bathtub as a souvenir—"

"That's incredible," was my inadequate reply.

"It was wonderful, amazing—there was a huge Durbar in Delhi. Thousands of the natives attended just to see Cousin Bertie carried in, sitting in a houda, on a large elephant. He was taken to an enormous throne—bigger than anything I'm sure Bertie had ever seen, never mind, sat in before, while the Princes and Maharajas paid tribute. It really was an astounding sight. There was something of a fairytale quality about the scene—like A Thousand and One Nights. I sketched most of it, since the illustrator fell ill..."

"I know I loved those illustrations."

"Well, the point of all of this," he smiled, as he leaned

over to kiss me on the forehead, "was that one day while I was busy doing a sketch of one of the elephants, a huge fellow, by the way, done up in silks and satins for his big day, with jewels pasted on his head, and on his toenails…"

"I remember that one," I cried, excitedly. "There was a little boy in a loincloth standing next to him, and the contrast of the boy and the bejeweled elephant—well, it was rather sad, I thought."

"I did, too. Although, it really wasn't so bad because it was extremely hot, and the boy was dressed the way I would have liked to be. Well, the Prince to whom this creature belonged watched over my shoulder as I worked, and kept exclaiming about the sketch. He was so effusive, that when I was finished, I gave him the picture. His gratitude seemed to know no bounds. This man had riches that passed beyond comprehension, and yet, he was so grateful for this little sketch, that he sent me an incredible gift that evening…"

"Really," this was fascinating, and I was becoming less self-conscious.

"Yes," he smiled again. "By the way, the picture you saw was drawn by memory."

He held up the box he had in his hand, and handed it to me. "This is what the Prince gave me."

I opened it, very slowly and drew in my breath in awe. Inside, nestled on some white satin, was the largest, most beautiful, pink pearl I had ever seen.

"This is beautiful," I began inadequately, "I've never

seen a pearl like this, even on the Romanovs!" I was really stunned. I gingerly took the pearl out and examined it by the firelight. It glinted and gleamed with an astonishing pink caste. It was truly magnificent.

"He wrote me a letter telling me something about it. I'll show it to you sometime, but the gist of it was this...The pink pearl was brought to him by a little Sinhalese pearl fisher from Ceylon. The pearl fishers in Colombo and other places on the Island can expect, perhaps, to find three perfect pearls in their entire lifetime. Well, it seems that Krishna had blessed this particular fisherman. This was his fourth perfect pearl, and he walked hundreds of miles in order to give it to this Prince..."

"What a brave man, to walk all that way," I said, impressed with his simple faith. I was imagining how perilous a journey it must have been with such a precious cargo and how this man had obviously thought his gods were watching over him.

"Yes, he was truly blessed, for no one ever robbed him on the way." Louis looked at the fire as he spoke. He was seeing the story as he was telling it to me. "He saw this as a sign that he was doing the right thing. When he presented it to the Prince he requested that it only be given to a woman who was, indeed, a pearl of great worth. When the Prince gave it to me, he wrote that he was a disillusioned man. He had never met a woman that could possibly live up to the faith the little pearl fisher placed in the gods and afterwards, in the prince."

I watched his face as he told this story. The fireplace lit the planes of his jaw and forehead as he stared at the fire. He seemed so far away.

"He wanted to give it to a young man, he said," Louis spoke this part almost as if he were in a trance, "because he hoped with all his heart that I would find a woman someday, that would live up to the promise he had made to the fisherman; a woman who was a pearl above price."

I said nothing. I was completely hypnotized by what Louis was saying.

"'A woman of valor who can find? She is more precious than rubies...' or in this case, pearls."

My heart swelled at the beautiful old Biblical Proverb.

"'The heart of her husband safely trusts in her; she does him good all the days of her life,'", I finished for him.

"And that is why I wanted to give this pearl, the most valuable possession I have, to you," he closed my fist on the pearl and pressed it. "I don't know if I can ever express my love any better than just telling you that I believe you to be the woman of whom the pearl fisher was talking..."

I felt a tear make its way down my cheek, as I buried my face on the lapel of his dressing gown. I had never cried from happiness before, but I think that was exactly what I was doing.

"You were the head of your family for five years, darling and you did a splendid job. Taking on such a task at the age of fifteen certainly took a great deal of courage. And don't, please don't be angry, but I believe you even, to a certain extent, took your Papa's place."

I put my arms around his neck, my heart swelling with love, and happiness and I kissed him. I loved the soft feel of his beard on my face, and stayed pressed against him for a few minutes. The fire was dying down, but I was not cold.

"I'm not angry, I just thank you so much, darling, with all my heart," I murmured as I looked again at the fire. "I hope that I can live up to the ideals of this incredible gift."

"You don't have to—you always are, every day..."

"But now it's not just a pearl that symbolizes a virtuous woman, whatever that might be, it is now the symbol of our love, the life and the family we shall have together," I whispered. I was never so poetic, but the words came out before I even thought. I trembled a little.

He began smoothing my hair away from my face.

"I sometimes wish that there wasn't one set of rules for men and one set of rules for women," he murmured as he began to arrange my hair on my shoulder.

"Ella used to play with my hair when we were girls. She used to say that it was my one beauty..."

"You're not going to start that again...?"

"No," I smiled, looking back into the fire. "What do you mean by sets of rules?"

"It's hard to put into words. Sometimes I just wish that you were the first woman I will have known, just as I am the first you will, if you know what I mean," he seemed embarrassed by this line of conversation, as was I, but pleasantly so.

"Well...I suppose it's good for one of us to know what we're doing, otherwise..."

He laughed softly.

"I can hardly believe we're talking about this..." he stopped, and leaned over again. He kissed my shoulder where he had arranged my hair, and I shivered, and sighed. I could not imagine anything more wonderful than my life at that moment. "You're not frightened, are you?" he asked very softly.

"No, I don't think so, at least, not with you," I began, slightly embarrassed. "I was lucky in that I had any number of well-meaning aunts, Grandmama, and even Orchie and Madgie, to tell me what...well to...what to expect," I stumbled.

"And is this what you expect, darling," he whispered, as he began to nuzzle my neck.

"No...well, I don't know," I murmured, thinking of how independent and self-sufficient I had been before today. I had always thought that I didn't really need anyone. It had seemed for such a long time, that everyone needed me, and I had to be strong. In a sense, I began to feel that I was giving up part of myself, but it was a part I was happy to relinquish. Submerging myself into Louis was a voluntary thing on my behalf, and I had the secret knowledge that I could somehow pull myself out, if necessary.

Now however, his lips were moving from my neck, lower to my shoulder, and I vibrated with the sensations. I now knew how a cat felt when it was being stroked. I had watched Ernie with one of our pet kittens, and saw how its tail quivered in delight when he caressed it. I could have quivered...

"Do you know that I love you?" he raised his face to look at me. I could see the light of the fire playing on his face. His brown eyes searched mine as I tangled my fingers in his beard.

"Do you know that I love you?" I responded simply.

"Then, no more talking..." and thus began one of the many times that Louis had the power to stop my tide of expression.

The joy I had felt that day in the church was nothing to the joy I felt in Louis' arms. My memories of that night and the next morning are memories of the heart and the body. They're not so much visual as they are visceral. His gentleness, his sweetness, and his strong passion, brought home to me, more than any words, how much I was cared for and completely loved.

When I woke the next morning, I reached over to his side of the bed, and felt nothing. My eyes popped open and I saw that Louis was sitting at the little table we had used to dine, and was writing.

"What are you writing?" I asked, sleep in my voice.

He got up and came over to me.

"Good morning," and I wrapped my arms around him and gave him a proper good morning kiss.

"Darling Louis, I could just laze in this bed all day long,

but what would the servants think?" I stretched very much like Ernie's cat, I think, and maybe even vibrated a little.

He laughed.

"Probably what they're thinking anyway, my love. That we're a honeymoon couple very much in love...," and he kissed me again.

"Hmmm," I murmured. "But you haven't answered my question."

"Just a letter to my parents, would you like to see it?"

"Certainly, if you want to show it to me."

He went over to the table and retrieved the paper. He climbed on the bed, and put his arms around me.

"Shall I read it?"

"No," I said, taking the paper. "I want to look at your handwriting."

My Dearest Parents,

I want to take this opportunity on the first morning of my married life to say to you what my heart was too full to express yesterday...You have given me the opportunity to bring home my beloved Victoria as my wife, and few men can have found such an angel as she is.... My happiness is so overwhelming that I cannot yet take it all in, and my heart is full of thankfulness to everyone who has helped me to find it...

How lucky I was to be loved this way. I put the letter down carefully, and kissed Louis for the thousandth time that morning...

I remember that first morning of our marriage so vividly. The pink pearl was hidden in a secret compartment in my jewelry box. The compartment contained several bracelets, earrings and necklaces that I had inherited from my mother, as well as all the jewels that Grandmama had given me on my wedding day. I, alone, had the key to that part of the box. I wouldn't even give it to poor Elsa, who sometimes watched me sadly when I opened it.

Although she looked at me reproachfully, I just couldn't explain it to her, or to anyone else. It took me a long time to show it to my eldest daughter, Alice, and, quite frankly, I don't remember if I ever let Ella in on my most precious secret. I'm not sure that even Louis knew where I kept it.

Of all the jewels and baubles I would own in my life, none were as precious to me as that pink pearl. Time and again, over the years, I would simply take the pearl out and look at it. Sometimes, I felt that it glowed when things were going well for family members, but it temporarily lost its sheen when tragedies occurred. I never had it set, or made it into a piece of jewelry. It was too precious to me to share with anyone except the members of my immediate family. I came to consider it just what I had said that night, a talisman of my marriage...and a source of great comfort.

Those days at the Heiligenberg were some of the most free and untroubled of my entire life. There was no family about and no controversies. Louis and I rambled through the house, and the environs, taking in the views of the valleys and the vista of the blue Rhine in the far distance. There were trees and vineyards to inspect and, had I not been an old married woman, trees to climb. Louis laughed and hugged me when I told him of my continued longing to climb trees.

"Always the tomboy," he would say then and many times afterward.

The Heiligenberg was situated next to the ruins of an old nunnery. Louis and I would make our way down the pathway to a spot next to a small point that overlooked the valley. We would talk about the nuns of long ago, who, with their donkeys would make their way to the pond for water, and then take it back to the monastery. It was so quiet up there, those sweet days that we spent; it seemed we could hear the tinkling of the bells of the little donkeys.

This was one of the few times that I had seen Louis in civilian clothes, and I must say that he was one of a unique group of military men that wasn't diminished by them. I've seen pictures of Nicky and Willy (who absolutely adored the most elaborate and sometimes comical of uniforms), and they always looked uncomfortable in civilians suits. They looked like little boys who were desperately unhappy being "dressed-up"—as though their collars itched and their suits didn't fit properly. Not so with Louis. He really was one of the most dashing men I knew—and that included Liko.

We did very little those days, besides getting to know each other—not as cousins—but as lovers and friends and close confidants. It was a relationship unlike any I had ever imagined. It seemed to me that my life was now really beginning. That all the years until the day I was married were pale shadows of what my life was and would become.

Every woman says that she is transformed by love, but I really was. Probably because I had no mother, I was unprepared for much of my feelings during those early days. I was simply overwhelmed with happiness—an altogether new and delightful sensation.

For me, it was strange not to want to escape every minute into a corner with a book. In the past, I had thought of books and the voracious reading I did as a refuge from Ella's mooning, from Alicky's sulks and from Papa's foibles. I believe I read less that week, than at any time in my entire life. We, two, however, were so close in our likes and dislikes, in the pursuits that we enjoyed and the cultural things that we craved. It was, sadly, then, when I truly realized how completely unsuitable Mama and Papa had been for each other. My life, as it was, was so joyful, that I could almost forget that I would soon lose Louis to the sea.

PART II

1884-1901

CHAPTER SEVEN

I

It was actually several days into our honeymoon that we received a long letter from Ella in which she described the events that taken place after we left the New Palace. It was then that I finally learned what had become of my father after the wedding ceremony.

Poor, dear, Ella, having to handle this distressing situation without me...

Papa, it seems, had done what he had threatened. Almost as soon as the wedding ceremony was over, Papa slipped away and virtually forced the Prime Minister to marry him and Madame de Kolemine.

When I read this sentence aloud to Louis, I was again, struck dumb. Louis and I looked at each other in astonishment. Louis recovered his wits more quickly.

"Well, to be fair, Victoria, this is hardly a surprise...he told you he was going to do it."

"But so soon after our wedding, I...I never actually thought he would..." I couldn't finish.

Louis grabbed the letter from me and continued to read.

"'Grandmama had to be told, so we all cast about for some poor soul to break the news. You, dear Victoria, were unavailable, and no one else had the nerve. It, therefore, fell to Lady Ely...' Lady Ely?"

"Grandmama's lady-in-waiting," I choked.

"Poor woman," he smiled. "As I was saying, '...fell to Lady Ely to volunteer to tell Grandmama. So, with great trepidation, she proceeded that very evening. Lady Ely was closeted with Grandmama for some time, who it seems, took the news fairly calmly. Uncle Bertie, as the senior male of the family, was called in...'"

"You knew all about this, didn't you?" I realized that he seemed very unsurprised.

He hesitated.

"Yes, I had a strong feeling. He said, often enough, he was going to do it, darling—to you, and later on to me. I just assumed that he would," he replied uncomfortably. "Then when he went missing during the wedding breakfast...well..."

"But you said nothing."

"Why should I want to ruin our wedding night, besides I didn't know for sure. You were upset enough, but, not nearly as upset as you would have been if you'd have known."

I smiled and put my arms around him, and rested there.

"You're right, of course."

"A proper little wife...." He held me close and kissed my head. "I wonder how long that's going to last."

"I wouldn't count on it," I murmured against his lapel.

"Oh, well, I suppose I shall have to bear it," he heaved a loud sigh.

Meanwhile, according to Ella, everyone, except the Queen was in an uproar. The Queen had decided, plainly and simply, that Papa must seek an annulment. She resolved that the bride must be informed right away, and that Uncle Bertie must be the one to tell Papa. After giving those orders, she settled back, satisfied that the matter was finished.

Papa, we were told, went about in utter shock. He, for some reason best known to himself, didn't understand the reactions of the people around him. What, I had to wonder, had he expected? The Prussians left the following day, Ella wrote, at Bismarck's orders. They were not, the Chancellor felt, to be polluted by morganatic marriages, past, present or future.

"Rats," Louis stated grimly, "deserting a sinking ship."

"It's strange how threatened they all are over this. Grandmama's just doing what's right, but the others...Willy...they are just afraid that something's being taken away from them..."

Louis looked at me for a moment, eyebrow raised, and

a faint smile on his face. I now sighed sadly and reached out for Louis' hand.

"Now I understand how you've felt at various times, dearest, especially at the hands of someone like Willy," I said slowly, realizing that Willy would be putting me in the same category. I held Louis' hand to my cheek for a moment. Somehow, being lumped in with him made me quite happy. It had the added attraction of annoying Willy. "It's nonsense...all of it...utter nonsense."

"He's already agreed to an annulment." Louis continued to peruse the letter, ignoring my ramblings.

I sighed again.

"So soon..."

The entire episode, when told this way, sounds rather sordid, and I am sorry to think that. Really, the tragic part was that Papa didn't actually find any happiness, thereafter, and mooned and moped for ages.

So soon, I was beginning to feel guilty about my happiness. We would be leaving here at the end of the week to travel to Chichester, near Portsmouth in the south of England. Louis would then take up his appointment to the Royal Yacht. Ella would travel with Grandmama back to England for her time alone before her marriage to Serge, and Papa would be left with Irène, Alicky and Ernie.

Back in Darmstadt—having settled matters to her satisfaction—Grandmama betook herself, Ella, and Aunt Beatrice, back to England. Papa was to visit Windsor quite soon after, but for now, unhappily, was hiding at the New Palace. All the different family branches decamped as swiftly as possible, and quickly decided he had brought great disgrace to the fine Hessian Family. Then, just as quickly, forgot all about it.

Louis and I finished our week at the Heiligenberg, and then traveled to our new home, on the coast of England, called Sennicotts. It would be one of a series of places we would lease though they all seemed temporary stopgaps to me. My real home, in my mind, was the Heiligenberg, then, after that was sold, my son Dickie's home, Broadlands, and lastly, finally, my apartment in Kensington Palace.

Those first few weeks, we had few visitors, though, Papa, having arrived for his exculpatory visit, came now and then from Windsor. Louis and I did our best to cheer him up, but he was quite depressed. I think what really kept him going was Grandmama's continued approbation. She was determined to show that nothing had changed, and I believe that helped him immensely. What probably didn't help was being around a newly married couple and an about-to-be-married Ella.

We, in fact, spent most of the time preparing to go back to Germany, and thence, to Russia. I was rather excited as we Hessian children had never been to Russia. Louis, of course, had been there several times, the last time being just a few years back.

He, Sandro and their Papa had been present at one of

the many attempts on Tsar Alexander's life. They had been making their way to dinner, a few minutes late, as it turned out quite thankfully, when a bomb went off. The Tsar and my Uncle Alexander were unhurt, but Louis always remembered the enormous force of the explosion, and the choking, thick, smoke. They found that many soldiers in the guardroom below had been crushed to death. It was no wonder that Louis associated Russia with brutality, just as I would.

Grandmama had several conferences with me regarding Russia. Once again, she expressed her reservations about Ella's marrying into the Romanov family, and once again, she warned me not to let my sisters go "all Russian". I wasn't worried about Irène. Her preferences already seemed to lie in another direction, but I was concerned about Alicky. She was such a self-contained and melancholy girl. I worried for her...

Ella's wedding, despite objections from the British and many of the German Royal houses, including the Prussians, was set to proceed in June and from all accounts, promised to be an entirely splendid event. I, myself, being tremendously excited, had only heard of the grandeur of St. Petersburg, and now I was about to see it all for myself for the first time.

II
St. Petersburg, May—June, 1884

It took us an entire three days by train to reach St. Petersburg. One always reads about how vast Russia is, but one can only comprehend it when one has spent days and days in a train watching its great expanses speed by. Having spent those days and days in the train, I could never say that the journey through such an enormous distance was in any way monotonous. There were stops in several Russian villages, as we drew closer to Petersburg and there was our fine escort of Serge's Preobrajensky Guard, joining us at the Russian border and caring, beautifully for us, as we approached St. Petersburg and the palace where we'd be staying—Peterhof.

Most importantly, there was my dearest sister Ella to spend time with and there were the children, especially Alicky, who at twelve, was more excited than I've ever seen her. And, most delightfully, there was more time alone with Louis.

I had brought the pink pearl with me, as I would on all my journeys. Besides being my talisman, I really felt that it was in very little danger since people didn't know of its existence.

Being in such close quarters with my family had made me a little skittish with Louis. After all we had shared this first month, I, somehow, began to think that everyone was aware of our intimacies. It was stupid of me and I lay it down now to immaturity, but I found public displays of affection intolerable. It was too important to me, too private. Grandmama chided me later for being unaffectionate, after all, she would point out, it was just family, but I knew that Louis didn't feel that way.

We sped through the countryside, going further and further north. As we did so, the days seemed to get lighter and lighter, until there was virtually no night at all. It was very strange, and exotic, but then, so was Russia. The terrain struck me as being beautiful, but extremely rugged. It was rocky and full of trees, very similar to other northerly cold climates, and, in particular, I thought of Scotland. There was, indeed, a mighty grandeur, as the view seemed to extend forever. The wide-openness of it was what really amazed me. It made little Europe seem extremely cramped.

The night before we arrived in St. Petersburg, Louis and I were lying in bed talking. Well, actually, I was talking and Louis was listening, as he often did. Louis already seemed to know me so well that it was a little disconcerting. He told me that it was easy to observe people while they talked. You could see the nuance in their expression and often what they really felt about what they were saying and to whom they were saying it. Since, I did enough talking for two people, I suppose Louis had plenty of time to observe me. Frightening thought, if it had been anyone but Louis.

I propped myself up by my elbow, talking my way

through my monologue, while Louis played absently with my hair. I finally got to the point.

"I'm worried about Ella," I stated, and fell silent, running, for a moment, out of steam.

When I stopped Louis looked up at me.

"Worried about Ella?" he repeated.

"Of course, aren't you?"

Louis plumped up a few pillows and sat up straight.

"Because of Serge?"

"Serge? No, not really, though he is a rather odd duck, don't you think?"

"Yes," he said bluntly.

"I'm worried about how Ella will get along here in grand Russia. She's such a simple, sweet girl. For a long time, as a child, I remembered her wanting to become a nun. I just hope that all this splendor doesn't overwhelm her."

Louis smiled.

"I don't think it will. Ella's sweet, but, Victoria, she's not that simple. She can be quite grand enough if the occasion demands."

I closed my eyes and sighed. I did have a sense of foreboding, and would always remember this feeling.

"What about Serge?" I asked.

He looked at me with a raised eyebrow.

"What?"

"Don't prevaricate. You thought I was worried about Serge...why?"

"Victoria..." he murmured coaxingly, as he leaned over

and began to kiss me; quite the best avoidance of an unwanted topic.

I thought about it later just before I fell asleep. I was listening to the steady cadence of the train wheels on the track. Louis knew something about Serge that he didn't wish to discuss. Later, I heard the rumors of enormous cruelty and strange ways, but I discounted the latter, while, never expressing my worry about the former. He was, I thought, a tragic man, but I conveniently avoided the truth of it.

We arrived the next day, Ella and Alicky nearly beside themselves with excitement. We'd all dressed carefully in our best day dresses and awaited Sasha, Serge and any other family members who happened to be about. I remember the day being quite warm and slightly sticky. One never imagines it being warm so far north.

It struck me as we waited that this could not be easy for Louis. Sasha had shown such a tremendous dislike for Sandro and such disdain for the Battenbergs in general. Meeting on these family occasions, even though they were first cousins, could not be particularly pleasant. At least, I comforted myself, Willy would not be here. He had vowed that he would never see Ella again after she refused him, and, was, foregoing the pleasure of a family gathering in order to keep his promise.

Instead, beside Uncle Bertie, one of the other senior members of my family, in attendance, was to be Uncle Affie of Edinburgh, Grandmama's second son. He had been, along with Mama, the one who encouraged Louis to join the British navy. His wife, Aunt Marie, who was Sasha and Serge's only sister, delighted in showing us her old home. I always enjoyed the times I spent with the Edinburghs and their children.

We disembarked for a few minutes and noticed to our surprise, crowds cheering as their Tsar and his brother came to meet us. This, I was told, was rather odd for Russia, as demonstrations of such a nature were not given to the monarchs—they were mostly feared, not loved. We saw, soon enough, that despite these demonstrations, which, I now gather were staged, there was a great deal of security for all the members of the royal family—and, with very good reason.

Sasha was giving everyone bear hugs in the old-fashioned Russian way, while, Serge, very stiffly and formally, kissed Ella's hand and the cheers increased.

"Who are all these people?" I whispered to Louis.

"Unless I miss my guess, they're here for the spectacle."

"What spectacle? Us?" I was incredulous.

"Just wait."

He was, of course, right. We were met by a host of elaborate looking carriages, the kind Grandmama took out once a year and went to open parliament. There was more of Serge's command, row upon row of the Preobrajenskys on horseback and ready to escort us—they were quite a sight in their colorful uniforms and glistening swords. They say, today, that the British monarchy knows how to put on a show, but I say, if they do, they owe it to the Romanovs.

I looked over at Ella, who was stepping into a coach with Serge and Papa. She looked radiant, but, curiously, calm, as though these were nice, but not necessarily important occurrences. I was momentarily satisfied that Louis was right, that being a Romanov would not turn her head.

Louis and I squeezed into a carriage with Alicky, Irène, and Ernie, and endured a monologue from Alicky. I never dreamt that I would have heard such enthusing coming from her, of all people.

"Weren't Cousin Sasha and Cousin Serge completely splendid?" she gushed. "I just adore Cousin Serge," which, strangely enough, I knew to be true, "he's such a gentleman."

I looked at Louis, who smiled faintly back, and raised his eyebrows slightly.

"What wonderful people to come to meet us..." she paused. Then a thought occurred to her—"Where are we going, Victoria?"

"To Peterhof," I answered in amusement. Peterhof was the royal compound just outside St. Petersburg on the Gulf of Finland. We would stay there for the week before the wedding.

Alicky nodded, and calmed down slightly. Poor child— whenever she became excited, the red color rose on her neck to her face, making it positively blotchy. Otherwise, she was growing into an exquisite young lady.

"You and Papa are to stay in the Grand Mansion," I told the girls and Ernie, "while Louis and I will be staying next door." The mansion next door, I thought, and had to suppress a giggle.

We would soon discover that everything in Russia was on a grand scale. The rooms were huge, the gardens were immense, and even the people were taller and broader than I was used to. It struck me that my family and I lived virtually a middle class existence in comparison to the Romanovs. Our little palaces in Darmstadt, and even Papa's exquisite summer resort of Wolfsgarten, must have seemed like little guest villas to our visiting Romanov relatives.

There was an enormous pull to all the grandeur and I saw that one could easily be sucked into this kind of life. I saw two of my sisters do so, and, yet, curiously, much as I was attached to my Russian cousins, never had the desire myself. I suppose it may have been that my life was so nicely settled before I had even seen the country.

Nevertheless, I was simply aghast at the excess. If that sounds strange coming from someone used to living in the lap of luxury, I will say that what I was used to was nothing in comparison to the lavishness of my cousins' court. It seemed magnified especially when I saw something of the way the other ninety-five percent of Russians lived. That was all my Mama's sense of social justice, and, even socialism, coming out in me. Those ninety-five percent seemed to live in dread of a very small ruling autocracy.

It was strongly brought to my attention in the mien of the servants at the palace. I particularly remember the subservient way they behaved to the royal family. They took the role of humble, domestic dog, and waited, warily, to see if their masters would beat or praise them. If it were praise, they would kiss their master's hand and call him "Papasha" or little father, and if it were not, they would wait with pathetic stoicism for their justly meted-out punishment.

I have to admit, I found it frightening. I remember, as a girl reading *Uncle Tom's Cabin* with Mama. Grandmama, who was fortunate enough to meet Harriet Beecher Stowe, had recommended the book to her. Grandmama told us that it was an important story illustrating social injustice and that it brought tears to her eyes.

I thought that the slaves in America had it worse, as they were not considered human beings, but only property. The Russian peasants, though considered human—barely, were, and in reality not treated like human beings at all. It is difficult to admit that if it hadn't affected my family so tragically, I might have been in favor of the Revolution of 1917.

We didn't see much of St. Petersburg since we were going straight out of the city. But we would be back just before the wedding. From what I could see, however, it lived up to its reputation as being one of the most beautiful cities in Europe. It was sunny, the avenues were broad, and as I glimpsed, the river Neva sparkled beautifully in its pink and orange stone banks.

Alicky had at last stopped talking, as though the exertion had finally exhausted her and sat back in the carriage staring contentedly out the window. Irène was feigning boredom, and Louis and Ernie engaged in a desultory conversation.

As we were traveling again, even for this short time, I continued my contemplative mood. Louis and I had more news of Sandro in the last couple of weeks. Sandro had followed Moretta and her family back to Berlin after our wedding. He was determined, it seems, to pursue Moretta and ask for her hand. An easier pursuit, I thought wryly, could hardly be imagined—at least as far as Moretta was concerned.

While Bismarck, Uncle Fritz, and Cousin Willy were outraged at such a proposal, I knew that Aunt Vicky and Grandmama were very much in favor of the match. Not only was it new blood, which Grandmama thought was extremely important for our family, but Sandro was one of the handsome Battenberg princes. His imbroglio with Russia and Bulgaria bothered her not a jot. In fact, she was under the impression he was deeply wronged. Grandmama actually counseled all the parties involved to wait and not make any hasty decisions. I knew, however, that Willy would not be moved in this matter. Not only did Uncle Fritz and Willy think that it would not do to offend Russia in this situation, but such a marriage would only let one of those dreadful morganatic princes into their immediate family. Of that, Willy, for one, was utterly horrified.

I smiled, and sensed that Louis was looking at me. He and Ernie had stopped talking and all of us, tired from the journey, were silent. And, considering the week that awaited us that was the best thing.

Soon, we reached our destination. Peterhof was immense, made up of several residences, beside the main ones—some very baroque and ornate, and others, in the Italianate style so well beloved. The gardens were beautiful, still green and blooming with the last of the spring flowers. All over there were fountains, pavilions and benches.

We were told that to really see all the gardens, one needed to take a carriage or trap. We did just that later, after one of our suppers. We, laughingly, piled into a carriage and Aunt Marie, whose fond childhood memories took place here, happily showed all the visitors the wonder of her gardens. I don't think I had seen her as happy as when she was now in Russia with her Romanov family. She detested England and everything about it. Here at home, she seemed to bloom like a flower, and when she was in London, she closed up like a clam. It was sad, actually, not to like one's married home. I, for one, was thrilled that my residence would be in England. But, then again, my marriage was so different than these spectacular royal marriages. I thanked heaven for it every day, especially when I looked at my pearl.

The days that followed were full of festivities, dances, dinners, lunches, games and outings. Sasha, who had always been warm to me in the past, had changed somewhat. Like Willy, I believe he was lumping me in with Louis and decided that as a couple, we weren't quite the thing. Many little slights followed, mostly done to Louis, who had given offense, mainly by his birth, but also because of his decision to become a naturalized British subject. Grandmama's dislike of the Russians was fully reciprocated by Cousin Sasha and he ranted against her, I was told, whenever there was an opportunity—though, thankfully, not in my presence.

Our days were full. We explored the exquisite gardens and marveled at the tremendous fountains. We delighted in the intricate patterns of the flowerbeds, resembling Versailles, and we stood next to the waterfalls, enjoying the refreshing water as it splashed on us during those hot days.

The Romanovs were not an easy family to marry into and Ella exhausted herself trying to get along with all the aunts, uncles and cousins, as well as, the brothers and sisters-in-law. Alicky and Ernie found the process much less trying. They fell in with the young ones, playing games, going on outings and attending little dances. I saw that they both thrived in the company of Sasha and Minnie's children: Nicky, Xenia, Michael and Olga.

Nicky, a sweet, handsome boy of seventeen, with warm brown eyes, took Alicky under his wing and Alicky blossomed. She was happy, carefree and actually laughing...she who had previously derived so much pleasure in being doleful. I began to think that Grandmama's admonition against going "all Russian" would be lost on her. I, however, was simply glad to see her happy and so playful.

The days passed quickly, and Ella and I agreed that I would come visit her every summer. Serge owned a delightful country home called Illyinskoje, somewhere outside Moscow on the Moskva River. We were determined to be there together each year. Though Serge always seemed stiff and unresponsive to me, I had to admit that as the day approached, he seemed almost excited. His admonitions to Ella lessened and they both glowed with what I suppose was anticipated bliss. I began to think that, if nothing else, Serge was an extremely refined and quiet gentleman—nothing like his bear-like brother, Sasha. Nicky once told me that his father could bend forks and other metallic objects with his bare hands. He also told me that Cousin Minnie hated him doing such things, though there was one point later, when his immense strength saved their lives. It had to be said that they were an unusual family.

We returned to Petersburg for the wedding. Ella's morning preparation for the ceremony was nothing like mine. No tantrums, no tears...Ella exhibited a serenity I would later marvel at, and yet come to expect from her. She was perfectly calm and tranquil. We began dressing her, my sisters watching as I and Ella's maid began the long and almost excruciating process.

She was stunning and far more elaborately and splendidly attired than I had been at my wedding. But, Serge was a Grand Duke of Russia, and extremely exacting in his requirements. He adored sumptuous jewelry and would later see that Ella had different pieces to match every single outfit.

Her dress, a court dress, was white with cloth of silver. It was immensely heavy and Ella told me later that from the minute she put it on, her shoulders ached. She wore the Grand Ducal Crown on her head as well as a diamond tiara, a necklace, and earrings all belonging to Catherine the Great. The earrings were so heavy that they had to be supported by a wire that dug mercilessly into her head. The finished product was beyond breathtaking and beyond my power to describe. She was exquisite.

There is an old sepia picture of a group of Russian Grand Duchesses, each one dressed magnificently, covered with jewelry, with an immaculate looking page standing behind her. As they stare out at me, they look so homely that they seemed like peasants or worse, monkeys, with baubles and bangles. Ella, however, was never eclipsed, no matter how much clothing or how many jewels Serge would require her to wear.

"Well?" she said to me, turning about for my inspection.

"I'm not going to join the sycophantic chorus," I nearly whispered, overcome by her radiance.

"Oh, Victoria," Alicky burst out in her twelve year old

way. "Ella's absolutely gorgeous and you know it. Serge will be so pleased."

"Do you think so?" Ella smiled. She was always eager to please Serge, so this was the right thing to say. "What I meant was, is everything in place. Are there any threads hanging and are all the jewels and tiaras where they are supposed to be?"

"And I thought you were fishing," and I hugged her as hard as I dared. I heard a small groan. "Will you be able to stand all of this?" I was truly concerned. I couldn't see her being able to divest herself of any of her finery until early evening.

"I'll be just fine," she answered, a trifle too briskly. "After all, I'll have to get used to this. Serge isn't exactly a casual person."

Irène giggled.

"Hardly."

"Oh, I almost forgot..." Ella went to her dressing table and got a coin. She handed it to her maid, and she stepped out of her shoe. The maid placed it inside. We all grimaced as she stepped down.

"Well," she shrugged, and tried to smile. "It doesn't feel any worse than the rest of this".

"What was that?" Irène asked.

"A ten ruble piece...for luck..."

We all smiled, and soon it was time to go to the ceremony. Since Ella had not yet converted to Russian Orthodoxy, there were two—the Orthodox and the

Lutheran rituals. Young Nicky was Serge's best man, and proudly held the crown over his much taller Uncle during the Orthodox ceremony.

The breakfast afterward was long and protracted. Louis had held my hand through the ceremony, putting me in mind of our much simpler one. Louis looked marvelous in his naval uniform, and once again, outshone me—not that I cared. I suppose, in a way, it was a slap in Sasha's face, but, after all, he was a Lieutenant, soon to be a Commander in the British Navy.

Because Grandmama had sent her yacht the *Osborne* to fetch all the members of the family who had attended the great festivities, many of the officers had been invited to the breakfast. I was completely outraged that Louis had been seated with his naval officers instead of with the family. I knew that it was Sasha's doing, and having the approval of the guest list, he sat him "below the salt" even though we were the family of the bride. I seethed with indignation, but Irène later told me that everyone simply thought that Louis preferred to sit with his officers. I, however, knew the truth and felt it strongly for Louis. I would have loved to have made a scene, but would do nothing to hurt Ella. Louis, I noticed, tried not to mind, but I was sure that he did. Later, when my father protested this insult, Sasha said he did it because the Prussians seemed to want it that way. We, all, however, knew that Sasha could have seated people any way he wished.

When the feasting was over, we all went with the bride and groom to the Sergueivskia Palace, Serge's home in St. Petersburg. The Emperor and Empress arrived before us, and met the couple at their own doorstep with bread and salt. According to Russian tradition, it is the parents who were supposed to do this, but they were, unfortunately, dead. It was, therefore, up to Minnie and Sasha to perform this parental task.

Louis insisted that I say nothing to Ella about what happened, and it was almost a physical effort to contain myself. Louis, however, was right. There was no reason to put a pall on Ella's festivities.

Soon afterward, we left Russia. My anger dissipated somewhat as we got under way. Louis was happy and certainly in his element. That was usually enough for him and had to be enough for me.

I prayed that Ella would cope with her new life, and that Serge would be more helpful and less pedantic, however, I wasn't optimistic.

Grandmama's yacht was a luxurious atmosphere in which to talk over all the events and grand spectacle to which we had all been witness. The sea voyage, being about three days, was enough to return us all back to everyday life once again. However, I was party to confidences from quite an unexpected quarter.

During our second day at sea, Alicky came into the salon and sat next to me, putting her hand on my arm.

"Victoria, what do you think of Nicky?" And, as she

THE ROYAL MOB

uttered his name, she blushed and got terribly red in the blotchy way to which she had a tendency.

"Alicky, you certainly get to the point," I smiled. "Well," I pretended to think, "let me see...Nicky, Nicky—oh yes..."

She pulled such a mischievous and sweet face that I could tease her no longer.

"I think he's a very nice and handsome young man." I can honestly say that I have never swerved from that opinion.

"You really like him?" she persisted.

"Of course, is there any reason why I shouldn't?"

She hesitated for a moment.

"At that dance we had at Peterhof...just before we came to Petersburg...?"

"Yes, dear...?" I wondered what she could possibly be worrying about.

"Well," and she blushed again. "Nicky gave me a broach."

"That's very nice, Alicky." I was still baffled. It was obvious she was very taken with Nicky...

"But," she hastened to add, "of course, I returned it."

"Why?" I was genuinely mystified.

"Because I didn't know if it was proper to accept and now I think that he doesn't like me anymore."

I would have to talk to Madgie about instructing Alicky about suitors and such, and what was proper and what was not.

"I'm sure he didn't think any such thing, dear," I said, soothingly.

"You don't? I do—he just turned around and gave it to Xenia. I don't think that was very nice, do you?"

Now I was getting confused. Alicky was making no sense whatsoever.

"Alicky…what is it?" I put my arm around her and drew her head on my shoulder. I could see that tears were slowly falling down her cheeks.

"It's just…well…I had such a wonderful time and now it's all over. And…I'm going to miss you and Ella. You both left Papa and us so quickly and too closely together…"

Mentioning Papa stung me painfully. What Alicky didn't know was that Madame made very strong mention to the family that she had letters; letters, which we were given to understand, were not of a subtle nature. She made no demands and certainly no one would have the audacity to publish such things, but Grandmama thought it prudent to have the letters returned sooner rather than later. Returned, I might add, for a price. I sighed. Madame de Kolemine, back again in Russia, had already taken up with another man and poor Papa was still waiting for the annulment.

"I know we have, dearest," I said softly. "It's strange how it happened all at once. But you'll be seeing us all very often and you'll come visit Grandmama—and before you know it, you'll have your coming out, and maybe Nicky will come…" I was rambling.

She lifted her head and looked at me, her face tearstained. She made an attempt in the tiniest of smiles.

"So, what do you think of Nicky?"

I can't say that I knew then that I'd lose another sister to Russia or that Alicky would one day be even grander than Ella—the Empress Alexandra Feodorovna. When it happened, however, I wasn't very surprised. They both fell in love during that visit, and in that, if nothing else in his whole life, Nicky was determined. Before all of that, however, there is much that comes between.

CHAPTER EIGHT

I
Windsor Castle, February 1885

I remember telling Louis that I, and only I, of all my brothers and sisters had been born in the Tapestry Room at Windsor. I see his face so clearly, struggling valiantly not to laugh, when I informed him of this very important fact. I had been so proud that I, above all the children in my family had been so favored. And because of that, that I, above all my family was closest to Grandmama. I was certainly very self-assured when I was a child.

I was even more blissfully happy than seemed possible in that winter of 1885. It was a few days after the birth of my first child...my beautiful Alice, as she was called. Naturally, she also had the names of many of the other women in my family, including, Victoria. But Alice was what we all called her—my Mama's name.

I thought often of Mama during those peaceful days after my labor and tears would often form in my eyes. I have never been much of a sentimentalist, but even during my day to day life, she was never very far from my thoughts. Sometimes, however, it seemed so strange to me that I was living my life without her. Mama was, after all, the most important person in my life until she died—and the most important presence afterward, until Louis came to fill the void. Much as he fully occupied a very lonely place in my heart, it really wasn't the same. Mama had been gone for nearly six years, and now it was for me to be all of that to one little girl—this little Alice.

I was very emotional after the ordeal of labor and the pure sweetness of having my new baby. It was so reassuring the way Grandmama and Louis helped me through these difficult moments. They were patient and soothing. Grandmama had, in fact sat with me, holding my hand and wiping my forehead, the entire day of my labor. Indeed, shs never left my side, just as she had done for my Mama when I was born. Many people marveled at her behavior—but they didn't understand Grandmama's incredible devotion to her family. Perhaps, sometimes, I would be of the opinion that such devotion was misplaced, but, certainly, and most selfishly, not in this case. I felt, as I lay there, that I knew what my Mama had gone through. Somehow, I felt closer to her here in this room.

It hurt me, though, and would always hurt me to think

that this was not Louis' first born child. That somewhere in London, raised by a woman I would never meet, there was another little girl who was missing a Papa. Most of the time I succeeded in ignoring that thought and certainly never reproached Louis for it. There would have hardly been a point. But, with the birth of each child, I clearly had that thought—that somewhere there was another sister for the children, a sister that they would never know.

Alice was beautiful, if I do say so, and would go on to be called one of the most beautiful Princesses in Europe. I would always say that it was due to the Battenbergs, then Ella would shake her head at me. She'd meant to point out that I was always running down my own looks, but then I'd be reminded of how beautiful she was, and, of course, Alicky. Then I'd know the beauty came from both sides.

There is a photograph I really love. It's one of those sepia pictures that usually look so stiff and glum, showing Grandmama, Auntie Beatrice and me, dandling Alice— fat, round-faced light-eyed Alice—on my knee. What I love most and what I've never seen in any of the thousands of photographs of Grandmama, is that she's actually smiling. She's not only smiling, but she has her eyes squeezed shut and she looks like she's in the middle of a giggle. I'm not sure what caused such merriment, probably Alice did something outrageous. But that part of Grandmama, seen so rarely that most people would not have credited its existence, is preserved for all time. It gives me such pleasure to look at that picture.

There is little doubt that Alice was outrageous. She was, generally, quite a sunny child. There is a story—an anecdote that I love to tell that happened when Alice was about four or five. She had been dressed to the nines, and presented to her Great-Grandmama. Alice had been instructed that she was to kiss Grandmama's hand. However, when the crucial moment arrived, she stoutly refused. Grandmama was affronted by this disobedience, and scolded, "Naughty, Alice."

Whereupon Alice replied, defiantly, "Naughty, Grandmama."

Naturally, I was mortified, and hurried her from Grandmama's presence. When I related this story to Louis, we both thought it was hilarious and had a good laugh. It is very much how I like to think of Alice. I didn't realize then that the child was almost totally deaf.

It was Louis' mother, Aunt Julie, who seemed to notice this from the start. I had thought that Alice was perhaps a little behind, not pronouncing words properly, and not looking around and speaking when spoken to—perhaps even a bit ill-mannered which distressed me. However, Aunt Julie urged us to take Alice to an auralist. Though it was determined that she could hear somewhat, it wasn't enough and we immediately engaged a teacher to instruct her in lip-reading.

Alice could lip-read in three languages by the time she

was fifteen years old. I was terribly proud of her, though I was determined not to indulge her in her handicap. I wanted her to appear as normal as possible and she was instructed by me and various governesses never to indicate by any sign that she had problems. She eventually learned this, though it was extremely difficult. Later, it was to help her through her life as a Greek Princess. Since no one ever knew of her handicap, she was neither treated specially nor pitied.

How I hated to be harsh with her in the beginning. Her tears of confusion when she was with a large group of children nearly broke my heart. Dearest Alice—who went on to have a tow-headed little Greek Prince Philip who would grow up to marry Uncle Bertie's great-granddaughter, Elizabeth. Alice, who in some ways resembled her Aunt Ella more than me.

Dearest Grandmama had other trials besides my lying-in to worry her those days. Auntie Beatrice, who had been biding her time since my wedding, had finally taken matters into her own capable hands and had told Grandmama all about Liko.

"It was dreadful, Victoria," she told me several months before Alice's birth. Seated in our drawing room at Sennicotts, we were talking about her problems with Grandmama. It was a late October afternoon and Beatrice had come to stay with me, ostensibly to keep me company during my pregnancy. Naturally, if Liko could get away from his duties...which he frequently did.

"I love coming here, Victoria. At least you have a fireplace lit and a person doesn't have to freeze to death. You know how Mama hates the heat."

I nodded. So Auntie was declaring her independence from Grandmama. There was a time when no word of criticism would have passed her lips, not even about something as innocuous as a fire. It was, in fact, rather early in the afternoon for a fire, but I had bad circulation and during my pregnancy I had a tendency to be cold. So, the fires were lit.

"I'm happy that you enjoy a good fire—but don't distress yourself, Auntie, I'm sure it will all work out." I found that during my pregnancy, nothing much upset me. I was in an almost vegetative state. An army of Sasha's and Willy's could come and insult my husband, all my ancestors, and myself and I would calmly wave them away. I wish I had this sense of proportion most of the time.

"Mama and I have been at loggerheads since I told her that I am determined to marry Liko." She clattered her teacup onto her saucer, and lit a cigarette. Auntie, too, had become a tobacco addict. I believe she must have started the habit sometime after our meeting in the garden when I first saw her with Liko. She, however, just like everyone else, could never, ever, under any circumstance smoke around Grandmama.

She blew a stream of smoke out, "Do you realize that we haven't spoken since I gave her the news?"

"Dreadful, I had heard something of the sort," I answered, gently. It was strange that I was calming someone else. Actually, I knew all about the matter from Louis, who heard all about it from Liko.

"She and I actually pass notes to each other...it's undignified...intolerable."

She got up and began to pace and waved her hands in the air as she talked. This was a changed Beatrice, indeed.

"Auntie, I'm sure things will turn out, you really mustn't trouble yourself."

"I'm sorry, Victoria, it's you that I shouldn't be upsetting, but Mama is at least as stubborn as myself. I'm determined, however, absolutely set on marrying Liko. It's as though Mama doesn't want me to have any kind of family or life of my own."

"I'm sure that isn't so. She just loves you so much and depends on you. She'd be so lonely without you. Look at my poor Papa—I can't imagine what will happen when Irène and Alicky go away."

But Auntie was not to be placated.

"Do you know what the strangest thing is? For all that Mama doesn't want me to marry, she was actually seriously considering me as a second wife for your Papa."

I had known about this strange situation. Louis and I had discussed the fact that they were trying to push a law through Parliament which would allow the widower to marry the sister of his dead wife—they were, however, unsuccessful. Louis told me that Grandmama was particularly keen.

"Thank heaven for Madame de Kolemine," Auntie exclaimed, as though continuing my thought. Though I would not have wished the heartbreak on my Papa, I could not picture my Papa and Auntie together. It was too strange and they would have never been happy. "Can you imagine, Victoria??"

I could not.

"I'm much happier with the idea of your marrying Liko. That means that you will be here and so will Liko, I believe."

I knew that Liko had no Schloss or any kind of home of his own, and being the wife of a German officer would hardly be suitable for Auntie. Really, the only way they could marry is if they stayed in England and Grandmama gave them housing and Liko some sort of occupation.

"I believe, that with Grandmama's penchant for handsome young men, she really will relent—in time."

Auntie smiled, and sat down.

"Of course, you're right, Victoria. And, if Liko will only consent to stay in England and perhaps even live with Mama, then she will, as the saying goes, not have lost a daughter, but gained a son. It's just miserable being at odds with Mama. We're usually so close to each other— and this not speaking is really about to drive me wild."

I nodded. Of course, though I had no Mama of my own, I would never wish to be at odds, as Auntie called it, with

Grandmama. It was something that everyone in the family avoided at all costs.

"I suppose we are rather a funny couple," she remarked, as she lit another cigarette. Really, she was worse about tobacco than I was. Had I, I wondered, corrupted her?

"What do you mean?"

"Victoria, open your eyes. Look at Liko—he's so very dashing and handsome—while I...well, I'm short and dumpy like Mama and certainly not as pretty as Louise..." she sighed.

"I don't think that Aunt Louise is so ravishing," I said, truthfully, though the prevailing opinion was that she was Grandmama's prettiest daughter. I remembered Auntie Beatrice's comments years later when Aunt Louise taunted her that Liko confided in her, Louise, more than he confided in Auntie, his own wife. Aunt Louise was married, extremely unhappily, to a peer of the realm, the Marquis of Lorne, later the Duke of Argyle and in her restlessness and dissatisfaction loved to make mischief in other households.

"The handsome Battenberg Princes do seem to have that affect on one..." I sighed. "Louis is forever telling me not to run myself down in the looks department. It's not easy when one's husband is the beauty of the family...but really, Auntie, looks don't matter much for very long. It is the regard that you have for one another that is important." I was reciting platitudes, and I wondered once again if Liko really cared for Auntie, or was just marrying her because his mother, Aunt Julie, had encouraged the match.

Several months later, as though they were both part of an endurance test, Grandmama finally gave her consent for the wedding which would take place in July of 1885. Her consent, however, was only given on the condition that Liko and Beatrice make their home with her. There were to be no love nests built away from Grandmama, and, as if to emphasize this fact, the wedding was to be in the family chapel at Whippingham, near Osborne. This actually suited Auntie Beatrice down to the ground. She was very much set in her ways and probably would have been miserable away from her Mama. There was only Liko who had to deal with the situation of living, in effect, with a widow and an old maid.

It's very much to his credit and showed a lot of character which I originally doubted that he possessed, that Liko made the very best of his life with Beatrice and Grandmama. Grandmama came to love and depend on him as much as she loved any of the men in her life. He became one of the very few men, other than Grandpapa, that were important to her. She often told me that he was like another son—certainly more satisfactory than Uncle Bertie, and, though not as intellectual as Uncle Leopold, nor as endearing as Uncle Arthur, Liko still took his place as being the son closest to her heart.

II
Varna and Sofia, Bulgaria, Spring, 1885

The exciting day was approaching. The day my darling Liko and Auntie Beatrice were to be married. The preparations had been furious. As usual, with the Battenbergs, there have been many unkind cuts, not only in the press, but also by our snobbish relatives. The Prussians were saying how dreadful it was that Liko wasn't of the "blood". Grandmama was especially annoyed that all this came up once again. It was, she said, most distasteful, like talking about animal breeding. She put an end to arguments and dissension, by quoting Lord Granville: "If the Queen of England thinks a person good enough for her daughter what have other people got to say?"

Louis had to assuage my anger at the unfairness of it all. But he was, as ever, patient which continued to amaze me as time brought us closer to each other. Our dearest Alice, who was now several months old, was becoming very pretty. I thought it great luck that she was so pretty, that it would smooth her way in the world. How could I, who had prided myself on my intelligence, have been so stupid? Being pretty won her a suitor at seventeen. And it was with some trepidation that Louis and I consented to her marrying at such a young age. I don't regret it now, though her marriage to Prince Andrew of Greece was certainly not what I would have wished for her. Yes, I suppose being pretty made things easier for Alice but her deafness balanced out the accounts.

Before the wedding, however, Louis and I had quite an adventure when I was fully recovered from my "lying-in". We decided, after repeated invitations, to visit Sandro in his princely seat in Bulgaria. If we made haste, and went in spring, we could stay for a month and arrive at Osborne in time for all the wedding preparations.

Bulgaria! How exotic and faraway it sounded. To Louis, who had been present when Sandro was first installed, it was just a rather primitive place. But, to me, it seemed like the Orient, bounded as it was by Turkey and Greece in the South and Serbia on the West. I could visualize mysterious, tented bazaars, with sinister characters selling food, trinkets and even the fountain of youth to unsuspecting tourists. I saw dark, musty churches, priests with long white beards, dressed in elaborate vestments, swinging censers burning frankincense, wafting perfumed mists to the ceilings and chanting arcane and wondrous masses that would make the hairs on my neck stand up.

My imagination ran wild with exciting pictures of an unknown and fantastical land. How typical of the insular European, who thinks that anything different is at the most bad and at the least strange and suspect. I do, however, feel that I was not, as many others including my husband, had been, patronizing of the unusual society that we found. I must also remark that I wasn't particularly impressed by their pitiful attempts to emulate European society. Their peoples were such a polyglot of nationalities and religions: Russian, Turkish, Bulgarian, Greek, and Romanian, Bulgarian Orthodox, Roman Catholic, Jewish and Muslim. If only they had assimilated all of these elements and made up something completely unique. I was, of course, naive, and very ignorant of the true nature of the country.

We started out on the night train from Vienna leaving Alice in Darmstadt with Orchie. Since she was still only a few months old, I felt extremely guilty about leaving her. Louis, however, with some foresight, convinced me that now was the time to go, if ever. Grandmama wouldn't hear of Alice accompanying us to that strange place—heaven knows what the poor defenseless child might pick up—so, against my better judgment, she was installed with Orchie.

We crossed over the Transylvanian Alps, through the Iron Gate, and finally to Turku-Severin, on the Danube. There, Sandro met us, all smiles. He looked very grand in his general's uniform, be-medaled, be-fringed, and full of sashes and swords. It was an elaborate kit that would have certainly warmed Liko's heart.

We were given a less than official welcome—that would happen later, when we reached Rustchuk and Varna. Boarding his yacht, the *Alexander*, we began a journey down the Danube—a Danube, I might add, that was wider and stronger that it was in its Austrian bed. Franzjos, Louis and Sandro's youngest brother, joined us for the voyage. The Battenbergs were all very happy to be together. They lamented that Liko could not be there with them, but he, of course, was obligated to the Queen and, now, Auntie.

In my opinion, Louis was the handsomest of the brothers, but Sandro certainly was a very close second. He was almost as tall as Louis was and had that same swarthy look, although a much longer beard. There was a certain sadness in his brown eyes that I wondered about at the time. Later, I would attribute it to his sad fate with Bulgaria, and his lack of success in winning the bride of his choice. At the time, however, I thought it was due to his concerns about the proximity of the Russian army, his fear of displeasing Sasha and by virtue of Sasha's enmity, displeasing Bismarck, as well. It was a heavy burden for a man of just twenty-eight years.

Franzjos was twenty-four at the time, and had been Sandro's right hand. I was glad for Sandro to have the company, but, otherwise, there was nothing so very remarkable about this youngest brother other than the love we all bore for him. He was neither as able as Louis, nor as handsome as Liko, but that was my youth speaking, again. Franzjos was a true intellectual with a great love of learning and had obtained a doctorate— something no other member of his family had achieved. Eventually, after much concentration and several detours, he was able to find a matrimonial match in the inimitable Battenberg fashion of "marrying up"—to Anna, Princess of Montenegro.

That wily old bandit, King Nicholas of Montenegro, had managed, heaven knows how, to marry his sons and daughters off to the crème de la crème of Europe. Two of his daughters would be Russian Grand Duchesses; another would become Queen of Italy; and, yet, another two, were married to rival claimants to the Serbian crown. It was all in aid of strategically placing his own family in feuding countries in order to insure the existence of Montenegro. Although his strategies were not successful, it was certainly resourceful for a family that lived in a two-story wooden home, euphemistically called a palace.

This, however, was all to happen in the future.

That evening, as we sailed peacefully down the river, Sandro and Louis discussed his situation.

"The people here actually seem to love me."

"Don't be so surprised," Louis chuckled. "You are lovable in your own way."

"It's hard to joke about any of this right now, Louis," he sighed. "I keep on thinking about Sasha and all that he's done to me. I must constantly be on my guard. I sometimes feel that my Russian Officers will desert me the minute he tells them to leave. There's no assurance of loyalty there. He's angry that I'm getting on so well here, despite not doing everything he says. To add to all of it, he's tremendously anti-German, which is amazing when you consider how much he and Bismarck concur on Bulgarian policy."

Bismarck and Sasha had agreed that there should be no marriage between Sandro and Moretta. When Sandro had gone to Berlin after my wedding, he had accompanied Uncle Bertie. One would have thought that that would have been recommendation enough for an ardent suitor, but this was not the case. Willy had always disliked his uncle and I believe it was because they were so different in their ways of dealing with people. Uncle Bertie was diplomatic, charming, and gentleman-like, while Willy was repellant, petulant and bombastic. The only reason Willy got his way as often as he did was because he was careful enough to fall in line with both Bismarck and his Grandpapa, the old Emperor.

"Moretta and Aunt Vicky write me letters constantly," Sandro remarked, lighting a cigar. "Do you mind?" he turned to me.

"About the letters or the cigar," I smiled.

"The cigar—there's nothing you can do about Aunt Vicky."

We all laughed at that for it was certainly true. Aunt Vicky liked Sandro very much and the notion had entered her head that he and Moretta must marry. She was incredibly romantic about the match, which was distressing to all of her Prussian connection.

"Only if I can have a cigarette with you gentleman..."

Sandro inclined his head, and lit my cigarette.

"It's a good thing Baron Riedesel isn't here," he laughed, naming his major-domo. "He doesn't believe that princesses smoke."

"I shall not be the one to disillusion him once we meet."

"The people here are excited to see a female part of the family. When Marie and Gustav visited last fall, they were sure that it was a harbinger of the arrival of the sovereign princess. I had hoped..."

He was no doubt thinking of Moretta.

"First your sister and her husband and now just me— I hope they won't be disappointed," I said.

"I should think not, darling," Louis took my hand. "They'll see the good taste of the Battenberg men, and it will just whet their appetite for more."

"Yes, but this confounded waiting that Grandmama imposes on us—it's making me damned restless. It's time I had a wife, I feel it, and the people here feel it." Sandro forcefully blew out a stream of cigar smoke to punctuate his words.

"It's not Grandmama, as you well know, it's Uncle Fritz and Bismarck and that ass Willy," I said and they both looked at me.

"As well as smoking cigarettes, I have also been known to sometimes use colorful language. I promise, Sandro, I won't do so in front of your Baron Riedesel."

I meant to cheer him, but nothing seemed to be able to do that just now.

"Grandmama can do it if anyone can," I said with great confidence and the two of them looked at me indulgently—as though I were a little girl again.

The following morning we reached Rustchuk and continued our journey by train, a train that was extremely elaborate. I almost thought I was back in Russia. Our carriage was blue with gold decor. It was, I was sure, meant to be for a king. We stopped in station after station, listening to cheering crowds for Sandro in each place. He was right; the people did seem to like him. Not only that, they seemed to like all of us, as well. They would shout, and someone would interpret that they were saying, "we like you," though now I wonder if the interpreter was just being kind.

The passing countryside was completely agrarian in nature. There were herds of cattle, extensive fields with all manner of crops, gypsy camps and small villages scattered over the landscape. The homes in the villages were built with white stucco walls and red tile roofs—a style that I've since associated with the Mediterranean.

The people dressed colorfully, their national costume being quite similar to that of Greece and Romania. The women wore bright, embroidered skirts, their hair done in ropes of braids interwoven with flowers. The men in their white cloaks, sheepskin vests, red sashes and blue embroidered jackets, could have stepped out of a Lehar operetta. They were a lovely people and it seemed that the country, though modest, was not poverty-stricken. I realize now that we weren't shown the real poverty. As usual, a country shows you what it wants you to see.

We reached Varna with more cheering and people throwing flowers at our arriving train. Varna was a beautiful town, situated on the cliffs next to the Black Sea. It was divided into two parts, the old quarter and the new quarter. The old quarter was Byzantine in nature and gave me the measure of exoticism for which I longed. The new quarter was European, with wide streets and European style shops and buildings, not nearly as interesting as the other.

Several of Sandro's retinue met us: Baron Riedesel, a tall thin gentleman with a pince-nez and great dignity, just what one would expect from a major-domo; Privy Councilor Menges, a most prosperous and heavy set gentleman; and, a horse escort of mostly, I'm sorry to say, Russian soldiers. I had to admit, however, they looked wonderful, mounted on their horses, with their breeches tucked into their boots and their Cossack-like caftans. The military band played the National Anthem, a somewhat different and, yes, Oriental sounding melody, then we all piled into carriages following our escorts.

The route to Sandro's villa, called *Sandrova*, was by the sea. The roads were lined with people, all looking distinctive in their exotic costumes. I sat with Sandro in the first carriage. He pointed out the differences telling me that this one was a Turk and that one was a Greek. It was all very confusing—but fascinating.

By the bye, we reached *Sandrova*, a large chateâu though not as yet habitable. We would use the public rooms for dinners and receptions, but we would not, in fact, be staying there, since *Sandrova*, like most of the new part of Varna, was in the process of being built. We would, instead, be staying at a monastery nearby on the cliffs: the Monastery of St. Demetrious. I was delighted by this turn of events. I loved not staying in a royal palace. I could almost hear the bells ringing in the early mornings and the monks chanting their prayers. It reminded me of the Heiligenberg and its ancient nunnery.

Our rooms were surrounded by a lovely wooden veranda, and a small flower garden. This being spring, all the flowers were riotously in bloom. The rocky walls were lined with bougainvillea, and climbing rose bushes. We spent a lot of time on that veranda. Both of us had our sketchbooks and gazed for hours at the view and sketching the landscape. It was all most salubrious and after just a few days at our monastery, I was feeling quite over my confinement.

Our first dinner at Varna was not a great reception or diplomatic affair, but rather a simple family dinner with the Baron, the Privy Councilor, and their wives. It was all very pleasant, though, when the wives talked about their children, I missed Alice. The food, itself, was delicious, with a band playing softly (or as softly as martial bands are able to play) while we ate. After dinner, a drum tattoo was followed by the National Anthem, the Lord's Prayer and Sandro, in his capacity as Commander-in-Chief, receiving the password for the night.

We retired early after the long journey and I marveled that this was like no royal court I had ever seen. The reason, as I could see, was because there was no princess and no other female family members living with Sandro and Franzjos. No ladies at court, and therefore, no court, it was as simple as that. It was really a young man's enclave with Sandro, uneasily waiting to see what would happen next.

We lived this peaceful but rather tedious existence for several weeks. I, going around looking in all the nooks and crannies of the old quarter followed by a worried Elsa and a rather bemused translator, while Louis, Sandro and Franzjos discussed strategies. I was a voracious tourist, getting my fill of the Bulgarian Orthodox churches in the old city, and the cathedral in the new part of town. While Sandro received petitioners and had military reviews, I observed the people. The veiled young women, who wore their wealth in coins around their faces, particularly fascinated me. This was to announce to possible suitors the amount of her dowry, and if that was suitable for the young man and his family, a match could be made. I had the uneasy thought that these people felt that royal marriages were made in a very similar fashion. Perhaps, they couldn't understand why their prince was not yet married.

In those noisy and fascinating Oriental markets, I brought all sorts of silly souvenirs. My purchases included a set of carved wooden animals for Alice that, with the help of the interpreter, I bought from an old wizened carver in a tiny, dark shop. She would enjoy playing with them when she was older. I also bought some embroidered shawls for my sisters, and Grandmama, but could hardly imagine them wearing them. Maybe Alicky would indulge me, but Irène would roll her eyes and I could see Serge giving Ella one of his "set-downs," even if she wore such a thing to please me. Grandmama, however, would no doubt try wearing it—at least once.

The days I loved best, though, were those days that Louis and I sat on our veranda and looked out at the blue, blue sea. It was a calm sea, and gave one a tremendous sense of well being and was, in many ways, a continuation of our honeymoon. But like most honeymoons, it ended too soon. Our royal duties, as the siblings of the ruling prince intruded upon our idyllic interlude. We were soon back on trains and aboard the *Alexander*, and, thence, on our way to our grand and royal reception at Sofia, the capital city.

CHAPTER NINE

I
Sofia, Bulgaria, April-May 1885

"You would think that you had never done any of this before," Louis remarked to me as I kept glancing in the mirror, checking my appearance. "As though you never received a deputation or had to participate in a reception..." he grinned.

We were approaching Sofia, the capital city, and I wanted to look my best so as not to shame my brother-in-law or the Battenberg name.

"Louis, I just want to look right. You know what an effort it is for me," I answered distractedly, as I made sure that my skirts were straight, my hat was not askew, and there weren't any stray hairs flying in my face.

As usual, Louis looked wonderful. He was wearing his British Naval uniform with decorations, since there would be a formal reception at the train station. I had put on my best day dress and had attempted to fix my hair the elegant way that Ella had. Elsa was hopeless; she just didn't seem to be able to manage my hair. Well, neither did I. Nevertheless, I was determined that everything would be perfect.

"Did you know that they actually offered me the crown before Sandro?" he asked, absently flicking off a speck of dust from his sash, and gazing out the window at the crowds that awaited us. They had already begun to cheer and throw flowers. Such a demonstrative people!

"Really?" I wondered why Louis chose this moment to tell me this. I vaguely remembered Grandmama relating something about it, but I had forgotten the details.

"Indeed. They even offered it to my Papa."

That I hadn't known.

"Really," I suppose I shouldn't have been surprised. The small principalities in Germany produced many candidates for crowns: there was Carol of Romania, originally a Hohenzollern-Sigmaringin, Leopold of Belgium, who had originally been a Saxe Coburg-Gotha, and naturally, amongst many others, Sandro. Later the Landgrave of Hesse-Kassel, my cousin Mossy's husband, would be asked to rule Finland, but he wisely refused.

"They made me an offer, but I was comfortably entrenched in the British Navy with the idea of advancement in my head. A crown was the last thing I was interested in."

He turned to me, and I brushed off his collar. Louis really didn't need anyone to brush his collar or confirm that he was looking elegant, but I believe he enjoyed indulging me.

"Dearest, you look fine—everything is in place." I couldn't quite allow myself to express the strong admiration I felt for him. I wasn't very good at it, anyway. "Well, it's perfectly all right with me," I continued, pulling out my small compact for the last time and going back to the subject of crowns. "I would have hated being a princess of a country—even one as interesting as Bulgaria. Certainly, I would not have wanted to be at Sasha's beck and call. I do so hate the fact that Sandro must be," I finished positively.

He nodded, looking out the window once again—was I imagining that he looked wistful?

"You're not sorry, are you?"

"Not at all. I was happy with my decision then and in the circumstances, I'm more than happy with it now. It's just that I feel the same way you do—I hate to see my brother have to struggle so with the powerful Russian bear."

I nodded. Usually men regretted giving up crowns. However, Louis obviously felt the British Navy was far more important to him. It wasn't odd that he thought of this now—since all of this could have been his, I suppose. But I believed very strongly then, as I do all these years later that he made the right choice, and that he was content with that choice.

The train came to a halt with crowds of Bulgarians cheering loudly outside our windows. Sandro gave us the word and we disembarked. Like Varna, a deputation of dignitaries met us, but unlike Varna, it was a much bigger and grander group—Sofia's elite, I was given to understand. They were all dressed in their very best to meet their sovereign's relatives and I tried to appreciate how much it meant to them.

A sweet little girl dressed in the bright blue and red embroidered blouse and skirt that the Bulgarian women favored, curtsied and handed me a lovely bouquet of spring flowers. After the appropriate thanks were given through a translator and Sandro said several remarks in Bulgarian, which made the crowds wild with delight, we were escorted to the State Carriage.

The carriage of honor was a luxurious open landau, lined on the inside with white silk. The cushions made a big whoosh as we sat down. Sandro sat next to me, while Louis followed in the next carriage. We were escorted this time with outriders in the blue and white livery of Darmstadt. It was quite nostalgic and made us all exchange smiles.

Following us in a happy and somewhat haphazard procession, were the carriages of the officers of the government, the social elite and riders who were just interested in joining the impromptu throng. The roads were packed with people curious about the brothers and sister-in-law of their prince, and there was much cheering along with happy demonstrations.

"Sasha's secret police have to pay people to cheer when he comes to town," I said, which elicited a small smile from Sandro. "That is," I added more seriously, "if he doesn't have to avoid them altogether."

I sometimes thought of the danger Ella must have faced living in such a country. There was always someone about who was plotting and planning. Their goal, I was sure, was the death of the sovereign and possibly any of his relatives who could get in the way, in fact, the more killed, the better.

I worried for Ella and hoped that I would be able to visit her after Beatrice and Liko's wedding. Such thoughts could hardly be considered paranoid since our Uncle Alexander had been tragically assassinated. Besides, as I was beginning to learn, the Russians were inveterate schemers. They engaged in constant skullduggery, not only in Russia, but here in Bulgaria, as well.

We drove first through the old quarter of Sofia just as we had in Varna. Once again, the Oriental character of the city impressed me. All the old, crumbling houses and shops were decorated with flowers and Bulgarian flags and many leaned out of their windows joyously flinging flowers. It was a lovely welcome, and, even with the perspective of years, I know that it was a sincere one. They did, indeed, love their handsome prince.

We finally reached the middle of the newer, more European quarter. Sandro had been disappointed with this city at first. However, in between struggling with

Sasha and Bismarck, he was able to get a building program started, renewing areas of the city and constructing new public buildings. Here, in this new part, the roads were wider and there was a huge square in front of the royal palace. Just the size for admiring crowds, I thought.

The palace could well have disappointed if we hadn't been warned beforehand. It had initially been built for the Russian Prince Dondukov-Korsakov, who had expected to be named Prince of Bulgaria. It was a rather dusty, two-story affair, with a lovely fledgling garden. We drove through the gates and disembarked; I, laden with flowers, and the seats covered with them as well.

The Baron Riedesel having preceded us, we walked through the doors and received a very proper reception. All the various servants were gathered in the hallway to gape at us, but also, to see to our comfort as well. It had to be said our rooms hadn't nearly the charm of Varna. I should never forget its deep blue sea, quaint monastery and the small seaside gardens that were so private. The enthusiasm with which we were greeted by all the staff, made our rather crude ground floor rooms seem just as warm and welcoming. It simply needed more imagination.

Again, Sandro and his brothers participated in deputations, receptions and council meetings, and again, me, along with my poor Elsa and yet another translator became tourists. We trudged through the old quarter of

Sofia. The capital was a city of great historical interest despite the fact that many of its beauties were crumbling. It had been inhabited, at various times by the Romans, the Bulgars and the Turks. My translator delighted in giving me a detailed background of the area. We visited places that had been built over Roman baths. Sofia, or as the Romans called it, Seridica, had many thermal springs in the town and its environs. In fact, we spent several days at Bad-Effendi, a fashionable hot spring just outside Sofia. It was typical of most European watering spots in that most people were more interested in showing off their wardrobes than improving their health. Since becoming a naval wife, my wardrobe could not compare with that of the sophisticated elite of Sofia, so it was good that such things never worried me. Nevertheless, everyone came to dinners arranged by the ubiquitous Baron Riedesel and seemed eager to see Louis and myself. More accurately, I believe they expected to be dazzled by the three Battenberg Princes.

I noticed as we traveled around Bulgaria, and as had been in Russia, all eyes were on my husband. I assumed they were speculating...such a handsome man, married to...well, not exactly a beauty. I knew they were wondering if he was, perhaps, not really interested in his wife—and possibly open for dalliance. I realized that this would happen often during the course of my married life and that I would have to ignore it. Louis was always polite and my reputation for being distant grew. I knew I couldn't embarrass him or myself by any jealous outbursts, but Louis heard my displeasure in private.

"I don't understand why you have to be so nice..." I once complained during one of our nocturnal talks.

He chuckled and reached for me. I put my head on his chest and he stroked my hair.

"Victoria, you must understand we can't afford to be impolite to people, especially here in Bulgaria. I don't want to offend anyone who may be giving strength to Sandro's leadership. Besides," he hesitated, "people talk, darling, and we have to be careful of our reputations."

I thought for a moment that Louis had always to be careful. I, of course, so sure of my position in life, never worried—I never had a reason.

"I think the reputation suffers the other way," I said bluntly, being in a petulant mood. "Just be a little less friendly," I reiterated.

"Dearest, my only interest in life, are my ship, my baby, and my wife..."

"I hope not in that order..."

"Naturally not..." he smiled, and quieted my fears in the best way he could...which usually did.

I enjoyed our stay in Sofia and was thrilled to see some truly ancient churches, courtesy of my guide. We wandered through the St. Sofia Basilica, with its three naves; the city was named after this fourteenth century edifice. We also visited the Rotunda of St. George, a small, red-bricked building amongst Byzantine ruins. This was the oldest standing building in Sofia, and had twenty-two existing frescos, some, actually dating back to the tenth century. In contrast, just being built was the parliament building that would house the National Assembly. It had been under construction for almost a year and would not actually be completed for many years. One could only get an idea of the final result by looking at the pillared and arched facade. The National Assembly, in the interim, was meeting at the Cadet House.

I had been exhausting myself with all the touring but was nevertheless feeling well and rested. I was quite pleased with my rapid recovery from childbirth. As strange as this may sound, perhaps it is good for a new mother to take time off to recover from such a traumatic experience. Naturally, not all new mothers have the luxury of Orchie to care for the children when husbands want to take trips to the wilds of the Balkans. At these times, I realized how spoiled I was and how much I really didn't think about my socialist ideals or that royalty had become an anachronism. I was content to bask in the knowledge that I had made an unequal marriage and was thumbing my nose at the Willy's and Sasha's of the royal world. I felt secure in my position and I could readily admit my hypocrisy.

During one late afternoon, I was taking a respite in the palace gardens. I wandered about, listening to the birds chirping and the soft wind rustling through the trees and tickling the little tendrils of hair on my neck. It was just starting to get warm and I had been told that the Bulgarian summers had a warm, balmy feel to them. As I sat on a bench next to a small pond, relishing the feel of the gentle breeze, I closed my eyes and wiggled my toes with pleasure.

"Victoria," a voice said softly. Startled, I opened my eyes.

"Sandro," I smiled and made room for him on the bench. "Have you escaped your endless meetings and commissions for a while?" I asked absently as he sat down slowly and stared ahead for a few seconds. I was feeling so lazy and content, just sitting with the sun sparkling on the pond. I looked at him and thought once again what a handsome man he was. I later heard a story that even Bismarck admitted that the Battenbergs were an extraordinarily good-looking family.

"Yes," he sighed, "once in a while, I just have to get away from all the discussions and beseeching..."

I nodded, and scuffed my shoes on the gravel.

"How are you enjoying our Bulgaria?" he grinned.

"I'm having a lovely time...there's so much to see and do, and it's so heavenly not having a court..."

"I've heard from Louis you've been doing as much as you can," he looked at me and I grinned at him. "It's funny you should say that about not having a court. I couldn't care less, but there have been a few comments about the lack of it."

"Not from me," I said, stoutly.

"No, Victoria," he smiled, now, "certainly not from you."

He looked at me as though he remembered me with powdered sugar all over my face from "*sneeballen*".

"Louis is an extremely lucky man," he said, unexpectedly.

I smiled. I couldn't help it, I was always under the impression that people thought I was the lucky one.

"How gallant of you, Sandro," I answered, with what I hoped was the right amount of both sophistication and warmth.

"I'm glad you think I'm so gallant, you're certainly the only one."

"No," I protested thinking of the smitten Moretta and knowing that Sandro was feeling sorry for himself.

He didn't answer, so we sat in silence. I was enjoying the waning afternoon, but I could see that Sandro was deep in thought. I had known him all my life and I wanted so desperately to help him through this unhappy time. But, I could not ask—not unless he wanted to tell me.

"I believe that you have discussed our situation here with Louis at some length, have you not?" he asked, finally.

I wasn't sure what reply he wanted so I answered with my usual bluntness.

"Yes," I replied, slowly, "But, I must admit I don't understand how it will all end."

"Most would say they don't understand how it all began," he replied with bitterness.

He drew out his cigarette case and made a great show of looking around to make sure no one was watching. I smiled.

"We wouldn't want to shock poor Riedesel, would we," he grinned suddenly and handed me a cigarette.

I giggled as he offered me a light, and then lit his. We both sat back again, and relaxed.

"It's all because the Bulgarians want a bigger country than the Congress offered them."

I said nothing. Fortunately, I knew a great deal about what had happened since Sandro had taken over in 1879. The Treaty of San Stefano, made at the Congress of Berlin, had ended the Russo-Turkish War and had established a Bulgar State—actually a Greater Bulgaria. Some feared Russia's influence on such a substantial state and others feared that it would intimidate the Ottomans. Yes, Louis and I had discussed it at length, as had I with Grandmama. However, I sensed that Sandro wanted to talk.

"Uncle Sasha is considered the liberator of this country—did you know that?"

I nodded silently.

"The Russians are their heroes here...but it's a much smaller country than the Bulgarians were promised..."

He broke off, and I just listened, with my mouth, for once, shut. I sensed he was talking almost to himself.

"When I arrived here, they all thought I would be a puppet. How I resented that," he muttered angrily. "I suppose I gave them a shock when I wouldn't fall in with their plans...I still have ideas...well, Papa, Louis and I went to Russia to discuss this, and that's when the attempt was made on Uncle Alexander's life."

I nodded. This Russian compulsion to violently eliminate rulers...who would be next?

"I even offered to abdicate before Uncle Alexander died, did you know that?"

"No, I didn't. Why would you offer such a thing?"

Unlike the Russians, I didn't think a crown was a trust given by god, but, certainly, they, in this case, felt that the crown was given by them and could be taken away just as easily. He stamped out his cigarette on the gravel and immediately lit another, while he peered into space.

"I was frustrated in my attempts to get the economy moving here. It seemed that the Russians vetoed everything I undertook....I didn't know which way to move," he smiled ruefully. "When Uncle Alexander died, I knew that there would be trouble. Sasha hated me and he didn't want me acting independently. Probably part of him hated the fact that Bismarck had supported my election."

"Well, but they seem to be agreeing far more these days," I added, ironically.

"Yes, I wonder if Moretta and I will be permitted to marry. Even Uncle Fritz seems against it. They've asked me to renounce her, officially, in a letter..." he trailed off. "We were secretly engaged two years ago. Did you know that?"

"I had heard of it from Louis..." I had begun to regret my uncharitable thoughts about Moretta. If she would make Sandro happy at this point, I was all in favor of it.

"I'm lonely, Victoria," he continued, as though I hadn't answered. "Several other ladies have rejected me, mostly, I suppose because they want nothing to do with this mess, and yet this vicarious crown seems to be all I have to offer to a princess of any consequence. It's a vicious circle...," he trailed off for a moment. He drew on his cigarette and looked at me. "When Aunt Vicky introduced me to Moretta, I thought, here is someone I could care about, who obviously cares about me and who would make an excellent princess for Bulgaria. She certainly has all the right credentials."

"I suppose, since Bismarck and Sasha are determined to keep the balance of power in Europe, it would make little sense and be a slap in Sasha's face for the Prussians to allow you to marry Moretta. The scale would be off kilter," I declared.

"And, the fact that I'm a Battenberg doesn't help. It's another unequal marriage and the Prussians don't have the same ideas about that as the British do—they're as bad as the Russians."

"They're worse," I said, thinking of all their talk of blood and breeding like one of Uncle Bertie's race horses. I sighed. I really didn't know where it would all end. "You'll see," I soothed, "everything will come out in the end."

He looked at me for a moment, as though I was

deluded, which I probably was, threw down his cigarette butt and patted my hand.

"For now, there's a coalition government in place, with me as the head...and so far it seems to be working out, if only Sasha won't interfere or agitate our neighbors against us. I know that Milan of Serbia is extremely anxious about our extending our borders as we wish."

I really had no reassurances for him. I knew from my reading that the Serbians felt threatened by the newly revitalized Bulgarian state. If the Bulgars went after what they wanted, the Greater state, there would be only one outcome.

"Victoria." He suddenly smiled at me. "I thought you'd have lots to say over this conundrum. Louis tells me that you have opinions about everything."

"Oh, at least two," I tried to keep my voice light, "but you don't need Louis to tell you that. You should remember that from all our summers together at the Heiligenberg."

"I do remember," he laughed for a moment—for once without a trace of bitterness. "The irrepressible Victoria— one of the few young ladies I know that reads more newspapers than practically anyone I know."

"One thing I will say," I began, serious now, "I've seen most positively and unequivocally that the people really do love and support you. Their welcome was completely genuine...it was very heartening to us..."

He leaned over and kissed my forehead.

"I'm glad you are—you both are...I think if I can just be

left alone. This country needs time to get on its feet—it's been stagnating under the thumb of the Ottomans for so long and it's such a hodgepodge of different peoples and religions—they really have very little idea how to govern themselves. We need to come up with some commonality. I sometimes think that my conflicts with Sasha and these problems with the Prussians are doing my countrymen no good. They don't need it."

I nodded, he was right—they most definitely didn't need it. But I wasn't going to agree with him out loud. It seemed to me to be a prelude to fatalistic talk—the kind that led to further thoughts of abdication.

"Just let the Bulgarians be themselves," I opined. "Don't try to make this into a copy of another European State—it isn't the same, and it wouldn't work. If they are strong, they can withstand all this jostling between the Emperors. No one likes to be in the middle...used as a pawn."

"You're right. I value that, because I know you've been out everyday looking at the city and the people."

"I love this city, it's still very raw, and somewhat primitive, but it's vital, energetic, it's just emerging from the morass of stagnation it experienced under the Ottomans."

"Quite dramatic," he grinned. "But, I like to think that you're right."

"I've been sloughing around for days now, and I have to admit that it's wonderful being in a city that isn't as refined as the European capitals we frequent. It's a complete break from the usual royal progress routine."

"You just say that because you'll be back in refined England and Germany soon enough."

He was right. It was fun, as they say today, to "rough it," but in the end, I'd go back to my pampered existence.

"You're right, I suppose, but I maintain my defense of this city. It could certainly teach Berlin a thing or two."

The sun was beginning to set and we both rose.

"Another boring dinner this evening with some of the diplomatic corps," he remarked, taking my elbow.

"I'll do my best not to humiliate you or Baron Riedesel."

"Oh, especially Riedesel," he laughed, kissed my hand very sweetly and we went in.

I have always remembered that conversation with Sandro. The fact that he voiced some of his deepest concerns to me was an honor. It was the closest we ever were and I really came to love him during our visit—which, I might add, ended much too soon for me.

As we traveled back to England, we went, naturally, to fetch our little daughter from Orchie's doting care. She was right—Alice hadn't missed us nearly as much as I had missed her. She was thriving, quite fat, and had already smiled for Orchie, which I must admit put me out to no end. We had a beautiful christening for her at the church at Darmstadt, which, only the Hesse and Battenberg connections were able to attend.

Everyone was preparing for the wedding at Osborne.

Ernie and the girls included, though Papa was still moping around. He had heard that Madame de Kolemine, far from being as unhappy as he, had definitely found someone else with whom she consoled herself.

We took a short detour to the Heiligenberg so that Uncle Alexander and Aunt Julie could spend some time with their newest grandchild. Louis and Uncle Alexander spent hours discussing Sandro's situation and trying to determine how best to proceed. It was, indeed, a knotty problem. Everyone was tugging at poor, new Bulgaria, who could probably not take the pressure much longer. Whether they would turn against Sandro, or whether they would fight the outsiders together, that remained to be seen.

I spent much of my time with Aunt Julie, whom I had known all my life. This lovely lady who was lady-in-waiting to Uncle Alexander's sister, the Empress Marie of Russia, had captured his somewhat wayward heart. After they married, they had both been banished from Russia and had made their way, back to Hesse—where Uncle Alexander was a prince. There, they had managed to produce a family of four princes and one princess, the beauty of whom had astonished Chancellor Bismarck.

The old Grand Duke of Hesse eventually gave Aunt Julie and her children the titles of Prince and Princess of Battenberg. Battenberg was a tiny, village in the mountains and the title was extinct. The young family throve. The princes were brilliantly successful in their

235

marriages, well—at least Louis and Liko—and the others were now being offered crowns. Not bad for a family that had endured social ostracism, contempt and a great deal more unpleasantness from various quarters.

Now that I was grown up and married to one of Aunt Julie's sons, I began observing her from the perspective of a grown woman. She was charming, self-effacing, yet, at the same time, could be tremendously iron-willed. She was always unobtrusive when she was with other family members and never put herself forward. I believe she had a real need for acceptance. Instinctively, she seemed to know that the correct route to acceptance would be the one that antagonized as few people as possible. Consequently, Grandmama truly loved and admired her.

She and I spoke much of Liko's marriage to Beatrice. She was a pragmatic woman without illusions about any of her children.

"I know that people think it's an odd match," she remarked to me one day, just before Louis and I went back to England. It was strange how she seemed to echo Auntie Beatrice's words.

"Why, odd?"

"Well, he certainly isn't her intellectual equal."

It surprised me that she would say this about her own son, nevertheless, I felt obligated to defend my childhood comrade.

"Liko has many wonderful traits even if he isn't a raving intellect," I conceded. "Well, for one, he's interested in absolutely everything. In addition to which, he has a tremendous amount of charm," I smiled. "He could charm anyone. I even believe that Grandmama isn't really as unhappy about this as she pretends."

"No, but she is imprisoning him," she stated positively. "He will have to stay always with the Queen. They'll never be able to have their own household. I would never have thought that Liko would agree to anything like that. I always considered him to be a man hungry for adventure. I never imagined he'd consent to Aunt Victoria's conditions, though I, myself, urged him to do so."

I always thought that she was behind his proposal. I wasn't sure that I liked being right about this.

"Auntie has a wonderful attitude about the whole thing. I believe she understands that she won't truly be happy living away from Grandmama, and Liko understands this, too. I think that he will fill a very strong need in that household. After all, you know how susceptible Grandmama is to handsome young men," I smiled, echoing more of the points Auntie and I had made in our conversations.

"It's going to be a beautiful day. But, have you heard? The Prussians will not be coming."

"But why?" I knew that Aunt Vicky never missed a chance to visit her mother—and a family event like this? It seemed a little strange.

"Willy has made it clear that he doesn't think that Liko is his equal. Even your Uncle Fritz is grumbling about having to call Liko his brother-in-law."

"I wonder how he feels about calling Louis his nephew," I said angrily. I was surprised to hear about such talk from Uncle Fritz. "But, Aunt Julie, Grandmama is furious over all of this nonsense. She thinks that Willy deserves a good beating, or as she puts it in the old Scottish way, a good "skelping." She also made a remark about how Dona shouldn't really be getting so above herself, after all she was an insignificant, poor little princess before Willy married her."

Aunt Julie and I chuckled softly. It may not have been nice, but we were both incensed.

"But there is also the other reason," she resumed. "It is because Bismarck and Willy don't want Moretta to be anywhere near Sandro."

I was genuinely surprised.

"I can't believe they would miss the wedding of a sister and aunt simply because of Willy's pettiness and worrying about the propinquity of Sandro and Moretta."

"You should believe it, Victoria, because it's true."

It was true.

II
Osborne, July, 1885

The marriage of Liko to my Aunt Beatrice took place July 23, on the Isle of Wight, at the St. Mildred's Church at Whippingham near Osborne. Louis, in his capacity as the Commander of the *Victoria and Albert*, met many of our Hesse and Battenberg relatives at Flushing with the royal yacht, and ferried them over to the Isle of Wight. I stayed at Kent House, near Osborne, with Alice, and was glad I had not accompanied Louis. The crossing from Flushing to Cowes, made in sixteen hours, was extremely rough, and amongst others, my poor sister-in-law, Princess Marie of Erbach-Schöenburg, suffered terribly from mal-de-mer.

It was, however, a beautiful July day with all of us going in procession to the church. The bride looked lovely, and thin. My plump Auntie had lost weight because of all the complications from her mother and because of all the insults to Liko in the English and Continental press. As I had observed during our talks, it made her very unhappy.

Liko, naturally, looked splendid, in one of those uniforms that he was so fond of—another sparkling white jacket with orders, and sashes. His breeches about as tight as human decency would allow and his boots, shiny as only his valet seemed to have the capacity to do—or perhaps it was patience and Liko's vanity? Finally, that handlebar mustache of which he was so proud was waxed to within an inch of its life. All this prompted Uncle Bertie to remark that Beatrice had found her Lohengrin. I smiled when I read that later, since we all found Liko's vestments a little much and it was something that Auntie had said herself. However, Beatrice was in heaven and loved his look, which she had always compared to the mythic German hero.

The Archbishop of Canterbury, who looked happy to have been asked, but a little white in the face, performed the ceremony. I suppose he was slightly ill from the trip over, as was most everyone else.

Afterwards, the wedding breakfast was served in tents on Grandmama's property. There were ten pipers in Highland dress piping their way around the table that held the huge bridal cake. I later learned it weighed about four hundred and fifty pounds. I looked around at everyone there: the Battenbergs, my Aunt and Uncle looking happy and content with this further proof of their acceptance; and, my Uncle Affie with his Russian Grand Duchess wife, Aunt Marie. She had more of a pout on her face than usual and didn't look very pleased with this further elevation of the Battenbergs. She made it a point to snub Sandro. Oddly enough, she spent most of her time talking to Marie of Erbach-Schöenburg, Louis and Sandro's sister, who had been her best friend growing up. I wondered if some of these people ever paused to reflect upon their actions and thoughts and how unconnected they might seem to the casual observer. In Aunt Marie's case, it wouldn't have concerned her.

Papa, of course, was sitting near Grandmama and the two of them looked as though they were consoling each other. Grandmama still carried on very much as though she were being left all alone, though Liko and Auntie were hardly getting a honeymoon. Papa—well—he, as usual, had the mopes. I suppose all weddings, after his own recent fiasco, depressed him. Never mind, everyone was making a fuss over my lovely Alice, which pleased me enormously.

When the couple finally went off, Grandmama looked very sad indeed. We all went back with her to Osborne House where an elaborate state dinner had been planned. She was cheered a little, I suppose, by the presence of her little great-granddaughter, but otherwise, was quite glum.

She kept reassuring Aunt Julie that it wasn't Liko that she had anything against. She rather liked him it was the idea that her daughter would no longer be hers. The strange part is that Grandmama never considered this kind of talk or behavior selfish.

CHAPTER TEN

I
Darmstadt, 1887

It was late August when Louis and I were awakened in the middle of the night. Louis' valet put a lit candle down next to our night table and handed him a telegram. I sat up sleepily and watched, with a pounding heart, as Louis opened the envelope. Telegrams, in those days, never contained good news. He stared at it briefly and then silently, stoically, handed the missive to me.

In brief, it was a frantic message from Aunt Julie. This was doubly distressing, as Aunt Julie was not given to hysterics. Officers of Sandro's general staff had foully kidnapped him, and Sasha was obviously responsible.

His plot had gone into full swing, and disgruntled Bulgarian officers snatched Sandro and Franzjos at gunpoint. Disgruntled, we were informed, because

Rumelian officers had been promoted over them. The brothers were taken to a steamer and whisked out of the country under the most dreadful of circumstances—locked in the hold, I found out later, and knocked about. This happened several days ago, and Aunt Julie had no idea where the two were, and if, indeed, they were still alive.

Louis and I stared at each other, frozen as Aunt Julie's words sunk in. His fingers loosened and the telegram floated slowly to the bedroom floor.

He got out of bed, and began pacing up and down. I donned my negligee and joined him. We probably looked like rats trying to find their way through a maze.

"I've got to help them—I must find them." He spoke, in fits and starts, trying not to let fear show in his voice. I nodded, slowly, shakily, trying desperately to think what to do. His two brothers were in serious danger and I felt helpless.

"I'm going, too," I proclaimed quickly and without thinking.

He looked startled, and then with a heavy sigh, sank down into his favorite chair.

"Don't be ridiculous, Victoria. You can't go. There may be danger. We, both of us, can't put ourselves in jeopardy—think of Alice."

"Don't you be ridiculous," I replied. "They're hardly going to execute the grandson and granddaughter of Queen Victoria."

What a fool I was, secure in the arrogance of my position. I would later understand how little such distinctions mattered to executioners and firing squads and how little our positions meant to showers of bullets. However, I must say now, it was not all due to Royal arrogance, but also, to the natural personality of the young—the attitude of immortality.

"Alice will be just fine," I continued, wondering only briefly if I would be. "We'll take her to Darmstadt and leave her with Aunt Julie..." I babbled. I realized that I was terrified at the idea of going to look for the brothers, but equally terrified that something awful had befallen them.

By the next day, we were packed and gone. Quickly, without much fuss, we arrived at the Alexander Palace, Uncle Alexander's home in Darmstadt. Uncle Alexander and Aunt Julie were in a state of extreme distress. Aunt Julie had not met us at the station, as she was too upset. Since she never took to her bed in these situations, we could only speculate on how hard she was taking this.

Upon reaching the palace, we went right to her suite. I did my best to comfort Aunt Julie, while Uncle Alexander filled us in on the details.

It seemed that all the worrying and despairing was for naught since Uncle Alexander now had the news that after four days Sandro and Franzjos were released. The two brothers had been unceremoniously dumped in Breslau in Eastern Prussia. Louis and I quietly persuaded Aunt Julie and Uncle Alexander to stay at home with

Alice, while we went to fetch them. They acquiesced since Louis stressed how much Aunt Julie needed rest and calm. After all, he reassured them, they were alive and well and just needed their family about them.

I'm amazed that we convinced them. They both knew that Franzjos and Sandros' lives had been in the balance. Later Sandro told us that they expected death at any moment. The officers, egged on by pro-Russian elements, were angry and trigger-happy. The tension was tremendous, and they feared continually for their lives.

Louis and I immediately boarded a train. I realized that we were both in shock and had been operating in an almost mechanical manner. I reached over and took his hand. We looked at each other as tears welled up in my eyes. I had certainly cried enough lately. It was times like this when I realized how precious Louis was to me. What if he was also in terrible danger? He squeezed my hand, a ghost of a smile on his face. Dear man, he was trying to comfort me. I put his hand to my wet cheek and smiled weakly.

As we rode along, Louis remained deep in thought, trying to decide, I imagined, what should be done about the Bulgarian situation. We already knew that the Bulgarian Assembly had voted to bring Sandro back as their prince. Louis was uncertain as to whether Sandro was up to going back and whether he had any desire to do so. As we traveled and Louis remained quiet and contemplative, I had a chance to think about the all the events of the past year; the family controversies as well as the imbroglio in Bulgaria.

Like most things that happened in my family, the furor over Liko's marrying Auntie passed over quickly enough, and was forgotten in what appeared to be domestic bliss. Liko took over as the man of the family, and Grandmama, far from having any objections, settled down to enjoying it immensely. In fact, I would have to say that she was happier than I'd seen her in years—certainly since poor Brown died. When the children came later on, raised as they were in Grandmama's constant company, I am sure that these were the most spoiled of all the grandchildren. They certainly were among the ones that knew her the best.

While most of us were enjoying our early married lives, poor Sandro's situation during '85 and '86 was not so felicitous. Naturally, he returned to Bulgaria after Liko and Auntie's wedding. In a strange act of acquiescence, he had written the fateful letter giving Moretta her freedom as soon as we left Bulgaria. Louis and I, however, knew that it was still very much in his mind to wed her.

Later that year, events began to move rapidly to their inevitable conclusion. The Bulgarians, abrogating the treaty of the Congress of Berlin, voted to unite themselves with East Rumelia. Sasha and his henchman had encouraged them to do this thinking that when the unification was accomplished, another prince would be called to head a "Greater Bulgaria". Sasha, however, never seemed to understand Sandro's popularity. To his chagrin, another prince was most certainly not wanted. The National Assembly and the Rumelian representatives overwhelmingly elected Sandro.

"It's a tremendous victory for Sandro," Louis remarked to me in great elation, at breakfast table, one morning in December of 1885.

I buttered a piece of toast thoughtfully.

After the Bulgarians had proclaimed themselves united, Sasha had withdrawn his support, obviously, because Sandro had not been ousted. Bulgaria's neighbors had become extremely uneasy over this. While Turkey was too enervated to do much about developing events, the strong armies of King Milan of Serbia poised themselves on the Western borders of Bulgaria and attacked the newly formed country.

Sandro, with a hastily put together staff of Rumelian, as well as Bulgarian officers (the Russians had been conspicuously ordered out of the country—Sasha had wanted Bulgaria to see that she couldn't exist without the help of Russia), was able to face the Serbs in battle at Slivnitza. And, what a battle it was!

Sandro was easily able to defeat the well-organized army of the King of Serbia. This completely astonished and rather shocked the allied powers and certainly the three emperors: Sasha, William I of Prussia, Willy's other Grandpapa, and Franz Joseph of Austria-Hungry. Sandro was ordered to fall back at the urging of Franz

Joseph, and, to his credit, he did so, but not without becoming a great hero to his people.

"Yes," I agreed, munching. "Sandro's position has got to be much stronger now than ever before. He's a genuine Bulgarian hero."

"I hope you're right," Louis put down the newspaper. "Papa is still pleading with him to put things right with Sasha. I think that now that he's in a strong position, this would be the right time to do so."

"It's difficult for him. He's lived alone in that country for so long. Remember he's young, he's tactless and he's made some unfortunate enemies," as though I were not young and tactless.

Louis nodded.

"The problem with Sandro is that he wants to do things for his new country—he's got liberal ideas, the kind that Grandmama loves, and besides—he's been there for six years and has shown that he really means to stay."

"Six miserable years, if you ask me," he replied, taking a sip of coffee. "There's no one criticizing him for that, Victoria, it's just that he's there at the sufferance of the Russians. When someone else has put you in your position, they expect obedience, or at least, gratitude. They also expect that you will fall in with their concerns, especially when yours are counter to what serves their best interests."

It may have all sounded convoluted, but Louis was right. He sat back, putting down his coffee cup. I could think of nothing that would defend Sandro's actions.

"I don't know if he can put things right," I remarked after a few minutes. "Sasha hates him so—I don't think he'll give him any peace in Bulgaria."

"I want to believe you're wrong about that, darling. But, you're probably not."

"Certainly now he still won't be able to press his suit with Moretta. Bismarck will be even more against someone whose very existence is ruining the balance of power."

"I'm not sure how much longer Sandro can last without a wife, some company, some family...something. He's temporarily encouraged after this victory, but generally, he's depressed and lonely. I think if the opportunity were right, he would leave."

"It seemed that way to me, too, while we were there," I thought of our talk in the gardens of Sofia.

"Sandro writes me that Aunt Vicky is quite excited by the victory. She tells him that Moretta is itching to cut her hair, put on men's clothes and fight beside him."

How embarrassing, I thought.

"It's certainly not very gallant of him to tell you what Aunt Vicky writes."

"No," he said slowly. "I suppose not...though you know very well there are no secrets between brothers."

"Well, certain things should remain private..."

Louis chuckled and I looked at him. Nothing seemed very funny.

"I was just reminded that you also wanted to cut your hair to join the English Navy."

"Yes, but I was a child, not nearly as old as Moretta. Besides, later I decided on something far more appropriate, being a school teacher."

Louis grinned.

"I never knew that."

"That's because I never told you, but I often thought, before I was married, that I would have been very good at instruction—I certainly read and talk enough."

He laughed. "I'm sure you would have, certainly better than Moretta."

"She ought to just stick to the navy," I said nastily.

I've said it more than once; perhaps I was wrong to judge Moretta so harshly. She was simply a girl who wanted to marry this handsome and romantic prince with whom she fancied herself in love. Later on, much later, she would fancy herself in love with a twenty-seven year old Russian waiter when she, herself, was sixty-three. Yes, perhaps I was being too hard on her. After all, she was empty-headed, and easily impressed.

I poured more coffee for Louis and myself.

Sandro was a national hero, but, as things turned out, he couldn't put things right with Sasha. During the spring of 1886, an alarm went off in St. Petersburg. Sandro was too well liked, and something had to be done about it quickly. First, they tried to remove him with disgusting rumors, some of the worst being his having venereal disease, or, conversely, having caught on to the Turkish taste, which in plain language meant homosexual affairs. This last really being ludicrous to anyone who knew him. However, this kind of smut seemed to have the reverse affect on the people, who were, as I've already said, extremely satisfied with their ruler.

Having failed in prior attempts, Sasha began to foment discord amongst the officers on Sandro's staff. Some had been passed over in order to give promotions to the new Rumelians that joined the army during the Serbian war. The officers unfortunately were susceptible to his agitation, and with their help, Sasha was able to do something so dishonorable and unscrupulous, that it makes me tremendously angry to think about it, even today.

So that's how matters stood as we sat on a train, heading to Breslau. Sasha had done the unspeakable— he had Sandro physically and unlawfully removed from the country. It was inconceivable to me that he could have done such a thing. They were, after all, first cousins. I suppose I should have thanked heaven that he didn't have Sandro murdered. I wasn't so sure that he would have been incapable of that.

When we arrived at the station in Breslau, the brothers, having been notified of our arrival, fell on each other with great relief. I think they were grateful that nothing worse than a terrible scare had befallen them. What a joy to be together again! I believe there were tears in their eyes. I stepped back so that they might have their reunion.

We went back to the small hotel at which they had been deposited. They looked tired, though Sandro looked the worst. He was unshaven and looked not just as though he hadn't slept in years. The anguish and profound disappointment in his eyes haunted me the rest of my life. Whenever I think of Sandro, it's hard to remember him as the heroic prince. Those despairing eyes are always there.

As Sandro related the events of the previous days, Franzjos actually drifted off to sleep. I could feel my heart breaking for him.

"We were locked in the hold of a filthy steamer and not given anything to eat or drink, it was hot and stuffy. Men that I had trusted were brutal to us—men that I had fought with at the Battle of Slivnitza. It's just so unthinkable that Sasha could have done this."

I looked down, and I believe that Louis, for a moment, was speechless. The naiveté of it all....

"There is some good news," Louis said softly, trying to sound cheery.

"What good can come of any of this?" Sandro's eyes glistened. I think if I hadn't been there, he might have burst into tears again. Louis told me later that they all wept when they were alone.

"The Bulgarian National Assembly, who was forced to reject you on the day of your disappearance, has voted to re-elect you Prince of Bulgaria. They refuse to be influenced by Sasha's plots and a small group of disaffected officers."

Sandro slowly put his head in his hands. Louis and I looked at each other.

"No...no..." was all he could say.

"Sandro, don't you see?" I said, hoping that I sounded encouraging. "They want you. They don't care what the Russians do, you're their Prince."

"It does matter what the Russians do, Victoria," he answered wearily. "They sponsored me, gave me the position of Prince, and like it or not, they're the giant on the Bulgarian borders."

"You can't possibly believe you're obligated to them in any way now," I burst out.

The two men both looked at me.

"It's a matter of honor, Victoria," Louis said in a strange voice.

"What rubbish. You don't owe them anything, and Sasha's behavior was certainly anything but honorable."

They both looked at me as though I weren't speaking intelligibly. I could see that they were convinced that this was a thing between gentlemen. That would be enough to set me howling, so I thought the better of further conversation—they had enough problems without listening to my radical ideas. I threw my hands up.

"I don't understand either of you, so, therefore, I'm going to bed."

And so I did.

The next day, Louis, Franzjos and Sandro went back to Bulgaria, and I traveled back to Darmstadt.

Later, I learned that Sasha sent a Prince Dolgoruki from St. Petersburg to take the reins of the Bulgarian government, being quite sure that he'd seen the last of Sandro. Sasha now believed that the Bulgarians would accept someone more amenable to Russia. Undoubtedly, he was very unhappy to learn that when Sandro and his brothers arrived in Bulgaria on the twenty-ninth of August, it was to cheering crowds. Sandro's welcome was more than enthusiastic. Not only did they have their handsome prince returning, but accompanying him were two equally impressive looking brothers.

The Bulgarian welcome, however, was not enough for Sandro. He no longer had the heart to be their Sovereign. These seven years of tug and pull had so dispirited him that he lost his youthful vigor and enthusiasm. He and Louis, following some bad advice of a Russian sympathizer, composed a very positive telegram to Sasha. They thanked the Tsar for his support and made it very clear that since Russia had given him his crown, if the Tsar desired, he, Sandro, would return it from whence it came.

Aunt Julie and I were sitting together in her sitting room, overlooking the courtyard.

"Sasha naturally told him to relinquish the crown," she said quietly, eyes down, resigned, working on a piece of embroidery.

"I can't understand it," a phrase I used frequently during those awful days. "Whatever did Louis and Sandro think he would say? 'Welcome back, old boy! Glad to see you, all is forgiven'?"

She looked up at me and sighed. Aunt Julie had always been a beautiful woman, the doyenne of a beautiful family, but now she looked tired and so very sad.

"He had to do it that way, dear. You mustn't fret. Sandro was given the crown by the Russians and the honorable thing was to return it in the same way. I'm afraid he's just tired of being a hero."

"That's just an excuse," I replied, in my customary blunt way. "Sandro has just had it. He didn't really want to go back at all; in fact, I don't know why he did."

"You're absolutely right, Victoria, he has had it, as you say. But I think we really don't have any idea what he's gone through all this time. Only he really knows where his strength lies and what his limits are. Perhaps we weren't wise to let him accept the crown—he was so young. It's never been easy. These last seven years have been lonely and difficult for him."

"I wonder if Bismarck will permit him to marry Moretta now."

"Ah, perhaps that will prove to be the proverbial silver lining," Aunt Julie smiled faintly. I knew that she, as well as Grandmama and Aunt Vicky, very much wanted that marriage. "I heard that the old Emperor himself had said that if Sandro came back to Berlin, he would permit the marriage. He added that there had been enough misery and that he wanted them both to be happy. Bismarck evidently agreed."

"Really?" I asked skeptically. Bismarck always struck me as a dog that had his teeth in a bone. When someone else tried to take it away, he clamped down with an iron jaw. I would think that he would never give up. "I hope that's true," I said absently.

It wasn't.

Even after Sandro abdicated and left Bulgaria, he and Moretta were not permitted to marry. Neither the old Emperor nor Bismarck would relax their views on the subject. Moretta wept endlessly but to no avail. Sandro having had all the fight knocked out of him decided that this wasn't worth it either. As the years went by, Sandro fell in love with a beautiful opera singer named Johanna Loisinger and decided that he would marry her instead.

I would not have it thought that Sandro was faithless. Far from it, he had not seen Moretta for three years and Johanna was a beautiful woman who worshiped him; a woman he could love without obstacle (well virtually without obstacle after Uncle Alexander died); a woman, whom, he, the morganatic prince, was above. Though Aunt Vicky continued to push for the marriage well into 1888, she was finally and most politely asked to stop by Liko. It was too late for Sandro. He just wanted peace.

Sandro married Johanna in 1889 and had two children with her. He accepted a commission in the Austrian army, and took the title of Count Hartenau. He said it was to save Grandmama embarrassment. It was surely a final break with the miseries of the past.

Moretta, on the other hand, moped and cried. She visited Grandmama and moped and cried. She lamented that she would never marry, that she was ugly and that no one wanted her. A match, however, was eventually secured for her with the suitable but lackluster Adolf of Schaumburg-Lippe. One imagines Moretta continuing to pine for her handsome prince in the face of the far more pedestrian Adolf—Moretta was never one to make the best of a situation.

I suppose, ultimately, she got all the romance she craved in the person of the handsome Russian waiter thirty-six years her junior. I have read her memoirs which were published in the twenties and it didn't seem to matter that she was bankrupted and deserted in less than two years. For a very short time, Moretta had her romantic prince and was happy.

But, I cried and felt deeply for them both, ridiculous and pathetic as they had sometimes been. Sandro died in 1893, leaving a young wife and family. In this, too, he had been far too young. The Bulgarians reclaimed their First Sovereign Prince—he was buried in Sofia.

II
Buckingham Palace, June, 1887

This business of remembering can be very upsetting. As I remember these things, it strikes me as odd, that I,

Victoria, have lived a relatively peaceful and happy life, right in the eye of many a storm. My sisters, brother, even Louis and his family have been buffeted about, and I have had, outside of Alice's handicap, very little happen to me. The vicissitudes of my life came from the follies and decisions of others and the subsequent results from those follies and decisions.

I contracted typhoid in the spring of 1887. It was an utterly dreadful disease and like diphtheria, it can be caught from contaminated water. I was alternately hot or shivering with cold; my skin broke out in a rash; and, my poor stomach was distended. The worst part was that this happened just before Grandmama's Golden Jubilee and I was utterly distraught with the idea that I would miss the festivities. Again, I was being wretchedly foolish and ungrateful since the disease, in those days, could easily have been fatal.

I must have an incredibly strong constitution. In my life, I have licked two serious and deadly diseases. However, I was truly lucky to have survived, but more than that, I was lucky that dearest Louis was constantly by my side nursing me through the worst.

Naturally, I was a terrible patient and when I finally began to feel better, I was extremely annoyed to be relegated to the sidelines. What was worse, during the entire course of the disease, Alice was not permitted to see me and I missed her dreadfully. She was just beginning to babble, and even though she was unintelligible, I enjoyed her emphatic attempts at conversation in her own private language.

I was greatly relieved when the doctor told me that I could, with caution, attend all the festivities of Grandmama's Jubilee. However, Grandmama warned me that I could only attend the ceremonies. It was important that I rest and not tire myself with parties and dinners. That was disappointing to me. However, after one day's activities, I was so dreadfully tired that I was most happy to be excused.

I was mostly allowed to lie down, but during certain of the ceremonies, when everyone else had to stand for hours at a time, Grandmama allowed me to sit. It was a very grand time and many of her brother monarchs, never mind Grandmama's family, came to pay their respects.

Since I couldn't go to any of the social events, most of the time I lay on a day bed in our apartments at Buckingham Palace. We had all come up with Grandmama from Windsor on the morning of the 20th of June and had taken places in a long processional going from the train station to Buckingham Palace.

Luckily, riding in a carriage wasn't very difficult for me. Grandmama led off in an open landau so as to be shown to the people. The enthusiasm of her subjects seemed to surprise her. She had hardly appeared in public since Grandpapa died twenty-six years before. Many of her subjects had never seen her before and many were annoyed about this, so much so that there had even been some strong republican movements afoot. However, I can say with certainty that, that day, as she rode through the streets and listened to the cheers of her subjects, there was no thought of removing the Queen-Empress—no thought at all.

The Thanksgiving service the following day at Westminster Abbey was even more impressive and emotional. Grandmama traveled, once again to the loud and heartfelt cheers of the crowds. Following her were some thirty Princes—her sons, her sons-in-law, some of her grandsons (even Willy seemed impressed by all the genuine adulation Grandmama received) and some very exotic creatures. Princes from Japan, Siam, Persia and Maharajahs by the handful from all parts of India were in attendance. There was even the mountainous Queen of Hawaii, those islands west of the United States, with the mellifluous name of Kapeolani.

The loudest cheers came, however, when Uncle Fritz, the Crown Prince of Prussia, and Willy's father, rode slowly by. He was extremely impressive with his gleaming white uniform and noble bearing. I knew that Uncle Fritz was ill, tragically so. What had been initially diagnosed as a throat infection was now thought to be cancer of the throat. He had a procedure called a tracheotomy in which a tube was inserted into the throat for easier breathing. How horribly painful it must have been for poor Uncle Fritz and how nobly he rode, even though, we all knew that he could no longer speak. We would never hear his kind voice again.

Aunt Vicky had insisted that English doctors be in attendance on the Crown Prince and this, as well as differences between their diagnoses and the German doctors, put Aunt in even more difficult situation with her Prussian family. Poor Aunt Vicky never learned to play the game with her in-laws. She was the most brilliant of Grandmama's children and the most beloved of Grandpapa, but she could not make her Prussian family or, even, it seems, her Prussian subjects, love her.

I sighed, and concentrated on the ceremonies.

When the Queen arrived at the abbey, the Archbishop of Canterbury met her at the door. All, naturally, were in their places as Grandmama made her way slowly to the altar, to the majestic strains of Handel. The Archbishop was wearing the velvet and gold robes that had been worn by the presiding Archbishop at Grandmama's coronation, fifty years before.

Grandmama looked splendid in her Jubilee dress. It was of black silk, so elegant and stiff that it rustled as she walked. On her head was her customary bonnet but it was a special bonnet with exquisite white lace woven with diamonds. She made her way to the coronation chair, under which rested the famous Stone of Scone—the prize that Edward the First had wrested from the Scots all those hundreds of years ago.

Then, Grandpapa's composition, the *Te Deum* was played. I could almost hear Grandmama thinking that her darling Albert was not there and what joy and meaning could she derive from such a moment without him? Then, as the music swelled, all her daughters, one by one, came up to the chair and curtsied to their mother and kissed her. When it was Aunt Vicky's turn, Grandmama embraced her warmly and for many more seconds than the other Aunts and Uncles. I felt a tear glide slowly down my cheek.

The service continued with more tributes, and as the finale we all rose as one, and sang *God Save the Queen*—it was at moments like these, overwhelmingly emotional as they were, that I felt so much pride and patriotism and great love for my Grandmama, for my country and for my family.

After this moving moment, we all went back to the palace to rest. Grandmama, would, of course, have a large dinner for all the royalties that evening, but I was, as I had the previous night, to rest. Really, I was beginning to find it very difficult, knowing that everyone else was having a good time. It strikes me as humorous that people in a position to have to attend state dinners, including myself, complain about the tedium and boredom attached to such events. However, when we are left out, we are utterly devastated. I had, however, commissioned my sisters to come up after dinner and tell me all. The best part was that I then had all my sisters around me. Ella and Serge were attending the festivities which was truly a treat. She was hardly getting out of Russia with all her duties, and I had not been visiting Illyinskoje during the summers as much as I had intended.

The three of them came in at once, a beautiful, silky hurricane of lovely women, dresses and scents. Ella, looking entirely splendid in her silks and jewels and the younger girls, Irène, with her longer dress and Alicky in her much shorter one, looked terribly sweet. They dressed alike, with only disparate hemlines, a practice we all seemed to adopt as siblings and with our own children later on.

"Victoria, it was wonderful," Alicky breathed as she sat down on my bed. I was regally decked out in a lacy dressing gown and was impatient for company as well as information.

"Let me tell her." Irène had also found a corner and sat down. She was twenty years old now and looking quite lovely. I knew that she and Henry of Prussia were in love, but I wasn't to breathe a word of it to Grandmama—which was actually quite a relief. I, as I had been over the years, was the one to speak of any and all unpleasant subjects to Grandmama, and, frankly, I was a little tired of it. Irène had actually promised her that she wouldn't get engaged to Henry, but I knew differently. Poor Grandmama, she seemed destined to be thwarted in all her matchmaking attempts for the Hessian children...except, unfortunately, Ernie.

"One of you tell me...you can't imagine how boring it is being cooped up, up here."

"Serge looked utterly and completely marvelous," Alicky breathed. "That man really does know how to wear a uniform."

We all agreed and Ella beamed.

When I look at pictures of Serge, even today, I have to say that he was tall, slender, and tremendously dignified. I had heard that he maintained that slenderness with the help of corsets, but I hardly believed that. There was never the look about him of being restrained—at least not in his dress. Serge had always been slim as a wand.

"Well, thank God you're better, darling. You gave us all quite a scare," Ella, said warmly, coming to my side to plump up my pillows.

"Can't I continue?" Alicky was insisting. She was, after all just a truly impatient girl in her teens.

"No, you shouldn't Alicky, really. You never remember who's who," Irène told her. And, Alicky, having been edged out, was quietly pouting.

"Get me those chocolates over there, mouse," I told her, pointing to some elegant bonbons Louis had brought me. She brightened up slightly as she brought them over, however, Alicky wasn't a particularly large eater, nor was she much interested in food. I wasn't sure how much the chocolates would cheer her.

"Grandmama looked beautiful," Alicky sighed, dolefully, with a mouthful of chocolate, and seated herself once again on the sofa.

"All the Aunts and Uncles tried to get her not to wear a bonnet, but she wouldn't give in," Irène said proudly.

"Grandmama wouldn't be Grandmama without her bonnet," Alicky added positively.

"After you were whisked away from the ceremony, Grandmama rode slowly through the streets once again. The crowds were immense, there was such loud cheering and they seemed thrilled to see her. Impressive, even by Russian standards," Ella remarked. "But, even more so, since they were truly impressed with Grandmama and truly happy."

"They don't see her much," I remarked.

"The Queen-Empress," Alicky put in. "Fifty years on the throne—it's amazing, Victoria, astonishing. I wonder if I would sit on a throne for so many years."

"What throne would you sit on?" Irène asked, disdainfully.

"I don't know," Alicky mused, as though she did know. "But it's not so unlikely, is it?"

"I think you can do whatever you like, Alicky—the world is out there for you," Ella laughed. I knew that it was in her mind to get Alicky to Russia and I also knew that Alicky would probably be only too happy to go. With all the controversy that surrounded our marriages, I really wondered what actual throne Alicky could aspire to, youngest that she was of four sisters.

"Will you all stop babbling and tell me about the dinner this evening?"

"Certainly, darling," Irène said, then stopped, evidently casting about for something interesting to relate.

"It was like most dinners except there was an awful lot of the family and other royalty hanging about," Alicky frowned. I suppose it had been fairly run-of-the-mill. "Oh, but Irène spent a lot of time with Henry."

Irène blushed.

"He's much nicer than Willy," was all she could say.

"Everyone's nicer than Willy," Alicky laughed. It was a hint of her old childhood irrepressibleness. It was rare. "He was boiling mad, Victoria. He went about complaining that he and Dona were being treated with—what did he say?—oh, yes," putting her nose in the air, "'exquisite coolness'."

"Monster," Irène giggled. "Oh, but this was good. You know that Queen Kapeolani is here?" she asked, pronouncing every syllable very carefully. I nodded. "She's here with her sister-in-law, Princess Liliuokalani."

Irène stumbled over that one, and we all laughed.

"I think Irène's doing very well with those names," Ella remarked.

"Well, the Princess was to be escorted into dinner by Leopold of Belgium, and do you know what? He left her standing there. He complained about her being dark-skinned."

"Horrid man," I said, passionately.

"Grandmama asked the King of Saxony to take her in, and he, too, left her conveniently standing around by herself. So, Grandmama whispered to Uncle Affie, who smiled and went over to the lady, and offered his arm."

We all smiled at Irène's account.

"I knew there was a reason I loved our uncle," I said with satisfaction.

"Have you seen the Queen of Hawaii?" Alicky rolled her eyes. "She's huge!" and launched into another fit of giggles.

Ella smiled as she watched our usually doleful sister laughing.

"She is very large," was her quiet comment.

"We're going to have to get Madgie to put this child to bed," I said, with mock sternness.

"I'm not a child," Alicky pointed out. "I'm coming out in two years."

"Practically ancient," I retorted.

The door opened and Louis entered.

"Ladies, you're tiring your sister."

"Oh, Louis," I protested. "I only wanted to hear about the dinner."

"Alicky and I have to go anyway," Irène began, "we have to gather up Ernie and go to bed."

"Gather up Henry more like," Alicky giggled.

"Alicky, you're disgusting. I'll get her out of here," Irène told Louis. "Goodnight both of you," and Irène took Alicky's hand and dragged her out.

"I have to find Serge; I'm getting tired with all this ruckus." Ella kissed Louis and me and left.

Louis sat down on the sofa and took my hand.

"What a lot of hooliganism, you must be exhausted," he said, tenderly.

"No, it's been wonderful to be with them again; especially after I've been so ill."

"I'll ring for Elsa; it's time you got into bed."

He got up and went to the bell.

"I suppose you're going down to smoke with Uncle Bertie?"

"Yes, and a huge number of other men," he grinned. "We'll all be cramped in one of the few rooms that Grandmama will permit such a nasty habit..."

I got up slowly and went over to him. I still wasn't quite myself; I felt extremely weak. I put my arms around him and leaned heavily against him.

"Poor, darling, you really are tired," he said, and kissed my head. I sighed, just enjoying the feeling of resting in his arms.

"Irène is going to marry Henry," I said softly.

"Yes, I've been observing them and they seem quite taken with one another."

"Perhaps Willy won't want any of the Hesse family— after all, it will make Henry your brother-in-law."

"He's already suffered with Liko," he chuckled. "Perhaps one more won't make a difference."

"Alicky says he's being horrid as usual."

"Yes, but, I'm most concerned about Uncle Fritz. I don't know if he's going to get well."

"It's so unfair—he and Aunt Vicky have waited so long."

"Indeed, nearly thirty years—not that fairness has much to do with it." I felt him sigh. "You should have seen Dona trying to keep her baby boys away from little Drino," he laughed harshly. Liko and Auntie had their first child in November of last year, a little boy named Alexander Albert, but like so many in our family, he acquired a nickname of misty origins—Drino.

"Ohh," I exclaimed, angrily. "I just don't know how she has the cheek to do that—Schleswig-Holstein-Sonderburg-Augustenburg indeed. Her title's bigger than any of the estates that go along with it. She's practically a nobody..."

"Darling, my democratic wife," he chuckled, and kissed my hair, "don't excite yourself, Dona is hardly worth it. Liko thought it was funny, and Beatrice didn't even notice. I don't imagine it occurred to her that anyone would do that."

"Louis, it would never have occurred to me, either, before our marriage. But now I'm aware of it all the time. Ohh, it anyone dares to snub Alice..."

"They'll have us both to reckon with, won't they," he said grimly. "For me, I don't care, never have." I pulled back my head and looked into his eyes, and wondered if that were really the truth. I somehow felt it was more a wish than a truth. "But for either of my darling pearls, nothing must ever happen to hurt them."

I looked at him for many moments, and smiled. How he could protect us from harm, I wasn't sure. But, how I loved him! His strength made our family inviolate. No one could hurt us—or so I thought.

CHAPTER ELEVEN

I

Windsor and Heiligenberg, Early Spring and Summer, 1889

The Golden Jubilee and its fantastic celebrations seemed like a dream as time quickly moved on. It had been several years, and things for Grandmama had quieted down considerably. She was approaching seventy now, certainly the twilight of her reign, and many of us, with trepidation, were thinking about her mortality. The thought of England or our family without Grandmama was so alien, so beyond anything that we understood as reality, that none of us dared dwell on it for long. Most of our contemporaries could not imagine England or the empire without her Queen.

I was staying with Grandmama and Auntie at Windsor for a few days, which I did very frequently. Louis was on one of his sea voyages, and I was carrying my second child. I had an overpowering feeling of lethargy that I hadn't experienced with Alice. I was always being reminded to move, but I just couldn't make myself do it. So, I often sat with Auntie, who was also pregnant and even more loath to move than me. Around us were Alice, and Auntie's babies, which now numbered two, Drino, and his sister, two year old Ena, who would one day be Queen Victoria Eugenie of Spain. Added to the mix were the inevitable nannies. Although, Auntie had been very anxious to get married, she was not particularly the motherly type and happily relegated the care of her children to others.

We were talking over Alicky. Last year had been an exciting one for her. She was confirmed and celebrated her sixteenth birthday. Now, she was eagerly looking forward to her first ball. Grandmama was very intent that Alicky come to England and spend time. She wanted to present perspective husbands that might negate the Russians that Ella and Serge were pushing.

"Mama would love her and Eddy to come to some kind of understanding," Auntie commented to me, one March morning, as we were sitting by the fire, drinking tea.

"Eddy?"

I wasn't really surprised since Grandmama had already discussed the possibility with me. Grandmama, as was her custom, was interested in the marriages of all her children and grandchildren. She put a great deal of time, thought, and energy into each one. It was either to be Georgie, Uncle Bertie's second son, or Eddy, who was of course, Prince Albert Victor, the eldest son. He was the one we used to follow over hills and into valleys in Scotland, when we summered with Grandmama at Balmoral. Unfortunately, he hadn't progressed much since then.

He continued to be slow-witted and barely seemed able to function in society. He had been put in the navy with his younger brother, where he had an extremely undistinguished career. Now, at the age of twenty-six, he was doing very little more than wearing uniforms and being somewhat pleasant. To make matters worse, he was a rather odd-looking fellow with an abnormally long neck and arms that seemed to hang much lower than they ought. His uniforms were made up specially, with high collars to hide the neck and longer cuffs to hide the length of his arms. Poor Eddy, Uncle Bertie made awful fun of him and told all the children in the family to call him "Cuffs and Collars"—not a very dignified name for the heir to the throne.

In actuality, it boded horribly for the throne of England, as it seemed that Eddy would have absolutely no idea how to function as a Constitutional Monarch; or, truth be told, any kind of monarch. Grandmama and Aunt Alix felt that what must be found for Eddy was some sweet and gentle princess with sense that could, as it were, guide his footsteps. Grandmama cast her eye on Alicky.

"Mama thinks that Alicky would be just right for Eddy. She is so sweet and simple. She's not a raving intellectual like you are Victoria. That would never do for Eddy."

I'll say it would not do.

"...and she is so lovely. I don't think that Eddy would consent to marry a princess that was not attractive."

"Alicky certainly is a beauty—but, I wonder if she's quite right for Eddy."

"Mama is very determined not to lose another granddaughter to Russia. She thinks about this all the time and worries so for Alicky."

"I know she thinks about it all the time. She writes about it to me all the time and I do understand, Auntie. What Grandmama has to understand is that I cannot force Alicky either way and I don't believe that Papa would be so inclined."

"Yes, but Ella is working hard in the other direction and is equally determined that Alicky would be quite happy near her."

"I suppose that's possible, but she's so young yet, not more than seventeen—surely we can just wait and see."

Grandmama was not one to wait and see. She took the bull by the horns and wanted Alicky quickly informed of her wishes regarding her marital future. As usual, I had been the one who was deputized to tell the uncomfortable news to Alicky. She, as I expected, did not want to think of Eddy in that way.

"He's a very sweet boy, Victoria, but I don't love him in

that way, I love him as a cousin and childhood chum," she explained to me.

"I think, Alicky, that Mama would certainly not want you to marry where you didn't want—but, Grandmama most emphatically wishes you to consider Eddy as a potential husband."

"I will think about it," she looked at me with her beautiful doe-eyes. "I suppose if Grandmama really wished it...But, I don't think I can do it..." Then, a faraway look came over her, and her thoughts were obviously a long way away.

"What is it, dear?"

She looked at me for a moment and smiled faintly.

"Nothing, Victoria, nothing. Please tell Grandmama I will think about it."

I smiled and hugged her. Sometimes I wondered where she was. She seemed to be slipping away from me, and I wasn't sure where. This wouldn't be the first time that I saw Alicky retreat into her own little world, and, tragically, it would certainly not be the last.

"I understand that the coming out ball in St. Petersburg was spectacular," Auntie commented, as I was jolted back to the present.

"Yes, Papa wasn't up to arranging such an event in Darmstadt and Irène is so busy with her new husband and now a new baby, that when Ella and Serge arranged for a ball in St. Petersburg—Papa didn't say no, nor do I think he wished to."

Nor, did Alicky, it turned out. Irène wrote me that Alicky was thrilled beyond anything when Ella had offered to give her first ball in Russia. Alicky had always loved Russia, I think in that way she had something of my love for exoticism and mysticism—but without my sense of proportion. She also adored the Russian relatives and as well as her adoration of Serge. She became very talkative about the event, writing me endless letters about her toilet and the events that would take place when she was there. Obviously, she was looking forward to her visit breathlessly.

Indeed, the Hesses went, once again, to St. Petersburg. I had no real desire to travel at that point, besides which, I was in no mood for the grandeur and excesses of Russia. I couldn't have gone even if I had wanted to; I was expecting Louise and had to stay home. I would have to rely on Irène, and Alicky to give me their accounts of the trip and its subsequent events.

One thing I did know however, when they returned from Russia, after a flurry of letter writing, it was again put upon me to give Grandmama bad news. Alicky was quite doubtful about Eddy. She had, instead, fallen, where I suspected she was going to fall all along—Nicky of Russia. I might add here, that Grandmama was not discouraged yet, nor would she be for some time.

We all met at the Heiligenberg, just after the birth of Louise and just before Louis and I went to Malta that autumn. We hadn't really had a good long chat together since the Golden Jubilee, and I cherished the moments I spent with my sisters before they went on to their new lives.

"Ella is worried about not yet having a sign of a child," Irène remarked, as the three of us tucked ourselves cozily up with cups of tea.

"I can understand why she's worried; she has been married for nearly five years. I really believe that is why she went with Serge to Jerusalem."

Ella and Serge had gone to Jerusalem the previous year, ostensibly to dedicate a church in honor of Serge's mother, our Aunt Marie. Nevertheless, I always felt it was a sort of pilgrimage for her. She had written me fascinating letters describing Jerusalem and the Holy Land itself as being both extraordinarily beautiful as well as dilapidated at the same time.

The Ottomans, she wrote, had neglected the land shamelessly, most of it being barren or derelict. There were pockets of Christians, Moslems and Jews living in the few cities that continued from ancient times, as well as the Bedouin, whom she said, wandered around the whole area along with their livestock and without thought of boundaries. But, sadly there was no development—no modern progress—of any kind. It was a land, she wrote, that time just hadn't neglected completely, but forgotten.

Jerusalem, however, was radiant. She rhapsodized about its loveliness saying that there was nothing more beautiful than watching the sun set on the walls of the city. There was a golden glow to the indigenous stone as the sun touched the walls. Serenity overtook the troubled city, as the muezzin called the faithful to prayer. She had gone to the burial place of Christ at the Church of the Holy Sepulcher, which she described as dank and dark, and had walked the stations of the Cross...there was nothing, she assured me more moving than this.

Louis had been to the Holy Land with his brothers and I was extremely envious. He had told me so much about the exoticism and mystery of the land that I always hoped to go. Even if I hadn't dearly loved to travel, I should have wanted to see where Jesus walked and where Joseph and Mary lived and worked. But never would I have thought that I would go to Jerusalem considering the circumstances in which I eventually undertook the journey.

"Yes, and seeing you have two children," Irène was saying to me, "...she's thinking that it's a sign from God. She's seriously considering converting to Russian Orthodoxy—"

"Converting?!" Alicky exclaimed. "How could she ever do that? That's absolutely beyond anything earthly—I could never change my religion. It would be—like not believing in Jesus the same way."

"Nonsense, Alicky," I retorted crisply. "It's all Christianity—I don't think it's that much of a leap of faith."

We both looked at her, and she started to color up. She was so emphatic, we were both taken aback.

"Alicky," I continued, less sharply, "if you marry Nicky, you'll have to change. He'll be Tsar one day, and it is against their laws to have an Empress that isn't Russian Orthodox."

"That's going to the problem. I probably can't marry Nicky," she said slowly. "I can't change my religion, and he knows that."

Once again, we both looked at her. She had been so insistent and conveyed to us often that it was quite possible that she could not think of marrying anyone else. Did she intend to remain a spinster?

"Does Nicky know that?" I asked.

"Yes, we've discussed it by letter, but since he hasn't formally asked me to marry him, I don't see why I should agonize over it now."

How could she not? Alicky seemed to have the ability to put on blinders, and, conveniently, see only what she wanted to see—so different from me. I always saw everything from every side. It not only drove me around the twist, but I really think that sometimes Louis wanted to tape my mouth shut when I was thinking out a problem aloud.

"Besides, I think that Cousin Minnie and Sasha don't want a youngest daughter for their Nicholas, do they?" Alicky said in a strange voice.

"I have heard that they would prefer a more eminently placed princess," I answered, as tactfully as I was able. "However, if you do wish Russia, there are many eligible Grand Dukes that you might consider."

That was certainly true. Russia at that time had more Grand Dukes, meaning more viable male members of its ruling family, than any royal house in Europe. This was nearly as bad as having no heirs—or at least it would have been in the old days when the heirs would have been killing each other to get closer to the throne. Now it meant that there were simply too many forceful men around to tell one what to do. This certainly happened with Nicky later on. But he showed them. Tragically, he didn't listen to anyone—excepting his wife.

"So perhaps if I don't marry Nicky, I should not go to Russia after all."

"Alicky, this is all needless speculation. If you don't marry Nicky, which seems a strong possibility since no one in the family is for it, including his parents and Grandmama," Irène began ticking them off on her fingers. "Perhaps you ought to consider Georgie or Eddy," she finished, reasonably.

"You're one to talk—Grandmama didn't want you to marry Henry, but you insisted."

There was no answer to that. But, what Alicky didn't understand was that Henry was a second son and to many people, not a particularly bright second son, so it didn't matter nearly as much.

"I just think that you ought to consider all the possibilities," Irène continued placidly. Irène never cared what people said about Henry, she was happy and the rest didn't matter.

"Grandmama also suggests Max of Baden," I cut in, not wanting the two of them to argue. "He's quite a handsome fellow, Alicky, cuts quite a dash and many other princesses have been interested in him."

"Maudie, for one," Irène interjected, naming one of Uncle Bertie's daughters. We had understood that Max wasn't attracted to her. She, however, didn't despair, she married Carl of Denmark, who was later elected to the Norwegian Throne—and they became King Haakon and Queen Maud of Norway.

"Oh, I don't know, it's all so confusing," Alicky said, and went into one of her sulks.

"Alicky, I don't want you sulking over this," I said with whatever authority I could muster. "If things don't work with Nicky, and it's very likely they won't, there are plenty of other princes who would be honored to have your hand. You're very pretty, you're the Queen's granddaughter and you are very sweet and kind. Don't worry if this particular match doesn't work out."

She put down her teacup, and I could see a tear falling down her face.

"Dearest, why don't you tell us about your time in St. Petersburg. I have never had a satisfactory account and Ella wrote me that you all had such fun." I hated to see Alicky cry. She did it far too often.

She sniffled for a moment, but then brightened up with the thought of Russia.

"You can never get tired of looking at Ella and Serge's

palace. The colors are so brilliant and—well, gaudy," and I chuckled, "but in a nice way," she finished quickly.

I remembered that huge edifice that was their town residence. It was a large baroque palace painted brick red with gold trimmings, with columns and statues adorning the front, and elaborate moldings above each window. It was enough to give purists nightmares. But that was Russia—everything was blazing and gigantic; everything except their charming country house, Illyinskoje.

I had already made several long visits to Ella's home on the Moskva and had been captured by its charm and serenity. It was a truly lovely place, a two-story wooden structure, with broad terraces facing the banks of the river. We spent many mornings on that terrace, sipping coffee or tea and eating our breakfasts. Here Ella reigned supreme and the insides were furnished with chintzes and imported British furniture—just like Mama's palace in Darmstadt. We always had such fun there, boating, fishing and bathing—it was quite informal.

Alicky, however, was talking and I listened as she described her coming out ball and what she wore—the usual white, albeit with gorgeous white diamonds and flowers. She told us every dance she danced and who she danced it with and told us how many times Nicky asked her to dance.

"It was the most heavenly six weeks in my life," she said, truthfully. "Nicky was wonderful to me and spent so much time taking me to the theater, the opera, skating and playing all sorts of wonderful games with all the other cousins. I adore the St. Petersburg winter—everyone has such fun."

She went on to wax eloquent about everything and everyone in St. Petersburg. It seemed that Russia was the only subject about which she talked more than I. She adored everything about it and that worried me. With all the opposition in so many quarters, I didn't know if things would turn out well.

Of course, what we all didn't reckon with was the fact that not only was Alicky in love with St. Petersburg, but she was also madly in love with Nicky and would struggle with the religious and familial factors for several years yet. She would do some very grown up and painful soul-searching about changing her religion. She stuck to her emphatic decision to not change for a long time.

II
Valletta, Malta, Autumn, 1889

Sometimes I think that memory plays tricks on one. This part of my life, when so many events of world importance occurred, for me is most strongly punctuated with the coming of my children. Events that had a lasting effect on the political situation well into the twentieth century pale in significance beside the birth of my babies.

It was a warm summer's day and I hardly expected to go into labor. Louis, Alice and I had spent most of his summer leaves at the Heiligenberg and this year was no exception. I had wonderful times visiting with Alicky and Ernie, who summered nearby in Papa's beautiful summer home, Wolfsgarten and many family members visited our hilltop home to spent a few days with Louis and me. We loved the place. For me, it was home. I had spent the day walking, well, perhaps not walking, more likely shuffling, around the gardens and courtyard areas, remembering our carefree days as youngsters, exploring, playing and falling in love.

This pregnancy had not been easy as it had been with Alice. Grandmama shot off letter after letter telling me to walk more, to exercise more, but I didn't listen to her. I didn't feel vigorous and I didn't feel like exercising. I like to think that the easy birth I had with Alice made up for the fact that she was later a very outspoken and headstrong child, while Louise, whose birth was far more difficult, kept closely to me for a very long time.

I sat down on the side of our courtyard fountain, when I felt a burning sharp pain. At first, I thought it was something I'd eaten for breakfast, but the pains continued and they quickly became recognizable. I went into premature labor, but happily, my baby, another girl, was born healthy and quite lusty in her protestations of coming out to the cold world.

She was called Louise Alexandra Marie Irène—that middle name after Uncle Alexander of Hesse, who had died the previous year. Dear Uncle Alexander—Louis had such a close relationship with him, as did all his sons. I believe there was a mentality amongst the men in the Battenberg family—'us against the world'—and Uncle Alexander was the rock. He stood by Louis through his difficult days as a cadet and an officer in the navy; he was at Sandro's side through his disastrous tenure in Bulgaria and was there to buck up Liko, when he was ridiculed in the British press, and by the various royalties. Perhaps his younger sons didn't suffer quite the difficulties of the older ones, but the unit was complete and self-contained. Now, its stalwart was gone.

From sadness can come some good—we inherited the Heiligenberg. Considering how much both of us loved the house, I think that Aunt Julie was pleased about it as well. It was to remain our summer home until after World War One.

Louis immersed himself in his career, now being the Commander of the *Dreadnought*. Though his time with the *Victoria and Albert* was pleasant in that it afforded him the opportunity of spending a lot of time with Alice and me, I believe that he was much happier with a real ship, rather than what he termed a pleasure cruiser. Naturally, when he received the appointment, there was a great deal of uproar, mostly starting with the word nepotism. It was, as it always would be with Louis: xenophobia because he had never got rid of his German accent and finally, anti-intellectualism. Louis simply didn't fit in with the typical British naval officer, and sadly, never would.

That summer, after the Jubilee, Louis brought Alice and me to Malta, that lovely island off Sicily, which served as the headquarters of the British Navy. Malta was Britain's stepping-stone to Africa and the Middle East, and thus, was extremely strategic. For me, it was a double pleasure, first because the weather was warm and balmy—so good for my circulation. Next and most important, we had the company of the family whose head was the Commander in Chief of the Mediterranean Fleet, my Uncle Affie and all the Edinburghs.

Aunt Marie was very happy on Malta. Perhaps it was not equivalent to her position as the Tsar's only daughter, but she was the First Lady of the island. Initially, when Louis and I arrived, we stayed with them at their residence, called St. Antonio, in Valletta, the capital city. It was an incredibly beautiful residence with so many gardens and exotic flowers. I spent hours exploring them with my family. I must admit, I enjoyed getting to know my little Edinburgh cousins. Though they were ten years younger and more, they were wild and independent and full of good cheer, especially the two oldest daughters.

The eldest was Marie, whom we called Missy. She would eventually become the Queen of Romania. The second was Victoria Melita, called Ducky, whose destiny, too, lay in Russia, the land of her mother's birth. I remember the third youngest, Sandra, who loved to tag along with us on her very small pony as well as the baby who was called Baby Bee even into advanced old age.

I also remember our wild gallops all over the island, which wasn't very big. It was very hilly and full of slopes and strange and fascinating geological formations—but there wasn't a river or a mountain in sight. The girls' mother roundly scolded them for acting like hooligans, although they didn't really hurt anyone, or disturb any of the natives. Nevertheless, Marie had some very definite ideas about how princesses should behave. Tearing around the countryside on nearly unmanageable horses was certainly not in the scenario. As for me, she would only smile faintly and shake her head. I suppose I should have comported myself in a more lady-like manner. Certainly Grandmama had taken me to task about my wild riding. But, somehow, I felt curiously free on that small island.

There were usually three of us, but sometimes four, when Sandra would tag along on Tommy the pony. We would end our ride at an al fresco tea or picnic at various fortresses on the island, presided over by my indomitable Aunt Marie.

Having a long history of being the scene of so many battles, and being a bastion of Southern Europe, Malta was chock-full of defensive forts and battlements. It was also the home of the Order of St. John, more popularly known as the Knights of Malta. These monk-knights would defend Europe against the infidel and help pilgrims and crusaders on their journeys to the Holy Land. My imagination fed on its eerie, mysterious and exotic surroundings—though it was a far more benign place, and kinder to my family than the even more wondrous Bulgaria.

Those teas of Aunt Marie's stand out clearly in my mind. Sometimes, there would be favored officers in attendance. All the girls had their pets among the officers and captains, as did Aunt Marie. But, at other times, it would be just family...naturally with the required nannies for Louise, who was just an infant and Baby Bee. And, when we were alone, we had some wonderful gossips about everyone and everything.

"It was so humiliating for me," Aunt Marie said one day, as we sat in some comfortable chairs next to the inevitable battlements. "I, a Tsar's daughter, had to go behind your Aunt Alix." She was referring to Uncle Bertie's wife, the Princess of Wales. This didn't strike me as humiliating or strange, but then, of course, I wasn't the Tsar's daughter.

"You must find it a lot easier being here," I murmured, not wanting to be placating, but anxious to leave that subject as quickly as possible.

"This is a lovely island, but it makes me feel claustrophobic—there's no space," she shivered for a moment, though it was quite hot in the autumn afternoon.

I nodded. Having been in Russia and seeing the vast spaces to which Marie was used, I could understand her feelings.

"Cousin Georgie will be coming soon," fourteen year

old Missy commented. She and Ducky were sitting by themselves under the shade trees, giggling and chatting. They came to us only for more tidbits.

"Hmm," was all Aunt Marie would say. Georgie, Uncle Bertie's second son, later George V of England, was rather strongly infatuated with Missy and I believe she reciprocated his affection. Aunt Marie, however, would have none of that. As determined as Grandmama was not to have any of her granddaughters go to Russia, Aunt Marie was determined that none of her daughters would stay in England. As much as I liked May, who would later be England's Queen Mary and Georgie's wife, I always thought it was a shame Missy didn't marry her childhood sweetheart—Missy would have made England a spectacular queen.

A warm gentle wind hovered over us and I sank further into my cozy chaise. I was regaining my strength after Louise's birth and enjoyed the rest and lovely feel of the sun soaking into my skin. I would have probably slept if Aunt Marie hadn't been in one of her gregarious moods.

"They are first cousins," Aunt Marie continued, abruptly, watching her daughters laughing and throwing food. "I won't have that. We have enough in this family. Missy, Ducky, stop that at once!" She raised her voice only slightly, but her word was their law, and order was immediately restored.

Aunt Marie was, if it were possible, less tactful than I. After all, just last year, Henry and Irène, first cousins, had married.

"Mama-in-law was concerned about those other two getting married," she remarked, picking up on my thoughts.

"Unfortunately, Irène didn't listen to anyone, once she fell in love with Henry," I replied, which was quite true. I was also defending my Papa, who was extremely complaisant about the entire matter.

"You girls were allowed to choose whomever you wished," she said, looking over at Missy and Ducky, who were no longer trying to listen to our conversation, but having a giggly, silly one of their own. "I don't believe in that kind of freedom. Choosing partners in marriage is a very serious business and I can't believe that if your Mama had lived, you would have had the freedom to decide where you wanted to marry. That will not happen with my girls. They're beautiful and they will marry where it is best for them. Choosing one's own partner is extremely perilous for young girls. They need the help of wiser heads..."

That meant, of course, that Aunt Marie would most definitely provide them with that help. She had, as I said, very definite ideas about Princesses. It was best to keep them in total ignorance until the last possible moment and then, spring a spouse on them before they knew what was happening. I suppose it didn't hurt Sandra or Baby Bee, but with Missy and Ducky, it had very tragic consequences. Though with Ducky, it would mean my own brother, Ernie. They were first cousins, though Aunt

Marie had so disdained such a connection and there would be heartbreak on both sides.

"To be fair, Aunt Marie, Mama had always expressed to Papa, that she wanted all of us to marry where we wanted, if it were at all possible. And, we were all in our twenties. I think we had some judgment." I didn't want to get into an argument with her, but I wanted very much to defend my parents.

"Princesses should be very young when they marry. I think that eighteen may even be too late." She looked speculatively at Missy. "She's very flighty and must be settled. We should not linger with it." She seemed quite determined about this, though I couldn't see what the hurry was. Marie had not been all that young, certainly in her twenties, when she had married Uncle Affie. Nevertheless, I decided not to pursue that line of conversation.

"I will admit that you made an excellent choice, Victoria—Louis is a fine man."

Normally such a remark would have really annoyed me, but from Aunt Marie, giving approval to a Battenberg was a real concession.

"Louis is extremely fond of you and Uncle Affie," I said, which wasn't strictly true. Louis was fond of Uncle Affie. "He credits Uncle Affie, as well as my Mama, for encouraging him to join the navy, which he loves."

"Yes, though I believe Sasha would have been so much happier if Louis had gone into the Russian Army."

I refused to pursue that line of conversation. I didn't want to argue with Aunt Marie about the dreadful things her brother had done to the Battenbergs. There was silence, so I cast about for a change of subject.

"So sad about Fritz, don't you think?" Marie beat me to it, though this also was not a particularly pleasant subject. My Uncle Fritz had died in the beginning of summer, 1888. It had, in fact been a terrible year for deaths in the family. Not only did Uncle Fritz die of throat cancer, but so, before him, did his father, the old Emperor. Poor Uncle Fritz was Emperor for a mere three months. Most people considered him an interim ruler. They were waiting for the poor man to die, which he did fairly promptly.

His last official engagement and the last time I saw him, was on May 24, 1888, when Irène and Henry were married. (The duty to tell Grandmama of their engagement, naturally, in the end, fell to me. She was fatalistic about it, though she genuinely felt that Irène would have an awful time with the old Empress.) He was already very ill and had risen from his deathbed, to attend the wedding. As usual, he looked tremendously dignified, in full dress uniform, but the wedding had a funereal feel to it, something like I suppose Mama's must have had, following so soon as it did after the death of Grandpapa.

"It is rather awful," I agreed.

"What's worse is that now Willy is in charge. I never liked that boy," she confided. "He was dreadfully indulged by his grandfather and has no self-discipline. Do you know that he has his younger brother so cowed that Henry won't write his own speeches anymore? He feels that Willy might as well write them so that Henry won't be scolded for them later on."

I had known this, because Irène told me. She was annoyed that some people, including his own mother, thought that Henry was unintelligent and she wanted me to know that he was not uttering his own words in certain speeches he made which were at the least simple and at the most, stupid sounding. She was determined that Henry would be brought round to what Grandmama called the right way of thinking. I felt that if anyone could do this, Irène could. She thought so well of him, that it was contagious. I came to the point where I also thought he was an especially nice person. He and Louis were also somewhat close, both sharing a love of the sea and both being in their countries' respective navies.

"I agree," I answered, not really enjoying the thought of discussing Willy yet again. "And now, Aunt Vicky has to suffer his arrogance."

"Your Aunt Vicky has some very liberal ideas that I don't think would be right for Germany."

"Certainly she's had no opportunity to try them, has she? But, Willy seems to agree with you. He immediately had her thrown out of the palace in which Uncle Fritz wanted her to live and insisted on confiscating all her papers."

The girls, Moretta, Sophie and Mossy, were evidently instrumental in making sure that this didn't happen. In the end, Willy didn't get his hands on all of Aunt Vicky's papers, but it was all so unpleasant. So soon after her widowhood, her own son was mistreating her in the extreme. I couldn't imagine a child of mine treating me this way.

"Sasha can't stand Willy."

You could have fooled me, I thought, bringing to mind poor Sandro.

"He certainly made a very good imitation of liking him when Willy went to St. Petersburg to discuss the Bulgarian situation," I said, not watching myself.

"No, he doesn't like him at all," she went on, as though I hadn't said anything. "He thinks he's mercurial, and not to be trusted."

Again, I decided not to say anything further. There seemed to be little point.

"So how do you like Malta?"

Ah, finally a subject that wouldn't get my hackles up.

One of the highlights of my stay that year had been the arrival of my family for a visit. Papa, Alicky, and Ernie had come from Darmstadt, but Irène, had come with her baby and Henry, who was Captain of the ship, the *Irène*, which anchored off Valletta. We had a marvelous reunion. Any doubts I may have had, I assured Grandmama, were absolutely wiped out. Henry was completely devoted to Irène. They were very much in love, and made a very happy and harmonious couple.

We stayed in Malta for the autumn, and into the winter of that year, but our lives were to be turned around by the events to come in the next few years.

CHAPTER TWELVE

I
The New Palace, Darmstadt, 1892

It was an unfair but pervasive feeling in my day: a family rejoiced more when a boy was born. My first baby boy, a beautiful child, was born in the early winter, though, how could he not be beautiful with such a father? We called him George along with his father's and Aunt Vicky's name, and for my sisters, I also gave him my brothers-in laws' names. So, he was George Louis Victor Henry Serge, but we ended up calling him Georgie. I think that my cousin Georgie, who later became George the Fifth of England, was extremely pleased with his namesake.

That year had been joyous with this birth, but it had also been tragic in the deaths that had occurred. In the beginning of the year, Eddy, Grandmama's heir presumptive died. The young man that my sisters and I had followed around the blue green hills and valleys of Balmoral, who had never been the picture of health or intellect for that matter, died of pneumonia in January of 1892.

Eddy was, I always felt, Grandmama's best argument for marrying as far out of the family as possible—and someone with strong blood. Eddy never seemed to advance beyond childhood. Because I knew him, I always have to chuckle when I read those half-baked theories about his being Jack the Ripper. Besides the evidence stacked against such an absurd accusation, Eddy couldn't baffle his pet kitten, never mind the great minds of Scotland Yard.

Just a month before this sad and unfortunate event, December of 1891, Eddy had finally got himself engaged to Princess Mary of Teck, whom we called May. Naturally, all hopes of Alicky's marrying him had to be put to rest and I think she could only approach the news of his engagement with relief. Grandmama, however, never one to take defeat, continued to talk about Georgie for her. After Eddy's death, Georgie, naturally, began to look more attractive, not only because he was, at least, intellectually normal and moderately good-looking, but, also, far more importantly, he was now the heir presumptive.

Worse of all for the Hessian family, we faced the death of our dear Papa. The doctors said the cause was heart attack and stroke, but I always felt that he'd given up the true will to live many years before. The sad and untimely death of Mama, as well as the ludicrous Madame de Kolemine debacle, seemed to rob him of his vitality. The births of grandchildren didn't seem to help and only the continued regard of Grandmama had cheered him. Apparently, he truly seemed to have given up on life. It was sad.

So, I and my brother and sisters were really orphans now. Grandmama, who had considered herself our mother for many years, with our husbands and children, provided much comfort, but for Alicky and Ernie, it was a different story. Ernie was now the Grand Duke of Hesse—an attractive young man of twenty-three, with a sensitive and artistic temperament. Unfortunately, it wasn't the temperament needed to be a ruler, though, as I have mentioned, the consequences of this in our little Grand Duchy were relatively benign.

As his first lady, Ernie was content to have nineteen year old Alicky, who, unless she was talking about Russia, continued to be shy and withdrawn. She had gone to Russia with Papa to visit Ella and Serge just months before he died. I knew for quite some time that any attempts to make her take Eddy or, now, Georgie, would be futile. Interestingly, she remained stubborn about the religious aspect. If anything were to defeat what seemed to be Alicky's only happiness, it would be her own rigidity. This was a harbinger of things to come.

Her tenure as the First Lady of Hesse was not agreeable

for her, or probably for those around her. For one thing, she didn't have Mama to teach her. I remember Mama telling me that when she was young, Grandmama would insist that she and her sisters do what she called the *cercle*. This was a process of walking around a circle of chairs—completely empty—and conversing and being pleasant as if these chairs were filled with the most interesting people in the world. It promoted the obvious attributes for a princess, namely to be sociable and agreeable no matter what the circumstances. Madgie, however, had never made Alicky do this, which was a great pity. Alicky did not converse easily with strangers, nor have a facile way with people. In short, she had no idea how to make herself appealing. She was the truest, most honest and decent of young women, but with people she didn't know, she lacked charm; sad for a Princess of Hesse and tragic for the possible future Empress of All the Russias.

We, sisters all did our best to help and I went to Darmstadt as often as I could get away, even during my pregnancy. Grandmama, who had rushed to Darmstadt to give Ernie an abbreviated course in ruling, continued to lament about what poor little lambs they were. She, however, had the perfect solution. She continually pushed for Alicky to come and marry in England. I knew what with all that was taking place that was a virtual impossibility, but did not yet know how to relate this to Grandmama.

298

"Surely Alicky can understand that she's ignoring the most important position in the entire world," she told me one day at Windsor, soon after Papa's death. Grandmama, with good reason, had a very healthy view of her position. She felt that being the Queen-Empress of a great empire was something to which a shy young Princess from Hesse could never hope to aspire. Having the opportunity put before her and actually casting it aside, was more than Grandmama could comprehend.

"I believe she understands something of it," I answered carefully. "However, I'm afraid that when all is said and done, Alicky will only do it if we absolutely insist. I really don't think she would, otherwise," which was nearly word for word what Alicky had told me.

"Your Mama and Papa had some very interesting notions about your marriages. Though," she sighed, "no one knows better than I that children will not marry where they do not wish."

"Grandmama," I said soothingly, "they simply wanted us to have the opportunities for love matches, as they did—as you did."

I hoped I wasn't treading on dangerous ground there. Grandmama only wanted memories of Grandpapa used for her own purposes—brought out only when she needed them. They didn't belong to, and therefore, couldn't be used by anyone else. She, however, didn't pay much attention to my comments. She was much too lost in her own thoughts.

"I have such reservations about her visiting Ella and Serge so much in Russia...not that I haven't seen that Serge is quite a gentleman—so civilized," she was now going onto a very familiar theme. Calling one of the Russian relatives civilized was a great concession for Grandmama. "Ella wrote me such beautiful letters from the Holy Land. If I were younger and inclined to be an adventurous traveler, perhaps I would attempt the journey. The Stations of the Cross would be such an inspiration..."

She began to muse, while I was quite taken up with the fact that my baby was kicking. I enjoyed it for it told me I had a lively youngster and in those days, that was a tremendous blessing—especially in our family.

"Ernie must get married," she said suddenly after a few minutes or seconds, I'm not sure which. I glanced up. "He's no better at ruling by himself than poor Sandro was." She paused and looked at me wondering, perhaps, whether I would be sensitive about that subject. "I had thought that Maudie would be good for him," she was talking about Eddy and Georgie's youngest sister, who was, as I have already mentioned, casting around for a suitable mate. "However, they aren't a very healthy group of children, all premature, you know—and with the hemophilia in the family..." she was thinking aloud. "No, I don't believe that Maudie would do."

She was silent for a moment. I was enjoying the sensation of my baby kicking and listening to the clock on the mantle ticking. This was really the last subject I wanted to discuss with Grandmama. I had always hoped that Ernie would decide upon his own mate, though he had shown no inclinations in that direction. No doubt, in the end, it would be from one of our cousins. However, whichever way it went, I so wanted him to be the one to choose—as Ella, Irène, and I had done. I felt that this was the key to happiness. If Ernie, who was just as melancholy as Alicky, were ever to be happy, it would be because he had found his soul mate: the woman with whom he would never be lonely or alone.

"She should be a girl that also has an artistic and intellectual soul, a girl who is sensitive and who would make Ernie a wonderful wife, and Hesse a good Grand Duchess."

Though Grandmama seemed to understand Ernie's nature somewhat, I doubted such a paragon could actually be found.

"Who is the young lady you have in mind?" I asked because I knew she had someone in mind, and wanted me to ask.

"It's young Ducky Edinburgh, of course," she replied forcefully, as though I must have been addled not to follow her train of thought. Grandmama, God bless her, at seventy-three, had not lost any of her acuity.

"Ducky," I repeated stupidly.

Certainly she wasn't the first person who came to mind for Ernie. Cousin Victoria Melita, the cousin with whom I tore around Malta on horseback, was Grandmama's choice. She was everything Grandmama said, with the possible exception of sensitive. Ducky was an exceptionally strong, honest and fearless girl, but for some reason which I couldn't figure, the match seemed a little strange, perhaps unbalanced to me. There was a restless spirit about the girl that I wasn't sure that Ernie would be able to handle or understand. Alicky, as spinster sister, certainly, would never be able to cope with her. However, I was, perhaps, a little too willing to accept Grandmama's judgment in this matter, maybe because it had always been rock-solid in the past and we were so used to listening to her.

"Such a nice girl," Grandmama continued, "so musical like Ernie. You know that they share the same birthday— surly that's a good omen."

I nodded absently. I failed to see that sharing birthdays would be so felicitous and certainly, as time went on, both Ducky and Ernie had to be, if not exactly coerced, certainly strongly urged in the matter. Ducky liked Ernie well enough, as, indeed, who would not? He was a dear, dear boy. Most of the cousins in our family got along admirably well. She did, however, seem much more fiery and passionate than he did and no matter how much Grandmama advised him, Ernie was reluctant to move on the matter.

Aunt Marie, as she told me later, liked the idea very well. It was one of my last days in Malta before I left for

Darmstadt for my lying in. We were having one of our now customary al fresco teas. The girls were off by themselves, giggling and thinking up mischief, as always.

"So she will live in Germany, not England," she pronounced with tremendous satisfaction.

I remember the day as being beautiful with a jewel blue sky and a mild breeze blowing. It was a sleepy afternoon on that lovely, flat island, the sort of sunny day that one could easily fall asleep with the warmth of the sun on one's face. The tinkling of a distant wind chime was an added lulling soporific.

I didn't answer, probably because her constant Anglophobia was starting to get on my nerves, but mostly because I was quite pregnant with my Georgie and feeling the serenity I had felt before Alice was born. Now, if this sounds contradictory, remember that had I been my usual feisty self, I would have argued with her about England and its virtues until the cows came home. Neither of us, I might add, giving an inch. As it was, I could simply not be bothered.

"Missy will love Romania," she continued on with her contentment growing by the minute.

Cousin Missy was engaged to marry Crown Prince Ferdinand, the nephew and heir of old King Carol of Romania. I found him a singularly uninteresting young man. He was good-looking enough, though he had ears that stood out like teacup handles and he looked perennially frightened—especially when he was around his very young and very innocent fiancée. When I got to know Cousin Missy, as an adult, I would better understand his fears. Missy needed a strong man to take her in hand and Nando, as we all called him, was definitely not such a person.

"No doubt," I answered. I was sure Aunt Marie hadn't the foggiest idea of what Romania was like, nor would she have a clue about how loveable it was.

"It seems a rather wild country, I believe. Something like Bulgaria...you've been there?"

Framed as a question, she was starting to irritate even placid me. She knew very well that I had been there.

"Yes, Bulgaria was certainly interesting, and very wild," I remarked blandly. Two could play the same game. However, I had no wish to rehash that business and did not elaborate. Aunt Marie, then, felt compelled to continue.

"I think Ducky needs to show Ernie she would be willing..." she left off delicately.

"I suppose encouragement wouldn't hurt."

"It wouldn't hurt if he showed a little more enthusiasm," she stated petulantly, "certainly the Queen is very interested in this."

Now I could see that she was becoming irritated. She wanted advice about my brother that I couldn't give, or, for me to at least agree with her analysis of the situation. Frankly, I wasn't sure that I could. Certainly a nice young woman could only have a salubrious affect on Ernie, but he was a bit of a mystery even to me. He was growing up while I was starting my married life, so I hadn't the time to know him as an adult. I did know, however, that he hadn't shown any great interest in getting married, nor did he seem very enthusiastic about Ducky.

God knows, I couldn't say all of this to Aunt Marie—not that such trivial details as reluctance would have bothered her. Ferdinand of Romania, I was told, had evidently shown little interest in Missy, thinking her very young, which at seventeen she certainly was. Indeed, Louis told me Ferdinand had a Romanian mistress, a lady-in-waiting to his aunt, Queen Elisabeth, whom he much preferred to marry. Naturally, the young peoples' wishes were not taken into consideration, nor were Aunt Marie's machinations to be ignored. I, however, was much more concerned with seeing my brother happy.

There were times, as I've said, that his melancholy nature nearly matched Alicky's and I would be reminded of his words when Frittie, our little brother, died. He had wanted us to all join hands and go to heaven together. He always exhibited a great fear of dying alone, and I believe it was something that was often in his thoughts. Later on I would be most tragically reminded of this.

"No matter, I believe things will arrange themselves properly," she remarked complaisantly.

I nodded slowly and returned to my own thoughts. I closed my eyes so that Aunt Marie wouldn't continue to question me. It wasn't nice, I suppose and I had truly enjoyed our time together, but there were sensitive issues that I wanted to avoid and until I understood Ernie's feelings on the subject, I wasn't going to discuss it further, even with my aunt.

It was much more fun, at that point to think about Louis, our children and our life together. Our pearls, as Louis called our children, were growing. It amazed me to think that Alice was already seven years old and that Louise was four, and that soon after leaving Malta, I would have a new little baby. We were quite a family.

I remember Louis' reference to the children and me as pearls that night during the Golden Jubilee. Louis had often asked me why I hadn't decided to do something with the pink pearl—setting it in a necklace, ring or broach. I suppose he thought that I would get more pleasure if people saw the precious gift that he had given to me. Perhaps, when I look upon it now, he wanted everyone to know that he was in a position to give me such a gift. However, at the time, something like that never occurred to me, insulated as I was in the cocoon of my royalty.

At the time, I thought he was more interested in everyone seeing the pearl as a symbol of our relationship, to be exclaimed over and admired. I, however, reminded him, that I was hardly interested in show. Anyone who watched me as I dressed and arranged my hair in the mornings would know that quite well.

Louis was moving up though many would have said because of his connection with the Royal Family. He had been promoted to Captain and was Naval Advisor to the War Office and Chief Secretary to the Joint Naval and Military Committee of Defense. This necessitated that we move to London. I was sorry to leave Malta, but London at least had the advantage of being near to Grandmama. And, happily, we would often return to Malta as Louis continued to rise in the Royal Navy.

Although Louis' new title sounded very grand, and, indeed, Grandmama was delighted in Louis' promotion, he was involved in many things besides his career. I've already mentioned Louis' talents as an artist; however, he was also quite an inventor. He devised a Course Indicator that the Royal Navy and Russia's Imperial Navy eventually adopted. In addition, I helped him to research and assemble a book called *Men-of-War Names*. This provided information about the way ships were given their names. Some people laughed at the title, suggesting that such a tome would be tremendously dull, but, then, Louis was hardly Charles Dickens and this was meant to be used as a reference. A work, I might add, that is still referred to today.

II
Coburg, Germany, Spring 1894

When one has such a large family, trying to remember all that has happened to each member is frustrating and, in the end, an impossible task. Not only is there the sadness of remembering the tragedies, but there is also the knot of relationships—the cousins, aunts, uncles and all that has happened to each one of their extended families. It was all quite puzzling, even to an intimate member of the family. Since I would never think of myself as the family historian, I will give over that task to someone far more qualified. As for my personal memories, I remember just as I like.

As I sit here by the flicking fire, I see my life as a series of images, not necessarily in chronological order, but in the order that things happened to my sisters, my brother, my children or myself. They seemed stacked one upon another, like piles of orderly pictures ready to be pasted in a giant scrapbook; they are images that exist apart, yet together. I could try my best to sort them out in some kind of formal order, but whatever makes them uniquely mine, makes it necessary to relate them exactly as I remember them.

I suppose as I near the end of the 19th century, I think of the great zenith of the family. Grandmama was getting on, but her mind was still in tip-top condition; Uncle Bertie, aging as he was, continued to do his best to live the life of a young playboy and in the process, annoy Grandmama; and, her grandchildren were marrying at a fast and furious rate, producing even more royal princelings. In addition, the sun continued not to set on Grandmama's empire. Europe was still composed of monarchies, many of which were ruled by members of our family, most powerfully so in Germany and Russia.

Georgie, meanwhile, had given up waiting for Alicky to change her mind and had asked May of Teck to marry him. While this sounds as though May must have been taking royal duties much too seriously, think of her relief in marrying such a nice normal fellow instead of one to whom she would actually have had to act as a guardian. Moreover, from what I understand about these two people, their devotion to each other grew out of their true grief at the loss of a fiancé and a brother.

I was delighted that in July of 1893, my beautiful Alice was selected as one of the bridesmaids at their wedding. I have a lovely picture of the wedding group where Georgie, in full regalia, and May, in a silver tissue dress festooned in orange blossoms, were surrounded by their attendants, all cousins and sisters. There were his sisters, Toria and Maudie, both unmarried at this point and as I've said, looking around for some suitable princes. (Their parents were oddly reticent in the case of their marriages. They didn't find it particularly necessary that any of their daughters wed, perhaps because the thought of more German Princes on the Civil List, was more than Parliament could bear. More likely, however, losing two perfectly useful daughters was more than Aunt Alix could bear. The two, who, eventually, did marry, did it virtually, through their own efforts.) There was Aunt Lenchen's daughter Thora of Schleswig-Holstein, looking as though she would really like to be elsewhere. She had great hopes of Georgie, which had, disappointingly, come to nothing. Having a great deal more sense than most of my cousins, it was a shame that some prince hadn't looked beyond her long nose and woeful expression.

Then, there were the beautiful cousins: there was Ducky, Sandra and Baby Bee of Edinburgh, all looking stately, and, in Ducky's case, quite stunning in the bridesmaid dresses. There were the little girls, looking so sweet with their white stockings and short dresses: the Connaughts, Patsy, and Daisy, the daughters of my Uncle Arthur, Grandmama's youngest and favorite son, Auntie Beatrice's Ena and my Alice, the two striking Battenberg girls. Naturally, I think that they were the prettiest, but that was simply prejudice, the Connaughts were also well known beauties.

It was during this time and for the rest of the year that Grandmama continued to lobby for the marriage of Ducky and Ernie. Both continued to be unenthusiastic, but both continued to listen dutifully to their parents in Ducky's case and Grandmama, in Ernie's.

Louis and I weren't nearly as much in evidence as we might have been, since, sadly, Sandro died in November of that year. Louis and his remaining brothers were broken-hearted over the loss, as was I. It was all so unbearably sad. I like to remember that quaint cliff side Monastery of St. Demetrious, where we stayed—those blissful warm days Louis and I spent drawing the rocks and plants and the beautiful sea. I was glad afterwards that we had spent that time with Sandro and that we, at least, made those weeks easier for him. Sometimes the waste of it still makes me angry; I always feel that like Papa, he just gave up the will to live.

Handsome, dashing Sandro! I shall always remember you the times we entered Varna and Sofia, cheered by the Bulgarians who adored you.

Well, anyway—all the urgings from parents and grandparents must have come to something, because eventually Ernie and Ducky agreed to the marriage. A truly luke-warm affair, though, both were certainly devoted friends, who enjoyed each other's company and hoped that their marriage would work. I have to say, frankly, that Grandmama was the only one that ardently felt this marriage was a good match. Never mind though, it gave us all a chance to gather together in another one of Grandmama's royal mob scenes. Indeed, this was called the Wedding of the Decade, as they had said of mine in the last one. Everyone was eager to come, and it seemed as we began to arrive in Coburg that spring, everyone had.

It was April of 1894, and we had all come to Schloss Ehrenburg. Coburg was another one of those quaint German market towns, surrounded by hills, and a fortress—the Coburg Citadel, called the Vesta. Schloss Ehrenburg was the town residence of the Dukes of Coburg. It was a lovely schloss without the wedding-cake look of some of the other castles in Germany. It sat on a square in which all the children of the town played, so how could it be too terribly grand?

I once again resort to one of the photographs of the day, a sort of "everybody who was anybody" kind of pose. We had a sitting with a certain Professor Uhlenhut. He was the court photographer and had us sitting in all kinds of poses and permutations. These photographs were printed all over Europe, and I see them in nearly every book on Grandmama ever published.

For this particular setting, there is Grandmama, surrounded by Aunt Vicky, dreadful Willy, the Edinburghs, we, Hesse sisters and husbands, and as many of the aunts and uncles and cousins who could attend—and who could fit in the picture. There was another attendee that day and standing in the picture next to Alicky—her new fiancé, Nicholas of Russia.

No one was surprised, of course, especially not Grandmama—she had been dreading this, perhaps, since Alicky had turned twelve and had visited Ella and Serge in St. Petersburg. Alicky and I had talked about this at length the night before.

"I know what I've said about conversion," she told me quietly, a new maturity surrounding her. Perhaps it was the maturity of someone who had finally made the most important decision of her life. "But I've talked to Ella, and she has told me that I would not have to compromise my beliefs. She's persuaded me that there are similarities between Lutheranism and Russian Orthodoxy that I can feel comfortable with."

"I don't think anyone would want you to compromise,

darling," I said, soothingly. At this point, there was nothing to say but what Alicky wanted to hear.

"I'm convinced more and more, that I would be at home in the Russian Orthodox Church."

"I believe that you will too, my dear. After all, we all respect Ella's beliefs, and she's certainly no hypocrite," which was true enough.

"I begin to see that it is my duty to support Nicky in his life's work."

She had such a far off yet determined look about her that I comprehended that somehow her mystical nature had embraced the concept of ruling Russia in the same way she'd embraced Russian Orthodoxy. Henceforth, she was a fanatic in both.

As usual, it fell to me to tell Grandmama about this newest family debacle. She wrung her hands and paced the room in agitation, though she was not nearly as agitated as I might have feared. As I've said, like everyone else, Grandmama already knew this was going to happen.

"Oh, dear. I wish I had the powers of old, and could categorically forbid this," she said softly. "This is far more calamitous than Ella's wedding—Oh! Why did Ella encourage this? It should have been just the opposite.

"Grandmama, perhaps it's all for the best. She wouldn't have wished anyone else."

"I tried to interest her in Max of Baden…Eddy…Georgie— but no one would do, only Nicky. Not that I have anything against Nicky. He's a charming young man, so sweet and unassuming, so like Georgie—people mistake them for each other, you know."

I nodded. They certainly had at Georgie's wedding the previous year. They were like fraternal twins. When they were together, they were easy enough to tell apart, but when separated....

"Tell me all that has happened," she sighed, and sat down. I decided quickly that a careful retelling of the facts was all that would satisfy her. She was not one to be soothed.

"The main problems were Nicky's family and the religious question and they've both been overcome."

"Umm," she said. "I know why the family is saying yes, Sasha's dying, but..." she left off.

It was true our powerful cousin, poor darling Sandro's tormentor, was seriously ill. He was suffering from kidney disease—nephritis, I believe they call it. It was a malady that could lead to kidney failure at anytime. The doctors were sure that he had damaged his kidneys saving his family from the collapse of the roof of the Imperial Train. Sasha had evidently held the disintegrating roof on his powerful shoulders, while his terrified family escaped. Though I felt that Minnie had been grateful for his unusual strength for once, the doctors were convinced that this incident had possibly caused major kidney problems.

"They haven't really prepared the boy for the road ahead," Grandmama mused, which would become all too sadly apparent as the years went on. I did find it ironic that Grandmama mentioned this. She had certainly done nothing to prepare Uncle Bertie for the road ahead, either. "But the religious aspect," she continued, "I was so sure that Alicky would stand firm."

I nodded. Grandmama didn't seem to want my opinions—she just needed to ruminate. Cups of tea materialized and ladies-in-waiting embroidered quietly in corners. I worried for Alicky and I worried for Ernie, just married to Ducky—but there seemed so little one could do. Our family had a tremendous stubborn streak that we all had gotten from Grandmama.

"So, what has Alicky told you?" she asked after taking a fortifying sip of tea.

"As you know, they were thrown much together these past few days, and I don't have to tell you how romantic weddings can be. When Nicky arrived, Alicky met him at the station and from then on, they were inseparable. She told me that they were closeted together for several hours, during which time, Nicky proposed. Alicky refused, he pleaded and pleaded, but Alicky was firm."

She nodded slowly, with a frown. I knew that she was wondering what in heaven's name had changed her mind.

"It wasn't mentioned again until after the wedding. The way I understand it, the evening after the ceremony concluded, Willy visited Alicky in her room."

"Willy?" Grandmama exclaimed. She frowned and I could see the anger glitter in her eyes.

"Yes, he tried to tell her it was her duty to marry Nicky. That it was her patriotic duty, as a German Princess to boost an alliance between Germany and Russia. She had to put her personal religious problems aside, he reiterated..."

"Well, of all the cheek."

"That's Willy for you," I smiled wryly.

She put down her teacup. I had the distinct impression that had Willy been here, she might have wished to give him a good "skelping", as she had wanted during Liko and Aunties' wedding celebrations.

"Did she listen to him?" she asked through clinched teeth.

Willy as usual had his agenda. He felt no compunction in trying to convince Alicky to convert for the sake of diplomacy and politics. However, when his own young sister, Sophie, married the heir to the throne of Greece in 1889—well, that was a different story. Willy was furious when Sophie decided to change her religion, which, after all, had been a requirement of marrying into the Greek family—something he had known all along. He was sure that she was going to hell and threatened to disown her. As usual, however, he never really had the courage to do it.

"I don't think so," I answered Grandmama finally.

"I should hope not. He's a bellicose little puppy. The things that he and his Prussian group want to get up to—well, they're anything but peaceful."

I don't think that Grandmama had second sight—just

more than her share of common sense, but through those decades before the Great War, Willy showed his hand often enough to those who were interested in taking note. Many times, when Louis and I would visit Irène and Henry at Kiel, Willy would take Louis on tours of his new battleships. Willy, you see, was quite proud of his navy and quite jealous of Grandmama's. Willy was never discrete with Louis and showed him absolutely everything. Louis always wrote detailed reports about all that he saw in Kiel and all that Willy told him about the German Navy in general. That's why it was doubly humiliating when—but, well, that's all much later.

"But," I resumed. Grandmama was determined to comprehend what had changed Alicky's mind and I was doing my best to explain. "After that, and don't continue to be cross with her please, Grandmama, Ella went into her bedroom. She began to explain to Alicky how Lutheranism and Russian Orthodoxy were similar and that she would not be betraying her belief in God, or any other of the dogmatic beliefs of the church, if she converted. She assured her that it wasn't that difficult. Naturally, since Ella had just done this herself several years ago, it was all quite credible to Alicky."

Grandmama shook her head.

"I don't like it, I just don't like it. Russia is an insecure and corrupt country. Alicky will be in constant danger, she'll have to be constantly watched and protected and she'll get so high and mighty."

Now, there I objected. Alicky didn't have a snobbish bone in her body, though people seemed to think just the opposite. It was just her acute shyness. There was, however, no use in gainsaying Grandmama at that point. She was not in any mood to be tolerant.

"I agree. I'm frightened for her too, Grandmama. I'm frightened that she doesn't have it in her character to be such a public person. I don't believe that she realizes how many people she'll come into contact with; that they will need to like or at least respect her; how many palaces she'll have to help run; and, how many appointments and ceremonies she'll have to attend—that she'll actually, in fact, have to be an Empress."

We both sat in silence. The terrifying thing was, neither Nicky nor Alicky was ready for this experience and I had an ominous feeling of dread.

"Grandmama, really, you mustn't be upset with Ella. I believe that she truly loves Nicky and thinks he's a fine young man. He and Alicky are very much in love; you only have to see the two of them together to realize that. Ella's thought was that she only wanted the best for Alicky and that Nicky for all intents and purposes is that person."

"I think that I know more about what's best for Alicky than Ella does, after all, I've been like a mother to her most of her life—such a pretty thing with her red-gold hair and her blue eyes..." she sighed.

I nodded—there was simply nothing else to say. Grandmama and I looked at each other for a moment. I could see that there was a suspicion of moisture in her eyes. Suddenly, she got up, and began walking around the room. I thought she was trying to hide her emotions from me and I was worried at her brisk pace. After all, besides having severe eye problems, Grandmama had rheumatism, and usually had quite a time moving. She spent most of her time in a bath chair unless it was necessary for her to show herself.

"Well," Grandmama said, in a sprightly way that nearly startled me. "She'll have to come to me this summer and we'll just have to prepare her for her new life, won't we?"

At that moment, I wondered if we ever could.

CHAPTER THIRTEEN

I
Windsor, Summer, 1894

I don't mention Irène very much. It's not because I loved her less, or because she interested me less. It was only that her life, in some ways like mine, was relatively serene and quiet. It certainly was so in comparison to the others in my family. She, Henry, and the boys were very dear to all of us. She had made a tranquil and devoted marriage, the only ripple being the initial objections of Grandmama. And, like my marriage, hers was warm and steadfast and, thankfully not in the public eye as were Alicky's and Ella's.

It was, perhaps, just as well because years and years before Alicky's only son was born with hemophilia—little Toddie, Irène's first born, endured the hardships associated with the disease. Later, Irène's last son, little

Heinrich, also suffered the disease and died at the age of four. Irène, I think, knew better than all of us what Alicky suffered. I doubt though that Irène, sensible and pragmatic as she was, would have made the same disastrous choices. Later, after the wars, we were never as close—couldn't be—but during those sublime years before the turn of the century—well....

Grandmama, in the stoic determination that she exhibited to me at Darmstadt, was ready to give Alicky whatever lessons in statecraft and being an empress that were possible during that summer before her wedding. I don't believe she ever had any high hopes for Alicky—I know that Grandmama didn't think she was up to it, though she never said so. Sadly, I felt that none of us did, though none of us would have ever admitted such a thing, not even to each other. Instead, I was determined to give Alicky the benefit of the doubt and decided to enjoy this last summer with her to the fullest. I very much wanted to get to know her better and gain her trust.

It was a very hot summer. Grandmama, who loved the cool airs of the Scottish highlands and draughty open windows, suffered from the stifling heat. Louis and I did our best to take some of the burdens of the engaged couple from her shoulders. She had always disliked being around affianced couples and Nicky and Alicky were the worst of all. They were very openly affectionate which, for some reason, bothered her.

It was a summer in which aunts, uncles, and cousins

poured into our lives. Though they had never paid much attention to Alicky before, they were now visiting someone far grander, the woman who would be the future Empress of Russia. I had a distinct feeling that they were in some way trying to curry favor with her. Having said that, it was always a pleasure for me to see members of my family—or I suppose I ought to say—certain members of my family.

Aunt Lenchen was in attendance, as usual. Between her, Auntie Beatrice, Aunt Louise and various useful granddaughters, Grandmama could not complain of being left to fend for herself. The most useful of these cousins were Aunt Lenchen's daughters Helena Victoria, whom we called Thora, and Marie Louise. Thora I have already mentioned was, unfortunately, still single. I say unfortunately, because I know that it was her dearest wish to marry and have a family of her own. She never accomplished this and spent her life doing charitable works and having a salon of sorts in London. It really was a shame that she did not become a consort, for she was really a very capable princess.

Her sister Marie Louise, though married in 1891 to German Prince Aribert of Anhalt, was destined to the unhappy limbo of the divorced woman. Today, of course, no such limbo exists, but, poor woman, she was married to Aribert for nearly ten years when Grandmama suddenly called her home and told her she was divorced. This was shocking news to Marie Louise, who had no inkling that such a thing was afoot.

True, as she told me later, Aribert couldn't seem to stand the sight of her and avoided her as much as was humanly possible. This was hardly fair to Marie Louise, who had done nothing at all to elicit such revulsion. The plain truth was Aribert had been found in what was then called a compromising position with another man. In order to hush this up, it was put out that the marriage had been ended by mutual consent. Marie Louise told me that she always considered herself married to Aribert, which seemed a rather senseless exercise to me. I remember Uncle Bertie remarking with acerbic acuity about how poor Marie Louise came back just as she left, the implication of which was obvious. I don't think he meant to be unkind, he just couldn't understand that there was still such naiveté in the world.

This, too, however, was in the future. In this overly warm summer, Alicky and I were able to get together and frolic for the first and it turned out, the last time in our lives. She had been a martyr to sciatica for quite some time and had taken cures in watering holes throughout Germany—but to no avail. Alicky suffered from spasms in her lower spine as the pain shot down her leg; it was really quite serious. I had always thought she was extremely young to suffer from such a disease and I often wondered if it wasn't as the doctors would say today, "in her head." Nevertheless, Alicky's discomfort was real enough.

In June, she and I traveled to Harrowgate, a small spa town just west of York, but further north of London. She was hoping to take a cure there. It would also give us a chance to spend time together before she was well and truly in Grandmama's clutches. Louis would soon be taking over as commander of the *Cambrian,* but was, for now, able to spend much of those first summer months with us. It was a peripatetic summer wandering from Windsor to Osborne to our little cottage at Walton-on-Thames, and finally by its end, to the Heiligenberg.

Alicky was thrilled about her engagement, and could talk of nothing else when we were together. She maintained to me that she had always known from the first time she had set foot there that her destiny was in Russia. Her satisfaction that she was proven right was immense. The entire event made her unusually grandiloquent—I hoped that wouldn't be another harbinger of things to come.

We, two, however, had a hilarious time at Harrowgate. I don't know what the local inhabitants thought of our bath chair races through their cobblestoned streets or what they thought of the shrieks of laughter coming from the spas where we dunked together in the rather repulsive waters. However, I had a dose of the Alicky of old that we had, in our family, called "Sunny." Sunny rarely emerged since Mama had died, but this summer was to be the exception. Nicky took up this old family nickname, but I had to admit that outside of those few summer months, for me, Alicky hadn't truly been Sunny since our mother's death.

"Nicky will be here the twentieth," she told me one day,

as we were settling together in a small boarding house. Alicky was incognito, hoping to have these last few unmarried days in peace and quiet. I think the locals, thereabouts, might have found her Russian tutor and an Orthodox priest a little odd, but it was evident they were helping in the scheme to guard her privacy. It became an unspoken conspiracy among one and all, not to answer nosy questions about the future Empress of Russia.

"You will be happy to see him."

"Yes, it's been an age, Victoria. Oh, it's so wonderful to know that I will be spending the rest of my life with the man I absolutely love and adore with all my heart and soul," and with that she began that painful blush of hers. Her cheeks and neck got blotchy just as they had when she was a child. She hadn't got over it. "You know what that's like," she looked at me.

"Yes," and I colored up a little. It was true that Louis and I had been married for over ten years and yet, I still, despite all of Grandmama's admonishments, couldn't talk as freely about my adoration as Alicky could. It still seemed so private to me.

"Do you think the Russian people will like me?" she asked. "...for I know that Nicky's family do not—they think that he could do better than a poor little princess from Darmstadt. But the responsibility of ruling Russia is great, Victoria. It covers, I believe, one-sixth of the earth's surface and he will need the love and support of a good wife at his side."

I nodded absently, for she was certainly right.

'Love and support'—ah, yes, I've heard that expression since, in a much different context. May and Georgie's first born David got on the wireless and told the British Nation that he could not go on without the love and support of the woman he loved—Wallis Simpson, a woman completely unsuitable. Funny, he was born that summer of 1894 and Grandmama was thrilled. This was an historic landmark. The first time there were three living heirs to the throne of England. His birth had made the throne more secure than ever and his abdication in 1936 had made it more precarious than it had ever been.

There was no doubt that Alicky did give Nicky all the love and support that was in her to give. From the minute she was engaged to him, to the end, they were completely and utterly devoted to one another and their children.

"Dearest one, I'm sure that they will like you, but you must put yourself out and try to be interested in all the little things people like to do and talk about. You must try to ingratiate yourself more with strangers and be less judgmental. You must make them like you." I stopped for a moment. Alicky looked at me as though I were speaking a foreign language. "If you go with the idea that no one is going to like you, they probably won't." I was advocating an active stance that only really worked for people who weren't as shy as Alicky. Heaven knows, I was no social butterfly, but I basically liked people and thought the best of them until proven wrong—I feared that Alicky was the opposite.

"I am actually glad to be going," she said quietly, after a minute.

"Because you'll be with Nicky—certainly I understand that," I smiled.

"No...yes...well, it's not only that, though that part is wonderful, but Darmstadt just isn't the same since Papa died."

I nodded. I knew what she meant. Having to be first lady had been a terrible strain on her. These were, however, the kinds of statements that had me questioning seriously whether Alicky was really fit to be the Tsarina of Russia.

"I did not enjoy being the first lady of the Grand Duchy...but, I must admit, and, Victoria, please don't tell anyone—"

"Never," I vowed, and I didn't.

"I really can't love Ducky as I should."

I hadn't known this. Yes, I had known that Ducky was an entirely different person, but I wasn't aware that they hadn't got on. Perhaps I had hoped that Ducky would teach Alicky a thing or two.

"What do you mean, dear?"

Alicky hesitated for a moment. She looked as though she were trying to get it right.

"She's so energetic it makes me tired. She always speaks her mind and tolerates nothing less from anyone else and you know how sensitive Ernie is—I see him cringe. She's constantly larking about and never worrying about her responsibilities as Grand Duchess and she's always egging Ernie on to do some silly thing or other. She just doesn't seem to care what anyone thinks."

That Alicky cared so much, at that point, was ironic. In later years, she never ever cared what anyone thought. It was her alienation of family and courtiers alike that partly led to her calamity.

I, too, had heard something of their capricious and hedonistic life from Grandmama. She, once again feeling the obligation of a mother, had written them pages and pages instructing them in their responsibilities, even to the point of exhorting them to write "thank-you" notes for their wedding gifts—but it all seems to have fallen on deaf ears. I also heard from Grandmama that Ducky had harbored some resentment that Alicky's engagement drama had taken place during her wedding festivities. It seemed to her that everyone was more interested in whether Alicky would accept Nicky than with Ducky and Ernie. This bothered her tremendously. She and Alicky would never get along and yet fate would throw them much together as time went on. The enmity between these two women would take a worse turn later on.

"Well, after all, they have only just got married. Perhaps they are having a little fun before they settle down to their roles."

"I don't like her. She's always poking at me and trying to get me to do things."

"It wouldn't hurt you to take some lessons from her,

Alicky. She knows how to make people like her—and she's tremendously energetic, which is a lesson for us all."

Tears welled in her eyes and I realized I had hurt her feelings. The truth was we heard that many in Hesse had not regretted Alicky's going. She had not endeared herself to the general populace.

"I'm sorry, darling. I don't want to hurt you, but you must remember that you will be a very public person from now on and you must at all times reflect positively on Nicky and the Romanovs, and more importantly, your new country."

She nodded slowly. I can't say I thought she was particularly convinced.

"And if I do forget, won't Grandmama be reminding me again and again and again?" She said, with a lightening change of mood and that extremely rare sense of humor. Both of us giggled.

We spent several days at Harrowgate and I could see that Alicky was truly embracing the new way of life with the help of the priest, John Yamishev and the Russian language tutor. It all had tremendous appeal to her. I could see that she had also inherited Mama's streak of mysticism, as had Ella. I, of course, had not, but the three of us did share that love of the exotic.

We'd had lots of messages from both Aunt Marie from Clarence House and Aunt Alix from Marlborough House. These missives invited Alicky and me to all manner of entertainments. We, however, never went for the very simple reason that we were on orders. Grandmama simply didn't want us to go. We were, she instructed, only to do "improving" things—things that would improve Alicky's physical conditions and her fitness to be Empress. I understood later that she was quite cross about our aunts' invitations. Certainly she wrote me long and angry letters about them. The truth was Grandmama wanted Alicky all to herself that last summer of her spinsterhood and resented any and all that tried to take her away. It was typical of Grandmama, and I, personally, didn't think it mattered in the long run, but Alicky and I agreed it was best to listen to Grandmama.

On Alicky's red-letter day, the 20th, Nicky came to us at our cottage at Walton. Louis had gone to Graveshead to meet the Imperial Yacht the *Polar Star*, and escorted the young tsarevich/lovesick swain to our charming cottage.

Louis and I melted as discretely away as we could, leaving the engaged couple virtually unchaperoned. They rambled through the gardens, deep in conversation. They rowed in a rowboat or I should say Nicky rowed heroically and vigorously. Sometimes they took picnics and had long walks, or as long as Alicky's condition would permit, exploring the banks of the Thames. They sat under trees together, Nicky reading as Alicky did embroidery. It was all very sweet and idyllic and so much of what an ordinary couple would do.

"It's unheard of," I exclaimed one evening as I looked

out our picture window and saw the two, in deep conversation, strolling arm-in-arm.

"What's unheard of?" Louis asked, sitting at his desk, going through the interminable papers he had to read as Captain of a ship and an up-and-coming man in the Royal Navy.

"The heir to the Russian throne and his betrothed having three unchaperoned days together—one might almost think they're ordinary people."

"I'm sure there's nothing they'd like better," Louis chuckled, laying down his papers. He came over to the window and put his arm around me. I sighed and leaned into him as I always did.

Nicky and Alicky had stopped and Nicky was pointing at something up in the evening sky. Alicky looked up, and as she did so, Nicky quickly tilted her chin towards him and kissed her passionately.

"Grandmama isn't going to like that," I said softly, as Louis took the cue and kissed my hair."

"What?"

"Louis, you are getting obtuse. She hates engaged couples. She was furious when you showed up at Osborne before we were married. She'll particularly dislike that they're so openly affectionate."

I could almost hear Louis shrug.

"Grandmama has a lot of tolerance for the younger generation these days. I believe that Liko has proved an excellent influence on her."

"Liko," I laughed, "hardly, my darling man, it's just Grandmama being susceptible to a handsome face once again."

Louis chuckled, and we both continued to watch the enraptured couple.

"You know, young Nicky is giving me some ideas." He turned me around and began kissing my neck and we both proceeded to forget about the children and Grandmama.

The following day, we took the couple to Windsor where Grandmama welcomed them with open arms. She might not have approved of Russia, but no one could help liking Nicky. He was such a warm and gentle man. The relatives, excluding Grandmama, were delighted with the affectionate couple. Some of the aunts went so far as to say that they had never seen Alicky so happy and called their absorption in each other sweet.

It was at that point that Grandmama closeted herself with Nicky for several long talks. I have no idea what they talked about and certainly, no record exists, but I am sure the most important thing on Grandmama's mind was her concern for Alicky's safety and security. Knowing her, she was reiterating how important it was to protect the family. She may have even stressed what measures should be taken.

Also, knowing Grandmama, I doubt she failed to discuss with Nicky her theories of ruling and statecraft. I'm sure she clearly expounded on the more liberal paths the Russian monarchy should take. We all, including Alicky, had cut our teeth on Grandpapa's vision of spreading England's parliamentary form of government throughout Europe. If she, indeed, imparted this to Nicky, it took a great many tragedies for him to implement the most elementary of democratic reforms. Nicky always took Serge's position that while democracy might have been a fine form of government, Russia wasn't ready for it.

Eventually, wanting to find a cooler place in mid-July, we all repaired to Osborne. Nicky, with great reluctance, had to return to Russia. Naturally, Alicky was desolate without her beloved, and, characteristically, moped. Even the delight of the birth of David, the future Edward VIII, did not divert her from her sulks. The only thing that could do so was a review of the engagement presents Nicky had bought her. They were all, predictably, incredible, and, to me, excessively large.

The day after Nicky left, Alicky had them all lain out on her bed. She stood over them tearfully as I made the appropriate noises of admiration. Spread before me was a diamond and sapphire broach with a chain, an emerald bracelet and a spectacular Faberge sautoir of pearls, worth, I was told, a king's ransom. I must admit, of all, I loved the pearls. Not, as you might think, because of my own incomparable pink pearl, but because pearls always reminded me of Alicky. She always wore pearls and was constantly photographed with ropes of them. In these photographs, the multiple strands never looked excessive.

There was one charming photograph with Alicky as Empress and her sweet boy, Alexis. Alexis must have been six or seven and he had taken a rope of Alicky's pearls into his mouth and was absentmindedly chewing on them while looking at the camera. That, to me, was Alicky personified. Her pearls were well and good, but nothing was more important to her than that little boy.

Grandmama, regretfully, sent us off to the Heiligenberg in August. She had taken one look at Alicky's new treasures and had said, "I hope Alicky won't get too grand."

When Alicky's acute shyness was translated to haughtiness, many others believed that she had indeed got too grand. It was only that Alicky simply was never comfortable with anyone but her family, and for an Empress, that was a tragic flaw.

When Grandmama wrote me that she felt that sweet, simple Alicky would get too grand, she was convinced that she would never meet her again as Alicky, but only as Alexandra Feodorovna, Empress of all the Russias. She was right to be concerned.

II
Heiligenberg, November, 1894

Sasha died.

I remember sitting in my morning room, just having my first cup of coffee, when I received the message. I was chilled for a moment and then felt myself go very pale. I must admit the death of the old Battenberg nemesis had much more affect on me than I would have ever thought. It's as though, even in death, he thumbed his nose at my family.

He died prematurely of nephritis, leaving Nicky and Alicky completely unprepared for such grave responsibilities. Certainly, we all felt badly for Minnie and the children, but I felt a lot worse for my sister. As they say today, Nicky and Alicky were thrown into the deep end, completely without life jackets.

To backtrack a little, Alicky and I returned to the Heiligenberg soon after Nicky left for Russia. Alicky wanted some time to relax and recover from the summer's festivities. Even though most of the time in England was meant to be a rest cure as well as a time for improving, Alicky was completely exhausted. However, on a positive note, her back and legs were much improved, and she was able to take up many of her normal activities.

We spent a lot of time rambling around the gardens of the palace and exploring the ancient nunnery that had always so charmed me. It was a lovely private time for the two of us, enlivened by a visit from Irène with her dear little ones. She was, as usual, as practical and commonsensical as ever and was determined to lecture Alicky on the best way to get along with frightening and possibly hostile in-laws. As this was something that Irène knew something about, I hoped that Alicky was taking heed. Later, however, I could see that she had not.

We had a lot of fun planning Alicky's wedding, although, in actuality, we knew that we would have virtually little say in any plans. All would be done according to ancient protocol and custom. It would be, if possible, even more stiff and traditional than Ella's wedding. Alicky was unhappy to learn that Grandmama felt that she could not, at this point, make the trip to Russia, but she would have to be content with Uncle Bertie once again representing England at the royal wedding.

It was early in October and Irène and her brood had returned to her home when we received the telegram. Alicky and I were drinking tea in the drawing room when Neumann, the butler, came in bearing a tray. A telegram, in those days, always carried momentous news and we both went a little pale as Alicky struggled to open the envelop.

"Cousin Sasha is worse...Nicky wants me to come at once to Livadia."

She looked at me, white as a sheet, and sighed. She was immobile for a moment, not seeming to know what to do.

Livadia was one of the tsarist palaces in Crimea. It was not the stately, yet charming villa it would be in Nicky and Alicky's time, but it was, nevertheless, a place of refuge. As Sasha had become worse, with little hope of recovery, the doctors recommended that the family go to a climate that would not be so difficult on the invalid as the ones in

St. Petersburg and Moscow. They had suggested Italy, but I believe that Sasha was aware that he had very little time and had no wish to die anywhere but Russia. So, off they went to their wooden villa in Livadia, near Yalta in Crimea.

Alicky and I continued to look at each other in a frozen state of indecision. However, doing my best to regain my equilibrium, I came to life first.

"Yes, Nicky's right. You must see the Emperor before he dies, Alicky. I believe it is very important that you go. We shall make the arrangements."

"Nicky says to come via Warsaw, and that Ella will meet me there."

"Excellent, I will confer with Neumann about making arrangements and have your maid start packing."

Alicky was to take only enough clothes for a few weeks. I would arrange to have the rest of her trunks sent from the New Palace as soon as was possible. I spoke to Neumann, arranging telegrams to be sent to Grandmama and Louis apprising them of the desperate situation. I knew that I could leave the children with Grandmama Julie, who happened to be staying with us. She was delighted with the task, enjoying Alice's company immensely. They were truly a devoted pair. Louis, who was busy getting the *Cambrian* in order, immediately sent me back a telegram instructing me to do what was necessary.

Without much ceremony and no honor guard, since there was no time to arrange one, Alicky and I boarded a train to Warsaw. Alicky, I believe, was desperate to be with Nicky, but with some trepidation as to what her future would hold. I could understand that as well as I could see that there was little regret in her face about leaving her past life behind. I suppose it had not been the same since Papa's death.

We arrived in Warsaw after what seemed like a short journey. Ella was there to meet us. There was no time to stay overnight or to have any kind of serious talks of the future. There was only time for us to sit together for a cup of tea as Alicky freshened up.

"I'm frightened for her," I told Ella.

"It will be as God wishes," she said with a fatalism I had never seen in her before. Ella usually cared so deeply for things. In this, I misread her—she was simply distracted and trying to decide what she could do to help.

"Neither of them is prepared to rule," I whispered.

"Serge and I will do our best to help, Victoria, but Nicky will no doubt be able, in time, to work it out."

That seemed extremely weak to me. I knew that statecraft wasn't something that could be improvised, though, unfortunately, it often was.

Alicky emerged and I kissed them both goodbye. As they headed to Livadia, I immediately got back on a train to Hesse. Ella wrote me several days later telling me what had happened.

They arrived at Simferopol where Nicky and Serge met them on about the 22nd of October. Sometimes it's hard to be sure about dates, since the Russian calendar was about ten days different from our Gregorian calendar. Alicky and Nicky were wonderfully happy to be together again; however, as the days wore on Sasha continued to get worse. Some days he would be restless and the family would be called every couple of hours for last rites. At other times, he would sleep through the night and the family would become optimistic again.

It was a roller coaster existence. However, about ten days after Alicky's arrival, the family was again called to Sasha's bedside as he was given Holy Communion. This time, according to Nicky, he kissed his wife and after a few light convulsions, he died. Nicky and his family immediately burst into tears and Alicky, as she told me later, cried hard because everyone else did.

Later on Alicky confided in me that Nicky had said, between sobs, "What am I going to do? I am not prepared to be a Tsar." I wasn't surprised at this admission, since Nicky had always said that he had not wanted to be Tsar. I had always dismissed these comments, hoping that his training would give him more confidence to rule. However, Sasha's lack of foresight and Nicky's lack of training dogged him for the rest of his life.

I'm not absolutely sure that Alicky grasped the gravity of her situation at the death of Cousin Sasha. As the days went on, she began to see that, again and again, she would have to urge Nicky to be strong and insist on being given precedence over Cousin Minnie, who wasn't the retiring dowager type. Certainly the rest of the family was no help, including the Grand Dukes, who tended to be far more autocratic and certainly bossier than Nicky. Well, anyone was bossier than Nicky. The following day, Alicky was received in the Russian Orthodox Church and I knew that there would be a hurried wedding. With no time for any of the family to attend, Alicky would go from being herself, to being the Empress of All the Russias.

Letters of condolence came from all sides. The letter that warmed Nicky's heart the most, Alicky told me later was from our darling Grandmama. She expressed the deep desire that their two countries ought to coexist in friendship and how happy she was that dearest Alicky was with him in this dire time. Grandmama obviously hoped for the best and her friendship was something that both young people desperately needed and, happily, could count on. It was so strange to think of them as the Imperial Couple.

Several weeks after the death of the Emperor, Nicky and Alicky were married. Ella wrote me that the event took place in the Arabian room of the Winter Palace. Although mourning was discarded for this one day, the atmosphere was grave. It was another one of those weddings that seemed more like a funeral. I prayed that it would bode well for them, as my Mama and Papa were mostly very happy together, but my heart was heavy as I read about the ceremony.

According to the reports there were possibly eight

thousand people present. It must have been a great comfort to Alicky that some of her family: George of Wales, Uncle Bertie, Uncle Affie, Aunt Marie and most importantly, brother Ernie, were in attendance. It seems an enormous amount of people to me, but then, as I've always said, everything about Russia seemed excessive.

Nicky, arriving before Alicky, was dressed in the uniform of the Hussars of the Lifeguard. Having taken over an hour just to put on her dress, she arrived at the ceremony wearing a circlet of diamonds on her head and her hair arranged down, in curls over both her shoulders. She wore a dress of silver brocade edged with fur over stiff petticoats. Her mantle was cloth-of-gold bordered in ermine. She was adorned with orders and broaches and ropes of pearls, and from every report, looked splendid and incredibly beautiful.

The ceremony, I was told, took about an hour and after kneeling for prayers, Alicky was declared the Empress of Russia. The two then went for photographs with the family, before changing to traveling clothes. They first stopped at Aunt Minnie's palace, the Anichkov Palace, where she welcomed them, as Serge and Ella had been welcomed nearly ten years before, with salt and bread.

Ducky did not come to the wedding since she was fairly far-gone with her pregnancy. Considering the feelings that my sister and cousin had for each other, this was probably just as well. Ernie was thrilled with the thought of fatherhood. He told me often enough that this was the reason he had married. Curiously, Ernie was also at the palace that evening and he and the newlywed couple had eaten supper together.

Immediately following, according to Alicky and with no ceremony whatsoever, they went up to their bedrooms. As time went on, it was sadly true that they never had a honeymoon—although to have heard Alicky talk and to look back at their lives today, it was also true that their entire marriage was a honeymoon.

CHAPTER FOURTEEN

Windsor, July, 1897

Those waning years of the century, like most years, were peppered with monumental events for my family. There was an Imperial Coronation, Grandmama's Diamond Jubilee and, unhappily, several devastating deaths. I visited back and forth, wandering from Moscow to the Heiligenberg to Wolfsgarten to Kiel and back to Windsor.

Alice was growing up to be quite a young lady and already showing signs of extraordinary beauty. In so many ways, she reminded me of Aunt Julie with her straight nose and fearless eyes. She was coping beautifully with her deafness and, as I have mentioned, was able to lip-read in three languages. She was bright, strong and had a bit of that love for exoticism and mysticism that other women of my family had shown. I hoped that she would also have some of my sense of proportion when it came to these things.

Louise, though not classically pretty, nevertheless, had the Battenberg bone structure: the long high-bridged nose, the intense eyes and the molded cheekbones. She might never be beautiful, but she would always be tall and thin, like her Aunt Alicky and look extremely elegant. She was as determined as Alice but seemed quieter to me. I had no idea where fortune would take her, at the time, but I believed that she was in for a relatively peaceful existence, something like Irène's and my own.

As for Georgie, he was an active, sweet five-year-old, always getting into everything and wanting to do anything that older boys and girls could do. In that, he reminded me of myself. He was, naturally, destined for the Royal Navy. There was never a thought of any other profession in our household. And, unlike some other children, far from resenting this predestination, Georgie embraced it, loving everything naval.

The three followed me around in my wanderings, though later, Alice would absent herself, wanting to go to finishing school in Darmstadt. There were whispers from some that I neglected the children with all my visits and travels. It would hardly seem to me to be the case since they often accompanied me.

As we closed in on the twentieth century, gossip and innuendo seemed to be the norm in social life and even in newspapers. And, who better to gossip about than people everyone knew—royalty?

Never mind, I always told myself and Louis would tell me this, as well. Our lives, because of the navy, weren't quiet and normal. We had always moved around a great deal, and would continue to do so nearly until Louis' retirement. If people talked, Louis would tell me time and time again, let them. We knew the truth of it. So off we would go, coming to rest stops accompanying Louis in London, Malta, Illyinskoje, or, best of all, when we summered together at the Heiligenberg.

In 1895, twin tragedies happened to my immediate family. My dearest mother-in-law, sweet, but always resolute, died in the early fall. I will always bless her for the determination in her character. Her sons and daughter always came first. She was tremendously ambitious for them and did everything in her limited power to make sure that their unequal birth would not hinder them. It was interesting to note that my Grandmama, who loved the Battenberg children, loved their mother as well and never, in any way, said or did anything that would make Aunt Julie uncomfortable about her less than royal origins. This sounds very patronizing when read, but during the hey-day of royalty, snobs like Willy and poor Sasha were certainly more the norm than my Grandmama.

Alice was very close to her grandmother, having spent a great deal of time with her. She told me later that she really felt that if it hadn't been for Aunt Julie, everyone would have gone on thinking she was a rude and backward child because of her deafness. I like to think that this wouldn't have been the case, but Aunt Julie, as I have already mentioned, was instrumental in getting us to recognize Alice's problem. Alice, I believed, missed her tremendously and for a very long time.

Louis, who had been at sea on the *Cambrian*, was very depressed for quite a while after her death. He complained that now he was truly an orphan and felt the loss keenly since they had been an unusually close family. It was an interesting dichotomy since both Louis and Marie had told me separately that Julie had never been the warm and tender type. I, fortunately, had always felt a great deal of warmth from my Mama, but then, as I have mentioned, our parents were unusual in their attentions to their children.

I comforted Louis the best way I could, telling him all the usual things—that he still had the children, Grandmama and me. The mention of Grandmama always seemed to have a salubrious affect. Curiously, this struck me like the legends of old when it was thought that rulers had magical healing powers. Grandmama's regard seemed to have an efficacious affect first with my own Papa and then with my dearest Louis. Later on, Louis would, indeed, become Grandmama's last chevalier and the executor of her will.

Though the group was so upset over Aunt Julie,

another death several months later proved much more devastating.

Dearest Liko, who had been the man of Grandmama's household for nearly ten years, was getting restless. I don't doubt that he was tired of ushering Grandmama and Auntie around, cutting ribbons at openings and having honorary titles, such as the Governor of the Isle of Wight, thrust upon him.

He was more interested in getting involved in some kind of action himself and frankly, as Auntie told me later on, it wouldn't have mattered what kind of action it was. Just when this malaise was hitting him the hardest, the British War Office decided to organize an expedition. They called it the Ashanti Expedition and its destination was the Gold Coast. The group was formed in order to do something about an African King, Prempeh of Kumasi, who was raiding the Gold Coast for slaves.

Liko told everyone that he was going not for glory, but because it was right. However I must confess it was terribly obvious to me that he was going because he was suffocating at Windsor. We all went to the station to see him off and, as usual, he looked incredibly handsome in his uniform. Auntie was crying, as was Grandmama.

"I told him I didn't want him to go. It is so dangerous down in Africa with all the diseases and tropical fevers," Grandmama complained, as we all drove back home.

"But, Mama," Auntie said softly, "Liko has promised not to catch any fevers. He has sworn to be most careful."

"Honestly, Beatrice, if a fever catches up to him, he'll not be able to fight it off with a sword," she answered in disgust.

"He's very healthy, Mama, I should think if the worst happened, he could fight off a fever."

Grandmama harrumphed and looked out the window. She was really annoyed that Liko had left them.

"Wasn't he dashing, though, that uniform," I said, having to get a word in for my errant cousin.

"Liko does look good in uniforms," was all Grandmama would concede.

"It has been a difficult year for them all—what with Aunt Julie's death. Perhaps a change of scene," I ventured.

"He hasn't taken into account how very much he is needed here," Grandmama, as usual, thinking of her own comfort. "He is the sunshine and the rock of our household, is he not, Beatrice."

"He is," she replied simply, with a small catch in her voice. Auntie looked positively pale but Grandmama didn't notice that.

"I believe the expedition will be a short one," I said, once again trying to comfort everyone. It was interesting that in my house, Louis was the one who was busy placating me; I was usually busy arguing my head off. "He'll be back before we begin missing him."

"I miss him already," Grandmama said petulantly, "and how do you know that the expedition will be a short one? All of this kind of thing takes patience and time."

I decided to keep still. Grandmama was not to be comforted, and Auntie was sitting in the corner of the carriage looking about as miserable as anyone could. It was different for her and Liko. They had barely been separated in these ten years, while Louis and I were often apart. I must confess I didn't like the partings, but the homecomings were wonderful. In an odd way, it was as though we were on a permanent honeymoon. The only ones who suffered were the children. They missed their father and for that, I was sorry. However, in his career, which I had known beforehand, frequent absences were to be expected. Alice, however, pointed out that she, her brothers and sister hadn't chosen it. She was right, but like most children of the time, she knew that she had to make the best out of every situation put before her. She did not complain—well not much.

Sadly, Grandmama's gloom over Liko's departure proved to be prophetic. He did, as Grandmama feared, catch a fever—malaria. It had seemed for several days that he would pull out of it and was actually on his way home. However, sadly, we were deceived—he did not get well.

Louis and I received the telegram (oh, how I hated those things!) the morning of January 20, 1896. Liko, whom we had thought to be rallying, had succumbed to the disease off the coast of Sierra Leone. He had been aboard the HMS *Blonde* on his way home, when he died. Poor man, they didn't even have the right accommodations for a body and had to put his in an improvised casket made of biscuit tins. The corpse was preserved in rum. There was nothing in my life since then, which approached the grotesqueness of this. It was even worse that some people, God knows why, actually thought it was amusing.

Poor Auntie Beatrice—though never very demonstrative, she loved her chevalier and missed him deeply. Her four children, three boys and one little girl, were without a Papa. I always felt that Grandmama was enough for Auntie, but certainly not for the children. When she was gone, more than one told me that Grandmama was more like a mother than Auntie.

Of her three boys, the younger two, Maurice and Leopold, inherited the dreaded hemophilia. Leopold died during a simple operation when he was a young man but Maurice had a somewhat more glorious fate. Although, like most hemophiliacs, he was a sickly child, he was nevertheless permitted to join the army when the Great War began. My nephew had the distinction of being the first member of a royal family to be killed, almost at the start of the war, when he was struck by flying shrapnel. It is a distinction all of us could have happily lived without—as unpatriotic as that may sound.

Another brother lost for Louis and another dearest cousin for me. As for Liko, I remember him the way he looked at my wedding. He was gorgeous as ever, wearing a white uniform, his boots polished in champagne and his tight buckskin britches. He wasn't just Auntie's Lohengrin—he was also my childhood hero. It was Liko with whom I played, Liko with whom I fought and even when we were pushing each other off trees, he was the cousin to whom I was closest. Even Louis took second place to him when I was young. Dearest Liko! I miss him to this day.

Like every other event, happy or sad, in my life, I did my best to simply move on. Perpetual mourning, as I've said, was not my style. I simply had not inherited Grandmama's morbidity. It wasn't as easy to maintain this attitude when a very dear member of my generation was gone, but I was determined. Anyhow, I wasn't the most sentimental of people. Members of my family constantly complained about this, but I often think that it was my brisk determination to get on with life that helped others get over these setbacks.

Better though, was our visit to Moscow in May of that year. We were to attend the coronation of Alicky and Nicky. I was determined to put away all of my misgivings and just enjoy the festivities. Grandmama sent her good wishes with me and was, as usual, not in Russia. In her defense, she really couldn't move around as much as she used to and an Imperial Coronation would have been too much for her. She had not let me go without reminding me once again, for heaven sakes, to be careful. Russia, she would repeat, was hazardous for members of royal families.

"I don't like you going there, dearest, really I don't," she expounded. It was a familiar theme and I half shut my ears to it.

"I know, Grandmama, but how would it look if Alicky's own sister did not attend her coronation?"

"Hmm," she sniffed. "Do you have to take the children?"

"Come now, Grandmama, Alice is eleven and it would hardly be fair for her to miss such a momentous occasion and such a tremendous family gathering. Louise is nearly seven..."

"...and Georgie?"

"Do you want me to leave him with you?" I smiled to myself; the image of Grandmama chasing a rambunctious little fellow was quite humorous.

She didn't answer. Instead she changed the subject.

"Poor dear Auntie, so good and uncomplaining about her terrible tragedy..."

"Well, there's hardly anything to complain about," I replied flippantly.

"Victoria, what a tone to take to me," she said severely. "Sometimes I think you should try to show some softness."

Here was another familiar theme.

"It's difficult for me to express what's in my heart," I answered simply.

She sighed and patted my hand. I think, as alien as that was for her, she somehow understood. We were silent for a moment, as I looked at her dear face. She was truly getting on now—nearly blind and extremely rheumatic. Poor lady, she could do very little walking and certainly no reading of state documents. Auntie was reading all her papers to her now. I often thought it was an enormous responsibility for Auntie and wondered if she understood the gravity of her position. Certainly, there were others that expressed the opinion that she did not.

I began to wonder what we would all do when Grandmama left us. More importantly, I wondered how I could possibly live without her.

"Promise me you'll take every precaution and listen to Louis. Don't go gallivanting off as you usually do."

I nodded, snapping out of my melancholy mood. She usually enjoyed tales of my junketing to unusual places and had been most insistent that I give her a detailed account of my visit to Bulgaria. She was most impressed and I think, a little envious. However, she was more concerned with my safety in this case.

The rest of our family traveled to Moscow for this glorious coronation. Uncle Bertie and Aunt Alix represented Grandmama, along with Uncle Affie and Aunt Marie, who were the senior members of the British family present. Joining us were the rest of the Hessians: Ducky, Ernie, and, the Prussians: Irène, and Henry.

The ceremonies took place in Moscow and we stayed with Ella and Serge. Moscow was very different than St. Petersburg. It was far more alien and Asiatic than the city of Peter the Great. The buildings were much more of the Old Russian style with the onion domes and the bright colors. It was just the sort of city that I would have loved to explore on my own. Its exoticism appealed to me immensely. Unfortunately, as a member of the Royal Family, I could not wander freely around the streets as I had done in Varna and Sofia—there was, as Grandmama warned, too much peril.

I comforted myself in riding around in the carriage whenever I could, and staring out the windows like an absorbed child. The city was completely wired with tiny electric lights that would be illuminated the night of the coronation. Wooden bleachers lined the streets, which were festooned with ribbons and every sort of banner. It seemed as though all the residents had planted beautiful flowers and plants to decorate the avenues along which the lengthy processions would wind. Above all, there were thousands of people who had come expressly to attend this lavish and momentous occasion, swelling the city to proportions it could hardly accommodate. However, for that moment in time, the joy of a new Imperial couple ruling Russia was deeply and spiritually felt. The fact that the country itself was plodding, when everyone else was sprinting towards the twentieth century, paled in significance to the astounding and wondrous ceremony that would take place. It was the zenith of the Romanovs, though they were oblivious to it at the time.

As in all the ceremonies in which I had taken part, the Imperial Coronation was astonishing in its length and pomp. Each event was more exhausting and exhaustive than the preceding one. By the time we reached the actual coronation, most of us were in desperate need of rest.

The day before, there had been a long, long parade of the Imperial Family entering the religious center of Russia—Moscow. The different guards and regiments rode through the streets to the moderate cheers of the people. As I had observed before, the Russians seemed to have much less enthusiasm for their rulers even on this day when their relationship was being renewed. The restraint of the crowd, however, was more than made up for by the grandeur of the parade.

Nicky, usually a shy young man, rode through the avenues on a white horse and a plain uniform. His face was serious as he held his right hand in a perpetual salute. I wondered what thoughts were going through his head and realize today that it was probably abject terror.

Alicky rode behind him in an incredibly ornate carriage of state. The crowds could see her through the windows and her face, too, was unsmiling and serious. She was warm and uncomfortable and people saw an unhappy face. She was, I believe, pregnant at the time and the strain of the ceremonies resulted in a miscarriage. She, nevertheless, looked beautiful in a white gown covered with jewels.

The procession finally ended at the Kremlin, where a special *Te Deum* was sung. Then, thankfully, Nicky and Alicky could rest up for the following day.

That night, we had a family dinner and I was able to

observe with great concern the state of affairs between Ducky and my dear Ernie. Whenever our huge family got together, we always had a wonderful time, though I saw right away that Ducky and Ernie didn't appear to have the camaraderie they had once shared. She and her sister, Missy, were spending much time with their cousins, the sons of our cousin Vladimir, Serge's brother. Boris and Kyrill were favorites of Missy and Ducky's. However, while it was obvious that Missy's flirting with Boris was in good fun, Ducky's with Kyrill seemed to have a quiet despair. I sighed—I supposed that everyone could not have the kind of marriage with which Louis and I were blessed.

The following morning, we dressed for the Coronation. Naturally, I felt I had nothing nearly grand enough for this once-in-a-lifetime event. Louis, lucky man, simply had to put on his dress uniform with sword and decorations. I had to settle for an off-white silk court dress with a tight bodice sprinkled with seed pearls and most of my jewelry. The pink pearl seemed to wink at me when I took out my bracelets and necklaces. It was, in general, a good time for my family.

Louis and I took our places in the Cathedral of Assumption and awaited the entrance of the Imperial Couple. The choir sang Old Russian hymns, which had weird and wonderfully close harmonies and gave me goose bumps. I was glad I didn't let Alice come to the ceremony—it was hot and stuffy inside and I, along with about five thousand other people, stood for nearly five hours. Had it not been so inspiring, I think most people would have howled from the tedium of it all.

Alicky and Nicky slowly and solemnly entered a cathedral full to the rafters. Nevertheless, you could have heard a pin drop. Alicky looked exquisite in an Old Russian Court dress of silver brocade and silver tissue. Over her dress, she wore an extremely heavy mantle and around her neck she wore a single strand of pink pearls. Like Napoleon, Nicky crowned himself and then Alicky, who was now the Empress Alexandra Feodorovna. We were awe-struck as they sat on thrones encrusted with jewels, while all paid homage to the newly crowned monarchs. The heat was intense. The choir swelled with Russian Chant. I fidgeted and felt that one awful bead of perspiration travel down my back. The priests continued their murmuring. With the heady smell of incense emanating from the priestly censers, one almost felt drugged and hallucinating; a fascinating feeling.

The Imperial Couple eventually rose and went out to the balcony to show themselves to the crowds. The rest of us filed out slowly. It was another of those rare moments that I felt speechless, realizing the enormous responsibilities Alicky had assumed and I was more than fearful for her.

Ella and I sat together in her boudoir that late afternoon, alternatively soaking and elevating our swollen and exhausted feet.

"Ella, you must help her—gain her trust and give her advice. You're right here, she'll listen to you."

"What's worrying you, Vicky?"

I sighed. I did not want to offend my sister, but I needed to confide in her.

"I suppose I've caught some of Grandmama's 'anti-Russian-itis'—" I smiled weakly at the joke. Ella smiled wanly.

"Is that all?"

"Don't you find it worrying? There were hundreds and hundreds of security men out there today. The Okrana," naming the secret police, "is everywhere. I must say it almost seems pointless to hang onto a country that clearly no longer wants you."

There, I'd said it and Grandmama would have been proud—though perhaps not of the revolutionary sentiments.

"What are you saying? You're starting to sound like Mama with her talk of royalty being an anachronism. Where does that leave us, Vicky?"

"You've seen those plainly dressed common people attending the Coronation and who'll be coming to the banquet tonight?"

She nodded, though I suspect she knew what was coming.

"Those are the families of people who have saved the rulers from assassins. Don't you think that's awful? Russia is a beautiful country, but it's also like a poisonous snake, just waiting to strike. Its target is obvious and I fear Alicky hasn't the wisdom or tact to rule in this autocratic atmosphere."

"And I think you're getting upset over nothing," she answered calmly.

"How can you say that? I almost never get upset over nothing."

Then I saw it. I realized that all that protection made her feel secure, while I only felt secure when such protective measures were unnecessary. Later, she told me that she thought she'd be able to handle Alicky if there were problems. How wrong she was.

We sat in silence sipping the tea that appeared as if by magic. Most things we wanted seemed to appear that way in Russia. It was unnerving as well as enervating.

There was a knock on the door.

"Come in," Ella said, as Serge entered. "Ah, Serge."

"Ladies," he nodded to me coldly. I smiled as best I could. "Dearest, I wanted to discuss the jewelry you will wear this evening."

Serge, I knew, had a say in all that Ella wore. I had seen him often come before Ella began dressing and they would discuss the outfits and jewels that she would wear for a particular occasion. I had always thought that a little strange, especially when I contrasted that with my Louis. He rarely took an interest in what I wore, except those times when he thought I looked nice. Then, in ill-concealed amazement, he would praise my outfit or my hair. I usually had to bite my lip to keep from laughing at his transparency.

I sighed and Ella looked at me sharply.

"I'll go back to my room" I murmured.

Ella and Serge had been married for over ten years and still he treated her like an errant schoolgirl—and still there were no children.

I took my feet out of the basin and before I could make for a towel, a servant woman, Ella's maid Varvara, was on her knees wiping my feet. What next, I thought, a kiss? I smiled at her and thanked her in my fractured Russian.

I wasn't sure I could find my way back.

Ella smiled.

"Varvara will show you," and she said a few sentences in Russian and little Varvara nodded.

"See you later," I said awkwardly as I left. I feared that I had offended Ella. I loved my sister and hoped not. More importantly, I hoped she would take heed of my anxieties and do her best to help Alicky.

That evening was an enormous banquet for nearly seven thousand people. Alicky and Nicky ate alone in a sort of tented-off section, while people entered humbly to pay homage to the Imperial Couple. The food was surprisingly good, being simple Russian fare and I ate as much as my tight bodice would permit. Louis was always highly amused by my appetite, but unlike others on Grandmama's side, I didn't have a tendency to plumpness. I maintained my slim figure very easily.

After the tables had been cleared, there was a ball, though only the most zealous of celebrants welcomed this. As the night wore on, we all went to the windows to watch the exquisitely colorful fireworks display. All those small electric lights that I had seen decorating the streets of Moscow and her buildings, were turned on all at once, resembling nothing so much as the stars in the firmament. The Kremlin, completely outlined in the darkness by the tiny lights, was magnificent.

The festivities continued on for days afterward tragically marred by a horrendous calamity. It was four days after the Coronation and a special feast for the common people was set up in a large spot just outside Moscow called Khodynka Field. There would be free meat and beer as well as a souvenir mug of the Coronation given to everyone who attended. From what I learned later on, people had been gathering from the night before in order to partake of the Imperial largesse. By daybreak, the crowds numbered in the thousands.

From this point, the story becomes slightly murky.

Some said that a rumor that there wouldn't be enough for all provoked the crush—and crush it literally was. Over fourteen hundred people were killed, either trampled or suffocated or both—it was heartbreaking—shocking.

That afternoon, when Ella and I were told, we burst into tears simultaneously, holding each other and rocking back and forth aimlessly. When Serge returned, having toured, in his capacity as Governor General of Moscow, the carnage in the Field, his face was ashen. It was the most emotion I had ever seen from him.

He walked into Ella's boudoir without his customary

knock and sank into a chair without a word. Ella and I continued to cling to one other, tears unchecked running down our faces.

"It was awful," he stated simply, "and they blame me."

We continued to sob, then, slowly, Ella took her arms from around me and went over to Serge, kneeling next to him.

"How can they blame you? It wasn't your fault. It was a panic. It's unfortunate, but every crowd has a life of its own...how could you have stopped it?"

I knew she was trying to comfort him, but he hardly seemed to notice that she was there. He was completely dazed. I knew there was nothing I could say and, as I usually did when Serge was present, beat a hasty retreat.

Louis and I discussed the situation at length.

"They should have anticipated something like this, it's plainly stupid planning." Louis was angry. As a dyed-in-the-wool navy man, he hated disorganization and waste.

"I understand that Alicky and Nicky are visiting the hospitals trying to comfort the survivors. Thousands were wounded."

"This isn't good," he mumbled. "It's not auspicious..."

"Don't be superstitious," I retorted fearfully.

But, he was right. And, it only got worse.

That night, there was to be a ball at the French Ambassador's. The French had spent exorbitant amounts to make the most lavish of parties and the ball had been planned for months. Alicky told me later that she and

Nicky had pleaded with the family to cancel the affair. Alicky had been crying most of the day, her face and eyes were red and swollen—they were both, she said, devastated. The uncles—Vladimir, Paul, and curiously, Serge—insisted that they attend the ball. After all, they reasoned, the French were allies and had spent a lot of money on the ball. They would be extremely insulted if the affair was canceled. We were all appalled, as were Alicky and Nicky, but the uncles were adamant and they were literally forced to go. Needless to say, many, including other members of the family and the court, were outraged that they attended these festivities. The image of Nero fiddling while Rome burned was mentioned, and often. After making an appearance, they returned to the palace and Alicky collapsed sobbing hysterically on a sofa. They were both in complete despair. But, it was from then on that she was called by many of her subjects—the German Bitch.

I visited Russia many times since that horrible day, and I sometimes felt embarrassed—as though people were glaring at my family and me—blaming us. I felt that they never forgot what happened. Though I did try to forget, it was never again comfortable for me.

Khodynka Field...I think Grandmama most definitely had that in mind during the summer of the Diamond Jubilee. I never doubted her subjects for a moment—this was certainly not Russia. I would have thought the outburst of affection her people had given her ten years before would have convinced her, but Grandmama was wise. She knew how fickle the crowds could be.

She didn't want a big "to-do" about her sixty-year anniversary, but as the time approached, she, herself, got caught up in the spirit and emotion of the moment. Once again services of Thanksgiving, processions and dinners were planned. They did not quite compete with the grandeur of the Golden Jubilee. For one thing, because of Grandmama's near blindness and other infirmities, she could barely make it up the stairs of St. Paul's, and for another, she was, as I've said, nervous. Crowds seemed to bother her more than had once done, but, when the all-important day finally came, she not only rose to the occasion, but she rose above it.

On that sunny June day, Grandmama, once again, heard Grandpapa's *Te Deum.* As ever, she looked regal in her black silk with panels of gray satin. She was veiled in black net, dusted with diamonds and had not, to Irène's satisfaction, abandoned her bonnet.

Alicky had taken such pride in Grandmama's wearing her usual bonnet, but I'm not sure Alicky would have been so proud now. She seemed to grow further and further away from all of us. She had suffered a miscarriage over the strain of the Coronation, but had just given birth to another beautiful daughter, Tatiana. Although she was well on her way to having a lovely family with two-year-old Olga and now Tatiana, I understood that she was quite in a panic after the birth. Another daughter, she muttered in despair. It was all so eighteenth century—but that was Russia for you, Grandmama remarked to me when we heard the news. If it were the least bit civilized, Olga would have been the heir to the throne and there would be an end to it. That was Grandmama for you.

After the church service, there was a long procession, nearly six miles, that wound from the South of London to Westminster Bridge and finally to the Houses of Parliament. Grandmama rode in the coach with Aunt Alix. My aunt had taken Grandmama's hands in hers, pressing them to comfort her as she was overcome with emotion. She told me later that there were actually tears in Grandmama's eyes as they made their slow progress through the city. It amazed Aunt Alix and, frankly, it amazed me that she seemed continually surprised and touched at the devotion of her subjects.

We had yet another family dinner that evening with various royalties and dignitaries from all over the world. The most interesting to me, since the exotic monarchs hadn't come to London as they had ten years earlier, was President McKinley of America. Like my mother, I had a certain interest in a government, completely of the people, which had not succumbed to another revolution, as had that of France. I had read much about the democracy of America and admired her much less bloody revolution—though it was always fashionable to favor France.

Everyone was dressed to the nines with every medal, decoration and sash that they could possible dig up for the occasion. Even Grandmama was looking quite as grand as she could in her unfashionable silks and satins and the inevitable widow's veil she wore.

President McKinley, however, stood out. He wore plain black evening dress and was all the more conspicuous because of it. I loved the simplicity of his plain dress and admired his simple manners. Again, I hope that it doesn't sound patronizing—the reality was he was quite a relief. A so-called anarchist unfortunately, shot him several years later. It was hard for me to understand, as there was very little controversy about the man. He was, I was told, about as conservative as they came.

The year following the Jubilee, Empress Elizabeth of Austria-Hungary, whom we called Sisi, was knifed and killed as she and a companion were walking in the streets of Geneva. This happened because the assassin, who was mentally deranged, wanted to be famous. However, the reality was that she had absolutely no protection—in fact, emphatically refused protection. This was, in my mind, the major reason this terrible misfortune occurred. These two tragedies made me rethink my attitudes about being close to the people, even when I visited little Hesse and beloved Heiligenberg. I was ambivalent at the time about the wisdom of shrouding myself in protection; I often thought that I was making a mistake. Events, sadly, proved me correct and it was a very long time before I went back to any of my youthful idealism.

PART III

1901-1921

CHAPTER FIFTEEN

I
Osborne, January 1901

In each person's life there is a explosive seminal event. Something that is so completely shattering that afterwards that person's life is changed beyond recognition. It is usually the loss of someone close, a parent or a child, or a complete life change. When it first happens—you have no context in which to understand or even cope with the event. When Mama died, I thought that was such a circumstance, so elemental, but so completely sundering. But then, I was young and I had many around me to help me to recover—Papa, all the aunts and uncles, the cousins, and above all, Grandmama.

Who, of this extended group was going to help me heal from the death of Grandmama?

We all knew that it was coming in those last years and faced the possibility with dread. Nevertheless, when she did die, we were completely shocked; did we think that she could live forever? All of England, the entire Empire and Western World, wondered what life would be like without the Queen; a woman that had ruled that Empire for virtually the entire nineteenth century.

More importantly as far as I was concerned was how I would live without her. I think my poor Aunt Vicky, who was unfortunately on her own deathbed at this time, said it best when she wrote: "...the best of mothers and the greatest of Queens, our centre and help and support—all seems a blank, a terrible awful dream. Realise it one cannot."

She had been slowly failing since before the Diamond Jubilee, but, nevertheless, managed to carry out her duties up until a week or so before she died. She was extremely distressed about the Boer War, but as ever, determined to block out the probability of anything but complete victory. The war made her very unhappy, but it never doused her spirits. There is a famous quote spoken when her minister, Mr. Balfour visited her during Black Week, a particularly bad patch of the war, which was, I believe, December of 1899. When he attempted to commiserate with her, she replied, "Please understand that there is no one depressed in this house; we are not interested in the possibilities of defeat; they do not exist."

I still get goose bumps when I think about that today.

She was indomitable in a way that can hardly be explained, never mind understood in this day and age.

It had been a difficult couple of years all around. One loves having an extended family, however, when there are so many—much can happen. For one, there were more deaths in the family. My darling Uncle Affie, to whom Louis and I became so close during our Malta years, died of throat cancer in 1900. He was too young to die, but he hadn't been a happy man for quite some time. He was, unfortunately, a drinker and had his lungs not failed, there was little doubt his liver would have done so.

His own son, my cousin Alfred, had, in the grips of venereal disease, attempted suicide the previous year and subsequently died of his wounds. Naturally, we were told at the time that it was consumption and in some memoirs I read today, that fiction is maintained. The truth, however, was that he had been ill for some time and had undertaken to end his life during my Uncle and Aunts' silver wedding celebrations. The doctors had insisted that he not be moved, but Aunt Marie, in a heartless decision that I still don't understand, decided that he should be moved to a sanitarium in Switzerland. Knowing Aunt Marie, she just wanted him gone—the imperfection out of her sight. Straight after the move, he died, alone, of his wounds—exacerbated most probably as a result of that move.

Poor boy! He was Aunt Marie's greatest failure. She couldn't make young Alfred into a good German Prince—

it was simply not in his character. There were several scurrilous rumors about him, such as an illegal marriage to a common girl by the name of Mabel Fitzgerald. This was all nonsense. My dear Aunt Vicky said it best when she said that he was a very taking boy, but his character was weak. He needed to be looked after and cared for which was not in Aunt Marie's disposition to do—she metaphorically ate her young. Weakness was simply not something she understood. The Edinburghs were a fearless family, but they were not particularly compassionate towards one another.

Uncle Affie's marriage to Aunt Marie, whom he had frankly married for her money, had never been a happy one. They spent much of those last years apart. I hadn't heard that they had sought consolation in the arms of others, but, there was no comfort for them together. In the end, I believe they disappointed each other mightily.

My news was much better than Aunt Marie's in that first year of the twentieth century. In June of that year, I gave birth to my last child and a healthy son. Now I had a full complement, two boys and two girls, even if they were spaced from youngest to oldest, fifteen years apart. We called this little one Louis Francis Albert Victor Nicholas of Battenberg. So silly, all of those names, but I had to name him after a whole host of people. Firstly, there was my newest brother-in-law, secondly the Albert and Victor were obligatory and self-explanatory and lastly, the Francis was for Franzjos, who always seemed to get left out. Now however, this youngest brother, for whom our newest son was named, was finally married.

Consuelo Vanderbilt Balsan, the former Duchess of Marlborough, had put it about that Franzjos had an interest in offering for her—and this, indeed, was quite true. This was the period when Consuelo was considered marriageable and she and her Mama were traveling about Europe meeting people. Alva Vanderbilt had brought her to Paris before her subsequent marriage to the Duke, purely and simply, to be auctioned off to the highest bidder; the more important the title the better. Certainly, Franzjos, as a minor royal, conspiring, still, to get back the crown of Bulgaria, was far more important than a common English Duke. Alva temporarily entertained great hopes.

I know that Consuelo wasn't to blame for this mercenary behavior, any more than Franzjos was in looking for a wife with money. Each had something that the other needed. What I do blame her for was not being very nice about him. She has said on more than one occasion that he was rather oily and had much too much Continental charm for her. I've never seen Franzjos that way, but, perhaps, that is because I've always thought that real charm was in very short supply.

He may not have been lucky enough to fascinate Consuelo, but he was, at any rate, charming enough to capture the heart of Anna, Princess of Montenegro in 1897. Louis chuckled at me when I put it that way. The

Montenegrin family was hardly an inspiration for romantic thoughts and to most people, I was the furthest thing from a romantic. However, to my husband, who, after all, knew me best, I was hopeless.

Franzjos found Anna and though they never had children, I believe they made each other happy. I didn't have the occasion to really know her well, though they came often to us. Even after Franzjos' death, Anna kept in touch with my daughters and was rather a favorite aunt of Alice and Louise. I always felt that, sadly, Franzjos lived in the shadow of his brothers. There seemed to be a feeling inside him telling him that he couldn't live up to the other three, though he continually tried. Franzjos, as I've said, wanted very much to regain the throne of Bulgaria for the Battenberg family. That was a feat that he couldn't possibly achieve. I can't imagine why he thought he could. But he tried for quite a long time.

There was another on that throne now—Ferdinand, formerly of Coburg—and this man was a completely different kettle of fish to Sandro. There would be no way possible that he would give up the throne if there were any alternative. To his credit, he did abdicate at the end of the Great War in order to save the Bulgarian Monarchy. It took a crafty, devious man to hold on to the Bulgarian throne and it wasn't either of my poor brothers-in-law.

Competition with older siblings is often a problem with youngest children, but I have to admit that it was never a problem with mine. My Dickie was born with confidence and charm to spare—I'm afraid that some have called it arrogance. Yes, we called him Dickie. I sat down with the children soon after his birth to discuss his nickname. There certainly couldn't be another Louis around, so what to call him? The best other choice was Nicky, though it was pointed out to us that that would mix him up with the Tsar. Though we spent many summers with Alicky and Nicky, I didn't see that there would be a great confusion, after all, you were talking about a small boy and a grown man. But, I was overruled and somehow, the nickname Dickie was decided.

There is another charming photograph, one of the final ones of Grandmama, where she is holding Dickie, this last great-grandchild that she would see born. She thought him a very large and beautiful child. What you don't know, looking at the picture, is that there is a maid in back of Grandmama's chair, holding the baby up for her. By that time she was getting that weak.

Grandmama thought it very funny that Dickie distinguished himself at his christening by knocking off her spectacles. She loved the activity of a healthy child more now than she ever had when she was a mother herself. And, even towards the end, she never lost her sense of humor, and her love of family.

Dickie was a sunny child with a great love for small animals, a slightly artistic bent and a true calling for the Royal Navy. He inherited the unfortunate Battenberg tendency of wanting to constantly prove he was as royal as everyone else and he inherited his Uncle Liko's vanity, being always concerned about his appearance. About being royalty, there was nothing much to say to him—Dickie was as he was. However, I so wished that Liko were alive to see this nephew that took after him so strongly. If I do say so, Dickie grew up to be an extremely handsome man, almost as good-looking as his father.

In that sad January of 1901, Dickie was only about seven months old and we were all at Osborne as my dearest Grandmama took to her bed. Dying did not bother her, though she lay there languishing for about a week. Her only concern that we make sure to carry out her orders for burial to the letter.

As in every other death in her life, Grandmama was much preoccupied with her own. It was vitally important to her that her effigy was completed and I must say that it was a beautiful one, lying as it was next to Grandpapa's at Frogmore. She was very precise about how she wished to be dressed—in a white satin dressing gown, with the order of the Garter resting from her shoulder to waist and her wedding veil over her face. In addition, she was extremely specific about the things that she wanted placed in her coffin.

Her retainers, without any of the family present, were instructed to put into her coffin all sorts of mementos and keepsakes. From what I have been told, among them were some of her favorite jewels, a photograph of John Brown, some shawls (I always hoped among them was the shawl

I bought her in Sofia), Grandpapa's dressing gown embroidered by my Mama and various other photographs—I don't know which ones. It was comforting to me to think of her with that dressing gown, made as it was by my Mama, pressed against her. It was a picture I held to my heart. It helps me even today as I continue to mourn her.

We were not, as I have said, present, so I really don't know everything else that the coffin contained. But I know that Grandmama was resting with well-beloved things about her. The Victorian preoccupation with death and mourning served her well.

Grandmama's last journey from Osborne to Windsor was one the entire nation took with her. I remember following her casket to the harbor where it would be conveyed to the mainland. I had an overwhelming feeling of numbness and incredulity. I felt like a sleepwalker. Alice, who was now sixteen years old, was my great comfort. I believe she was one of the few great-grandchildren who had been privileged to know Grandmama really well and because of that understood how I felt. I also realized that the whole country, indeed the entire known world, was mourning with me. As a member of a royal family, one gets used to that, but as a human being, I marveled at the thought.

Uncle Bertie had gone to London ahead of the family. He naturally had to be proclaimed king by the Privy Council and the Cabinet. There, he made what was thought to be a startling announcement—he proclaimed himself Edward the VII. Startling, I suppose, because Grandmama so wished him to be King Albert. He explained that it was because Grandpapa, as Albert the Good, ought to stand alone in people's hearts, and that he, Edward, would be different.

Naturally, I believed something quite to the contrary. Much, I am sure, was owed to the resentment he had felt for this man who was constantly brought up to him as a paragon of perfection. This was coupled with the manner in which his mother treated him, especially with regard to his future position. She never let him look at a state paper. I am sure that not being King Albert the First was our middle-aged Uncle's first declaration of independence.

He returned, before the body was borne away, to oversee the arrangement for Grandmama's military funeral. She preferred this to a royal funeral and I can see that the less flamboyant dignity of the military was much more to her taste. Louis and I returned to London and, along with other family members, did what we could to make sure all the visiting dignitaries were suitably quartered and comfortable. As with all such occasions, London swelled to many thousands more than its usual population.

Louis, the children and I were at the Admiralty, but I was in such a state, I wouldn't have cared where we were housed. That entire week took on an air of unreality. Even

Willy, who had been awarded the Order of the Garter by his Uncles Bertie and Arthur, right after Grandmama's death, managed to stay respectful, somewhat quiet and extremely sorrowful throughout the entire process. In addition, Bertie's son Georgie, now the heir apparent to the throne was quite ill with German measles. He was very upset at not being able to participate in Grandmama's funeral.

Grandmama's coffin was brought from Osborne on the 1st of February and made its sad and slow procession through London on the following day. There were many people—family members and other royalties—following the coffin through the streets. It made its way, in virtual silence, through a grieving, black draped capital. The procession, two hours long, eventually ended at Paddington Station from whence the coffin would be taken to Windsor. Then, the sad, flag-draped coffin would take a much smaller journey to Frogmore where Grandmama would be laid next to Grandpapa in eternal rest.

It was when the funeral train arrived at Windsor that an unexpected event occurred. Thank heavens Louis had been there to see that it was put to rights, though it made his fellow military services extremely jealous. When Grandmama arrived at the station, there was a gun carriage with two pairs of horses waiting to bear her up to the mausoleum. Because the horses had been waiting for several hours, they were evidently no longer inclined to move. When the coffin was placed on the caisson, the forward horses balked while one of the back horses reared up and collapsed in a heap, hopelessly entangling all the horses in the harnesses and lines.

All the uncles and Willy stood aghast having no idea what to do about the situation. They were standing about, as Louis told me later, somewhat dumbly, until it occurred to him what must be done. He suggested that the lines be cut and a whole group of his sailors pull the entire carriage up to Windsor. After that and some other alternate plans were discussed, it was decided to convey this singular honor upon Louis' men.

They were thrilled to do this last task for Grandmama, but Louis said that the others of the Calvary and artillery were much put out. It was either this, he remarked, or they would all be standing there still, trying to find solutions. It did make for an impressively moving procession to the chapel.

We were all present for the last service at St. George's Chapel at Windsor; all that is except Alicky, who was at this time pregnant with her fourth child, and could not travel. My sisters and I talked it all over several evenings later with my Alice now considered grown up enough to be with the adults.

"Papa was wonderful with his quick thinking at the station," Alice said proudly in her curiously flat voice, I was proud of how she held her own in any group. People barely noticed that she watched faces intently, hoping not to miss a word.

I bit my lip to keep from smiling; her pride in her Papa was enormous, as was all the children's.

"He certainly thought fast enough, which was more than you can say for the others," Irène said. She was no doubt thinking of her brother-in-law, the redoubtable Willy, who was now fifty-six years old and as childish and petulant a bully as he ever was. He had also expressed to me that he was completely put out. Why, he asked, should Louis be the executor of Grandmama's will? He, Willy, was much closer to her. I had often thought Willy was delusional, but never so much as at this point. It would hardly have been appropriate for him, a foreign monarch, to be executor of Grandmama's will, nor, for these last years was he particularly close to Grandmama. As usual, Willy was getting caught up in the moment.

"It was a good and politic idea, however, to let the Royal Artillery pull the carriage to Frogmore. They seemed to be so jealous of Louis' men. I think that decision averted a possible problem," I remarked, trying, as I usually did, to put Willy out of my mind. I succeeded for long periods.

"Diplomacy seems to be one of Uncle Bertie's best suits," Ella responded.

"Well, if he can handle Willy in the years ahead, I'll agree with you," Irène responded. It was one thing to call Willy a petulant bully in the context of our family, it was quite another to think of him as the ruler of a very powerful country. A country, which by all accounts was building up its army and navy at a rate that could only be interpreted one way. In hindsight, it's astonishing that the great powers permitted such an armament build-up for twenty years without seeming to know the inevitable consequences. More astonishing was that they let Germany do it twice.

"Between Uncle Bertie and Louis, perhaps all will be well," I said, trying my best to be an optimist and thinking of all the excellent reports on the German Navy Louis was writing to Naval Intelligence. Since 1899, he had been Assistant Director of Naval Intelligence. Soon, he would be the Director.

"Nicky wrote some lovely condolence letters to Uncle Bertie. He's such a sweet boy," Ella sighed. "Alicky still has girls, and the Russians are getting very nervous. What if this next baby is another girl?"

"She seems highly prolific; perhaps she will have a boy still. Besides, this is the twentieth century, Ella, perhaps they can change the laws—this preoccupation with male succession is positively medieval." I disliked this talk of male heirs. After all, Alicky had three girls. But, I had to remember, Russia was still trapped in the eighteenth century.

"Vicky, trust you to bring something like that up. I don't think it would go very well in Russia. But, I don't worry about Alicky—she's feeling very healthy and vigorous with this pregnancy, so perhaps it will be a boy."

I looked at Alice, whose blond good looks and huge brown eyes were turning her into another Hessian beauty. All this talk of babies was perhaps a little adult for her.

"Perhaps," I said quickly, deciding a change of subject was in order, "but wasn't it glorious weather until after Grandmama was interred?" It remained sunny but rained straight afterwards.

"The thought of Grandmama being there is rather sad, don't you think?" Irène sighed, "But, at least she isn't by herself."

That was one of the first things I thought when we left the chapel—should we leave Grandmama by herself? It was then that I really wept. And though I would weep many times more in the future, there was nothing so hard for me as the thought of leaving her there, alone. Though, of course, she wasn't alone, she was with the person with whom she wanted to be more than anyone in the entire world.

"I liked the idea of all the orange blossoms—orange blossoms, the smell of them, always remind me of Grandmama," I said quickly, not wanting to remember the hurt that dreadful thought gave me, and brushed a tear from my eye.

"I must admit that I liked it best when the public wasn't there," my daughter stated, enjoying the fact that she was included in this conversation. "I liked it when Uncle Bertie, Aunt Alix and all of us got to look at Grandmama in her crypt."

We all had filed passed the two effigies. They were,

indeed, beautiful. Uncle Bertie and Aunt Alix knelt at the grave, which must have been difficult for Aunt Alix, especially with her rheumatism.

I didn't like all the ceremony and pomp, or even the moments alone at the crypt quite as much as my daughter. For me, it was much too sad. But, really, I shouldn't have been sad for Grandmama. She was where she really and truly wanted to be all these years, lying next to Grandpapa with a splendid effigy above her that pictured her as youthful and beautiful as Grandpapa. In her final great ceremony for the British people, Grandmama did not fail to please and it all went flawlessly.

II
Darmstadt, 1903

Family weddings were always highlights of those years when there were so many of us, and usually not as tragic as funerals. We got on with our lives as best we could after Grandmama's interment and Uncle Bertie ascended the throne. Though his coronation was initially postponed, it eventually occurred with all due pomp in August of 1902. Eleven kings, I think, attended his crowning, which, while grand, could not compare to Nicky and Alicky's. Ironically, Uncle Bertie was determined on a course of making the court elegant again after the quiet days of Grandmama's reign. That he didn't succeed entirely, I believe was just as well. Great Britain was well pleased with their middle-class monarchy.

We were thrilled that Louis, who was, after all, one of Uncle Bertie's favorite cousins, was appointed the new King's Naval Aide-de-Camp. That meant, among other things, that we spent more time in London than anywhere else. Our household changed somewhat in those years. Louis felt that I should have a lady-in-waiting. I believe that he felt this strongly since the years became more dangerous. In view of all my travels to Russia, he was insistent that I should travel with someone besides my maid. This was not the reason he gave me—he talked about the fact that as a Princess of Hesse and the wife of a rising navy man, I needed some assistance. Miss Nona Kerr, a Scotswoman, the sister of one of Louis' officers and the daughter of an admiral, was commissioned for the job. I found her invaluable as time went by. I hope that she didn't live to regret having to deal with me. For my family, she was a godsend. She was a delightful and lovely young woman, who enjoyed spending time with us and didn't seem to mind my eccentricities. I'm afraid I was quite difficult for her, but she was good and respectful and didn't take any of my nonsense—even my penchant to always have the last word.

In addition, Elsa decided to retire and Pye took up the post of my lady's maid. She was a young woman when I engaged her and has loyally stayed with me all these years.

Alice had gone to finishing school at Darmstadt which at the moment wasn't the most peaceful of places. After Grandmama's death, Ducky and Ernie's marriage crumbled. I knew they hadn't been happy together almost from the beginning, but I had always hoped that they'd find some common ground. I don't blame either of them. They were mismatched from the start. Truthfully, Ernie had no idea how to cope with Ducky's passionate nature. I always felt and eventually knew that Ernie had never shown much interest in women in general. This along with Ducky's falling madly in love with her cousin Grand Duke Kyrill Vladimirovich, sounded the death knell of Grandmama's last royal match.

After Grandmama died, Ducky left Darmstadt and went back to Coburg to live with her mother, Aunt Marie. When she left Ernie, she also left her little daughter of six, Elizabeth. She was roundly criticized for this. I knew better: Ducky loved her daughter passionately, the only way she knew to love, but she also knew that as a Princess of Hesse, the little girl had to remain in Darmstadt. Nevertheless, I suppose there were just as many critics that felt that she was an unfit mother.

Alicky emphatically took sides with Ernie against this cousin whom she'd never liked and made it clear that she would never be welcome at the Russian Court. I was not so set against Ducky, out of respect to my dearest Uncle Affie, but I can't say I was unaware of how much she had hurt my little brother. Ernie certainly hadn't been much in love, but his pride was hurt and by extension, Hessian pride was hurt. I also felt bad that some of the fabric of my Grandmama's family was unraveling.

These events didn't much concern my Alice, who had met a young man in the Hessian 23rd Dragoon Guards. This dashing fellow, who was nineteen at the time, instantly fell in love with my beautiful daughter. They met the year of Grandmama's death and though only in their teens, decided they wanted to marry. The young man was Prince Andrew of Greece and Denmark, a tall, be-spectacled fellow who was the youngest son of King George I of Greece.

Alice was in heaven when she told me how handsome, romantic and intelligent he was. We, Louis and I, were not.

"She's too young," I complained to Louis, as we discussed it about a year after Grandmama's death.

"We certainly don't disagree there, Victoria. Not only that, but my real concern is whether he's really the most suitable choice for Alice."

I was silent. Greece had only become a monarchy in the last fifty years, and King George, who had been Prince William of Denmark, and Aunt Alix's brother, had only gone to Greece in 1868. The Greeks seemed a bellicose people with expansionist ideas. I wasn't sure I wanted to place my daughter in a volatile Balkan state, even if she'd be nowhere near the throne.

"Sophie's married to Tino," I offered, trying to see a

bright side. My darling Aunt Vicky, who had died, it seemed, just weeks after Grandmama, had permitted her daughter Sophie to marry Crown Prince Constantine and Sophie was always saying how much she loved Greece. "She says the climate is marvelous, so warm," I continued inanely, thinking of my horrible circulation.

Louis smiled faintly.

"They'll have to wait. I'm not going to permit such a marriage until Andrew's twenty-one. Maybe waiting will take care of the situation better than forbidding will."

Unfortunately, it didn't matter. Alice persuaded us to announce her engagement that year and, although they did wait, as Louis insisted until Andrew was twenty-one, they got married in October of 1903.

Alice married! I marveled, and I was just forty myself and still in many ways feeling just married. It would be another royal Wedding of the Decade.

This one, we decided, should take place in Darmstadt. Besides the place where the couple had met, it was a convenient meeting place for the entire "Royal Mob." All my sisters, including Alicky, and their husbands attended, along with as many aunts, uncles and cousins who could manage to come. We were disappointed that Uncle Bertie wasn't able to attend, but Aunt Alix came along with Georgie, May and some of the British contingent. I'm not sure if anyone else felt it as I did, nevertheless, it was always at events like this that I really felt the loss of Grandmama. For all her calling us the

"Royal Mob" and saying that these occasions were tedious and tiring, I believe she secretly enjoyed them.

Ernie was recovering from his troubles, but, naturally, for the first time, there wasn't a strong Edinburgh presence at one of our big family events. It was just as well since Alicky's hostility towards Ducky and by extension, the rest of that family was palpable—and Alicky was by no means any longer just a troublesome younger sister.

Louise, who was fourteen and one of her sister's bridesmaids, looked slim, elegant and quite grown-up in her long dress. As I've said, Louise wouldn't come close to her sister's beauty, but she had a tremendously attractive way about her and was extremely intelligent. She began to lose some of her quietness and I began to think of her as excellent company, which, indeed, she had become.

The royal festivities culminated with the wedding, which was a rather hilarious affair. I've always thought that our subjects would be amazed at how silly all of us got at these parties. A lot of it has to do with being with so many members of one's family and being able to behave naturally and not constantly be on one's guard. No less a factor was a great sufficiency of champagne.

When Alice and Andrew left in their new motorcar, a gift from Nicky and Alicky, some members of the family, to the dismay of the ever-present detectives, began chasing the car. There were cheering crowds determined to get a look at the newlyweds, as well as others just out to get a glimpse of the entire royal splendor that had converged on their town. Nicky, evidently feeling very free and secure in Darmstadt, was the ringleader of this gang chasing the car. They caught up to the car and flung another slipper at my poor daughter along with more rice. Alice laughingly flung the slipper back at Nicky, whom it was reported, she called a silly ass. I will never believe this of my dignified daughter, however, she told me when she finally looked around, there was Nicky, in the middle of the street, convulsed with laughter.

Yes, our weddings were extremely raucous affairs and sometimes the memories of our merriment hurt—it was so hard to separate them from other events.

Louis and I were exhausted that evening, but so keyed up that we couldn't sleep. We would have to return to London immediately since he was now Director of Naval Intelligence.

"Grandmama would have laughed over all the silliness today. It was just her kind of wedding—not too much dignity, some good jokes and quite a bit of good feeling."

"I hope she wouldn't have been as apprehensive about Alice's going to Greece as she was about Ella and Alicky going to Russia," he responded with a seriousness that led me to believe that he was the one who was apprehensive. Well, I was too, but what were we to do? Alice was a young but determined creature when it came to getting her way.

"Grandmama might have been. After all, she was against Uncle Affie's taking the Greek crown." The crown of Greece had been offered to my Uncle Affie before William of Denmark was considered. "She didn't think we should be taking crowns in these foreign parts. I know that she would have counseled Sandro away from Bulgaria had she been asked."

"My parents didn't ask her, though I imagine she thought they ought to have. I always thought that it was a good thing that I was only fourteen years old at the time, or they might have tried me and my parents might have made me take it."

I hated to admit it, but he was right. I've already stated that both my parents-in-law were ambitious. If they had not been, under the circumstances, they would not have sent Sandro to Bulgaria. However, it's unfair to them to say the he wasn't willing—for he was more than eager.

"You were already in the navy by then, I don't think your Papa would have made you go."

"Perhaps not. I think that Grandmama being against it for her own son was strong enough reason not to and I think Papa would have at least taken that into consideration."

"Well, I'm as glad you weren't asked to take Greece as I was when you didn't take Bulgaria. I don't want to be a reigning Princess or Queen. I'm happy as I am, besides, can you imagine me as a queen with all my bad habits and eccentricities? Courtiers would be paid to listen to me talk all day or roll my cigarettes," I said, smiling absently, as Louis laughed over the description.

"You'd certainly never be forgotten."

"I'm afraid I'd have been the sort of queen someone would have thought of throwing out the window."

Louis nodded a little too enthusiastically for my taste so I decided to pay no attention and sat down at my dressing table. I had a desire to take out the pearl on Alice's night of nights. I rolled it around in my fingers savoring the touch. I owned this pearl for nearly twenty years and it seemed like just last night that Louis and I sat cozily by the fire and he told me the story of the pearl fisher. I prayed that Alice would be as happy as we had been all these years. People never thought it to look at us, but we were happy and still very much in love.

"At least the Russians are behaving these days," I said idly.

"Behaving in what way?"

"They aren't nearly as insistent about your sitting with your officers," I giggled. Though it was true, Nicky couldn't have been a better brother-in-law to Louis. With their influence and that of Ella and Serge's, the Battenbergs were welcome once again in Russia and given all due honor. The snubbing of past years was over at last.

Louis smiled faintly; it had all been an annoyance to him, like mosquitoes or lice. He never for one moment complained about it—never. Sometimes his uncomplaining nature puzzled me.

"Your brother is looking pretty miserable these days."

I had been very close to Ernie in these last years—trying to help him the best I could to get over this terrible misfortune. I believe I was able to help him a little, but he needed constant distraction and that was difficult for me, being busy with my own family.

"Can you blame him? He's raising a little girl on his own, and Ducky sits with Aunt Marie waiting for permission to marry Kyrill—permission, I might add that Nicky will never give."

"I think Ernie may actually be lonely, though I never thought of him as needing a lot of company."

"It's funny you should think that because you're completely wrong about it," I answered. "Ernie never wants to be alone. It's a fear from his childhood."

"Well, if that's the case, I think the best thing for him would be to find another Duchess. Then he can just forget about Ducky."

"I don't imagine Ducky would be easy to forget," I responded.

"No, I'd have to agree with you there. Ducky is not the sort of woman to be forgotten or ignored," he said slowly. "She's complicated in a way that I don't think I could understand."

"Well, I think it's well that you only deal with my complications," I smiled, and put the pearl away in its secret compartment in my private jewelry box.

Though our conversation ended on a light note, we both continued to worry for Ernie, and hoped that he would find someone new. We knew that he could easily forget Ducky if not for the scandal she was creating—it was humiliating. As time went on, he was not alone in his desire to forget Ducky. Her eventual marriage became one of the great scandals in our family and Alicky took it even worse than Ernie did. Alicky wanted very much to forget Ducky, but Ducky would not go away.

CHAPTER SIXTEEN

I
Russia, Greece, and Heiligenberg, 1905

1905 was a strange, awful and yet wonderful year.
When I think of it, it becomes such a jumble of horror and
tragedies—events I'm thankful Grandmama did not live to
see. It would have given her absolutely no satisfaction to
think that she had been right about so many things. But
then, there were the joys of new birth, promotions and, as
always, adventure.

I came to my beloved Heiligenberg to rest and to shed
a few tears over things. Irène was there for time, but I only
began to feel better when I had time on my own. Time I
could spend renewing acquaintance with my favorite
books and getting to know new ones. Time for exploring,
once again, the nooks and corners that I loved in our
Schloss, hiking around the environs, talking with Louise
and playing with little Dickie and all his beloved animals.

Georgie, dear boy, was now at the Royal Naval College at Osborne. Uncle Bertie, it seems, had no use for his old childhood home and gave it, lock, stock and barrel to the Royal Navy. It comforted me to think of Georgie being so at home there, but, I must admit, I was a little put out with my uncle. I had difficulty imagining how he could so easily give away Grandmama's precious home. I suppose the memories of his childhood give him little pleasure. Or perhaps, it wasn't opulent enough for him.

My boys would follow their father into the Royal Navy. I was not unhappy with this, but I wished somehow it wasn't such a given. I would have liked them to explore different areas, perhaps go to university. They were men that would have to make their way in the world since Louis and I were only slightly more solvent, having inherited properties and monies from Uncle Alexander, than we had been when we were married. I had a fleeting desire that they follow other professions. However, in the end, as maudlin as it may sound, they followed their hearts.

My brother and sisters had heartbreak with their children in the years since Grandmama's death. Irène lost her last little boy, Heinrich, to hemophilia. Poor little fellow, he was only three years old. That left her with just two boys: her eldest, Toddie, who also had the dreaded disease but seemed, somehow, to manage and even grow up; and, little Bobby—Sigismund, who was without the disease. It is a mystery to me and a gift from God that I'm sure I didn't deserve, to think that while my two sisters passed down the hemophilia gene to their boys, I was lucky enough not to do so. I remember trembling so when Dickie was born. I hadn't been quite so aware with Georgie, but, after my sister's experiences—well....

Alice, also, was blessed and did not pass it down to her precious boy. I often wonder why I was so favored; it seemed to me to be such an arbitrary and cruel thing. I also often wondered if there wasn't a small seed of anger in Alicky and Irène and even Auntie Beatrice about this. I'm sure they would never have consciously thought so, but I, being spared, thought about it quite a lot. It was so unbearably sad for my sisters.

Irène, naturally, was even more empathetic than the rest of us when Alicky's little boy, Alexis was born. The country had waited nearly ten years for Alicky to produce an heir in 1904. Unfortunately, what they didn't know and what was revealed to only a select few soon after the birth was that this sweet and beautiful boy had hemophilia, as well. I hated to see what this was doing to Alicky. Since they so feared the country knowing, they hid the truth. In the process, Alicky, who was not exactly a social leader in St. Petersburg, was becoming even more insular and private.

My sister, as I feared, did not do particularly well in court; perhaps because she was completely outshone by her mother-in-law, the Empress Marie, our cousin Minnie. Nicky never seemed to do anything about that.

Alicky couldn't, and, indeed, had no desire to ingratiate herself with the leaders of society or even with the other members of Nicky's family. She never hid her views regarding that society namely that she found it degenerate and unwholesome. That was questionable, but she made very few friends among them. Sadly, later, when she desperately needed the support of her peers, the support was not there. Perhaps, had the family been more united, things wouldn't have turned out as they did.

Then, she was also so shy and extremely uneasy in crowds. She was never spontaneous and had no way of showing the deep affection she had for the Russian People. She never smiled or seemed friendly. To the people who saw her, this translated as being cold, distant and unfeeling. She was hardly this to the people she loved. Especially with her husband and children, she was capable of a warmth and compassion that very few others were privileged to see. We, her family, understood her solemnity and the reasons for it, but others weren't to know.

The beginning of 1905 marked a watershed in Russian history. Towards the end of January, workers under the leadership of a priest, organized a strike and, from all accounts, went on a peaceful march to the Winter Palace. They were interested in presenting a list of grievances to their Tsar and quietly walked through the streets to do so. When they reached the huge snowy square of the palace, Serge's Probrajensky Guard was set up and waiting in front of the ornately columned and statued building. They presented a long line of mounted soldiers with swords drawn. They were stationed there to meet the crowd, having been told there might be trouble. Though the crowd had remained peaceable during their walk to the palace, the Guard's orders were to disperse them by any necessary means. Nicky, in any case, was not there but at Tsarskoye Selo. What happened was a tragic melee where scores of people were killed and wounded. It was another stupidly handled fiasco.

Alicky wrote me letters pouring her heart out, but she just didn't seem to understand. As was in her character, she mourned profusely the people that had been killed, but she placed no importance on the voice of the people in the future of Russia. I will not be the one to call her foolish as many others have already done so. This, however, was one of the many tragic links in a chain started almost at the beginning of the last century, which led to the fearful downward spiral of the Romanov family. Perhaps, the only good thing to come of this horror was that Nicky finally realized, contrary to my other brother-in-law's opinion that constitutional reforms were necessary and he proceeded to set up a limited representation. Many, of course, say that this was too little too late—and history, I'm sorry to say, proved them right.

The following month, after this "Bloody Sunday," another horrific event occurred. Serge, since this latest unrest began, had been fearful for his life. He had spent his governorship of Moscow in a most repressive fashion. He had been particularly brutal to Jews, which had distressed Ella tremendously. However, since he never listened to Ella on political topics and certainly never discussed such things with her, there was very little use in her protesting strenuously. However, because of his tenure, he was intelligent enough to know that he was now in trouble.

Serge, cruel and callous as he was by this time, wanted to take even more repressive measures than before in order to squash the dissidents. As the riots and strikes continued, he realized that his solutions to them would not be countenanced even by the Russian government. Since he could not be effective in the way that he wished, he decided to step down. In addition, he refused to appear together with Ella because he knew himself to be extremely unpopular, which was obvious, and a target for the kind of assassins that had eventually murdered Uncle Alexander. Therefore, as a precaution, he resigned. Ella wrote that this made her particularly unhappy since she and Serge loved Moscow, and had always principally lived there.

On the 17th of February, I was sitting in our house in London. I remember it so precisely because Louise, Louis and I were having tea on a blustery February day. Louis would shortly leave for his new commission, the HMS *Drake* and his new appointment as Rear-Admiral. We were talking about the ship's refitting and were excited about Alice's imminent lying-in. We planned to travel to Athens for the event. Louis would not be able to come in April, as he would be out at sea. However, he would, he promised, try to get leave to come for the christening.

The butler softly knocked and entered with a telegram on his silver salver. Hateful things! I hoped it was just a naval emergency since Louis had been appointed Rear Admiral. I went through a catalogue of my family, which as time went on I was wont to do every time I saw one of these dreaded missives.

Ernie was fine, though his dear child, Elizabeth, caught a rare form of typhoid while she was with Alicky, Nicky and their children. They had been, as was their custom in autumn, at the hunting lodge at Spala, Poland, when Ernie received the news that Elizabeth had died. I look back at pictures of this little Princess and am continually struck by her beauty. She would have been another of the Hessian beauties. I'll never forget Ernie's face when I went to him, just a month after Alice's wedding.

"It was so quick," he cried, tears coursing down his cheeks.

I comforted him as best I could, though who truly feels comforted at the death of a child? Little Elizabeth was his life, especially after his divorce from Ducky. The New Palace was particularly lonely with no sisters and only Ernie clattering around. Naturally, I worried for him; worried enough so that we were all particularly relieved when Ernie finally found another princess to marry. His depressions upset me tremendously and I knew his fear of being alone. Our prayers were literally answered when Eleonore of Solms-Hohensolms-Lich consented to be his wife. She was a sweet, simple girl, therefore, nothing like Ducky. She was much more suited to Ernie, who had no idea how to cope with complicated women—not that he'd ever been much inclined to try. Their marriage was smooth and serene and Ernie finally got what he really wanted—two beautiful boys, George Donatus, Don, and Ludwig, whom we called Lu.

Please God, not, Ernie, I prayed silently as I watched Louis slit open the envelope; and, please, not little Alexis or one of Irène's remaining boys. Louis scanned the missive and I saw him visibly pale. My heart began to pound.

"It's Serge," he said flatly, and with no preamble. "There was an explosion...he's dead," and once again, as if in a nightmare, I saw a telegram flutter slowly to the ground.

I found that I could not react. I simply looked around the room and for some strange reason, thought how much my taste, as well as the tastes of my sisters looked like my mother's. Then, for a moment, the room began to spin.

"What?" I exclaimed unnecessarily, shakily taking a sip of tea and willing the room to steady itself.

Louise was frozen and pale. She, like my sister Alicky and some of the other children in our family had a great deal of love for Serge. I certainly never understood it, but it was true. She began weeping quietly into her handkerchief.

Then, suddenly, it began to hit me. Ella, I thought to myself, Ella, and began to tremble—

"Oh dear god...poor Ella...I must go to her..." I whispered shakily.

"I'm not sure that it's a good idea, Victoria. Feeling is no doubt high against the Royal Family. Russia is extremely volatile, as it is—I'm concerned about your going."

"Well," I said my heart beating painfully. "There's no question that I will—I have to go to Ella."

He sighed, making what looked like a physical effort not to argue with me.

"You must be extremely careful and take Nona. I'd go myself, only I can't—I've got to be on the ship—" he agonized.

Taking a deep breath, I went to his chair and took his hands.

"Don't worry about me, Louis I'll be fine, I promise. I won't take any unnecessary chances. Naturally, I will take Nona, and I will take Louise. No—don't worry about her, she'll be fine—you know as well as I do that she has ten times more sense than I," I said lightly, trying to comfort him. "I'll let Nicky surround me with security, certainly that's one thing they do very well there—and I promise I won't go out exploring the way I usually do."

I could see that he was arguing with himself. His face

was telling me that he was wondering if he shouldn't give up the commission on the *Drake* and come.

Louise got up and put her hands on ours.

"Papa," she said resolutely, "I will take care of Mama. Nothing will happen to either of us, but you know very well we must go to Aunt Ella."

She was such a confident sixteen-year-old. She inspired both of us with her self-assuredness. Louise, I always thought, unlike her sister, was not likely to fall in love soon. In many ways, two sisters could not be less alike in looks and disposition. Alice would later, as I've mentioned, show an extremely spiritual side, while I always thought of Louise as my pragmatic daughter. Her pragmatism, however, made her seem rock-solid, which was just what was needed at that moment.

Louis got up and paced.

"You must promise to never to go out unnecessarily and take whatever security Ella or Nicky will provide. I will insist on this, Victoria and I want no discussion about it."

I nodded mutely. When Louis insisted, which was very rare in our relationship, I had enough sense to know there was good reason for it. Louise and I looked at each other and looked back at Louis.

"Yes, Papa," was all she said. Though Louise would eventually prove herself to be another of our family's excellent talkers, I was glad to see that she also knew when to be silent; much more than I did.

We repeatedly gave assurances and eventually, with

trepidation, we made the arrangements to leave the following day. Nona accompanied me, as well as my stalwart Louise. It took me no time at all to pack, just black, black and more black. However, at the last moment, I put the pink pearl in my little jewelry case. I think, somehow, I needed its comfort, its security, but just mostly, its presence. In a way it was like having Louis there, and how I would have preferred that he accompany me. Louis, because of his job, could rarely accompany me. Only a real emergency could take him away and since poor Serge was already dead, there was hardly an emergency. Besides, I was a naval wife and though I wanted him desperately to come, I knew better than to voice such thoughts aloud.

We were able to make the trip quickly and with the minimum of fuss. Willy, of all people, actually met us at the Berlin Railroad station. What was unique about this meeting was that it was quiet and he came incognito— well as incognito as Willy could bear to be. There were actually very few people who knew that he was there. We had a quick cup of tea together and he most especially wanted me to take his best wishes and greatest sympathies to Ella. This was unusually nice of him, not only because he made the effort, but also because he really hadn't spoken to Ella since she refused him and married Serge.

After only a few hours we parted and were sped on our way. Being only minor royalty, as far as I was concerned, had many advantages. No one felt compelled to make a fuss over you and consequently, speeches and appearances were unnecessary. All the better when you were in a hurry, as we were, and we arrived in Moscow three days later.

I was amazed at Ella's calm. She seemed to be going about her business, making arrangements for the funeral, informing the family and comforting everyone else. I had rushed to her without bothering to unpack and she welcomed my urgency with a faint smile.

"Dearest Vicky," she said calmly and quietly, "you are here at last."

I studied her face. It was familiar, of course, but she was deathly pale and there was a hollow look in her eyes. For the first time, I didn't think that she was beautiful. It was as though the light had left her face. She looked like she was functioning on pure will—as though there was no more strength.

"Of course, darling."

I was longing to burst into tears, but somehow felt if she did not, than neither should I.

Her servants hovered and watched over her, some tearful, though mostly for her sake, not for Serge's. Again, things started to appear as they always did in Russia, as if by magic. I was, with very little interest, sipping a cup of tea and hoping that she would talk and perhaps unburden herself.

"There is a lot of unrest here," she murmured.

"Yes, I've read about it," I replied, thinking of how poor Louis was so worried.

"They've closed the universities—the students are so unruly."

"I can't understand that," I said, in my usual outspoken way. "If you close the universities, you have a lot of young people on the loose, just itching to make trouble. At least, if you keep them open, some of them might feel obligated to go to their tutors and lectures."

Ella smiled and muttered, "They feel that the universities are hotbeds of revolutionary activity."

"That may be so, but they eventually grow out of it."

She looked at me and actually chuckled.

"Oh, Vicky," she said with just a light catch in her voice and a tiny spark in her eyes, "you do cheer me so."

I smiled weakly. Sometimes my blundering paid off.

"I had to pick them up," she said in a far away voice, her mood completely changing.

"What, darling?" I asked as I took her hand. Her eyes were moist and I was wondering when she would break down. According to her maid, who met me at the entrance to the house, she had not yet done so. This maid, one of Ella's servants from Darmstadt, spoke to me in German.

"Her Imperial Highness hasn't cried or screamed or even become angry," she told me as she took me straight to Ella's room. Though I couldn't imagine Ella screaming, she did have a point. "She's just as calm as she can be, sending telegrams and telling people the news."

I couldn't imagine taking Louis' death so calmly, but I underestimated myself. I would take much in these years that were to come. I approached each crisis with a calm that I think would have pleased my mother—and completely puzzled Grandmama. However, this also exacerbated my reputation for being cold, which would continue. Well, I had to hold on.

"There was much blood on the snow in Red Square. Yes, red was a good name for it," and inexplicably, she giggled. I must have looked alarmed because she squeezed my hand. "I'm all right, don't worry I'm not going to get hysterical—I don't have the energy, sometimes I just...forget...."

I nodded slowly, but said nothing. I wanted her to talk.

"There were bits of Serge all over and all I could think was 'Hurry, hurry—Serge so hated mess and blood.' You know how immaculate he was—it would have distressed him. A strange thing...we gathered him up and put him on a stretcher. He wouldn't let me go anywhere with him in public, you know," she was rambling; "he did worry that this might happen. Perhaps he even knew...."

Again, I just nodded.

"I went to the prison yesterday—where they're keeping the man that did it. Serge would have wanted me to—he would not have wanted the man to have died without some kind of confession—Serge was a very religious man, you know," she looked at me and I nodded.

I knew that Serge was religious, though it never

seemed to fit in with his other characteristics. I guess it was because most of the religious people that I had knew were mainly kind and compassionate. Serge was not that.

"I suppose I wanted to find some answers," she continued, not waiting for me to answer. "You know how people always say that such murders are senseless? I wanted some sense; I should have known that I wouldn't get any. I asked him why he did it..."

Good gracious, I thought, what courage. I pressed her hand, fighting back my tears.

"He told me that he'd acted according to his principles. In such cases the principles seem distorted, and unrecognizable, don't you think?" she asked conversationally. "I gave him an icon and promised to take care of his mother—I'm sure that was the right thing to do, don't you think? That's what Mama and Grandmama would have done."

Obviously, Ella was in deep shock. I felt the tears down my cheeks, especially at her mention of Grandmama and she patted my hand as she sipped some of her tea.

Louise and Nona had come in while we were talking. I thought that Ella wanted people about her now. She was not, I supposed, in the mood for retrospection. Her little niece, Marie, also came in while we were sitting and tried hard to comfort her aunt. Marie and her brother Dimitri, the children of Serge's youngest brother, Paul and his dead first wife, Alexandra, had lived with Ella and Serge for quite a while. I believe they had been there since Paul had made a morganatic second marriage and it was not deemed suitable for Dimitri and Marie to live with their father. Serge, however, loved these children deeply and was extremely demonstrative towards them. Such gestures were very unlike him, however, the children loved him back and were both extremely distressed. As seemed to be the case these days, Ella ended up comforting Marie, who had collapsed into her arms in tears. Later on, Marie would insist that Ella had been cold to her throughout the time they had lived together, but when she needed her most, she had not been.

We all tried to help Ella, to some way alleviate her sorrow, but she remained calm, except for some occasional strange rambles, as though she was sleepwalking.

Aunt Marie had rushed to Moscow to mourn her brother. However, Aunt Marie wasn't necessarily capable of being comforting. She tried, but her nature was quite brusque. She went about saying how accustomed the Romanovs were to such things, which helped no one. As was the norm those first days after the tragedy, Ella was comforting her. She continued to function and most people believed that she shed no tears for Serge, though I knew better. After some days, she shed them with me, but told me that she had resolved to remain calm until the whole business was over—and she did.

We attended funeral services for Serge and many people, even though he was not well liked, came to express their condolences to Ella. It was, as I observed, because Ella was so admired. People seemed to care about her and she certainly showed how much she cared about others—always.

As with most Russian ceremonies, this one was long and laborious. There was much standing, lots of chanting and prayers and incense. That's how I came to think of these occasions—just prayers and incense. To Ella, as I watched her face, they were much more. There seemed to be a mystical serenity that took over her face while the choir sang—a sort of comfort and joy that I didn't understand. I had never felt so far away from her as I did at that ceremony. There was something that she knew and felt of which I knew nothing. But, then, I was not the mystical type—and had to struggle to understand my sisters, and later on, my daughter.

When it was finally over, we, as the family, marched slowly and mournfully out of the Kremlin. Later, Serge was buried in a crypt of the Chudov Monastery in the Kremlin—and again there were more solemn ceremonies and prayers.

I had just about had it when we finally returned to Ella's home. She and I nearly collapsed with exhaustion afterwards. Over the cups of tea and my inevitable cigarettes, we once again soaked our feet and talked over things. I couldn't help but remember the previous times we had done this, usually with Serge coming in at some stage to speak to Ella. He never failed to make me feel left out of these conferences. I usually left the room. Anyhow, he could never stay away from her for long—it was as if he had to have a certain amount of her presence in order to get through the day.

I remember, as a child, Mama gave me something. I believe it was a pretty little book of poetry—even then I was fond of books. I treasured that little book, drinking it in with my eyes and keeping it on my night table, so that I could look at it before I went to sleep, and if, by chance, I woke up during the night, it would be there. When I would awake in the morning, the first thing I saw was that beloved book of poems. I thought that was how Serge felt about Ella, as though she was a treasure that had to be glanced at and handled frequently.

Louise, who had never been through such a protracted ceremony for anything, including Uncle Bertie's coronation, excused herself, saying that she was exhausted.

"I'll come and wake you for supper," I called after her. Ella looked at her retreating figure, and sighed. I knew that although Paul's children were with her, she still mourned all the children she didn't have. Considering how fecund Alicky, Irène and I proved, I knew that she felt that it had been Serge and not she that was the source of their infertility.

"I am just over forty, Vicky, and childless," her voice trailed off for a moment. "I suppose I have several choices," she paused, "I can live the life of the disconsolate widow, mourning forever..."

"Like Grandmama..."

"Precisely," she smiled at my mention of Grandmama. We both knew that neither of us would ever go through that kind of protracted mourning. "I should never do that, Vicky. I don't believe God wants us to mourn for our fellow beings in that fashion—it's just too much."

I didn't disagree.

"Or I could go to the Riviera and roam about looking for young lovers...."

I must have gasped. She was hardly the type to do something like this, there was such a purity about her, most of the time I couldn't even imagine her having Serge as a lover—I was probably right about this, as I found out later. But she smiled at my gasp.

"Are you trying to shock me?" I said weakly, gathering my wits.

"I don't think so I'm just thinking aloud, do you mind?"

I was glad none of the younger set was about or even Alicky, who had become even more pious and prudish than she had been as a younger woman.

"Or, I could do something worthwhile with my life. Make myself useful as Mama would want me to do."

She'd been useful enough during the Russo-Japanese War the previous year. In what seemed to have become a family tradition, she was ordering ambulance trains and getting nurses organized and working with the wounded. Some of them even convalesced at Illyinskoje. Now, she had a faraway look in her eyes—one I'd seen in Alicky when she thought she had the spiritual calling to help Nicky with Russia and later on in my own daughter Alice. I, being more realistic, never got such looks in my eye.

"Yes, I think that's what's to be done. I shall do what I've always thought I ought," she smiled at me as though that were settled.

I must admit, though I tried to help Ella as much as I could, I'm not sure to this day whether I did. As the days wore on, she had about her a composure that was in no way comparable to the shock she'd suffered before.

I was extremely relieved when several days after the funeral, she did cry. We were reminiscing about our times at the Heiligenberg and the tramps we used to take to the Jugenheim for "*sneeballen*". It was, oddly enough, the "*sneeballen*" that set her off. She was laughing at the remembered sight of me with powdered sugar on my face and the laughter turned hysterical and then into weeping.

She wept inconsolably in my arms for several hours that day and smiled at me afterward. She was in some ways restored. I must admit that I did not mourn Serge very much—I had grown somewhat fond of him during the years that Ella and he were married. He seemed to dote on her so and was so good to her that you couldn't help but be impressed. But he had never been my kind of person, nor was I, his—I believe we repelled each other. He had always struck me as the type who could never quite believe that women were also people.

After spending some time with Ella, I traveled on to Athens to be with Alice. I was concerned about Ella, naturally, and we wrote back and forth frequently during that period. The letters I received from her in Greece were encouraging. My sister was not only going to pull through this crisis, but she was going to carry on to a new life.

She had many ideas about what she wanted to do. Remarriage was never part of the picture, though I had hoped it might be. I suppose I thought it still wasn't too late for Ella to have a family. Ella's ideas, however, had to do with nursing, building hospitals and much more farfetched, at least in my opinion at the time, founding an order of nursing nuns.

I did not believe the Metropolitans would ever let her, a convert to Russian Orthodoxy, do this—especially in the way she proposed to do it—it all seemed too Protestant for them. Ella had her own ideas of the way a nunnery should be organized. She wanted her sisters to be able to go out in the world and have holidays with their families. It was, I thought, because she never wanted them to forget that they were human beings, so that they could better take care of other human beings.

I expected that the church hierarchy would refuse to implement Ella's ideas, which they did, but, then, I expected her to be discouraged about this and she was not. She continued sending them proposals and having discussions about such a nursing order. It seemed that my sister, Ella, had a true calling—and a lot of determination.

II
Athens, 1905

I, who loved to travel, was excited about a trip to Athens. Here was another exotic destination into which I could delve. Not just the ancient ruins of the Parthenon awaited me, though I was extremely interested in archaeology and had, naturally, done a great deal of reading about them, but, also, the markets and bazaars that had a distinctly Ottoman flavor. I must admit that after all my other exotic destinations I was getting quite adept at understanding the eastern mind. All things considered, I was quite expert at haggling and the Mediterranean weather warmed my soul, as well as my bones.

I believe that my guide enjoyed my appreciation for the streets and markets of his city.

"Greece is not just an ancient ruin, there for the pleasure of the Western visitor," he held forth. His name was Pavlos and he was a student at the university in Athens. "There is so much more to see here than the Parthenon and the Acropolis. We are a country that is struggling with her neighbors," meaning the Balkan countries and Greece's particular nemesis, Turkey, "and trying to regain our historic borders."

How often I had heard such a declaration. Historic borders reminded me very sadly of Bulgaria, and, much later on would remind me of Nazi Germany. I usually fail to see the validity of any of these claims, but that is because I am not an ultra-nationalist.

"We are very happy with the present royal family," he said with a smile. This might seem a sycophantic statement, but the truth is, that from all reports, Aunt Alix's brother was very popular, as was his son, Sophie's Constantine, whom we called Tino. However, I always thought what this young man said also implied that "we're happy with them now, but one false move and out they go." I might have been right about this because, sadly, that was the attitude. This was a family that was constantly in exile and on trial.

"They are such an improvement on the Wittelsbachs. King Otto wanted to dictate to us, he did not want to reign, he wanted to rule—and all those Bavarians he brought— I am thankful that he left peacefully."

I nodded, as I climbed up to the Parthenon. I loved the ancient pillars and pediments and the view it afforded of the city. I was only half-listening to Pavlos' history lesson.

"The Greek people wanted your dear Uncle, the late Duke of Saxe-Coburg, to replace Otto—but instead, it was finally decided that Prince William, Queen Alexandra's brother, would come instead."

Once again, I nodded absently. I knew the history of my family and was much more interested in the internal colonnades and the other temples of the Acropolis.

"We are quite happy with this choice," he said less enthusiastically, most likely because I wasn't joining into the discussion as eagerly as he would have wished. After that, he kept to architectural descriptions and ancient history, which I had come to hear.

Some days into our visit, in April of that otherwise terrible year, Alice presented us with our first grandchild. She was named Margarita, with the title Princess of Greece and Denmark. She and her next sister, Theodora, called Dolla, who would come two years later, were destined to be very good friends with our boy, Dickie. There are many family pictures of Dickie playing with the two little girls. I sometimes thought that he must feel like their cavalier. I also surmised that he was happy that he was the older of these three. He found being the baby of our own family was difficult, though I was completely happy to have another one around. His oldest sister was already married and having children and his older brother was about to enter the navy. His next sister was already a young lady and considered an adult.

As for me, it felt so strange to be a grandmother. I know that Grandmama was only a little older than I when I arrived and I was by no means her first grandchild. I, however, always thought that I had not changed. I certainly felt little different that I had those days when we all came together at the Heiligenberg. What a shock it was to me that I was approaching middle age.

The christening of baby Margarita, took place at the royal palace in Athens. Best of all, Louis was able to attend. We were thrilled that Aunt Alix, who was now

Queen Alexandra of England, was there visiting her brother, King George of Greece, and was also able to be with us. In addition, much of Alice's new family, King George and Queen Olga of Greece, their sons, Tino, with his wife, my cousin Sophie, Andrew and all the others were in attendance. This peace and serenity that we felt in Greece, alas, was not to last much longer. I wish now that I had understood the precariousness of the Greek throne before Alice married into the family. Perhaps I could have prevented so much heartbreak.

Never mind, it is never good to dwell on that which is unchangeable. I enjoy remembering that christening because we were all there and, in its own way, it seemed like one of our grand celebrations.

CHAPTER SEVENTEEN

Illyinskoje, the Gulf of Finland, June, 1909

So much of a coincidental nature happens during one's life. I've never been particularly religious, though I was raised with strong religious convictions. But, there is a point when I truly wonder if some supreme puppet-master is pulling my strings, and then, of course, stepping back. When I despair, I am sure that the master is laughing at me, but when there are wonderful times I know that is not so—that I am somehow in his grace.

There was another event that happened in November of 1905 that I remember as being very pleasant. I suppose it just didn't belong with the sadness of Serge's assassination and the deaths of some of our children. At the time I remember being extremely envious and put out that I couldn't go, not that it was customary to take wives on cruises.

Louis in his capacity as Rear Admiral, Commander of the Second Cruiser Squadron and the *Drake*, made a good-will trip to the United States. How I had wanted to go! I'd always been curious about that country ever since I'd read *Uncle Tom's Cabin* and more recently since I had met the unfortunate President McKinley. I'd read much about the formation of this new and grand country and read much about the beauties and varieties of scenery to be found there. It didn't sound exotic, but it did sound vital and energetic and, well, fun. I had heard that it was enormous, nearly as large as Russia, but yet, I knew that it was quite different.

Louis and his squadron were shown such gracious hospitality when they arrived in Baltimore Harbor. The Americans had treated all the British Officers with such friendliness and great consideration. I suppose it helped a great deal that the British didn't look upon the Americans as foreigners. It was perhaps more true to say that we looked upon them as eccentric cousins. I traced this back to Grandpapa and his tact in dealing with President Lincoln during those first dark days of the American Civil War. Afterwards, and after a few false starts, America and England came to a rapprochement that has held fast. So much so that today, I would venture to say England considers America her best friend, and I believe the reverse is true.

Louis had the good fortune to be received by the President, Mr. Theodore Roosevelt. Louis told me he was such an exhilarating person. I had seen newsreels of Mr. Roosevelt and his energy just walking along the street or speaking to a crowd was so infectious that it was very apparent on film. I had rarely seen such a vital and vigorous man. He was also incredibly knowledgeable about naval matters. He had been Secretary to the American Navy just before he became Mr. McKinley's Vice-President. As both men were admirers of the famous Admiral Mahan who wrote *The Importance of Sea Power in History*, there was much for the two to discuss. Louis told me that he and the President had talked of their concern about Willy and his naval build-up. It comforted neither of them to know that Willy also kept a copy of this vital book on his night table. Louis' only complaint was that he left the official White House dinner hungry. He and the President were so deeply in conversation that he had waved away dishes and touched little on his plate.

When he returned, I remember being particularly anxious to hear his accounts about the interesting land of America. We, in Britain and, indeed, in Europe had always had a strange view of the States and I'm sorry to say that in our ignorance, it wasn't always a positive one. We pictured Americans as either red Indians or going about dressed in buckskins with raccoon-skin caps and chewing tobacco. We, women especially, were sure that we'd have to spend most of our time frantically holding up our skirts and dodging faulty aims at the spittoon.

Louis quickly disabused me of my ignorance. He had

only seen the eastern part, but I had resolved that perhaps one day, he and I would travel all over the North American continent; it would be a glorious expedition. As he spoke, I could see a new land, beautiful, nearly pristine, with a population eager to modernize, progress and to throw away all the restrictions of the Old World. Later on, I was to think that Louis belonged to a place like that. Not, sadly, the British Navy that ultimately did not appreciate him the way that many, not just I, thought they ought.

That did not mean that Louis did not continue advancing his career in the Royal Navy. It was interesting that most people recognized that Louis' rise was due to hard work and diligence, not to connections. Some wondered why he didn't join the German Navy, where Willy, when he got over his aversion to Louis' semi-royal status, would have no doubt given him many more advantages and regular promotions whether or not he deserved them.

1906 was punctuated by another Royal Wedding. My Auntie Beatrice's only daughter, Ena, my tall, blonde, beautiful niece, was to be married to Alfonso XIII of Spain. Alfonso was a small, dark, odd little fellow, who stood up rather poorly to my Junoesque niece. Moreover, she was not his first choice.

Alfonso had already made the rounds with my other cousins, first setting his sights on Princess Margaret, whom we called Daisy, of Connaught. Then, when Crown

Prince Gustav Adolf won her, he cheerfully shifted the photographs in his wallet and his attentions to her sister, Patricia, whom we called Patsy. Some of us were good at changing our minds over important things like marriage—one needed look no further than May or Cousin Minnie, who had actually been engaged to Sasha's elder brother, Nicholas before he died. The rest of us, who were somehow less changeable, for good or ill, would often sit and marvel at such behavior.

Patsy and Daisy were the beautiful Connaught sisters that were bridesmaids along with my Alice at Cousin Georgie's wedding. Patsy, however, wasn't the least bit responsive to Alfonso. She reminded me of my Louise in that she wasn't interested in kings—she was far more interested in marrying for love. She ultimately did marry the man of her choice, but she had to wait quite a long time for him.

But, as to Ena, or Queen Victoria Eugenie as she is known in history, she married Alfonso in a solemn ceremony in Madrid in May of that year. It was one of those events that many of us attended. As was often true, this wedding took place under threats of violence. The church was crowded with family and press and after their vows were said, the couple rode in a procession to the royal palace. En route, a deranged young assassin threw a bouquet of flowers at the couple. It concealed an exploding bomb.

Pandemonium ensued as the horse guards scrambled

around the crowds looking for the murderer. Twenty-four people were killed and dozens injured, while the newlyweds could only try to calmly change carriages and proceed to the palace. I could only think later that like Khodynka Field, this boded ill for the two.

Auntie Beatrice and I discussed this traumatic incident later that night.

"Ena was wonderful, wasn't she," she said, her face white and her voice still trembling with fear.

"I can't imagine what Grandmama would have said." I was also shaken, though I had not been anywhere near the procession. The rest of us had proceeded back to our various lodgings by a different route. "This isn't Russia after all."

Not the most cheering remark to have made, but it was true. Spain was not expected to treat its royalty the same way the Russians did. One didn't expect bombs and assassinations.

"No it isn't Russia", Auntie retorted sharply. "But, Alfonso, poor man, has had many death threats."

"Perhaps Mama was right and we royal families should just forget this monarchy business", I said, thinking of all that my mother had told me about privilege and aristocracy. "Now is the time, as our countries industrialize for a new order one that doesn't include 'haves' and 'have-nots.'" I was rapidly warming to this topic and gesticulating with my cigarette.

"Victoria, Mama was right, you are a gasbag," Auntie

said with disgust. "This is hardly the time for your socialist nonsense."

"Oh, Auntie," I laughed, not the least offended. "You have to admit that something here isn't right. It's neither modern nor democratic."

"Hmm," she lit a cigarette. "Democracy...? How I wish you'd been a schoolteacher as you always wanted to be, then you could harangue your students instead of unsuspecting members of your family. Not all countries are ready for democracy, Victoria. I see nothing democratic about assassination attempts, and I don't see your sister Alicky making any inroads in that direction in Russia."

"I feel that Alicky has become more Russian than the Russians. She seems to have rejected every liberal idea that we were taught in Darmstadt. She and Nicky are caught up in the antiquated idea of the divine right of kings. Though, admittedly, even if she and Nicky wanted to change things, the Grand Dukes—the uncles—would hardly let them," I sighed. "Grandmama was afraid something like this would happen, and she was right."

"Alicky has taken on autocracy with all the zeal of a convert, Victoria. She'll die before she lets Nicky give up a shred of his 'God-given' powers."

I nodded, and we both sighed, because we both knew what Auntie said about Alicky was the truth.

"It's hard to believe in true democracy," she went on, "because with true democracy would be the death of the monarchy and I've always believed in the efficacy of monarchy...it's a symbolic force that can create tremendous unity."

Auntie shook her head faintly, and then wiped a tear from her eyes.

"I suppose the way that Grandmama and now Uncle Bertie reign in England would be an excellent example for both Spain and Russia," I mused.

"Victoria, I can't say that you're much of a comfort in this situation."

I loved her veracity. She never let me get away with anything.

"Believe me, if Ena had been hurt I wouldn't be taking this with so much equanimity."

"But twenty-four other innocent people have been killed."

Well I knew that, I could hardly forget it. While I could forget no detail about any of them, I suppose I just didn't want to cry anymore.

Poor Ena and Alfonso—their lives were also tainted with hemophilia. Several of their sons were affected with it as well as with other physical disorders. Unlike Nicky and Alix, the sorrows of their children's misfortunes, rather than unite them, divided them.

My last little Edinburgh cousin, Baby Bee, who had also been a candidate on Alfonso's list, married, instead, Infante Alfonso, a first cousin of the king. It was said that she spent a lot of her time making mischief and trouble between Ena and her Alfonso, but I like to think not. If so, I've also heard that trouble would not be difficult to make. Instead, I always like to remember Baby Bee, beautiful creature that she was, as a baby that couldn't join Ducky, Missy and I on our wild, beautiful rides through Malta.

Speaking of Malta that was a place to which I never had to say goodbye. I was there often with Louis and the family as he rose in the ranks. By 1908, Louis was appointed a Vice Admiral, and later that year Commander-in-Chief of the Atlantic Fleet. Those were the most idyllic and sweet days of my family and the end of my youth. I traveled constantly, bringing Nona, Dickie and Louise with me. My Georgie flourished brilliantly in the Royal Navy, and Alice continued to present me with grandchildren, now numbering two little girls. I can hardly say that I was reconciled to the fact of being a grandmother, but I tried to be philosophical. The fact that they lived in a foreign country often let me forget.

Alice seemed to be happy with Andrew. I believe their times in Greece were the happiest of their marriage—their many exiles did not improve their relationship. Great adversity, it seems, would not strengthen their bond either.

As for myself, I spent a lot of those years in rented homes in London: 4 Hans Crescent which comes to mind and later, Sheerness—but there were many others. Later, we resided in the beautiful Mall House at the Admiralty where, Louis, as the Commander-in-Chief of the Atlantic Fleet, was housed. Louis, who was a progressive man, continued to move up in the navy. He wanted more than anything to institute needed reforms which, as he often said, would bring it into the twentieth century. Consequently, he made enemies among the conservatives and those who harbored jealousy.

It is incidents that took place in 1909 that stand out in my mind when I think of my family and my travels. I packed up Dickie and Louise, who was twenty and avoiding marriage proposals, for yet another jaunt to Russia. Louise had fleetingly been among the crowd thought of for King Alfonso, though, obviously, nothing came of it. King Manoel of Portugal also expressed a strong interest in her and actually proposed to her, but she refused him. I was glad about that very soon afterward. King Manoel fled into exile only two years later. My girl was, I suppose, like me, not to be impressed with crowns. That, however, did not mean that I didn't want to see her settled—but I would never have wished any of my girls to spend their lives in exile. It is a dreadful and divisive life.

In all events, our first stop on this latest journey was to see Ella at the Nicholas Palace in Moscow. Since the death of Serge, she had embarked upon an entirely different life. Her bedrooms and sitting rooms no longer displayed the sumptuous furnishing and precious objects that Serge had so adored. She began to institute what she hoped would become a plain life devoted to self-perfection, and dedicated to service. She became a vegetarian, spent most of her days either in prayer or helping the sick and the poor. She began to sell much of her worldly goods.

"I mean to divide my personal possessions among you, my family and then return anything that belongs to the crown or the state—whatever remains, I'll sell and put the money aside for my convent fund."

Ella, Louise and I were chatting in her rooms, as we had done so often before. Nona was sitting unobtrusively in the corner darning some of Dickie's socks. I had always told her that it was the maid's job to do those things. Nona, however, was one of those women who always wanted her fingers busy. I would laugh at her and call her Victorian and she would sweetly thank me. Yes, she did know how to handle me. In addition, she was extremely fond of Dickie and gave him the stability that our constant travels attempted to erode.

Her duties were nebulous, though she was ready and capable of doing anything I wanted. That way she became an indispensable part of my household. However, it wasn't just the administrative end of things—it was the companionship of a calm, sensitive, nice person. One that was neither argumentative, nor was she a compliant ninny that I could wrap around my finger.

So different from me!

I often wonder how she stood me at my most querulous and impatient. I didn't get better as I got older, just more pugnacious. But, at least I recognized it and found myself constantly apologizing to her. In the end I was lucky to find such a strong and supportive soul.

Ella told us about her proposals to the Metropolitans and how they were obdurate about granting her permission to found a monastery. They were hesitating, in part, because such a place—a convent that housed nuns devoted to nursing—had never existed in Russia. It would be called the Monastery of SS Martha and Mary. The nuns would wear gray habits instead of black and they would eat meat in order to be strong enough to work in hospitals.

"And, they'll get a good eight hours sleep—no interruptions in the middle of the night for prayers. There's no point having them work hard if they don't eat properly and get rest, they simply can't be at their best," she told me.

All that went through my mind was that these women would in some way be her children. Nevertheless, I saw a lot of Grandmama and Mama's pragmatism and dedication to public service in her thoughts. She was determined to initiate a service that was desperately needed.

We talked of these things, as well as family matters as we packed again for the journey to Illyinskoje. I always loved Ella's summer home and felt that we were away from all the troubles of the world. I was really sorry when she decided to sell the property, which she did quite soon.

She told me after Serge was killed, that she would keep it until Marie and Dimitri had lives of their own.

What I enjoyed most about Illyinskoje was the more relaxed atmosphere, since there was no need for the tight security that Nicky, in light of Serge's assassination, had insisted upon. However, as time went on, that proved not to be the case. We were not permitted to leave the grounds because threats continued against the lives of the Imperial Family. Illyinskoje was never the same.

Later, when Ella had established her nunnery she would drive the police to distraction. She would insist on being accompanied only by her faithful maid, Varvara, who had joined her order as Sister Barbara, when she went to the worst cesspools of Moscow to minister aid to the poor and the unfortunate. Many was the time that the Chief of Police would wring his hands in despair, telling her that he was unable to protect her and plead with her not to go to these terrible places. Ella would respond saying that God would protect her and that he wasn't to worry. In the end, the people she helped never hurt her.

There was one sleepy June day at Illyinskoje that remains in my mind for no reason other than the fact that we were all together and everything was happy and peaceful. We were lazing about on the veranda, watching the children. Louise and her cousins were down by the green banks of the river, shoes and stockings off, splashing and chasing each other around squealing with delight. Even though Louise was as tall and elegant as

Alicky and nearly twenty, she derived more pleasure from playing with her young cousins than gossiping with us older ones.

That day there were so many young cousins about, including, Alicky's four sweet girls. The eldest was Olga, about fourteen, and turning into quite a handful for her mother. Alicky was aghast and had whispered to me, genuinely distressed, that this oldest child actually had the temerity to talk back to her. Tatiana, twelve at the time, reminded me most of the typical Hessian princess. She was tall, slim and beautiful and, from what I could see, had a mind of her own and a decided air of authority. She was the leader of the children in her family. Then there was ten year old Marie, who had apple cheeks, enormous blue eyes and masses of brown wavy hair. My Dickie, who was somewhat younger, told me seriously, that he meant to marry her when he grew up. It was no joke to him and he had a very strong feeling for her that lasted his entire life. He had a particularly lovely drawing of her that he took with him wherever he traveled. I believe he still keeps that drawing near him today. The youngest sister, Anastasia, was about eight that summer and the very devil of mischief. She wasn't as pretty as her sisters, but there was something taking—memorable about her. Perhaps, it was that her personality made her stand out from the rest or perhaps it was just hindsight on my part, because of what came later. Anastasia was definitely herself, a merciless tease and prankster, who was sometimes even a bit cruel. Alicky, however, was always quick to make sure she understood her actions and she inevitably apologized to the person who was the butt of one of her jokes.

I always wondered why so many legends of her survival grew around her, for there was really nothing so very romantic about her. She was short, chunky and not particularly pretty and is beauty not the thing upon which most legends are based? Tatiana or Marie would have better been cast in the role of the lost princess—they were the real fairy tale princesses in that family.

Alexis was not there that afternoon. He was usually allowed to play with his sisters and cousins, for they understood that he had to be treated with the utmost care. However, today he was with his father. Sometimes it broke my heart to see this handsome five-year-old carried around by one of the sailors deputized to make sure he never fell or hurt himself. He was such a boisterous, energetic and fun-loving child—being restrained must have been so frustrating. I was surprised that he didn't have more tantrums and wasn't more spoiled than he was.

Then, there was little Margarita and Theodora, or Dolla as we called her, my own precious granddaughters (how I still felt strange saying that!), who were very small. Dickie had appointed himself their nanny. We rocked with laughter as we watched his efforts to keep them dry and upright. He was run quite ragged and reminded me, when he would pick up Margarita, who was about three, and certainly not baby-sized, of a mother cat taking her kittens by the scruff of their necks. Naturally, the girls had a nanny, but she was wise enough to let Dickie think he was in charge. Grandmama would have said, "Of course! She's a sensible Englishwoman!"

Ella, Alicky, Alice and I watched the scene as Don and Lu, Onor and Ernie's boys, who were little more than toddlers, themselves, were trying to get involved in what was evolving into a melee. They were all chasing one another, presumably to gain possession of a ball. They were laughing and yelling in English, as sailor suits, white dresses and hair ribbons flew in all directions...and my Louise was in the center of it all.

"Such a dear girl, your Louise," Alicky remarked lazily, as we all sat comfortably on the porch, letting the sun warm our faces. "She's so good with the children. She ought to have some of her own." Alicky sighed as she tried to get comfortable in her chair. Her sciatica often made her uncomfortable, especially when she worried about Alexis.

"Shall I get you another pillow?" Ella asked her, ever vigilant, ever caring.

"No thank you, but some tea perhaps...?" And, as usual, practically as the words left her mouth, the deed was done. Magically, a samovar, plates of lemon, rock sugar, cakes and biscuits of all descriptions appeared.

"Wonderful," I breathed, "I'm parched."

I always loved it when we sisters could sit quietly. Irène could not come that year and poor Onor was upstairs with a migraine, so it was just the three of us. The rarity of such gatherings of the sisters was sadly becoming the norm rather than the exception.

Alicky tried to make herself comfortable once again, with the maid shifting her pillows. Annoyed, she waved her away; Alicky had always hated to be fussed over.

"I suppose you know that Nicky is permitting Kyrill and Ducky to return to Russia," Alicky said painfully. It was obvious that she had waited to introduce this particular subject when Onor wasn't around.

"He has only done so after the death of Kyrill's papa. The poor man didn't even get a chance to say goodbye to his father. I suppose that is enough punishment, don't you think? After all, it's not as though Ernie isn't happily settled with Onor," Ella said gently.

Alicky was not to be placated. She truly seemed to hate Ducky and by extension Kyrill. She told me that it was for religious reasons, but I believe that the fact that she would have to receive the divorced wife of her own brother galled her beyond words.

Ducky's divorce from Ernie had been finalized at the end of 1901 and she went home to her mother in Coburg with the express purpose of marrying Kyrill. Nicky, however, at Alicky's behest, forbade the marriage. Kyrill, who was Nicky's heir at that point, was biding his time. He had no intentions of jeopardizing his position as heir apparent by marrying someone of whom the Tsar did not approve. This was so typical of Kyrill, whom Ducky's own sister, Cousin Missy, described as the "marble man." I sometimes thought that no one but Ducky actually liked him.

When Alicky finally gave birth to Alexis in 1904 and Kyrill was no longer as close to the throne, that is when he decided to marry Ducky. They certainly could not marry in Russia, so they married at Aunt Marie's in Coburg in the fall of 1905. When Alicky heard, she was livid. At her urging, Nicky stripped Kyrill of his allowance and all his decorations, appointments and titles. The young couple went off to a pleasant exile in Paris and waited for Nicky to have a change of heart, for Alicky certainly never would.

"It was only at the urging of Uncle Vladimir—his deathbed wish—that Nicky relented," Alicky murmured. She had that faraway look in her eyes—the one that said that she was thinking of what an awful sin Ducky had committed. When had my sister become such a religious fanatic? Or, had she always been this way, and I had chosen not to see it?

"Perhaps Nicky feels the family should stand united, not be divided. Anyhow, what's done is done. They've been gone for five years, and, well, dearest, you don't have to receive her except officially—it was Uncle's last wish— you would not want to be responsible for not fulfilling such a desire?" Ella said soothingly.

Uncle Vladimir was a popular member of the Romanov

family and I believe that Ella was trying to moderate Alicky's views about the family and the Russian aristocracy in general. It seemed, from what Ella had told me in private, to be a hopeless cause. Alicky felt that Alexis' hemophilia was a judgment on her for sins—though she never specified to Ella what those sins were. Accordingly, she was going to live a life as free of sin as was possible. That meant keeping away from sinners—and in Alicky's eyes the family and the aristocracy were sinners by definition.

Her determination to stay away from sinful society strengthened as the years went by. As she became more isolated, Alexis' illness made her more paranoid. She feared that the people would find out about this weakness in the Tsar's family, and would blame her. She feared that they would find her entire family weak and unworthy to be the custodians of Holy Mother Russia. Poor Alicky had many fears.

"Ella still struggles to get her ideas accepted by the church hierarchy; it seems so unfair," I remarked trying to change the subject.

"You know," Alicky began, "at first I didn't like the idea of Ella's doing this. However, I know now how sincere she is—well, if they don't give in soon, something will have to be done. Sometimes these priests get above themselves."

Alicky was becoming overbearing and autocratic, which wasn't a surprise, though it was most disappointing. Grandmama had foreseen it, knowing that Alicky would eventually think too much of herself.

"Never mind," Ella said quickly. "I'm sure that God will see to it in his own good time."

"I'm sure God will and so will Nicky."

"You will now have the time to devote completely to your projects, now that little Marie is married," I said. Marie had married Prince Wilhelm of Sweden that year.

"Yes, that is also true—Wilhelm seems a nice boy—not that Marie was any trouble. I believe that Dimitri will now join the army."

"Nicky and I will do all we can for Dimitri; Nicky also looks upon Marie and Dimitri as his own. They are both such good children," Alicky commented.

Considering what Alicky thought of most of the Russian relatives, this was quite a concession.

Ella smiled.

I often thought that God laughed at the Hesses. There was certainly some kind of strange heavenly manipulation that ran through our family. And, except for very few cases, it never seemed for the good. Whatever imp was at work was no doubt shaking with laughter. Dimitri, so dear to Alicky, was one of Rasputin's assassins. While this seemed a tragedy only to Alicky, it crushed her to think that after all the regard and favor she had showered upon him, he had been responsible along with her niece by marriage's husband, Prince Felix Yussupov, for the death of the man she considered a savior.

We were silent for a moment looking out at the shenanigans on the lawn. It was wonderful to see that they were a loving group of children. Louise was detaching herself from the group. Hair disheveled and red with exertion. She had finally had enough.

"I can see which child takes after you, Vicky," Ella smiled.

Louise, panting, threw herself on a chair and made a comment about hooliganism. I could see Alicky recoil just slightly at her exuberance, but, I suppose Alicky had never been so robust and full of life as had Louise or even her own young girls. It was most strange when you think that Louise was not always at the pinnacle of health herself. In the end, it was just a question of attitude. High spirits were too much for my sister, who, along with her other mental and physical discomforts, was now suffering from a heart condition.

The children had settled down and were on the grass laughing and talking. The nannies had carried away the littlest ones and the others were pelting each other with grass.

"Should we serve them their tea right there?" Ella suggested.

"Yes, so much better than having them here with all the noise," Alicky stated. She was flushed and fanning herself. She had told me on several occasions that she had great difficulties with the extremes of weather in Russia.

Soon tables and servants appeared with food. There were some food fights going on and a lot of shouting. I saw that Dickie was following Marie around like a loving dog and fetching cakes and delicacies for her.

"I believe we'll have a match there," I remarked to Alicky and laughed.

She finally smiled, though it was one of those reluctant and thin-lipped smiles for which she was famous.

"They are terribly sweet, aren't they? Just don't take her away from me too soon."

"No, I believe we have to wait until Dickie gives up Sonnenbein," Louise giggled, naming Dickie's precious teddy bear.

We all laughed heartily at that—even Alicky.

"But Louise, dearest," Ella began, gently, "what's holding you back?"

"Serious talk, Auntie?" Louise grinned smartly. "Like all of us, even the ones that are only half-Hessian, I want to marry someone I love. Isn't that what my Grandmama and Grandpapa wanted for all of us?"

We were all quiet at that, though I'd heard it enough from Louise.

"I'll wait 'til I find someone like Papa or Uncle Nicky," she mused. "But I don't think it will be a king," she smiled at me. "And, I don't think I'd want a widower, the memories of the dear departed would always get in the way," and laughed again. Louise, like her Romanov cousins was addicted to laughter and had an excellent sense of humor.

"Louise you're outrageous," Alicky scolded gently. However, she joined in our laughter.

Louise made a lot of sense. It was probably a good thing that she had no ambitions to be a queen. In the scheme of our royal families, it would hardly be likely that she'd be considered for a crown prince. As for widowers, I wasn't sure where she had gotten this strange idea, though it did prove ironic later on.

"I mean, what a thing to say," my already matronly daughter Alice admonished.

"I don't know why you say that, it's just between ourselves."

"She's right, Alice. We should be able to talk to one another. After all, usually we need to be so careful. There are few with whom we can be comfortable."

Later on I remembered that Alicky had said this. It was after she stopped speaking to Ella, who was pleading with her to banish Rasputin from the court. Alicky had frozen Ella out of her presence and out of her life. It had only been for a time, but it had been an extremely crucial time.

"The girls are growing up so beautifully, are you thinking about anyone for Olga?"

It was a harmless enough question. Ella, as always, was the peacemaker.

"Olga has told me many times that she wants to stay in Russia, so I suppose it will have to be one of the Romanovs, though I'm not so keen on that."

"As the eldest daughter of the Emperor, she may be seen as having certain obligations. It seems to me that Olga could look to a crown prince if she so desired," Alice remarked. I suppose these thoughts came from living in a royal palace—she never heard them from Louis or me.

"That may be so, but I would so prefer it if my girls could marry for love—as we all did."

In spite of Alicky's feeling, I thought that she kept Olga, and later Tatiana, too close. Perhaps, I feel that now because had Olga married outside of Russia she would not have suffered the fate of the Imperial Family.

We all nodded in agreement as we watched our children. Perhaps, there is truth in what one of my favorite authors says, that happiness in marriage is simply a matter of chance and that is why it is better to know as little of one's future partner as possible. I never felt this way, but that was because I was fortunate enough to grow up with Louis. Even though he was not always there, we saw each other enough on leaves to know who we were, without artifice or concealment.

Such was the situation for Ella and Irène, though Serge always seemed to want to change Ella. Poor Serge—Ella seemed very content in her life and especially her project and though she wore black with a black veil, almost nun-like, I felt that in some strange way, she had firmly closed the door on that other part of her life. I also felt that it hadn't been quite as difficult for her as many might have thought.

"Louis has come along beautifully in his naval career, hasn't he?" Ella smiled at me, as she always did when she brought up Louis. I always believed that my being so happy with Louis gave her great joy. She was, and this is not only my belief, an extraordinarily unselfish woman.

"He is now Commander-in-Chief of the Atlantic Fleet—a tremendous responsibility in the British Navy." I could have bit my lip for the bragging that I was doing. Oh well, it was not as if he were my child—he was only my husband.

"Nicky says that one day he will be First Sea Lord," Alicky stated. "He is proud to have such a fine officer for a brother-in-law."

Praise coming from Alicky was so rare that I hardly knew what to say. I blushed a little, and Ella and Alicky both giggled.

"You would think that the two of you had only been married a month instead of over twenty-five years." Alicky smiled in a relaxed manner which, even among her beloved sisters was unusual.

I thought that this was nearly as shocking as being a grandmother and it was something that I articulated but rarely. It was hard to believe that Louis and I had been married for twenty-five years. It was a bit difficult to realize.

"We, girls have been gloriously lucky," Ella remarked. "We have all married where we loved and I can say that we have been happy in our marriages. It makes us unique, don't you think?"

"How so?" Alicky asked.

"If we look at all the marriages we know of," I took up the baton from Ella. "We have to admit that they aren't the very model of domestic felicity—you only need to look at Mama and Papa—"

"Victoria!" Alicky admonished sharply and eyed Alice and Louise. Alice was busy eating cakes, but Louise was sitting with a little grin on her face.

"I'm only saying that while Mama and Papa were happy together, they weren't as compatible as you and Nicky, for example, or Irène and Henry. They didn't have a happy commonality of tastes—"

"It is true that they were very different people," Ella added. "You don't remember them very well together, dearest, and Vicky and I were more fortunate."

"Alice and I didn't know Grandmama Alice and we hardly knew Grandpapa—"

"Then you have nothing on which to base any opinion," Alicky said sharply. Alicky evidently had a picture of her parents of which she wanted no intrusions from anyone else—no matter how true they might be. So like Grandmama.

I caught Louise's eye and shook my head. I didn't want her sparring with Alicky over this or anything else. She didn't believe in the freedom of expression that I encouraged in my house. Louise was sensible enough to hold her tongue after that.

What would become harder to take than the fact of my twenty-fifth anniversary were the events of the coming years. It was as though all the hopes, fears and underlying currents and themes, good and bad, of my youth were being realized. And, no one in my family was spared.

CHAPTER EIGHTEEN

London and Russia, 1912

As the new century wore on, I am amazed that we did not act upon the ominous harbingers of things to come. The signs seem so clear to me now that it's unbelievable that I was so obtuse—though what I could have done to effect any changes is entirely debatable. I, suppose, however, it would never have mattered if I or anyone else had been so blessed with the gift of prophecy. People never listened to soothsayers anyhow. So things and events continued to plague and pleasure us much in the way they had always done.

Sadly, Uncle Bertie died in May of 1910 after a short reign of nine years. Louis and I truly mourned this man who had played such an important part in our lives. It was Uncle Bertie who befriended Louis during his young and difficult years in the navy; it was Uncle Bertie who insisted on Louis' staying with him whenever Louis was on shore leave, so that Louis actually had his own bedroom at Marlborough House; and, it was Uncle Bertie who insisted that Louis be his Naval Aide-de-Camp as he had been for Grandmama and as he would now be, for Bertie's son, Cousin George. When I contemplate what his life might have been if Grandmama had understood his character better—ah, well.

Uncle Bertie's funeral was a grand affair. As usual, many royal families attended. There was the so called March of Kings, in which nine sovereigns took part in the funeral procession, following the coffin as it wound slowly through London. Among those included in the procession were: Alfonso XIII of Spain, Willy, Manoel of Portugal and more interestingly for me, at least, Mr. Theodore Roosevelt, the former American President whom Louis had been privileged to meet during his stay in America.

My daughter, Louise, complained bitterly that she was sick and tired of going to weddings, funerals and christenings. She was just beginning to understand that being a member of such a large family had its responsibilities, sometimes sad, as well as its privileges. This was our life, I told her more than once.

That year also marked the birth of another grandchild, a granddaughter, named Cecilia. I remember so clearly watching Alice playing with her new little girl.

"It seems to me that we, Hessian women are fated to

bear daughters, daughters and more daughters," she said as she leaned over and kissed her baby. "Look at Aunt Alix," she pointed out. "It took her four girls to get her one little boy. Do you think it will take me another girl?" she smiled.

It was, however, quite true. It took both Alicky and later on, Alice, four daughters before they finally had sons. My Alice now had little Cecilia and would have another girl, Sophie, before she would give birth to her tow-headed boy, Philip—and that was more than ten years away.

Ella, by virtue of Imperial Order, was finally given permission by the Synod to build her convent and in April of 1910, she, herself, took the veil. She had chosen some land on the banks of her beloved Moskva River and continued the construction of the Convent of SS Martha and Mary, which had actually begun several years before formal permission. It would eventually encompass a convent house, a beautiful onion-domed Church of St. Mary, as well as a hospital, an old age home, a home for consumptive women and lushly planted gardens. There were also plans for an orphanage. This endeavor utterly absorbed her and she never again took any social engagements. Instead, she would visit her sisters and be present only on so-called family occasions, the same thing that she had decided for all the nuns of the convent. However, unlike most convents in Russia, these women would not be completely cloistered. They would be allowed to visit their relatives on a regular basis. It was so like Ella to be so caring.

She and I spent many happy hours conferring about all aspects of the convent and what it would and would not comprise. We discussed the way in which the nuns should set up their days, when they should be required to say prayers and when not. What their mode of dress should be and even what they should eat. Again, because this was the first of such liberal institutions in Russia, we would have to improvise answers as the problems and issues would arise.

I was happy that I was able to help Ella in her noble work. Louise, Nona and I had spent much time doing charitable works in London and other places where we had lived. However, I never felt that we had accomplished as much as Mama had in Darmstadt; though every charity that I worked for, every hospital visited, made me feel, in some ways, closer to Mama. It was only when I was working and planning with Ella, that I truly felt I was achieving something of importance. How much I still missed Mama after all these years.

Ella, in her new life, was not in attendance the following year at Georgie and Mays' coronation.

It was a grand occasion, on a typically beautiful June day in 1911. Though it was not the custom for the dowager Queen to attend the Coronation Ceremonies and poor Aunt Alix, quite rightly, stayed away, there was quite another reason that her entourage encouraged her to stay away.

She was evidently lamenting, to the embarrassment of

all, that George not Eddy was to be coronated. Poor Eddy! I suppose it should have been his day, and Aunt Alix in her grief and delusion, ignored the sad fact of his demise. However, England was certainly eager enough to forget a prince that would have been ill-qualified to serve as its ruler. Only his Mama, to the discomposure of her court, remembered poor Eddy.

More interesting, as far as I was concerned, was that May and Georgie were the first Imperial Couple to go to India for the Coronation Durbar at Delhi at the end of the Coronation year. The durbar was a time when delegations of Indian Princes and Rajas would pay homage to the representatives of the Queen-Empress or the King-Emperor. However, this would be a far more festive event in that the Imperial Couple would actually attend. With all of the stories that Louis had told me about his fantastical cruise, I could just imagine the opulence with which my cousin and his wife would be received.

It was also paramount, at that point, that a new crown be made—named appropriately enough, The Crown of India. I closed my eyes those winter days of 1911, when Louis and I were freezing in our newest of billets and imagined the bright, sunny days and the warm perfumed nights of the British Raj and the Crown of India in all its magnificence. Now that is something that I would have dearly loved to see.

Closer to home, Louis was not only appointed Georgie's Aide-de-Camp, but also Second Sea Lord. My husband was now one of the top men in the navy—an extraordinary thing—though not surprising because of his unusual capabilities and I wasn't the only one who thought so. I would constantly get notes and letters from the men under his command telling me what an able and fair leader he was—how intelligent, organized, and dedicated to his men.

"I sometimes wonder how far I will actually be able to go," he mused out loud to me one morning just before his promotion.

I was frowning as I looked out the window at our house, the Admiralty House at Sheerness. This was the freezing billet of which I spoke and I must admit that this was not one of my favorite places. I longed to be at the Heiligenberg or even London that winter—at least there I could shut the windows.

During that previous summer, we had had a glorious time. Louis was busy training aeroplane pilots for the navy—his idea and, at the time, an entirely new concept—and I had my first flight in an aeroplane. Dickie and Louise went up with me for a very short flight, but it was incredible. I was temporarily speechless as we soared through the clouds, seemingly being carried on a pillow of wind. I ventured to look down and though we were not very high up, it was a revelation. The fields below, dotted as they were by grazing animals, looked like ants and the proverbial patchwork quilt. Dickie and Louise were laughing and screaming as we sat cramped in the small quarters allotted to passengers. I could not utter a single syllable.

So this is what God sees, I remember thinking.

That summer may have been glorious, but this winter was horrid. It was cold and damp and we were obliged to keep our windows open lest they shatter. It happened that there were gunnery defenses nearby who were constantly firing. It would not do to have the windows closed. Therefore, it was extremely noisy as well as being icy.

"Well, I hope that wherever it is, it's out of here," I drew in my breath as I shivered, pulling my shawl closer around me.

"Poor, darling," he laughed and then sneezed.

"This weather isn't doing you any good either—oh, for Malta or Greece or some other warm and beautiful isle!" I moaned.

Louis laughed again.

"I agree—much as I love England, I would prefer not to be here during the winters. They are pretty awful."

"I suppose we should look on the bright side—we could be in Tsarskoye Selo, completely blanketed with snow," I chirped brightly.

I had been in Russia in the summer after Georgie's coronation in order to attend Olga's coming out ball at Livadia. Nicky and Alicky had rebuilt the palace on the Black Sea and it was one of the most beautiful and restful places I had ever seen. It was not ornate and grand like the palaces of Tsarskoye Selo or Peterhof and any number of other Russian palaces; rather, it was built in the style of an Italian country villa, bright, sunny, with a restful, friendly and completely casual air about it that made it the perfect vacation spot. All of Russia's troubles, which were escalating, could be forgotten at that most tranquil of homes.

"Yes, but at least at Tsarskoye Selo, we can close the windows," and we both laughed.

I poured us both some more tea.

"What do you mean how far you can actually go?" I asked as my hands gratefully embraced a steaming hot teacup, willing my mind not to dwell on Russia and its problems.

"I don't think it's an unrealistic goal for me to want to eventually be First Sea Lord, do you?"

"Of course not, Louis, it's obvious that's exactly where you're heading. Doesn't Admiral Fisher think so?" I asked, naming one of Louis' closest and most powerful friends at the Admiralty.

"The Admiralty loves our connections with the royal houses on the continent. They are grateful for all the reports I write to them detailing Willy and Henry's blatherings about the Prussian navy and strategies and everything else the two of them can think of to brag about."

I hadn't known that Louis was so annoyed about this subject. I realized that he hadn't loved spying on his cousin and brother-in-law, but I didn't know that he disliked them so.

"Henry's not a bad sort," I said weakly. It seemed that many in our family spent much time defending Irène's husband.

"I don't dislike Henry in fact, I can stand the fellow pretty well when we are talking about our voyages and the navy and such. I just dislike the position I'm in at the moment. When we visit, they take great delight in showing me everything. Then when I return, I report dutifully to Naval Intelligence—do you think they're really stupid enough to think that I am not reporting to Naval Intelligence?"

I had no answer. It certainly would have occurred to me, however, I wasn't the pompous, braggart Emperor of Germany.

"I just wonder when they're going to decide that my relationship with the Germans is a touch awkward for one and all."

"Louis, they know you well enough to know just exactly where your loyalties will always lie. Good heavens, you've been a British subject since you were fourteen years old. I can't imagine they would think differently. It's enough that Georgie and Winston believe in you implicitly," I said, naming the man currently heading up the Admiralty, Mr. Winston Churchill.

"I just wonder whether Winston and Georgie will back me up when some of my enemies decide that I am secretly working with Willy to undermine the entire British Navy."

"That's ridiculous. How could they think that? I'm astonished that you could doubt for a moment how everyone feels about you at the Admiralty, after all these years. Louis, I had no idea you lacked confidence in this matter," I said positively.

He looked hurt and put down his teacup.

I was looking at his face and realized with a shock that Louis was fifty-seven years old. Though he was still a very handsome man, he was not the man I always pictured in my mind's eye as my husband. That picture was the heroically handsome young Louis that I and all the ladies saw in those early days. Now I was looking at a man, vigorous still, but, older. I had to readjust my thinking. Never mind that I could never recognize the woman in the mirror. Certainly, I was never a beauty, but now I, too, was getting older. I was older than Mama had been when she died and that was an extremely sobering thought. The thing is that as I got older, I truly think I got better looking. That wasn't bragging, but I look at pictures of me in those first several decades of the century and I must admit I began to look like a rather elegant and dignified older woman. I am not sure where the elegance came from as I was just as heedless as ever about my hair and dress.

"The problem is that I have as many enemies as friends, and they don't play fair. They will accuse me of being pro-German when push comes to shove, no matter how much we all protest otherwise."

"If it's just because you have German family? Well, so

does Georgie, have you thought of that? Accusing you of disloyalty will be like accusing Georgie and May and just about everyone else in family of disloyalty. It's nothing that Lambton, Beresford and the others want to start, they would be completely over their heads," I asserted, naming some of the gentleman who were always opposed to Louis.

Louis sighed.

"Just don't be surprised if you hear opposition in the Admiralty when I'm in line for any further promotion."

"Darling, there's always been opposition at the Admiralty when you've been promoted—now is not the time to let it start bothering you—"

"We are doing our damndest to get the navy in a state of readiness, and we have a lot of opposition, by some of the reactionaries."

I knew he was talking about the aforementioned Beresford and Admiral Lambton, men who had become Louis' enemies quite some time ago. They were both of the group that opposed progress in the navy and resented those who pushed for it. They were also of the group who were so xenophobic, that they would kick harmless dachshunds on the streets to express their anti-German sentiments.

Louis' friend, Admiral Fisher, may have worried when we went to Germany, but he also was concerned when we visited the Greek Royal Family at Mon Repos, on the island of Corfu. Sophie and Tino were thought to be pro-German, though, actually, nothing could have been further from the truth. Sophie was very pro-British, a feeling she inherited from her mother, my Aunt Vicky. Tino, whose aunts were on the thrones of England, and Russia, was solidly neutral.

It was strange that Fisher worried, since Louis continued to gather intelligence on these visits. Nevertheless, Louis' enemies evidently wanted to misunderstand. As Louis predicted, they made much of our junketings to the continent and even made insulting remarks when Louis went to his brother-in-law, Gustav of Erbach-Schöenburg's, funeral.

When Churchill became head of the Admiralty, there was great consternation in the camp of Louis' enemies. Winston was a great admirer of Fisher, and, therefore, extremely well disposed towards Louis. Again, snide comments issued forth about the possibility of having a German as the First Sea Lord. The newspapers, always eager for slander, published these innuendos. Louis never answered these calumnies. He simply continued his work, hoping that it would, in the end, speak for itself.

As we edged nearer and nearer the precipice of catastrophe, our conversation at Sheerness would come back to haunt me—dozens of times. Our visits, however, didn't cease. In hindsight, perhaps we were indiscreet. Perhaps we should have stayed at home, but, how could I know that such hysteria would come at the beginning of the war? How could I have predicted that I and, in a way, the Royal Family, itself, would be victims of that hysteria?

The following year, I went, with Nona, Dickie and Louise, my boon companions, to visit Ella. I was so eager to see my sisters and most interested in the progress of Ella's convent. Interestingly, we stayed at the convent, living the lives of the ascetics. It was quite a sobering experience to a fairly nonreligious person. I believed in the basic tenets of Christianity, celebrated holidays and went to church regularly. However, it is quite a different thing to live with your religion constantly. I could never actively participate in such a life; I supposed I was just too worldly. However, I truly admired Ella and later, my own daughter Alice, for being able to do so.

We lived quietly for several weeks, touring the facilities, and observing the lives of the nuns. None worked harder than my sister. I found it difficult to realize that this was the same woman, covered with jewels who had made such a splash in St. Petersburg society all those years ago; the same woman who would actually change outfits during the evening of a ball simply to astonish her guests. I hardly recognized her, but, nevertheless, I was not surprised in the direction her life had taken.

"Alicky is very angry with me," she said to me in one of our first conversations. It was hard for me to get used to Ella this way, with a wimple and a veil and I had a tendency to stare which amused her. She'd say, "It's just me, Vicky," and I'd be embarrassed.

I looked at her questioningly and she continued.

"Father Gregory is a terribly malignant influence.

Alicky is convinced that he stops Alexei's bleeding. There's nothing anyone can say that can convince her otherwise."

"Surely she doesn't think..."

Ella raised her eyebrows.

"Does she not? You remember how she was as a child? That love of the mystical...; have you any idea what she did, trying to ensure the birth of a male heir?"

I certainly had. Alicky had consulted any number of holy men, soothsayers and self-proclaimed prophets, endeavoring to make this possible. It was the Montenegrin Grand Duchesses, who brought Father Gregory Rasputin to the Court. There didn't seem very much holy about this strange creature. He was dirty, licentious and a complete hedonist, what the Russians called a "starets"—an itinerant and ignorant holy man, who had no official orders.

But, for what seemed at the time an unexplained reason, he had the power to alleviate Alexei's sufferings. To a mother riddled with guilt, as Alicky was, this was a man truly sent by God, and no one could say nay. And, if they dared to object, well, they were sent away, exiled, and reviled by my sister.

"I was asked by the family to try to talk Alicky into ridding herself of this man. I tried to tell her how everything he does scandalizes society—the debauchery, the—" she paused, a look of revulsion on her face. "...and she answered me quite firmly that everything society does scandalizes her—though I can't say that I disagree," her voice trailed off.

I knew that she was thinking of the disreputable lives of the Grand Dukes; the marriages to divorcées that Ella looked upon as adulterous, and the complete disregard most Romanovs had for duty.

"You know, of course," she began, "that Gregory believes that he can only be saved—purified—through excessive sinning and depravity and so it has become his mission in life to live as base an existence as possible."

I had heard of these things, but was only completely convinced of their veracity when my sister spoke of them to me.

"He spends his time in drunken orgies, seducing women, and granting favors with his great influence. Do you know he noises it around that he would love to meet and seduce little Irina?"

"No!" I was aghast. Irina was Nicky's sister Xenia's daughter. She was married to Prince Felix Yussopov, a special friend of Ella's.

"Yes, he has been that bold."

She rose and began to pace the floor of the tiny sitting room she allowed herself. I could see that she was in great mental distress.

"I told Alicky these things, thinking she would be as shocked as you and I are—as we all are—but it's no use, Vicky. She will hear nothing against Gregory Efemovich...nothing. In fact, she asked me to leave her presence. It was a true dismissal."

"That can't be," I breathed. "We're sisters. Nothing, certainly no dirty deviant could ever come between us."

"It has and I'm at a loss as to what I should do next. Alicky won't see me or listen to anyone else in the family and Nicky condones this. I always knew that he was gentle and compliant, surely not the most ideal of autocratic rulers, but I had no idea how much Alicky twisted him around her finger. It is beyond good sense. This can only have tragic consequences—there is still a great deal of unrest in this country."

I knew that, everyone who read a newspaper or was interested in politics knew that—it had always been this way. Exiled leaders were continually trying to stir up Russia to rise against its nearly three hundred year old royal family. Many different parties with many different beliefs, meeting in England and Switzerland and countless other places were waiting for their chance to rid Russia of the Romanovs—most likely to their own advantage. It was frightening.

"I'm afraid for Alicky, really I am."

She was not afraid for herself—Ella never could be, even when the worst happened. She had the purest faith of any human being I've ever met. Nevertheless, I had no idea what to say to my sister. I had always had a bad feeling about Russia, certainly no need to go through all of that again. Grandmama, dearest Grandmama— perhaps she'd want to give Alicky a good "skelping." But, no, Alicky was one of her dearest girls and she would have

461

found a better way to talk reason to her. It was at times like this that I missed her wisdom and good sense. And, it was at times like this when I felt that she was really gone and only a void was left.

"So, she will not listen to you," I said, finally, quietly.

"It appears not," Ella answered, tears in her eyes.

She sat down and took out her handkerchief. She dabbed at her eyes and then took a deep breath.

"There is something else, Vicky."

I nodded and waited.

"I must tell you some things—only you—before I will really be at peace with this new life I have chosen."

She paused and I could see tears forming in her eyes once again.

"Dearest," I took her hand, gently. "What is it?"

She looked out the window and then dabbed at her eyes again. She sniffed like a little girl and I squeezed her hand.

"Do you remember, a very long time ago, that you asked me what I saw in Serge?"

Where on earth had this come from?

"Yes," I replied, faintly.

"Don't be distressed, dear, I really must tell you these things. It's like a confessional for me. It will only do good."

I nodded again.

"At the time, I suppose, I saw what I wanted to see; a tall, slim, handsome young man, who was religious, and extremely devoted to me. He seemed lost, especially after

Uncle Alexander and Aunt Marie died and he seemed so angry at the way Uncle Alexander died...."

"Yes, it was awful."

"Everyone thought that Serge and I were happy, the perfect couple. You remember how upset I got, oh, years ago, when there were rumors to the contrary."

"Dearest, this will be too painful; you mustn't tell me anything you don't want to tell...."

"But that's just it, I do want to tell you. Serge was not the man I had thought him to be—he wasn't...he couldn't...he loved me, yes—but like a thing," I recoiled, "perhaps a sister, or probably more accurately, like a daughter."

"A daughter?"

"Serge just wasn't interested in—well, having a wife. He loved me, I suppose, but not in that way."

I must have continued to look blank.

"...oh, good heavens, Vicky, I'm trying to tell you that our marriage was a sham. If you've wondered why I didn't have children, wonder no more."

I was staring at her, again, blankly, because a ghost of a smile came to her lips.

"Don't be so shocked, dearest; at this point in our lives I expect you've heard a lot worse than this. The reason I wanted to tell you, is that I didn't want you to think that I hadn't seen his peculiarities—that I wasn't aware of his cruelties and the unfeeling way that he treated others. I knew of it—only too well. That was why it was such a puzzle that he became so devoted to Marie and Dimitri—not that I begrudged the poor orphans someone's love. I really, in my heart, didn't. But, I wondered—could he be capable of a normal fatherly relationship with them—I worried."

"Ella, why didn't you tell me this? That must have been quite frightening for you. Louis and I suspected something, but you've been so quiet all these years. You've given the facade of a happy couple—why couldn't you have unburdened yourself to me?"

She paused for a moment.

"Perhaps because I didn't want you to say 'I told you so.'"

"You don't mean that." Such a thing was so completely out of character for me to say and for her to think.

"Well, you are incredibly outspoken." I winced and she took my hand. "No, dearest, I don't suppose I do mean that. However, this is a confessional, isn't it, and I wanted to tell you everything—even my most evil thoughts."

I looked at her for a moment. I didn't know what to say to her. That my dearest sister had to be in the presence of such an unhappy and perverted man for so long—and that she hadn't told me—it wasn't to be borne. Once again Grandmama had been so right and the rest of us had been dangerously obtuse.

"Dearest Ella, I don't know what to say. I hate it that you felt that you couldn't confide in me."

"Don't hate it—I suppose I really could have, perhaps I

didn't need to do so as much as I do now. There are some things that one just cannot tell a priest. You are strong, you can bear it and you'll forgive me for not telling you, oh, years ago."

"Of course I do, it's just the fact that you've had to bear this all on your own for all these years. I wish your pride hadn't got in the way."

There were so many conflicting thoughts running through my head—anger at myself, at Serge, compassion for Ella, the feeling of helplessness. It was Ella's turn to squeeze my hand.

"But, I do feel better now that I've told you. I always felt," she continued, "that living in that marriage was my duty."

I embraced her and thought about that remark. "Her duty..." At the time I thought it extremely Victorian of her, but later, I used it as a model for myself.

"I wish you had remarried."

"No, no, I don't—not now—I'm perfectly content with my convent. More than content—I've never been so happy—so fulfilled." She smiled at me. I hoped that she was telling me the truth—at last.

I tried to believe her, but this conversation troubled me greatly. It was one of the absolutes of my life torn down before my eyes. I wondered which ones would follow.

What Ella had told me about Alicky and Rasputin continued to plague me throughout the rest of my visit. When I went to Alicky for several weeks at Peterhof, the specter of it rose again.

"I just don't understand," she complained, as we sat together in her boudoir. The afternoon was warm and I could hear the children playing outside. I hid a smile as I saw Louise and Olga, very grownup, joining the fun. Olga was becoming something like Louise, practical, fun loving and slightly rebellious. "Father Gregory assuages Alexei's misery and suffering. The pain he goes through is immense, Victoria, you can't even imagine," she paused, and looked outside. "He is sent to me by God. I don't know why Ella can't comprehend this. And she calls herself a religious person...."

I watched her daintily dab her forehead with lavender water. The heat seemed to affect all of her. Her sciatica would flare up and her head would ache. I knew this was a subject headed for problems. I didn't want her to dismiss me as she had Ella, for I hoped at some point she might realize that she needed me—and that I could be of some use.

"Dearest, you mustn't ascribe to Ella anything but the purest motives," I ventured, trying to pick and choose the right words; the words that would convince her that my concern was only for her.

"What do you mean?"

"Simply this, Alicky—we weren't raised this way—we weren't raised to believe in magic and superstition."

"Are you saying religious faith is superstition? I wouldn't have thought that of even such a godless person as yourself, Victoria."

I fought against retorting angrily against such an ignorant supposition. However, it would not serve any purpose.

"Alicky, I certainly don't believe that true faith is superstition, but I believe, like Mama, like Grandmama, that there are many ways to look at something."

"Are you doing this because Ella asked you to?" she asked coldly and I began to think I was seconds away from being dismissed.

"No, of course not—I've wanted to speak to you about this for a long time. I have felt that perhaps you would wish to discuss this with someone you could trust. Someone without ulterior motives—I only care about you and Nicky and the children."

Her face softened at the mention of her family and it made me realize the route I must take.

"You love Russia very much, don't you?"

She nodded.

"I believe that the Russian Tsar and Tsarina consider themselves the Father and Mother of their peoples—am I not correct?"

"Yes, the peasants call me 'Matuschka'—that means little mother."

I understood that from my limited Russian. I also knew that this was the title that Alicky loved most of all her titles and designations. She and Nicky had considered themselves very in touch with the people of Russia. I saw no evidence of this, but, perhaps I just wasn't there enough to understand it.

"Alicky, you are the Mother of All the Russias and all the Russians."

"Yes," and she got that transformed look on her face.

"Darling, you must remember that being that mother is a greater thing that being Alicky, mother of Alexis and Olga and the rest."

"What do you mean?"

"I mean that you must think of all your children now, not just Alexis—"

She continued to have that transfigured look. She actually appeared to pondering what I was saying.

"There may come a time when they will need you, darling, and you must be wise. You must think about all of your family."

She nodded slowly, and took my hand.

"Victoria it's so good to have you here—it's like having Grandmama and the English Family here—sometimes I miss her dreadfully, don't you?"

"Every day."

She smiled and it was not the tight-lipped smile I had often seen on her. It was a tender and nostalgic one.

"I will think about what you have said," she murmured gently.

I decided to leave it alone—and for a while, my conversation with Alicky had beneficial effects. For a small amount of time, she stepped away from Rasputin.

Unfortunately, it didn't last long.

I sometimes blamed myself. I would ask why I hadn't

talked more sense into her? I had always been a fearless child, and I hoped that I was that way, within reason, as an adult. However, blind faith that flew in the face of reason, good judgment—*that* I feared; that I couldn't understand. When it came to trying to dissuade Alicky from her faith in Rasputin a second time, I wasn't willing to face her wrath, and in that, I was a coward.

CHAPTER NINETEEN

I
London and Sandringham, Winter 1912

Usually, in the summer, I visited Alice at the family's lovely summer home, Tatoi just outside of Athens. It was a peaceful villa and was the place Alice loved most in Greece. However, this year, Greece continued to have troubles that were rapidly becoming chronic. Between 1912 and 1913, she fought a series of wars called the First and Second Balkan wars. Without trying to understand much about an extremely complicated and bewildering situation, it was all fought essentially for territorial expansion.

Macedonia, which had previously belonged to the Turks was now wanted by many countries, including my old friend, Bulgaria, as well as Serbia and Greece. The first battles in 1912 were between Turkey, whose

Ottoman Empire was dying, yet still limping painfully along and the aforementioned countries. The following year, Greece and Serbia fought Bulgaria. The outcome after both wars was the Treaty of Bucharest. Greece greatly expanded, adding the southern part of Macedonia, some of the Aegean Islands and Crete.

Naturally, during this troublesome period, I worried constantly about Alice and the girls. Andrew was at the front in Turkey, which, in itself was frightening. I sent Nona, upon her request, to Greece in order to help Alice. There, true to our family inclinations, she was working and organizing hospital facilities. Nona wrote me that the atmosphere in Athens was one of high exhilaration—typical of wartime exuberance. I remembered the words of my guide, the young student, Pavlos and his attitude towards the Royal Family. The Greeks would no doubt rid themselves of their current rulers if all did not go well—the Family just wasn't that well-entrenched and the Greeks weren't that attached.

Things didn't quiet down much for Alice as 1912 wound down. However, I was, at least, calm at this point. In December, Louis was appointed First Sea Lord, despite the grumblings of his critics. I remember that particular Christmas so vividly. We had all gone to Georgie's sprawling residence, Sandringham. It was a lovely, white Christmas—not grey and nasty, but snowy, as we all loved it. We met Irène and Henry there, and it seems to me that this was the last carefree Christmas we all spent together before the war. I missed not having Alice and her family with us, but Dickie, Georgie and Louise attended the festivities and I contented myself with that.

My Georgie was becoming quite a young man now. He was doing well in the navy and well thought of in his own right. He was extremely intelligent and analytical, having graduated fourth in his class at Osborne Naval College. I knew that like his father, he was extremely attractive to women. Nevertheless, he would smile a charming smile and tell me that he had no intentions of marrying for quite some time. He was here, he said, to have fun with his cousins. I was happy that he, like Louise, had a great deal of family feeling.

Sandringham was a large Georgian, edifice, constantly expanded and rebuilt to accommodate the family. In its latest incarnation, it was more gingerbread Victorian house than anything else. I loved the brick facade. It was tremendously homey. It had originally been bought for Uncle Bertie and Aunt Alix when they first married and served as their private country residence. Most of us agreed that it was far cozier than Balmoral—certainly much warmer.

I remember, with great fondness, Uncle Bertie's house parties. They were always invitations worth receiving, as Uncle Bertie was an incredibly fine host. The shooting weekends were always attended by interesting people, not just aristocracy or family, but the intellectuals, the celebrities and the prominent people of the time. I loved them—and was always thrilled when Aunt Alix invited us. Those days of brilliant society were gone. Now, it was the middle-class comfort of Cousins George and May.

The family had our usual festivities before Christmas. The children had a wild and wonderful time helping with tree trimming. We all joined in with the Christmas charades and games. Trying my best to pick them out on the piano, we sang far too many off-key carols and inevitably ate far too much Christmas pudding.

Louis and I spent our late evenings sitting together in front of the roaring fire that I insisted upon in my suite of rooms. I would wait for him to come up after cigars and brandy with the gentlemen. There was a lot of talk about hostilities between the allies and the so-called Triple Alliance of Germany, Austria-Hungary and Italy. Louis often told me that the whole thing made him quite nervous. None of us, with our German ancestry, wanted to fight Germany, he would tell me, but none of us would hesitate if we were called upon to do so.

I remember distinctly that particular night, just before Christmas Eve. I was talking to Irène and smoking my inevitable cigarettes. We were discussing the next spring visit Louis and I would make to their estate in Hemmelmark. We always enjoyed those visits and it usually gave us an opportunity to see the Russian family as well. We talked about the fact that Willy's only daughter, Viktoria Luise, was getting married to Ernst-August of Hannover. That would take place in March. Just another of those royal gatherings Grandmama had sniffed at, but really enjoyed. Then we would leave to spend some time with Henry and Irène. I enjoyed being with Irène. Compared to Alicky and even Ella, she was so calm and restful, with no controversy swirling about her.

Louis opened the door and with a joke that Henry was looking all over for her, Irène bade us both goodnight. Louis watched her leave and shut the door before he sank somewhat painfully into the chair she'd previously occupied. My poor husband, who spent his life at sea, was suffering from rheumatism, periodically aggravated by attacks of lumbago.

"Tired?" I asked, absently stubbing out my cigarette.

"Yes and no. It's a good kind of tired, the kind you get after spending a day at sea."

"Umm," I said, stretching my legs and closing my eyes. I was thinking about getting ready for bed.

"I just had the most extraordinary conversation with Henry and Cousin Georgie."

"Umm." I was thinking about my nice cozy covers, my hot water bottle and the fire that, along with Louis, would warm me the entire night.

"Victoria, I'm very serious. We were the last three left in the drawing room downstairs and Henry asked Georgie what he would do if Germany and Austria attacked France and Russia."

That woke me up with a start.

"What?"

"He sounded like he was reciting the question by heart. It was as though he'd been commissioned by Willy to ask it."

"Ask what?" I wasn't comprehending.

"Pay attention, I'm trying to tell you that Henry informally asked us if England would act if her allies were attacked."

"Attacked by whom?"

"You're being obtuse this evening—by Germany, darling."

I digested that for a second and sat up. This was extraordinary.

"Well, what did Georgie say?"

"He said, and I remember this precisely—'Undoubtedly yes—under certain circumstances'."

"So?"

"That's the amazing thing. Henry seemed pleased by the answer. He left happy."

"Does that mean that he doesn't see any circumstance in which England would intervene?" My sleepy brain was trying to put this together.

"I don't think he meant that at all. But, that is what Henry may take back to Willy."

"But that's ridiculous," I said, light dawning on me. "Irreparable harm could come from such a report—they'll take it as some sort of tacit permission."

"I agree. I just hope that Willy will discuss this with Georgie himself and not rely on second hand reports, even from his own brother."

"I wish that Henry would stay out of politics," I uttered in disgust. "He should stick to tinkering with his gadgets."

Henry was the sort of person who was the first to get some new and different contraption. He loved the idea of steam automobiles and we had many hilarious times riding around in his car with steam and heat engulfing us. That was what Henry was good at—where his talents lay—not in speech making and certainly not in politics.

"Victoria, you're getting carried away. I merely thought his reaction was odd. I don't believe it is the end of the world. It's not as though it's going to happen. They aren't prepared for such an attack—and it isn't the Middle Ages when kings can just order their countries to go to war."

It was not perhaps the end of the world, but it would later seem that way. In addition, I later remembered Louis talking about the German Navy's unpreparedness and wondering whether anyone could be prepared for such eventualities. Sometimes I think that we had prepared all our lives, dreaded all our lives, what ultimately happened.

Henry, indeed, felt that George's reaction was just the one Willy wanted to hear. After conveying this information, in that fateful summer of 1914, he was sent back once more on the same mission. This was only days before the hostilities of the Great War began. I suppose Willy wanted confirmation of the previous talk.

Cousin George told Louis in the strictest confidence, who, naturally, told me, though, very discreetly and only after belligerencies had begun.

476

They had, Louis said, virtually the same conversation they'd had at Sandringham, and again, Louis remembered word for word what Georgie had replied.

"His answer was that he didn't know what 'we shall do, we have no quarrel with anyone and hope we shall remain neutral.' But if Germany declared war on Russia and France joins Russia, then he said we'd be dragged into it. We had to do it, Victoria," he said looking straight at me. "We had to back up our allies. Then he said, at the end, that he and the government would do all they could to prevent a European war—fat lot of good all that does now."

Once again, Louis told me, Henry seemed happy and satisfied with the answer and went back to Willy with the news that George and his government would not act. Naturally this wasn't at all what George said, nor what happened. Most of us wonder until this day why Henry would have made such a misinterpretation of statements that seemed obvious enough. Later on, when poor Henry was implicated in all sorts of nefarious deeds, including being responsible for starting the war (which, of course, was utterly ridiculous), these conversations were brought to light and discussed, it seemed to me, ad infinitum.

It's absurd that Willy had not sought clarification and Henry admitted after the war that he'd misinterpreted George's statements. It seems that he had transmitted to Willy his version of the comments, which seemed an assurance of neutrality, rather than just the hope of it. I know how much Willy trusted Henry, but it seems to me to be poor judgment to accept such important declarations without further clarification.

II
En-route to England from Russia, London Summer–Autumn, 1914

I had to rush home in some panic that August of 1914.

I had been visiting Russia just after the Arch-Duke Franz Ferdinand and his morganatic wife Countess Sophie Chotek were tragically assassinated in Sarajevo. From then on, especially when fighting began on the Western Russian front, I had a frantic, almost manic journey out of Russia until finally via Scandinavia I was able to reach England.

I remember standing at the railing of the boat in the North Sea and thinking back to the last time we all met. It was at the wedding of Viktoria Luise and Ernst August, the same event Irène and I had talked about at Sandringham.

Potsdam, 1913

In March, we all gathered together at the lovely New Palace at Potsdam for the nuptials. There was a feigned amount of camaraderie, all forced, between the Emperors Nicholas and William and George for, by now, it seemed the lines had been drawn and it was only a matter of time.

Indeed, it was the last time all the German Royalties met with their English and Russian cousins and counterparts.

Willy, as usual, was in his element, hosting his family and feeling quite important. Alicky didn't come pleading illness, but dear ineffectual Nicky was there. So, we, sisters couldn't be together at this last meeting of the "Royal Mob." This was between Henry's ill-fated talks with George and we all steered clear of any controversial subjects...which seemed the most intelligent thing to do.

I recall the evening of the ceremony. The bride and groom participated in the traditional torch dance. With pages lining the room with torches, the bride would dance with her father, her father-in-law, then with the other Emperors present that evening. It was beautiful to watch. I gazed about—and later I thought that I was like a cinema camera, giving the audience a panoramic view of the room and all its personalities. I would focus on certain groups and individuals, watching their reactions and imagining their conversations. It was like watching a charade—the pretense that we were a loving family and that nothing whatever was wrong.

I was seated with Auntie Beatrice, who was also perusing the room and reminiscing about the older people there. I was only half-listening to her, as usual, since I enjoyed my own thoughts much more. I saw my Louis talking to Henry and looking naturally quite handsome and even more distinguished as First Sea Lord. I wondered what important things Henry was telling him, since Louis was listening carefully to every word. There was an obvious frown of concentration on his face that told me he was memorizing the conversation. Henry, however, was babbling on fearlessly, as though there were no enemies or problems or battle lines drawn in the world. Louis looked over at me and just very barely smiled, with a raised eyebrow. Thankfully, Naval Intelligence was no longer soliciting such reports from Louis; however, I knew that in this case, in such a gathering, they would expect some kind of accounting.

My eyes moved to Willy, looking overdressed in one of his beloved uniforms, like the groom on a wedding cake. He was talking and talking to Nicky, who was, again, as usual, doing nothing but listening. No doubt Willy was telling Nicky again and again why Russia should never fight Germany. How they should all be friends, allies, cousins and support each other in every eventuality. I could imagine him asking Nicky what he would do if hostilities began and Nicky trying to be clever, which he could never be, answering that it would depend upon where the hostilities began and upon whom.

The reality was that Nicky looked as though he wanted to get away from such bombast and I had a feeling, he was thinking about his Alicky reclining in her Mauve boudoir, his girls going without him to hunt for mushrooms on the grounds of Tsarskoye Selo and poor little Alexis, who had had an extremely severe bleeding episode in Spala that previous winter and had not yet fully recovered.

There was Cousin George, now, having got away from Willy, waltzing around the room with the bride, while May was talking to her dear Aunt Augusta of Mecklenburg-Strelitz, a lady in her eighties. Aunt Augusta was a Cambridge and sister to May's Mama. Poor old soul, she was very unhappy when the war started. It was, as it was for many members of the royal families, so incredibly difficult to have allegiances that were contrary to one's inclination.

Near the punch table, I saw that Willy's six tall sons had gathered together. They were all bon vivants and not averse to getting drunk on any happy occasion. All six would survive the war, though later on, one of the sons, in despair over the defeat of Germany, would commit suicide. Dona's youngest son could not bear to live through the end of the Second Reich and poor Dona, pined away and died probably as a direct result of Joachim's suicide. Willy was obviously incapable of teaching them anything about having a backbone—well, I suppose for that, he would have had to have one himself.

The bride, the new Duchess of Brunswick-Lüneburg, was radiantly happy. This was most definitely one of our family's love matches. Willy hadn't really liked young Ernst August nor the Hannover royal family, since they had refused to bow, even after all these years, to the suzerainty of the Hohenzollerns. In later years, our immediate families would have a connection when her daughter, Frederika married King Paul I of Greece, Sophie and Tino's third son.

My gaze turned to the English part of the family, led by George, May and Auntie Beatrice. Aunt Alix was not present. She still found it hard with big family occasions, though that didn't last. There was Auntie Beatrice's sons, Drino, Leopold, and Maurice—all three looking young and handsome and none, at that point, married. Leopold and Maurice were afflicted with hemophilia and would never marry. Eventually, however, Drino did marry and produce one daughter who had, to say the least, a rather checkered career.

Missy was there, now the Crown Princess of Romania—outrageous and luminous as ever and waltzing over to me. I wonder if she ever thought of those exhilarating rides we had all over Malta—it didn't seem that long ago.

"Ah, Victoria..." she said a little breathlessly, eyes shining, as a servant appeared with glasses of champagne. She smiled graciously at the man and took a glass. "How did he know?"

"How do they ever know?" I muttered.

She didn't hear me, she was in a heightened state of excitement and too busy watching the waltzing couples.

"Your Dickie is getting so tall," she said, as we both watched Louise teasing him. She might have been asking him to dance and he needed persuading.

"Yes," I replied.

"Not happy at the moment, though."

"True, but it's nothing particularly complicated. It's the fact that there isn't anyone his age here that he knows. He's a gregarious boy, but he does prefer his cousins."

"It's too bad Nicky didn't bring the girls—Alix keeps them much too close. The older two are already out and they should be here on family occasions."

I didn't want to agree too vigorously—I was loyal to my sister, but Missy was right.

"You know they all will come to us next June, a visit is planned."

I nodded, Alicky had told me. She liked Missy well enough, but could never forget that she was Ducky's sister.

"We entertain the hope that perhaps Olga and my Carol might enjoy each other's company," she said, delicately.

I had heard from Alicky that there was some kind of matchmaking. She was not particularly pleased nor did she think that Olga would be—but, naturally, she told me, Olga would not be told. That made me slightly uncomfortable because that was not the way things were done in our family—at least we, sisters had not been treated that way. However, one thing was clear—one could never tell Alicky about her children—she always knew best. However, in the end, neither of the young people, having any inclination toward each other, were persuaded in that direction.

Perhaps in this case, however, Alicky was right, at least from what I knew about King Carol of Romania later. He had one of the most chaotic private lives I'd ever heard of. There was his penchant for unsuitable mistresses (Are there any other kind? I would ask myself, but then would think of Madame de Kolemine, who may not have been a suitable wife, but as a mistress, she was ideal.) and the extreme abuse of his immediate family. I should have been glad, but, I can't help but thinking now—at least Olga would have lived.

"She does, perhaps, indulge them too much—keep them too close," I murmured. "Perhaps, it's time for the older pair to begin their own lives."

"My Mama never believed in princesses getting married too late. I believe she thought that we might get some of our own ideas. Not be amenable to the plans of our parents...."

"So she once told me," I said, remembering my conversations with poor Aunt Marie on Malta. How annoying I thought she was then—well, I suppose I did still, she was nearly as opinionated as myself.

"We shall see," Missy said as she put down her glass, and another equerry swept her back onto the dance floor. As always, she had more energy than any two people.

I saw my Louise finally taking Leopold, who was exactly her age, onto the dance floor—it seems she had no luck with Dickie. Leopold was in a gorgeous uniform and had an elegant mustache. He reminded me, a little, of Liko, though with only the echoes of Liko's elegance and beauty. Louise was so outgoing with her family, I wished that she had perhaps chosen a groom from among them— but, whenever I suggested this, she would smile her little

smile and shake her head. I couldn't figure out what
Louise was waiting for—nor did she confide in me.

Dickie, who had time off from Osborne Naval College in
order to attend the wedding, looked bored. What he told
me later confirmed what I had said to Missy. It was
because there was no one there his age and he felt silly
asking any of the older girls to dance. I reminded him that
Louise had wanted a dance and he just looked at me and
smiled. Certainly I was aware, his look implied, that she
was an older girl and his sister. I knew that he was
missing Marie and wishing that she and her sisters had
attended with their father.

Gallantly, Dickie approached me and asked for a
dance. As we whirled around the room, all those dance
lessons having served him well, I told him not to worry,
that we would see the Romanov cousins very soon.

I scanned the room once again for Louis. He once told
me that he never danced at the social affairs that the navy
put on aboard ship. Chivalrously, he explained that he
only wanted to dance with his wife. Then I saw him and he
was looking back at us with a faint smile. I hoped that he
would perhaps tap Dickie's shoulder and cut in, but, as
he told me later, Henry wouldn't stop talking and he
didn't feel patriotic stopping him.

My Georgie, unlike Dickie, was having a wonderful
time flirting with the girls. His cousins were delighted
with him, but, he was not fated to marry one of the family.
He, like Dickie, made a marriage with an incredibly

strong woman. Louis would tell me that they were both looking for women like their mother, but I wasn't so sure. Those ensuing years sapped a lot of my strength.

Russia, 1914

The last summer I had with Alicky and Ella was an idyllic one. Since things were starting to get a little ticklish and Louis wanted me to stay put, I had revised my plans and hadn't intended to do any of my usual traveling. We had heard a great deal of criticism for our constant visits to Hemmelmark, the Heiligenberg, Wolfsgarten and Darmstadt, so it seemed prudent simply not to go anywhere.

Louis and I had our own house now, on the Isle of Wight—Kent House, near Osborne. Aunt Louise and Uncle Lorne had given us this house and we had spent the previous Christmas of 1913 there. I wanted to spend some time redecorating and getting the garden in order— I always loved gardening and was thrilled to finally have a place where I could design the garden and watch it grow.

In addition, we had spent some weeks during the previous summer of 1913 at Wolfsgarten with the entire family. Alice and her brood, Alicky and all hers, back from their Romanian visit, along with Irène, Ernie, even, Ella and myself spent that final summer together as a family. It had been a magical, halcyon summer, framed and beautified now by the fact that it was the last.

I can close my eyes now and hear the shrieks of laughter from all the children, splashing around in the pools and fountains of my brother's verdant estate; Dickie continuing to follow Marie around like a love sick swain and all of Alice's and Ernie's children playing all the games we, Hesse children had played. Sometimes their voices get mixed up, in my mind, with our own—darling Ella's, Irène's and mine. The picture of white dresses, sailor uniforms and hair ribbons flying is constant and timeless in my thoughts—though I can't always make out the faces.

As 1914 was ominously ushered in, Dickie was in Naval College and my Georgie, had been promoted to Lieutenant in the Royal Navy. Louise, who was twenty-five now, was rather at loose ends. She wanted to get away and Louis, who was having mobilization exercises with the Navy, wasn't interested in going anywhere, even if he could.

Louis had finally got his way about conducting these exercises. It was a question of seeing whether this new, modern navy could prepare itself for war in a hair's breadth of time. These exercises were not only important for us to determine our strength, but also for everyone else to take notice—a showing of the flag, as it were. Dickie was thrilled when the cadets were also assigned hammocks on ships and he could serve along with Georgie on his ship the *New Zealand.*

Louis had the difficult choice of either standing down

after exercises were over or keeping the navy fully mobilized. It was, I believe, in July of that year, and many in the upper echelons of the navy wavered. They felt that if they did demobilize that they might be caught completely unprepared, but if they didn't, it would seem like an aggressive gesture. Louis made the decision and we blessed him in later years—we didn't stand down that summer and, were, therefore, ready when the worst happened.

I would have been just as happy to stay at the Isle of Wight. I was having such a good time redecorating my new home and planting my garden. I might have gone to the Mall House in London and worked with my charities and read my books. I always enjoyed going to the opera or theater with Louis, who was increasingly busy at the Admiralty. This would have made me quite content as we all had a nervous "wait and see" attitude as the summer came. Louise, however, insisted that she wanted to visit the Heiligenberg and to see her cousins in Russia. Though I was slightly hesitant about the German destination, I was later glad that we had that last opportunity. Never mind that it may not, as I've said, been the most prudent of trips to make that summer.

When we reached Russia, I found my youngest sister and Ella on somewhat better terms—at least they were speaking to each other. They would never have the same sisterly camaraderie that they had in their youth, Rasputin had ruined it. He had demonstrated on numerous occasions that he really hated Ella. However, she was, at least, no longer uninvited.

I chose to spend that summer touring around the country with Ella. I had always wanted to make such a trip, mostly because there was so much to see in a country the size of Russia and also because I didn't really like spending time in the Court. It was an anxious place, even though at this point Rasputin wasn't there. Nevertheless, the family was for all intents and purposes alienated from Alicky and Nicky. The only people they really saw were Nicky's sisters, Olga and Xenia and Ella and Serge's wards, Dimitri and Marie. Though I was a welcome visitor, I sensed a tenseness in Alicky that was paralyzing. She seemed to be waiting for someone to do or say something that would displease her. There was that thin set of her lips that forbade any opposition. And, there was also the awful fear that poor little Alexis would have yet another bleeding episode.

So, Ella and I, along with Nona and Louise, traveled and had a wonderful time. We took a steamer along the Volga River and made many stops on the way with Ella visiting convents and such, and me visiting sites of less religious interest. I think that Louise and I enjoyed that trip though in retrospect it seems rather ghoulish to have derived any enjoyment from it whatsoever.

I say this because of the morbid coincidence that we actually visited the Urals and Ekaterinburg. We literally drove by the so-called "House of Special Purpose," one of

Nicky and Alickys' last prisons and stopped in the little mining town of Alapayevsk—the site of Ella's imprisonment and death. Naturally, we had no idea at the time, but I remember that the residents thereabouts were not particularly happy to see members of the Royal Family, no matter how distant.

It put me in mind of my feelings of guilt and anger after Alicky and Nickys' Coronation and the incident at Khodynka Field. Though Nicky and Alicky had been as devastated as the rest of us over that incident, they later deluded themselves that no matter what might happen in the big cities or with members of their family, the peasants loved them. There was nothing anyone could say that could persuade them differently and in this more remote part of their country, I could easily see this was not true.

Though Dickie was supposed to join us that month in Russia, I was relieved to get a communication from Louis telling me that Dickie wasn't coming. Later as July was winding down and ultimatums between waiting belligerents flew across the telegraph lines, Louis sent us an urgent telegram that Louise, Nona and I must come home at once. This was the beginning of that frantic journey back to St. Petersburg.

There were several problems on the way. The first and most serious one was that by the beginning of August the British fleets were ordered to commence hostilities towards Germany. I was the most patriotic of British citizens, but I would be less than honest if I didn't say that I experienced great pain when thinking about my beautiful homeland, England, fighting against my once beloved birthplace.

It was agony to think that I must now be enemies with my sister and with my darling brother, Ernie and his family. Poor man, once again, he was being left alone by most of his family. If these were my feelings, I could only imagine what Louis was thinking—being, as he obviously was, a Prince with a German last name and in the thick of things. I knew that my Georgie was at his post with the fleet, but I later learned that Dickie was down from Osborne Naval College so that Louis and Dickie were able to spend those anxious days together.

The next and more immediate problem was that Louise and Nona came down with a particularly virulent form of tonsillitis. Poor dears, they were terribly ill and so miserable. We, nevertheless, had to board the train back to Petersburg and, with Alicky's help there were doctors waiting at every train station to try to help the poor invalids. Thankfully, they finally improved by the time we arrived in St. Petersburg, though they were both extremely weak. I practically had to carry them, as well as the luggage, back to England.

Alicky opened the Winter Palace for us for the short time we were there. It would prove to be my last occasion to see Alicky and my nieces and nephew and I was, in hindsight, at least, grateful to have had that opportunity.

We were met by the British Ambassador, Sir George Buchanan, who would help us arrange our trip home. We were in such a rush and there was little official escort, so, with a great deal of reluctance, I left my jewels in what I thought would be Alicky's safekeeping. I never saw those jewels again, luckily, my pink pearl was not among them—something made me leave my little jewelry case at home. Jewels, however, were the least of my losses.

I remember waving one of my little white lace handkerchiefs in all the chaotic confusion that ensued as the train pulled out of the station. I saw the motorcar in which Alicky and Ella sat. Alicky, stoic as ever, but Ella looked more emotional and more distressed. It was, as I mentioned, good to see them together. I hoped that they would help each other through whatever would come, but I wasn't sure. Today, I have that picture of the car in my memories. That was the last time I saw either of my sisters. It is hard, even now, to contemplate.Our little group continued by rail to the Swedish border, and I remember a particularly odd incident as our train rushed in the direction of the frontier. We were stopped for a few minutes next to another train, with Royal Crests on it, going the opposite direction. I was able to find out that Cousin Minnie, who had been visiting her sister, my Aunt Alix, in England and her daughter Olga, were on that train. I left my train and knocked on the windows of theirs. For a few strange moments we chatted as if we were drinking tea at the Winter Palace. Then, almost simultaneously, our faces fell and I bit my lip. I would not get upset. In those few minutes, I was just barely able to say goodbye, then it was over, I rushed back to the car and our trains slowly departed.

From this train we transferred to another, which traveled to Norway, where we were able to take a ferry that would put us down in Newcastle. As I stood at the railings of the ship, Nona and Louise, still fairly weak, though convalescing, I thought about when we would see our relatives again—my sisters and my brother.

Then something completely uncharacteristic happened—I started to weep.

It wasn't just tears of distress it was a full blown cry. I think I had an inkling then that my world was over. The beautiful summer worlds of Livadia and Wolfsgarten, the sound of children laughing and playing, melding my past and present, my domestic paradise, the scene of my love and youth—the Heiligenberg were all lost to me—if not temporarily, then perhaps for always. The bereavement that I experienced, standing there looking out on the North Sea, was akin to the loss, once again, of Grandmama, for this was the world that she had made. I was glad that there was no one except a few unknown passengers, scattered on the deck, to witness this. I would, as always, try to be the strength of my family, their bulwark and for that I would continue to be the stoic. But, for now, I cried.

Naturally, some of the usual optimists were saying that

the war would be over by Christmas, but most of us knew that was wishful, even foolish thinking. What I didn't know was the disastrous toll these hostilities would have on our family—Grandmama's family. It wasn't just the fatalities, which were devastating enough and which were far beyond anything I could ever have imagined, but even worse, we would, in many cases, loose our names, our lands, our very identities, especially if they sounded German. My immediate family, in the panic and hatred that total war causes, would lose much, much more.

CHAPTER TWENTY

London, October, 1914

"I have resigned," Louis stated to me, bluntly.

It was a cold, blustery evening, near the end of October. Louise, Nona and I had just returned from the Red Cross, where they had both signed up for nursing courses. I might have preferred not to go out on such a night, especially since London was filled to the bursting point with soldiers, but they had insisted. Louise and Nona wanted to go to France as nurses. Neither Louis nor I voiced any objections—they had my blessings and my envy.

I regretted that I couldn't go too, but I had other responsibilities. I had a son in the Navy and another one who was about to enter Dartmouth Naval college. Most would say I was doing my bit, but I never had the feeling it was enough. I did, however, sign up to go to the auxiliary twice a week and visit the hospitals in London. Nevertheless, I was restless and wanted to do something more.

As we entered the house, a woman was being shown out by the butler. She was quite young with a very sad expression as she brushed silently passed me. I could see that she was somewhere in her early thirties and quite a beauty. I looked down the hall at Louis' study. He was standing there rapt, emotional and obviously very sad.

I was puzzled. Louis was certainly not in the habit of entertaining strange ladies in our house, but decided not to mention it until he did. I was very curious, but I knew that it would be best for him to tell me in his own time.

I ordered only tea, since we'd be having supper in an hour, and went into my sitting room. I began re-reading *The Prince* by Machiavelli. Why I was reading this particular book at the time I do not know, except that I had a habit of reading everything I could and re-reading everything that I loved. It seems ironic today as I contemplate it—but perhaps I was trying to understand, not so much Willy, whose mind I never thought so very complex, but some of the men active and retired in the Royal Navy; the men who were now ruining my husband's career after more than forty-six years of dedication. Surely, that was Machiavellian. But no, to truly have been Machiavellian, it would have had to profit the state in some way or other and I could not fathom this.

As I sat thinking, eyes shut, about a passage I had just

read, I heard the door open and Louis entered. Slowly I closed my book and looked at him. I saw the lines of long hours of hard work on his face, as he told me of his decision. But what was worse was the sorrow. Sorrow of this kind was something I only saw at the death of his parents. But, it was a death, the death of his life and the heartfelt dedication that he had given to his country.

The look of numbness and, yes, resignation on his face elicited two unusual emotions. The first was to protect him—this was only unusual because I had never felt particularly protective of Louis. I always knew he could take care of himself, as only a young fourteen-year-old left in the navy of a foreign country could. But there was also helplessness—nothing I could say or do could help him and so I put down my book with trembling hands and looked down.

"What has happened?" I asked in a low voice and he told me.

I was not shocked. I saw with every passing day which way the wind blew and that his resignation might ultimately be the only outcome. So much had happened before that there was only this last indignity to be revealed. Louis, who had been the object of prejudice for most of his career, was now the object of xenophobia from the tabloid press, the clubs and the public.

Digs from writers who hid behind such pseudonyms as John Bull and Bottomly (most appropriate), were becoming a constant in our lives. There were accusations of sending secret signals to German ships and other allegations of allegiance to the "germhuns"—as the press called them. Louis was even accused of being a German spy. He was being blamed for every ship sunk since hostilities began and every man drowned.

There were even whispers that I had talked too much to my sister Irène, who was, after all, Kaiser "Bill's" sister-in-law. Though this made me angry, everyone that counted knew that not only had Louis gathered information from Henry, but I, too, had been able to extract some tidbits from my sister. I wasn't proud of this as a sister but, as a British citizen, I didn't hesitate, either. Today it is easy to understand these fears, for several wars after, cooler heads finally prevail. The measure, I think, of strength, comes when you resist taking the easy solutions and stand by those whose loyalty should never have come into question. But so few people have cool heads in a crisis.

Our butler quietly brought in the tea, briefly interrupting my thoughts. Louis, unusual for him, poured for both of us and then sipped silently.

The whole situation made me doubly angry since we had just recently received the news that Maurice, Liko's son, had died of wounds he had received at Mons. My thoughts and prayers were with poor Auntie, too. After losing a beloved son, she now had to suffer this insult to her husband's family name. And for once, I was glad that Liko wasn't around to see that the sacrifice of his life, for no matter what the personal reasons and that of his son, was completely ignored by people who were determined to smear the Battenberg name.

But, it wasn't just the tabloid press—it was those members of the Admiralty past and present, that had always hated Louis. They had always been jealous of the love Louis' fellow officers had for him and continuously circulated the information that he had German properties, German servants and that his promotions had only been the result of nepotism.

Louis handed his resignation as First Sea Lord to Winston Churchill.

...I have lately been driven to the painful conclusion that at this juncture my birth and parentage have the effect of impairing in some respects my usefulness on the Board of Admiralty....

"I will try not to let this embitter me against the country I love," Louis said quietly.

"I don't know if I could have your stoicism, my dear. It would make me angry that not only was I not appreciated, but I was vilified by the rabble."

"But, as an officer in the Navy, it has never been my intent to be appreciated. I have always just wanted to do my duty and belong. Appreciation wasn't even a part of what I wanted. As for the rabble...I can't believe that you of all people would call the people that."

"Oh, I dare call them that because they are all moral rabble in my mind."

I sighed. It was useless to argue. It would only agitate him more and he was suffering from a great deal of physical pain with the gout that afflicted him on occasion. It was also useless to tell him that there was no one there that could take his place. Indeed, Winston, George and Herbert Asquith, the Prime Minister, had all lamented this fact constantly, though it evidently gave them no more courage to stand firm for Louis.

"Grandmama would have fought for you," I said in a small voice, not wanting to agitate him, but feeling that he needed to know that there were people that would never have let this happen.

He tried to settle his leg in as comfortable a position as possible and I heard a small gasp, as he put his cup down. I had that feeling of protectiveness. I wanted to spare him both the physical and emotional pain, like I would spare my Georgie or Dickie, but I knew that he wouldn't want any fuss, any more than they would.

"Grandmama is no longer here," he said quietly, letting his breath out slowly. "And, unfortunately, there has been so many letters and telegrams saying that it doesn't seem right that a man with a German surname acts as the First Sea Lord—well, everyone had to bow to the pressure. I am just sorry for you and the children..."

"Nonsense," I responded passionately and saw a ghost of a smile appear on his face. "The girls will get through it, as will Georgie," I paused and took his hand. "It's little Dickie that I'm concerned about."

Dickie, indeed, took the resignation extremely hard and hated what he saw as humiliation to Louis. He was inordinately proud of his father and the resignation seemed to take away some of the strong foundations of his life. I had heard that he stood at attention to the flag at Osborne, with tears running down his face. I think, perhaps, this influenced him greatly in his later successes. He was the type that was going to show everyone else that not only was he as good, but he was better. Poor child.

"I went to the palace to see George," he continued, squeezing my hand. "He seemed more angry about the whole thing than I am."

"That's just it, Louis, I wish you were a little angrier about this."

"There's no point. This is part and parcel of the kind of bigotry I've always had to contend with. I'm actually used to it and, at this point, it's for the good of the country not to emphasize. This is going to be a long, drawn-out war. I've seen it coming, as have most of us, for a very long time. I can't see how fighting for my position will make it any better. I'm afraid many families, including our European relatives, will be destroyed."

"I can't think about that—I'm sick about Irène and darling Ernie. I can't help but feel that he will be so lost..."

He looked at me for a moment. I felt rather ashamed that I lamented more for poor Ernie—but he seemed so ineffectual and forlorn and Louis, even at this low point in his life, had never been that.

"George has appointed me to the Privy Council."

I said nothing, just huffed and puffed a little at the consolation prize that George handed my husband.

"He at least wanted to show, as you call it, some appreciation," he laughed, mirthlessly. "David came over while you were gone," he continued when I said nothing.

David, what we called George and May's first son, and the future Edward VIII, would go on to be a very good friend to our Dickie, something like Uncle Bertie was to Louis. I always thought, however, there was a strange loneliness about the man.

"He was very angry about what has occurred. He wanted to assure me that he was against it."

"That was very loyal of him," I remarked.

Yes, David was loyal to his friends, but I never thought he had many real ones—certainly none that could convince him to do his duty. His penchant for married women was well known and I always wonder whether modern psychologists might not say it was because he was looking for a loving mother figure. His father figure had certainly left a lot to be desired. George and May were notoriously shy, never being able to express their love for each other except through letters and unable to show any affection to their children.

This search for love reached its ultimate conclusion with Mrs. Wallis Simpson. David was a man who was utterly without inner resources, according to Dickie and someone who needed constant amusement. That was, indeed, Mrs. Simpson's charm and her forte—she kept him constantly entertained, through his short kingship, abdication and his rather odd existence afterward. It must have been very exhausting for her.

Fortunately for England and for the second time, a younger son proved to be an entirely capable monarch. George VI, whom we also called Bertie, wasn't as intelligent or charismatic as David—but he had several things that David lacked—the ability to concentrate and a fierce devotion to duty that had somehow escaped his brother. The abdication crisis was years in the future at this point, but there was something about David that I could never put my finger on—something sad and desperate and restless. Sadly, I don't think his marriage to Wallis was the answer, though he certainly tried to show the world that he was happy enough.

"Yes, it was good of him," he muttered.

We were both silent, I, trying to master my anger and disgust and Louis, well, I think he was trying to work out what he could live for now. I hoped that his family would be enough, but his career was the frame of his life and now he had lost it. To paraphrase Edward Grey one might say the lights went out of his life, and it was true.

"You may be wondering who that young lady was that left when you arrived."

"If you wish to tell me, you were ever popular with the young ladies," I said, not at all bitterly.

Then he smiled again.

"Dearest, Victoria, it's not what you're thinking."

"I'm not thinking any such thing," I replied defensively—though I was actually glad he thought I was in any way jealous. It was a distraction.

"I decided that, in view of what was going to happen with my career that everyone connected with me closely should know."

I couldn't think what he meant.

"That, my dear, was Jeanne Marie. I arranged to meet her for the very first time. From what I understand, she only learned, perhaps, in the last ten years that I was her father. Lillie, it seems, was posing as her Aunt."

"Dear me," I said inanely. I didn't really know what to say, it was such an about-face and something that I hadn't thought about in donkey's years. Little Jeanne Marie was the one I lamented about on the birth of each of my children and she was, I believe, about thirty three years old at the time.

"Margot Asquith," the wife of the Prime Minister, "informed the girl of this fact—even before she was married. When she found out, she was, she told me, so angry at her mother that they have never really made it up. She has married a very rich young man in society, an Ian Malcolm, who is actually a good friend of Winston's."

It was interesting, but I suppose out of good taste, Winston never invited them when he was inviting us.

"She has four children."

"I'm glad she finally has a regular family."

And I was.

"Poor Lillie—Jeanne is furious with her, but for some odd reason she's not, it appears, angry at me. I suppose that's not really fair to Lillie, but the girl came quite willingly when I sent for her. She didn't even voice any recriminations as to why I had not contacted her before this. Very curious."

"I don't think it's so very curious," I retorted. "She's obviously a very intelligent, well brought-up girl and realizes that doing or saying anything now wouldn't change anything. I am glad I got to see her. She's pretty, though not quite as pretty as our Alice," I said with childish satisfaction.

"She takes after her mother, who was beautiful enough, but I'm glad I was able to do something honorable for her at last. I'd always felt that I hadn't quite done right by her—that I was conveniently sweeping a problem under the rug. My only excuse was that I was young at the time and let my parents tell me what to do." Men have such interesting consciences. I wonder if Louis had ever thought of his daughter all these years. "I wanted her to know this humiliation before the rest of the world found out. If her children know anything about her parentage, I hope she'll explain this all to them."

"Or not," I answered.

I wasn't sure that Jeanne would ever tell her children about Louis, though I felt sure that her husband knew. Naturally, there would be a thousand other ways that the children would eventually find out, there was always someone ready to give out such interesting tidbits.

Since then, I have often thought about her when we've had family gatherings. It wasn't that I was sentimental enough to think that her absence was felt, even by Louis, but the truth remained that I felt, as I had that first day after I delivered Alice, Louis had a child that none of us really knew. It was an unpleasant feeling.

"Louis, I hope that you realize that while you've lost a great deal, you still have a great deal."

I realized, even at the time, how lame that seemed. But, I suppose it was, in a way, the covenant I had made with myself on the ferry from Bergen, Norway. I had my cry and my despair and now I was going to be the rock for my family. No matter what came later and no matter what the cost. In the end, the cost was unbelievably high, but I think, at least, I hope, it was worth it.

The only positive thing to be derived from all of this was that Louis was put on half-pay and we were able to retire together, to our house on the Isle of Wight. It was delightful to be so near Osborne, where I had spent some of my happiest days—it was a place that always reminded me strongly of Grandmama. It was, indeed, probably the most extended time I had ever spent with Louis and it was wonderful, in spite of the reasons for it. We had always known that we had many things in common, but it was all borne out when we lived with such quiet joy together on the island.

Louis loved taking long walks on the shore and I loved gardening. He had also begun to work on his memoirs, though they would only cover up to the time we got married. I think the idea of writing a book about Naval Medals of the World was more his style and it was on this that he preferred to work. Louis had not set out to write something that would keep the reader up at night but, it was, again, a reference that is used until today.

During our evenings before a roaring fire, we would read to each other, peruse the newspapers and talk about the theaters, operas and ballets we would attend on our trips to London. Even in wartime, it seemed, there were plenty of entertainments, had to be, I suppose, for the soldiers swarming all over the city.

We visited there whenever we could, hoping, of course, that we could catch our Georgie on leave or see little Dickie who had graduated from Osborne and now was going to Dartmouth Naval College. We would go to plays and museums for those snatched few hours and talk about the things we loved. Those days were not free of worry about our boys, but were also days that I felt that I was getting to know and love my husband all over again.

Understanding him, I knew that my sailor prince missed the sea more than anything in the world. We sometimes visited Georgie and Dickie at their various postings during that period, and, as they showed their father proudly about, as surely as I could see the pride in their eyes, I could see the longing in his. I remember one particular day, when our Georgie was showing us around the *New Zealand*. He had been invited by Admiral Moore to stay aboard and sail with the ship for a few days. For a moment, there was a light in Louis' eye that had been lost on that awful day in 1914, just a few short months before. But he shook his head and explained that they might have trouble if he was aboard.

That was January 1915 and it was memorable for a very nice reason. We got a telegram that Nona was to be married. Though Louis was in London, I was not, so I was unable to attend the ceremony that united her with Colonel Richard Crichton. It was all terribly romantic, for the Colonel was an officer that she had nursed in France. What made it even happier was that I did not lose Nona. We were often together and even, at a rather impecunious point in our lives, lived in a house that belonged to them— Fishponds at Netley Abbey.

Among my other activities, I continued my correspondences with all my relatives, including Alicky and Ella. I had heard conflicting reports as to whether they were on amiable terms and whether Alicky was heeding her excellent advice. I tended to think that she was not. According to Ella's letters, she was becoming more controlling and if possible, even more convinced of her place in God's plan.

"...I had hoped I would be able to guide her and that she would have trust in God and in me as His instrument. I was so sure that Alicky would be pliable, but, Vicky, I was so wrong. As the war drags on, Alicky believes that Nicky has been sent by God as a savior to Russia and should lead the army. She is constantly pressing him to replace Cousin Nikolasha, while she advises him on government matters at home, including the appointment of ministers. She is no more qualified to do this than little Alexis. I am, once again, not a welcome visitor at the Alexander Palace..."

I received this letter in 1916 and I must admit that it was hardly news to me. In that year, Prince Felix Yussopov and the Grand Duke Dimitri, Ella and Serge's ward were able to assassinate Rasputin. The stories of this murder are ghastly and the time it took to kill the starets inordinate, but I, like many people wished that they had done something about him long before. I had wanted it and yet dreaded it since I am not an advocate of murder. Alicky was, of course, in complete despair. She was further distraught by a letter written by Rasputin that I later learned predicted the downfall and death of the Imperial Family within a very short time, should anything happen to him.

She was quite upset that the nephew of whom she had taken such care, who had lived under her wing as well as Ella's, Dimitri, had been the one to eliminate her direct line to God. She exiled them both, Dimitri and Felix, and in the end, without knowing it, she had done the most compassionate thing she could. Because of this, they were both spared the Bolshevik's murderous execution squads.

So as the war wore on, I worried for all of the Romanovs, though not as much about Ella, because I knew how much the people of Moscow loved her. The climate, even after the death of hated Rasputin, was one of great peril for the family. The talk of revolution was even more outspoken than usual and those same revolutionaries promised a truce with Germany when (not if) they came into power. As time wore on, I heard less and less about the Russian family.

Closer to home for me was the wedding of my son Georgie in November of that year. At a ceremony which took place at the Chapel Royal at St. James's Palace, he married the Countess Nadeja de Torby, the daughter of the Russian Grand Duke Michael Mikhailovich, whom we called Nada.

Miche-Miche, as the Grand Duke was called, had contracted a morganatic union with the daughter of the Duke of Nassau, who happened to be the granddaughter of Pushkin, the great Russian poet. Even with such illustrious antecedents, she was not accepted and therefore, their marriage was spurned at the imperial court. Miche-Miche was exiled and he spent most of his life in Britain. From that moment on, he made it his project to pester Nicky into making his wife an Imperial Highness, which Nicky refused to do. Nevertheless, Miche-Miche continued to lobby for this even when he wrote a rather ludicrous fictional memoir of his life in exile called *Never Say Die*.

From what I understand, Miche-Miche was trying to placate Nicky with the marriage between my son and his daughter. Since he was aware of what great esteem Louis was held by the Tsar, he was certain that his own fortunes might improve by uniting his family to mine. He wrote several letters to Nicky in which he took the opportunity, after describing Nada and Georgie's marriage ceremony, to ask for money. The truth was, Nada and Georgie were quite devoted to one another and it was unseemly that her father was so determined to profit monetarily from the venture.

Because of the climate in wartime London, I did not know my new daughter-in-law very well and would have to wait until well afterward to appreciate her. I was always happy later that Louis seemed to like her very much and was very satisfied with Georgie's choice. She was something of a flamboyant creature, but very sophisticated, which appealed to my intelligent son. She was dark, petite and pretty and I think in the insecure world that Georgie now lived in, she seemed almost family to him and something left of the world before. The marriage seemed rather quick to me and I believe my son was interested in putting his life in order. It was not unusual for men during wartime.

Another issue of great concern to us was the capricious regard the Greeks had for their royal family and what affect that would have on my daughter and her family. King George, the Danish Prince who had been invited to rule, had been assassinated in 1913 at Macedonia. As is often the case with assassins, this man was a cowardly creature who shot poor George in the back. That brought me to Alice and naturally I worried very much about her. In June of 1914, she had what would be her last daughter, Sophie, named, as I understood, after the new Queen, my cousin Sophie. I could almost hear her complaints from here: another girl? Will I be like Aunt Alix and have to have many girls until I have one boy?

But worrying about the sex of a child was insignificant at this point. Greece, or at least its new King Constantine, was very insistent on its remaining neutral. People here in England, the Allies and so forth, thought they ought to declare one way or another. I understand that their Prime Minister, Venizelos, was puzzled by this insistence. The Greeks wanted to fight, and the Allies had promised them lands in the Asia Minor in return for their support. Venizelos went so far as to set up a rival government to Tino's. During this altercation, the beloved summer cottage of the Royal Family, Tatoi, was burnt down by arsonists. Alice told me later that they had all pitched in to fight the flames, but it was no use—Tatoi was lost...the least of their worries.

By 1917, it was recognized by Venizelos that the King was not heeding the will of the people and therefore he must go. Tino, along with his eldest son George who was thought to be pro-German, went into exile. Their second son, Alexander became the next King of Greece, though virtually under house arrest. Alice, I knew, was doing what she could, trying to protect her children and waiting for the pieces to fall where they might. Soon, they had to follow Sophie and Tino into exile in Switzerland. Luckily, that was where Alice and Andrew waited out the war.

Eventually, in September of 1917, I was overjoyed to see my girl. Andrew had elected to stay in Switzerland, but Alice had brought all her beautiful girls with her. Though there was a great deal of resentment against the Greek Royal Family, people just couldn't get it into their heads that they really wanted to remain neutral, happily, this resentment didn't extend to my daughter. So, they were allowed to visit and I had my first opportunity to see Sophie. They came to the Isle of Wight and spent some time with us at Kent Cottage.

"The war seems so far away from us here," Alice said to me in her flat little voice, as we worked in my garden. Working in the island air was becoming quite a pleasant pastime for me. "I worry so for Aunt Ella—but I'm so proud of her. I sometimes think that had things been different with me—if I had stayed single like Louise—that I might have become a nun."

"You do resemble your Aunt Ella in that regard," I answered. "But your first duty is to raise your children, my dear."

"I know," she said distractedly. "I sometimes just don't feel I have the strength."

I found that an odd statement considering how

heroically she had conquered her disabilities as a child. My only guess was that her marriage had not given her the strength that one might hope. The whims and vagaries of the Greece people had buffeted them around for as many years as I could remember and I saw no signs of it stopping. I could only hope that between us, in our family, that we could try to provide the stability that the girls would need as their lives went on.

"Dearest," I said, as I straightened up from pulling a weed and looking at Alice's pale face. "Are you well?"

She didn't look at me.

"I don't know, Mama. Sometimes I get such poundings of my heart and slight pains in my left shoulder and arm."

"You should see a specialist. Remember, Aunt Alicky has heart problems. It could be that you do, too."

She didn't listen to me then. When do children listen to their parents? But eventually, Alice had to go into a sanatorium in Switzerland for heart problems.

"I shall try one more time," she said.

"Try what dear?"

"Well, I do want a boy—so does Andrew, so I think I'll give it another go—maybe it will help."

Alice seemed so distressed and so unsettled. I'm not sure, even today, what she thought having another child would help—though most indications point to her marriage. What had started out to be two young people very much in love was ending up to be two older people with little in common.

"Four girls is rather a lot," I smiled, trying to shake my own unease at her words. "But now that you have them, would you really trade them for boys?"

"Of course not—it's just—well, I do like boys."

This talk of boys did not distract me from the main issue. Her statements made me realize that I ought to talk about some of the anxiety I felt from her. I hesitated, I suppose, because Alice had always seemed to know her mind so clearly. I think it was, perhaps, because of her deafness that she had more time for introspection. She always appeared to me a person who had thought things out and understood herself better than most. But I plowed ahead—I would not have been content with myself in later years if I had not.

"Darling, are you and Andrew—well, are you all right?" That was so typical of my lack of sentimentality that I saw Alice smile.

"Mother, you do get right to the point, don't you?"

"With the way things are these days, I see no reason not to," I replied briskly. "Who knows what country you'll move to next—or what will change. You have a large family—you will need to provide strength for your girls."

I had a right to feel everything was so precarious. To add to our discomfort, Louis and I had also given up our titles. In June of that year, George feeling apprehensive about his own German antecedents renounced all his German names. The Royal Family was no longer of Saxe-Coburg Gotha, but now, Windsor. The Tecks, of whom May,

Queen Mary, was the most illustrious member, now became the Cambridges and Athlones. And, most importantly to me, the Battenbergs were no longer princes or Serene Highnesses, but now became British peers with the name Mountbatten.

It was a strange thing. With all my egalitarian notions and all my socialist and progressive ideas, this upset me. I told myself that it was because of Louis. They had got their title less than sixty years before and now, it was being swept away. Louis became the Marquess of Milford Haven, I was the Marchioness. Milford Haven, it seems, was a town in Wales. Georgie was the Earl of Medina, a river on the Isle of Wight and Louise was Lady Louise Mountbatten, as Dickie was Lord Louis Mountbatten. I even told Nona that I didn't think that the peers would like having us among them, but that was a cover-up. It was just one more nail in Grandmama's coffin. It was one more deed that changed our world beyond recognition.

Sadly, I also gave up my Hessian titles. I didn't really have to, but I thought it would be better to divest myself of any German names. Though, Louis thought this was very noble of me, I didn't feel noble. For the first time, I truly felt alienated from my sisters. I had an awful sense of not belonging to anyone anywhere.

"Oh, Mama," Alice came over to me, interrupting my thoughts, which must have been written all over my face. "Please, don't worry about Andrew and me. We're content with our lives, though we wish we could be back in

Greece. However, the way things are now, I don't think we would be particularly welcome. Once events straighten themselves out, I'm sure our family will feel less vulnerable."

That was an unusual way to put things. Besides, I thought that an invincible family unit would be a bulwark against all negative outside forces. However, for once, I understood that I ought to be silent. My daughter was, after all, thirty-two years old and well capable of taking care of herself.

If we had little news of the Greeks until they came to visit in 1917, we had even less news of Nicky and Alicky as 1916 turned into 1917. Alicky, in some of her last letters, told me that she, Olga and Tatiana were nursing the soldiers and had set up a hospital in the Alexander Palace. I also knew that Ella had opened her doors to the wounded. How I envied them doing such good work. How I had always wished to do so. I believe that Louis' resignation barred us from activity, but more importantly, visibly participating in any war work. Perhaps I was mistaken but I very strongly felt that we should melt in the background, so as not to antagonize anyone. How I wish that was not so, but it was.

Strangely enough, I was able to get some tidbits about Irène. This was through Margaret of Connaught, Daisy, who was my Uncle Arthur's daughter and now married to the Crown Prince Gustav Adolf of Sweden. She became a go-between for our family. It was a way for us to know whether our German relatives were well in all this destruction. That is how I had heard news of Irène during the war—through Daisy.

From the few pieces of mail I received, all seemed well with Irène and her family. Ernie was well too, but hated the war so much that he did not go with the troops, but stayed home and worked in the hospitals. I understand how he felt, but the example to his people was unexceptional.

Louise and Nona had, after some training courses, both gone off to France to nurse the troops. If I hadn't been practically considered an enemy alien, I would have run to do the very same thing. I wanted to help so desperately. Luckily, I was able to visit them in France on several occasions and even walked through the wards with my daughter, comforting where I could, and doing something of which, I believe, my mother would have been proud.

So, we waited.

CHAPTER TWENTY-ONE

I
Kent Cottage, East Cowes, Isle of Wight, August, 1918

So much ended that year, and all endings are something akin to death. At the time, however, I thought it was much worse. It was the death of our purpose and all that made us stand out in the world. It was the end of everything that had made sense to our family.

Oh, the hypocrisy! For years, I had sprouted and sputtered about the uselessness of royalty and the wonders of socialism and progressive thinking. I might not have showed it, but such thoughts dogged me through those later years. The systems I praised to the skies had been the killers of a large slice of my family. And I...? How ashamed I was that I was no longer a princess, but just a commoner amongst other peers. They, at least, had been made so because of their accomplishments: the scientists, the financiers, the industrialists. What had I accomplished to be placed higher than anyone else? My feelings were, to say the least, ambivalent.

These were my silent laments after that awful summer of 1918. I say silent because I never, by a face or gesture shared these gnawing feelings with anyone. For that, at least, I continue to be grateful.

As the world knows, the revolution in Russia came nor was it shocking that it was unbelievably vicious. Certainly, since I had always said that Russia seemed completely immobilized in the past, something like a wolf in a trap, I was not surprised at the ferocity—the utter brutality of it. Having said that, however, how could I have been prepared or even begin to predict the consequences for my family?

Nicky abdicated for himself and Alexis in early 1917. He relinquished the throne in favor of his brother, the Grand Duke Michael, who, several hours later, also abdicated.

That was that.

It was a rather ignominious end for a dynasty that had lasted 304 years. Nevertheless, when I heard the news, I was actually relieved. Nicky and Alix had, neither of them, actually wanted to rule over such a country and now they were finally rid of that responsibility.

They will exile the family, I thought, and they will go to Switzerland, or more likely, England since their inclinations, contrary to propaganda, were for the most part English.

"It is all for the best," I said, rather complacently, to Louis one morning at breakfast. It was end of March and I was thinking of my garden and how it was going to look after all my work; the snap-dragons I'd tied up, the daffodils, the impatia, and alyssium borders—and what English garden would be complete without rose bushes full of bursting buds?

Louis was sipping his coffee without answering me. He had a frown on his face. Usually, I didn't worry about his lack of response; everyone knew that I could chatter endlessly to myself. Louis had spent the last several years with the sound of my voice, though he had learned to combat it with a simple "Shut-up, Victoria." This never offended me, since I knew that I often didn't know when to stop. However, in this case I wanted and needed his verbal agreement.

"I'm not sure you're right about this," he said finally.

I stopped thinking about my garden because I knew deep down what was coming. I'd certainly feared it and thought about it enough times since Ella and Alicky had gone to Russia. Nevertheless, the hearing of it made my heart drop to the floor.

"You don't think they'll just eject them from Russia, do you? Surely we need not worry about them? They're not really in any physical danger...? This is the family of their allies, either English, or if worse comes to worst, German."

Of course I was intelligent enough to know the answers

to these questions, but I suppose I hoped that others would see it differently and persuade me differently. The reality was that I knew very well that the family was hated enough to be treated—well, perhaps the same way that Louis XVI was treated in France. "About Ella..."

"As to Ella," he interrupted, "you've read enough Marx, probably more thoroughly than most of us, to know what he thinks of religion. There are Marxist groups that are agitating to take over Kerensky's provisional government and if they triumph, there will be no room for Ella and her kind in the new order." He sighed and put down his cup. "Kerensky's well-intentioned enough about exiling the family, but he's weak—he simply doesn't have enough support. If the others seize power, they will most certainly cry for blood..."

I gasped even though I knew very well that this was a possibility. I was letting my concern for my family cloud my judgment. I knew better than anyone else that this was not going to be a revolution in the style of America, where a highly literate and fairly well-to-do population was separating from the Mother Country.

"They won't be all right, will they," I said at last, my voice was quiet and trembled slightly.

"I should have thought that was obvious, dearest. They're in for a very difficult time and you may need to prepare yourself."

Louis was not given to exaggerations nor, it seems, did he wish to deceive or even comfort me at this point. His words sent chills down my spine. It was foolish to be optimistic.

As the year wore on, we heard about their house arrest along with those among their household who wished to remain. Willy, of course, made a lot of noise about saving the Hessian princesses, especially the love of his youth. This was hardly helpful. George had offered asylum to the Imperial Family—offered, and then later withdrew that offer. From what I understood, George thought it was bad policy to offer asylum to an autocrat, even if he was an ally and his first cousin. It seemed incredible that they actually tried to deal with the revolutionaries that took over after Kerensky's provisional government fell.

I like to think that had George and May known what the revolutionaries had in store for Nicky and Alicky and especially the children, they would never have withdrawn their offer. However, it is a niggling thought and I cannot be sure, but May always felt that Alicky snubbed her because she was the product of a morganatic union. I don't know that this is true, but it may very well be. Poor May! If that was so, it would seem to me that she later had something unbelievably dreadful on her conscience.

Naturally, Lenin, who had Willy's aid in getting back into Russia after years of exile, had no truck with the Allies. In fact, in November of 1917, he signed a treaty with Willy to end hostilities. So that was it, Russia was out of the war. It had gone from monarchy, to democracy, to socialist paradise, read chaos, in the space of one year and we had no idea what had happened to Alicky and her family or Ella, and no way of finding out. As 1917 turned into 1918, I tried to exert some influence and even tried to talk to Lenin's wife about the whereabouts of my family, but my efforts were met with resounding silence.

One day near the end of the summer, my cousin Marie Louise came to visit us. Marie Louise was the cousin who had had the misfortune of marrying and then being summarily divorced by young Aribert of Anhalt. Marie Louise and her sister Thora had taken a house in London together since they both lived in a state of unwedded bliss. They were, I thought, particularly lucky in that they still had both their Mama and Papa. Yes, Uncle Christian of the glass eye and Aunt Lenchen had celebrated their Golden Wedding Anniversary just several years before. Truthfully, these two ladies lived an interesting and useful life in London, probably far more so than if they were married to princes. I admired their good works, their cultural salons and their courage.

I had invited Marie Louise to spend three weeks with Louis and me—I felt that she would be stimulating company. The war was winding down and Marie Louise spent a lot of time with George and May and could tell us the latest news. We met her at the pier and I noticed that she seemed to be whispering something urgently to Louis. I didn't much pay attention as I was seeing to the luggage and getting Marie Louise's trunks loaded up into the motorcar.

We went quickly back to the cottage and I had expected Marie Louise to be chattering away sixteen to a dozen, but she was curiously silent. When we reached the cottage, Louis gave instructions to the butler as we went in and I was astonished when he asked Pye to take Marie Louise to her room.

"Louis, that was rude, I will show Marie Louise to her room," I hissed as I watched her figure go up the stairs.

"She'll be joining us for tea in an hour. Victoria, please come into the library with me."

Louis looked extremely tense as we entered the room and he shut the door. My Georgie, I thought, something's happened to my Georgie...I tried to get hold of myself and could not stop my hand from trembling.

"Sit down, Victoria and don't say anything until I'm through."

Louis' voice broke and I frowned but held my tongue.

"Marie Louise gave me a letter from Cousin George..." he paused.

"Give it to me," I said, thinking that whatever it contained would be easier to read than for Louis to struggle to tell me.

"No, uh—no. Dearest, I have some very bad news. George writes that Nicky and all the family—I might as well just say it—" he took a ragged breath, "were all shot to death in their prison at Ekaterinburg."

Nicky, I thought, the children would be without a father but they'd survive. Poor Nicky, he said Nicky...but then I stopped. My hand continued to tremble more violently and I watched it with fascination. All the family...?

"Louis, I thought you said all the family but surely that isn't possible, who would shoot children? Who could they get to shoot children?" I asked in a low, hoarse, voice. I heard it calm and measured.

"All the family, the girls, little Alexis, several of the servants...it hardly seems possible..."

I took hold of my hand and looked out the window. Everything was still there, the sun, the garden, the sea out in the horizon and all the same, but how could that be?

"Marie...?"

Poor Dickie, he would cry when he heard about Marie—about all his cousins.

"All."

"All," I repeated quietly.

I began to feel like I was suffocating. I tried to catch my breath but I couldn't. I started to hyperventilate and Louis took my face in his hands. Tears started to run down my face and I tried to shake my head "no," my arms began to flail, but I could not move my head. Louis was holding my head and I couldn't move it.

"Ella?" I croaked as I tried desperately to catch my breath.

"There's no mention of Ella in this letter, darling. We don't know where she is at this point. But you should prepare yourself in that regard too."

I tried to quiet my breathing. This would never do, I had

to control myself and I had made myself a promise. I stopped waving my arms and I slowly took Louis hands off my face, staring off into space and suddenly, my whole body began to tremble violently. He jumped up and got an afghan from one of the couches and began rubbing my shoulders. I drew the afghan around me and began to rock back and forth. I couldn't stop thinking about Nicky and Alicky—those beautiful girls in their sweet white dresses and hair ribbons; that frail, pale, little boy who held the fate of an Empire in his ability to clot blood. It seemed so strange and funny that I began to giggle.

"Shh, shh," Louis held me closely and tightly and rocked with me. After what seemed like an eternity, my tears turned into real crying. I wept and moaned for what seemed like hours, and Louis just held me. Soon, I began to calm down a little. My hands still trembling and my heart was beating painfully. I got up, extricating myself from Louis' arms and paced back and forth.

"We knew that this was coming," I chanted as I walked. "We knew that this would happen. They were foolish and inept—but oh, Alicky—the children..."

I went on this way for a while and then suddenly, looked at my watch.

"I must go up to Marie Louise—we have a guest," I said as though I was clutching onto the anything in life that seemed normal. I couldn't think about it, I decided—if I did, I'd break down completely and really become hysterical. I had to go on—to go on.

"Dearest, I don't think she expects you to exert yourself right now."

I looked at Louis. He had tears in his eyes. This will never do, I thought.

"But I must thank her for coming, and telling me," I said in a strange voice.

I left the room, with Louis' tear-stained face in front of me as I climbed up the stairs. I knocked and entered.

"Victoria," she said a face full of concern. She put out her arms and I went into them. We stood there and I felt somehow better for the moment I was in her strong embrace. I felt tears coming again and didn't want that. I stepped away.

"Marie Louise, I'm so glad you came and brought that letter with you. Thank you."

"I'm so very, very sorry, dear. We are all devastated."

"Poor Ernie," I said in a distracted way. "I wonder if he and Irène know about this."

"I'm sure they don't, unless there was a way for Daisy to let them know."

Dear Daisy, from what I learned, she was copying letters in her own hand so that it wouldn't offend people of either side to see from where the letters truly came. Poor Daisy, she would die in childbirth soon after the war, leaving a husband and five children.

"Come," I said in that same strange voice. "We are having tea in the drawing room."

"Victoria, I must call George. I promised I would when I

was able to tell you the news. He's held it back from the newspapers until you could be told."

How considerate of him, I thought, that would have been a shock—to read such news in the papers.

"There's a phone in the hall, let's go," I replied.

We walked slowly, arm in arm, until the end of the hall where the phone stood on a small table. I handed the receiver to Marie Louise and told her that I would see her down in the drawing room. I walked down the stairs once again. I was watching myself do all these things. It was like someone else was doing them. I was an actor in a play or some kind of improvisation where I was required to do normal things no matter what happened.

I rang for tea and asked the butler to inform Louis that it was being served. Marie Louise and Louis entered at the same time. Their faces were both white and full of concern for me. I had a feeling that they had conferred before coming in and were wondering what they could do to help. I knew there was nothing. I just had to go on and I wanted to go on without discussing what happened.

We drank tea and had sandwiches and cakes. I was amazed that food went into my mouth and that I even tasted it. We engaged in a desultory conversation and avoided the subject completely. As a matter of fact, for the next three weeks while Marie Louise stayed with us, we avoided this topic. When we were through with tea, I asked Marie Louise to come out in the garden with me and I gave her the job of getting rid of weeds, as I cleaned up the rose bushes. And we gardened...and we gardened...sometimes Louis joining us, though I thought it was hard for him with his gout acting up and his joints aching. We talked very little, the subject of Ekaterinburg was never again brought up and we just worked with the soil and the flowers and the green plants.

I slept badly and tossed and turned. Louis woke me several times a night for many nights telling me that I was calling for Alicky and Ella. Sometimes I had nightmares as I pictured the family being herded in a cramped, dingy, cellar and being executed by a firing squad—it was awful seeing the scene run with red. Sometimes I saw all of us, including my little sister May, who had died when Mama had died so long ago, playing with our beautiful doll's house at the New Palace at Darmstadt. That was quite odd since I hardly ever played with dolls, but in these visions, Ella would beckon over with her sweet smile and I would go—just to be with her again. I often woke up with heavy eyes even if I hadn't been up half the night. Louis said that I cried and moaned in my sleep.

Poor Marie Louise—what an awful visit it must have been for her. But she was wonderful and I've never forgotten it. We all simply gardened together and when she left, I hugged her silently. I watched her boat sail away and went back to my house and sat at my desk and wrote her a letter. I thanked her for not talking about my tragedy and I thanked her for spending the time with me, being so splendid, though it must have been difficult and painful for her.

I had letters of condolence from everyone and I had a secret hope. I hoped that somehow Ella would have escaped from all of this. That Ella, with her goodness and her piety, did not kindle the rage of the revolutionaries. That perhaps they left her alone to do her work. So I waited for word.

I watched my garden and as the fall approached my roses had one more bloom. The white ones reminded me of my nieces—especially the ones with a faint blush on the petals. The red ones reminded me of little Alexis. Nicky and Alicky I couldn't think of at all. I was beginning to feel a great deal of anger for the way in which they handled their situation. I hadn't thought my sister was so blind and stupid and I hadn't thought my brother-in-law was that weak—but I knew it, hadn't I? All the Romanovs, I thought, had been criminally ineffectual and I would come to resent, for many years, the ones who were able to escape. Yes, I was extremely angry and I kept on being so for some time. I suppose I had to be—it kept me from being sad and weepy those months.

That fall also brought good news, though it seemed anticlimactic after my disaster. The war was over and armistice was signed in November. With a stroke of the pen, it seemed, more of our world ended until it was barely recognizable. Willy was no longer an Emperor and went quietly and cheerfully into exile in Holland. The grand-nephew of the late Emperor Franz-Joseph of Austria, who had reigned in Austria-Hungary for two years as Emperor Charles, was now also an exile. As for all the Princes, Grand Dukes, Dukes, and Electors in Germany—they were all, including my brother Ernie, finished.

Interestingly enough, Ernie was allowed to stay in Wolfsgarten. He abdicated like the rest and no longer had any real power, but the people seemed to like him, so he kept his land and his title and he and Onor and the children continued, for the most part, just as they always had. Ernie worked with the convalescents and Onor was the benevolent mother figure to the Hessians.

Henry and Irène took up residence in Hemmelmark as though nothing had happened and all was seemingly peaceful once again. Later on, there was the controversy about Henry's misinterpretation of George's words in 1912 and 1914, but outside of that, their lives went on much as before. Both of their surviving boys married, which I was happy about.

Cousin Minnie, Nicky's mother and the Dowager Empress, along with her daughters, Xenia and Olga and their husbands, were eventually permitted to leave Russia. They were spirited away in a British gun boat, which upset me a little. Why, oh, why couldn't they have saved Ella and Alicky. That however, was wasted effort—Ella and Alicky would have never left Russia. Their loyalty was complete.

Ducky and Kyrill were able to escape, even though Kyrill was marching, at least in the beginning of the Revolution, under the red flag. That may explain why he wasn't arrested right away, but finally, he was forced to leave by the skin of his teeth. He and Ducky escaped through Finland and eventually made their way to France. Kyrill announced that he was the Curator of the Romanov throne and Cousin Minnie wouldn't speak to him, much. She refused to believe that Nicky and the family were dead and consequently never felt that he had the right to hold court.

My Cousin Missy continued to be Queen of Romania, but that was because Romania was on the side of the Allies. Tsar Ferdinand, who had become the monarch of Bulgaria after poor Sandro left the country, abdicated in favor of his son Boris and very quietly left the country. Of the others who retained their thrones, there was Alphonso, Ena's husband, though not for much longer and there were the Belgians, the Italians and the Scandinavians. So a continent full of monarchs went out so quietly that hardly anyone noticed.

Our lives, which I had thought ruined by Louis' resignation, were certainly changed—but catastrophe, thank God, did not happen to us as it had my dearest sisters. England was our comfort and stronghold. They might have wanted us to give up our German names, but they seemed to want us very much, as we hadn't been wanted in Europe, especially in the difficult times of the war. We were stability and history and tradition to them and I really feel that they knew it.

Louis and I did our war work by sheltering some of the

wounded and sick men that came to the Isle of Wight. Several of these men convalesced for long periods at our cottage. It was good for Louis, for he was able to advise the men as he had advised his junior officers. They looked up to him and he began to feel useful again. I had learned that there is nothing more important than feeling useful. He kept up with several of these men for years afterwards.

I had another grandchild—Georgie and Nada had a daughter, Tatiana. They, of course, couldn't know at the end of 1917 that Nicky's Tatiana would be killed, but I have always thought, in my own mind, that this child was named after her—even though her life was not destined to be a happy one, either. Poor child, she was severely retarded—Georgie and Nada tried, but there was little they could do with her.

As time passed, I began to think of Alicky and Nicky with a little more charity. My anger began to dissipate and I felt that I had, perhaps, been unfair to them. I missed them both, Nicky and his gentle ways and Alicky, who so much reminded me of my childhood with her rare bursts of humor and her loving kindness to her children. They had not wanted their lot in life. It was their supreme tragedy and Russia's that they had only wanted to be ordinary lovers with an ordinary family life. This would have to be the way I thought of them in the years to come—soft, sepia memories.

I had continued to hold out hope for Ella, but I was to learn several months later that this, too, was futile. Louis and I were told that Ella, along with Grand Duke Serge

Mikhailovich, several Princes and attendants had been murdered in Alapaesk, near Ekaterinburg. How strange and mysterious, my darling Grandmama would have said that we had visited these sites just four years before.

Ella, my darling sister—I know that you met your death with courage and unshakable faith and completely without fear. I know that I would have been a complete coward under the circumstances that I would not learn of until several years later. I wrote to Nona:

> If ever anyone has met death without fear, she would have and her deep and pure faith will have upheld and supported, comforted her in all she has gone through so that the misery poor Alicky will have suffered will not have touched Ella's soul and maybe had she lived, years of solitary suffering would have been her lot, for I have recently heard that all her work in Moscow has been destroyed.

Hindsight provides us with much wisdom, but it seems so unnerving and ironic that Grandmama had never wanted Ella and Alicky to go to Russia. She knew that disaster would come to them there and with all the signs that had taken place during her lifetime I even believe that, sadly, their eventual fates would not have surprised her. I'm just glad she didn't live to see it.

And now, there was no one to call me Vicky.

II
Fishponds, Netley Abbey, 1921

Unfortunately, with all the work I did on that beautiful garden, we had to give up our home at the Isle of Wight. How I missed it and the time that I spent there. I always saw that rose garden in my mind—the white and red roses and the chattering snap-dragons that laughed at me in my grief. Everything, I suppose, goes back to the earth and we go back to it for comfort, but I was still in a state of disquiet. We waited for details about Ella and Alicky and they didn't come.

Closer to home, we were in a slight financial pickle as Louis was no longer able to draw on monies he had invested in a platinum mine in Russia and various properties in Germany. This major part of his fortune was for all intents and purposes gone—and we seemed to be back where we started from, living on his navy half-pay and some of my properties that remained intact. In addition to all these financial losses, we also were compelled to sell the Heiligenberg and with the devastating financial conditions in Germany, didn't get half of what the estate was worth. From a pragmatic point of view, I was miserable about this as I had been about our financial reverses, we wouldn't have our beautiful home to leave to Georgie, but from a sentimental point of view, I wept for the Heiligenberg, the scene of so many of my youthful larks and later, my marital happiness.

Instead, we repaired to a little house on Nona's estate called Fishponds and I was determined to enjoy this time, close as it was to my dear friend and her new husband. I think this move as well as all else that took place, including Louis' retirement from the navy in the beginning of 1919, added to the aging I began to notice in him. Louis was about sixty-five at this point and he looked sad and tired—as he had looked during much of the war. The reverses in the fortunes of our family took their toll on him. A man hates it when he sees his fortunes severely reduced. We lived well, certainly we never starved, but it was nothing like we had before. One cheerful note in our woes was Nada's giving birth to another baby—little David, who would eventually be the Third Marquess of Milford Haven.

We also continued to struggle with the rumors and misinformation that finally began to seep through to us in England about the fate of the Imperial Family and Ella. There were more differing accounts of the events than there were stars in the sky and everyone came forth with a new and miraculous escape or an even grislier version of their sad ends. Later, of course, between Irène, myself and poor Cousin Minnie, now living in exile in Denmark, we would have to contend with all the imposters parading themselves before us. They claimed to be the Grand Duchess Anastasia, or Marie, or Olga, or Tatiana and even, for God's sakes, Alexis, who could have never survived such an ordeal—it was so cruel.

I did a very scaled-down version of what had once been such grand touring to visit family. I visited Ernie and Onor at Wolfsgarten, who were contented with the domestic life and raising their boys, Don and Lu. These two were growing up into nice young men. Visiting Irène was a little harder. Her two surviving boys, as I mentioned, had married. Bobby, the boy who was born without hemophilia, was considering a move to Guatemala or Costa Rica in order to open a coffee plantation.

She and I avoided topics of the war, which was best. We should never agree on those, but we did agree that we missed our sisters. We had both really lost the sister that we had grown up with, she with Alicky and I with Ella, our closest companions and in that loss, we, I think, became closer—but in the end, things would never be the same between Irène and me.

One day, in the beginning of 1920, my telephone rang. I rushed to get it, as I always did and found myself chatting with Auntie Beatrice. We gossiped and talked over things the way we always did until she got to the point of the call.

"Darling, I have been reading one of the illustrated newspapers and there is an entire article about how two coffins are resting in a small chapel in Beijing."

"Beijing—how strange," I murmured, having absolutely no idea what she was talking about.

"It says here that these are the coffins of Grand Duchess Elisabeth Feodorovna and her assistant Sister Barbara."

"What?" I exclaimed.

"Yes, dear, I'm trying to tell you that they have been found. Not alive, unfortunately, but they are in Beijing."

"But how did they get there?" I asked, trying to gather my wits about me. This was one of the odder developments in an otherwise tragic story.

"I shall send you the article, but it seems a Father Seraphim pulled their bodies out of the mine shaft in which they had been pushed...oh, dear, is this too awful? I should just send this..."

"No," I said in my calm actor's voice. "Please, explain what happened."

"Well, it seems, he was able to pull them out and take both the bodies by wagon all the way overland to Beijing China. It says here that the Grand Duchesses' greatest wish was to be buried in Jerusalem."

"Yes, that's true." Ella had often told me that, especially in the later years.

"Well, the man couldn't go any further, so there he and the coffins sit, in Beijing."

"I must go," I said automatically, I must go get Ella.

"Of course you must," Auntie replied, soothingly. "I'll send you the article—it's an extraordinary story...the dear man, how courageous of him to have taken them all that way. Russia is such a chaotic mess right now..."

"Yes," I was nodding slowly, and took the receiver from my ear and stared at it for many seconds. Auntie's voice continued, but I didn't hear it. Ella, I thought, at last I will be able to do as she wished.

I hung up the phone without saying goodbye and went to Louis. He could see that I was determined and agreed with me that we should make all the arrangements, including the financial ones for the burial and set out as soon as possible.

We made inquiries first of all, to find out whether this story was true, however, I was not at all surprised to find that it was. Ella was able to inspire true faith and loyalty and this Father Seraphim was evidently inculcated with the necessary zeal to take Ella wherever she wished to be. Moreover, we would find out that he was determined that she be buried in the proper Christian manner. We were told over and over again, how many of the faithful and most particularly the peasants looked upon Ella as a saint and therefore, there was nothing they wouldn't do.

With the Foreign Office's help, we were able to make all the necessary arrangements. It wasn't as difficult as one would imagine—I suppose it still helped to be a member of the Royal Family. With a series of telegrams, we were able to coordinate arrangements with Father Seraphim, as well. He and two assistants would take the coffins to Suez where we would meet them. From there, we would board a train and go together to Jerusalem.

More telegrams were fired off to Jerusalem, to the Governor and the High Commissioner, Sir Herbert Samuel and we made preparations for the coffins to be interred at the Church of St. Mary Magdalen. It was convenient for us that Palestine, after the finish of the

War was a mandate of the British Empire and thus, accommodations of all sorts were much easier to make.

So, I would finally get to go to Jerusalem—a city I had dreamed about since Ella and Serge had gone for the dedication of the church. How well I remembered her letters to me and how Grandmama and I had envied their progress in the Holy Land. How we could see them landing in the ancient harbor of Jaffa and climbing the Hills of Judea to make their way to Jerusalem.

As the time approached for our departure, I admitted to myself, that in a strange way, I was thrilled with the prospect of this trip even though the reason behind it was naturally distressing. Once again, I would be able go to exotic climes, and once again, I could explore. I saw myself riding a camel, examining an archeological dig and walking through the shouks and marketplaces. I saw myself walking in the footsteps of Jesus on the Via Dolorosa, as I went through all the Stations of the Cross. I saw myself go to Calvary and the Church of the Holy Sepulcher, where He was buried.

For the first time in a very long time, I began to feel revitalized and I think when Louis saw this, he permitted himself to feel this way too. Perhaps this trip would rejuvenate us—and I could escape the terrible loneliness I felt—the feeling that we had no place in this new world.

CHAPTER TWENTY-TWO

Jerusalem, the British Mandate of Palestine, 1921

The act of burying my sister in the city she requested was one of the hardest and saddest tasks I had ever had to do. It therefore seems quite incredible that after this was accomplished, I enjoyed the remainder of the trip as no trip I had enjoyed in a very long time. I would have felt wicked about such an admission (even though it was only to myself), if I couldn't very clearly see Ella shaking her head at me as she had done so many times before, telling to me to relax and enjoy life and try to be as happy as she was.

It was also comforting to know that wherever Ella was, she was, indeed, happy. The complete happiness that goes with the knowledge that one has truly accomplished what one wanted with one's life. If there is any regret in her spirit, which I, to this day, doubt, it would only be that she had not a longer time to do the things she desired and to help the people she loved.

Louise and several others, including Kitty Kaglianinov, Ella's lady-in-waiting from the old days, accompanied us and we spent the first leg of our journey in Italy. I had been there and as much as I loved Italy, I was anxious to be on the cruiser that would take us first to Alexandria.

Egypt in January is perhaps, for a Westerner, the only bearable month. Otherwise, the weather is so hot and humid that the natives, themselves, can hardly stand it. When we arrived in the harbor, one got the impression of unmanageable crowds of people. As our motors took us to our hotel, it seemed to me that it navigated through a roiling sea of humanity that swelled back and forth against our car, like waves. Those waves were people crossing the streets and, it seemed to me, taking their lives in their hands as they ran by and dodged cars.

Louise and Louis were preoccupied—one exhausted after the voyage and one with all the arrangements. Neither of them could be persuaded to walk through the streets with me. But I couldn't stay still and took along a translator, as well as poor Pye. My faithful handmaiden had gamely come along on this exotic journey with us and now accompanied me on my reconnaissance of the city.

I made my way through one shouk after another, seeing the immense poverty and the sense of decay. I had a feeling that this city had not yet entered into the twentieth century. I saw that it was sealed inside an eddy of time that hadn't caught up to the rest of the world.

The strange thing was that it wasn't as if there wasn't

new building going on. The British had been in Alexandria since about 1880 and the city had been the chief port of the British in the Middle East during the War. There was a municipal renewal program going on since the middle of the nineteenth century, according to my translator. How upsetting, though, that the great Library of Alexandria, one of the seven wonders of the ancient world, was destroyed—that would have been a sight to see. However, I suppose, it would require a great deal more renewal and some civic effort to return the city to its previous greatness under the Greeks and Romans.

I cannot say that I regretted leaving Egypt, though I would have loved to have seen Cairo, the great museum and the pyramids. We easily caught our train to Port Said, since it was two hours late and were thrilled when we reached the port to learn that coffins had arrived just hours before. It was quite late when we got there and the coffins had been placed in a small Greek Orthodox Church. Finally, I was able to see Ella again, though it was with great sadness that I only beheld her photograph in a wooden frame, placed on the coffin. Nevertheless, at least now my fears could be put to rest at last. My dearest sister was, in a way, safe and finally on the way to her last destination.

Our train was fitted with luggage compartments that would fit the coffins and all of Father Seraphim's effects and those of his two assistants. This was all arranged by General Allenby, a soldier famous for liberating Palestine from the Turks and who was at this point, British High Commissioner of Egypt.

At the train, we were finally able to meet Father Seraphim. He was a big, bluff, bear of a man with a long beard. He looked like the hearty village priest, who knows something of the world and therefore is perhaps better with his flock than the more acetic types. He came to our cabins to tell us of his experiences since that awful day in 1918.

"I was hidden when the assassins brought the party to the mineshaft at Alapayevsk," he began, through a translator. Neither Louis nor I, with our rudimentary Russian, could have understood the priest without help. "They were taken to Sinyachikha and were made to walk to the mouth of the shaft. Blessed Saint Elisabeth began to sing a hymn in English, I believe called—'Gentle'— 'Light'..."

"'Hail Gentle Light'," I murmured automatically, picturing the scene in my brain. How frightened I would have been, but I knew firmly that Ella was not. There was nothing to frighten her, the pure soul that she was.

"The commander pronounced their sentence of death and selected the Martyred Saint Elisabeth first. I saw her kneel at the edge of the shaft..."

I put my hand in Louis' and could see immediately that his knuckles were getting white under the pressure of my grip. I would not break down—Ella would not want it.

"She said, as our Blessed Savior said, 'Father, forgive

them for they know not what they do'..." he hesitated for a moment.

"Please continue," I said in a voice that I hoped was calm and gentle.

"She was struck unconscious by a rifle and thrown many feet down."

I gasped softly and I think I nearly broke the bones of Louis' hand, but he said nothing. I looked away from the priest so that he would not see a renegade tear that made its way down my face, I so wanted to maintain control. Ella would have been in control—she would have organized everything as I hoped I was doing.

"The rest were dealt with in the same way, except that one of the gentlemen who protested the outrage, was shot before being flung down." We learned later that that had been the Grand Duke Serge Mikhailovich. "I could not come out, much as I wished to, and the soldiers also threw down hand grenades so that though they were mostly alive when they were thrown down, they were mortally wounded by the grenades. When the soldiers left, I could hear them singing hymns down in the shaft. As the early morning dawned the hymns began slowly to die out..."

Later, he told us, when the White Russians were able to take over Alapayevsk, he was able to go down into the shaft with the help of the soldiers and see the state of the bodies. Ella, it seemed, had been trying to care for the others who had survived the fall. She had torn her nun's veil and bandaged their wounds. When she finally succumbed, her hand, he said, had stiffened into the sign of the cross.

"At first I took them to my church in Alapayevsk, but I knew that the Grand Duchess could not stay there long. The Bolsheviks wouldn't care for such occupants in my little sanctuary and they were, unfortunately, coming back, so I had to remove them."

This he was finally able to accomplish about a year later. He told us of his trek eastward and was actually able to get Sister Barbara and Ella on the Trans-Siberian Railway. Later, after many ordeals, he got the coffins on the Chinese Eastern Railway, and eventually made it to the Russian Mission in Beijing. It was here that the *London Illustrated News* got hold of the story and my Auntie Beatrice, useful as ever, had pointed it out to me.

Father Seraphim rose.

"I shall go to be with Saint Elisabeth now," he said quietly and walked back to the little room next to the coffins that was set aside for him.

When he left, I went naturally into Louis' arms and he held me while I tried to collect myself.

"Steady, my dear," he murmured, as I cried, once again.

"I thought I was done with all this crying," I said, thoroughly ashamed of myself.

"Darling, you set too strict standards for yourself. You are allowed to grieve for your sister—sisters and you can shed tears for them—it's as simple as that."

"You are a comfort, Louis," I snuffled, and took a proffered handkerchief from my husband. "Oh, dear," I sighed, moping my face.

Our train reached the Suez Canal that evening and arm in arm, Louis and I leisurely strolled over the bridge to a second train. This one, provided by the Palestine Government, would take us through the Sinai Desert and into Jerusalem. I must admit that it gave me quite a thrill to cross into the desert that Moses and the Children of Israel had wandered for forty years. It was dark as I tried to soak in the marvel of engineering that was the Canal and heard no sounds except the chatter of the porters transferring our bags.

"I know you're trying to take this all in, but it's hard isn't it?" Louis asked taking a long draft on a cheroot he'd lit.

"Yes, I suppose if our purpose was not so awful, I would be more susceptible or at least make much more of an attempt. I wish we could stay and see the canal by daylight. Perhaps I'll feel better tomorrow."

"Unless I miss my guess, you'll be bouncing back by supper."

Cheerful me with my stiff upper lip.

I suppose that was the reputation I had cultivated. I had certainly kept my promise to myself, made at the beginning of the war, but I hope it wasn't becoming a habit. Certainly one doesn't want to make an exhibition of one's self, but it wasn't good to stifle feelings either. They inevitably came back to haunt one.

That night, I couldn't sleep. I watched the quiet and somewhat forbidding desert go by my window. It was quite dark and I could imagine all sorts of shapes and things in the darkness. I even imagined that Ella was telling me about her sad ordeal once again. However, as she told it, it was with an air of someone who had already passed from this world and what had happened simply didn't matter anymore, she was beyond earthly pain.

I'm fine, I imagined her saying. Truly, I am well and happy.

To this day, I don't know whether it was a vision or my very strong desire. I like to think that it was the former.

We reached Jerusalem the following day and were met by representatives of the Colonial Government and the High Commissioner as well as the Russian Orthodox clergymen. The coffins were loaded onto trucks decorated with green ribbons and two priests in black and silver funeral vestments sat with Ella's coffin. We followed in cars provided by the High Commissioner and eventually reached the city itself.

Now modern Jerusalem extends beyond its crusader walls and constant construction seems the order of the day. Unlike the decay I had sensed in Alexandria, I sensed no such thing here. Here, ancient laurels were not rested upon. The Jewish immigrants from Europe were building the western part of Jerusalem into a new and vital city. As we drove through that city, towards the road that skirted the walls of the Old one, I was thrilled to see commerce and the business of living going on here as it would in any other city. Jerusalem, however, was not just any city—anyone could see that.

As our car made its way down the rocky road that led to the Mount of Olives, many of the faithful began following the cars and trucks. They were determined to participate in the funeral of the beautiful Grand Duchess and her dear assistant. We drove to the Church of St. Mary Magdalen, the church that Serge and Ella had dedicated in 1888, and I marveled at the beauty of this edifice, gleaming white in the winter sun. It had five onion domes and if one didn't know better, they could have been in Moscow. Later I was able to see the Latin plaque of dedication with Aunt Marie's name on it. As our cars came to the entrance, there was a bit of a struggle. So many had come for the funeral services being held today, tomorrow and the day after—I was wondering if we'd be able to climb the stairs to the church.

Louis, as usual, took charge in the mob scene. He helped direct the unloading of the coffins and held on to the brass handle of one of them as we climbed the stairs to the entrance of the church. He told me later that there was such a crush, that people were tripping and falling on their faces everywhere.

I was in the back of all this, content to let the coffins get to the place of honor where they would lay throughout these observances. Luckily, with the help of Kitty Kaglianinov, we were able to get up to the church and our seats, which had been, thankfully, reserved for us. It was a long drawn out service with a congregation that flowed out the door and onto the terrace of the church. Just as the services I remembered in Moscow and St. Petersburg, this too had the required chanting and the waving censers full of incense. Luckily, the weather in Jerusalem in the winter is cool and dry and so we did not suffer during the long orders and prayers.

We sat through similar services the next several days and after each one, I was happy just to get back to my hotel and rest. Louis and I refused invitations from the Government House. It seemed like a bad idea to have cocktails and tea dances when we were attending the funeral services of my sister—not that I wanted to. Actually, when it was all finished, I spent the next week doing what I loved, sight-seeing.

Without Louis, who had felt compelled to meet several times with the High Commissioner, Sir Herbert, I was able to explore the old and new cities of Jerusalem to my heart's content. Naturally, I dragged Louise along and sometimes even poor Kitty, but I don't think they minded much. Louise had the same instinct to explore that I did—loved archeology as much as I did—and we went through as many ancient sites as we could.

We did go back to the church, hoping to explore it in a more quiet time. However, it was difficult, because there were still many visitors. Father Seraphim, who had elected to stay at the church with Ella and Sister Barbara, always welcomed me. Louise and I, however, didn't care for the crowds and usually stayed away.

We wandered about the so-called Old City, which was divided up into quarters: Jewish, Moslem, Christian and Armenian. It was a fascinating place. When one stepped into another quarter, the entire character of the place seemed to change. The Arab Shouk in the Moslem quarter was particularly engaging. My guide, Fuad, told me that because the two of us were obviously Westerners, we would be victims of every sharp bargainer in the entire area. I knew that, but I enjoyed myself anyway—coming away with little coffee urns, wooden crosses I was assured were from the original true cross, painted tiles, colorful shawls and little bottles of water from the river Jordan. I'm sure I overpaid, not being a great bargainer, but, though it enraged Fuad, for whom such things were a matter of honor, we were having a marvelous time.

A car took us all over the city and through the Valley of Kidron. One memorable day, Louis came with us and we drove to Bethlehem, where we saw the Church of Nativity in Manger Square. I was thrilled to think that there, in that tiny dark place inside the church, the little family rested when there was no room elsewhere. I would have loved to go to Nazareth, but we didn't have the time and there was so much to see in that area just around Jerusalem.

Eventually, we did have tea with a few friends, who after they had tactfully felt us out, wanted to know what had happened to Ella. Members of the Russian colony came to see us believing we had news of the Imperial Family. They didn't believe the story of the assassination in the cellar and they weren't alone. Cousin Minnie never believed that her son and his family were murdered in this awful fashion. She chose to think that they had somehow survived the ordeal and were hiding somewhere, though where was anyone's guess. She went to her death believing this.

One warm February day, just a few days before we planned to leave, Louis, once again, accompanied me on one of my outings. It was a crisp, clear winter day, just a little warmer, with a few puff clouds in a cerulean blue sky. The contrast between the color of the sky and the golden stone, which was the rudimentary building material of the Old City, was breathtaking.

Fuad had taken us through the shouk with its pungent smells and large fly population. I'd already bought more souvenirs than was my allotment and Louis didn't like being pestered by the shopkeepers. We took a sharp turn out of the main shopping area, and walked towards the Dome of the Rock, also known as the Al Aqsa Mosque.

"This is the very spot where Ibrahim, a prophet of Islam, nearly sacrificed his son Ishmael."

Naturally, we Christians and the Jews believe, as is related in the bible, that it was, in fact Isaac, that was nearly killed by his father, Abraham, in a brave show of faith. I remember the philosopher, Kierkegaard, had called it a "leap of faith." I was awed by such faith—though perhaps I should not have been. It was present in my own family in the person of my sister, Ella.

We went onto the Temple Mount and slowly walked around the golden Dome of the Rock. It was an impressive sight. The earliest mosque, Fuad told us, was built on this site in the seventh century by the Umayyad Califs. Around the dome itself, was a flowing Arabic inscription describing Mohammed's Night Journey. It is said that his very feet were on the rock. I continued to wander around the building, looking at the exquisite tile work, while Louis and Fuad went into the mosque. Since I didn't fancy taking off my shoes or kneeling on the prayer rugs, I left this part of the tour to them. I was incredibly impressed by all the archeological excavations. It seemed that something was being excavated in just about every quarter of the city. There was much to be discovered and I promised myself a tour of the sites before we left.

Louis emerged from the mosque looking a bit stiff as he was shaking out his leg. Fuad suggested tea and Louis and I, gratefully, agreed.

"My uncle has a wonderful café. You can sip mint tea and watch the world go by," he smiled.

He led us through more narrow cobblestone streets to a small café with several tables outside—all occupied. With a few shouted words in Arabic, a new table was brought out, I had to bite my lip to stop from smiling, I was waiting for him to shove occupants out of their seats—

though, he evidently decided to spare us that spectacle. An old man swathed in a kaffiyah and long white robes, completely unimpressed by the commotion, sat at the next table smoking a water pipe. To me, the pipe looked quite intriguing. I wondered what was in it, but Louis shook his head firmly when I wanted to order one.

"God knows what's in that thing."

Whatever it was, the old man looked quite happy.

Fuad's cousin, Mahmoud, placed mint tea and plates of sticky, sweet cakes before us. He asked if we wanted anything else and Louis raised his eyebrow, so I did not ask for a pipe.

"I shall go and talk to my uncle. Tell little Mahmoud when you wish to leave." He smiled and bowed graciously. I had been told the Arabs were famous for their hospitality and the proof was before me.

I sipped my tea and watched the sun, hanging low in the winter sky, just begin to set. I lit a cigarette, having offered one to the old gentleman, who shook his head and smiled—sadly, a nearly toothless grin. I drew on it and let out a slow stream of smoke with a contented sigh.

"It's been a wonderful day."

"Yes, it's quite curious, isn't it? After the initial shock and the period of mourning, I have a sense of contentment bringing Ella here. I loved her dearly, but I can't say I feel sad at the moment."

"I'm glad you feel that way, darling. So do I. I just can't be unhappy thinking about Ella and the fact that we were able to make this happen...her dearest wish—well, I'm happy," I said, and yet tears came to my eyes. "I do miss her dreadfully, though. Next to you, she understood me best. I just wish she'd had the same affect on Alicky," I moaned for the thousandth time.

"Alicky was a troubled and unhappy woman in a situation she hated and at odds with Providence who visited the scourge of hemophilia on her son. I'm not sure she could ever have got over that, even if she had lived. It's not the kind of state of mind that sees reason."

I agreed with Louis's analysis of the situation. It may have been simplistic in the larger picture, but quite right for the private woman.

"Grandmama would have loved all of this. It would have appealed to her sense of the mysterious."

"Yes, that is true. Grandmama was always looking at life's mysteries."

I couldn't imagine what he was referring to unless it was the séances that Grandmama was reputed to have in her effort to contact poor Grandpapa. I was not there, so I don't know if she really did it, but they were along the same lines as the rumors that she and John Brown secretly married. Both, I always felt, were absurd.

"How do you like my sightseeing tours? You've never accompanied me in the past."

"In the past, there had always been work to do—besides you always had your sisters, your brother, your children and your nieces and nephews..." he was ticking them off on his fingers.

"Are you implying that I would have preferred all of them, sisters and brother, nieces and even children, to you?" I was amazed at this revelation.

"Not for the most part, but I always thought that Ella was your closest companion—and that you didn't need me as long as you had her."

He looked away. It was hard for me to believe, but I saw, at that moment, that Louis was just a little jealous of my devotion to my family. I had never seen that before, I was so busy with each and every one of them.

"Darling, that's simply not the case. I had no idea you really felt so neglected." I hadn't thought of this. "Because, you know," I grinned suddenly. "I could say the same thing—I've always been a navy widow."

"I suppose I've felt neglected, that is, well—sometimes...a man wants his wife home when he gets there, not traveling to Russia or Germany."

"Louis, all you had to do is say—I thought that you wanted me occupied since you couldn't be home. I was always jealous of your going to so many interesting places. I still long to go to North America."

"Were you? I did want you occupied, but I wasn't always sure that I had a say in it either way."

"You never asked," I replied bluntly.

"I suppose I didn't. It's just that now—I see how much I've missed."

I was speechless for a moment. Louis never ceased to surprise me.

"Do you know that is the nicest thing you've said to me in a very long time? Well, I suppose it's a little of the pot calling the kettle black, isn't it? But, we have nothing but time now to make up for it, don't we?" I smiled. How I wish I hadn't beguiled fate with that remark.

"Well, the reality is that I'm just trying to give poor Louise a rest—you've been running her ragged," he said attempting levity. He was already trying to get past a heartfelt moment.

"Yes, Louise," I repeated, thinking of my younger daughter, just past thirty now and no wedding in sight. "I don't mind if she wants to be independent, after all, she was a nurse in the war. She saw things you and I can't even imagine. The stories she's told me..."

"You visited her there. Didn't you see it all for yourself, first hand?"

"Not some of what she described. I always had the feeling she was sparing me."

"Maybe, but she's such a wonderful, bright, compassionate young woman. She'd be just right for someone's family."

Someone's family? I wondered what he'd meant.

"I agree. I wish more than anything that she would have one of her own—I don't like to think of her being alone when we are no longer here."

I took Louis's hand and we both sat. The late afternoon was quiet—just the stray donkey cart or bird flying past. I think people were just stirring from their siestas.

"Poor Alexander," I said, apropos of our children.

"Which Alexander?" Louis asked patiently.

"Tino's Alexander," I said, expecting him to follow my train of thought. Sophie and Tino's son, who had been left to rule Greece when Tino and his son and heir, George, went into exile, had died several months before of blood poisoning from a monkey bite.

"Bad luck that, but, Alice writes that the people seem happy with Tino again. She's thrilled about being with child."

I nodded. Even saying "with child" embarrassed him. Men—they never seemed to face reality. Oh well, the Greeks were at it again. They were fighting Turkey and Andrew had applied to be readmitted into the military. Who knew what would happen next.

"I wonder if Alice will finally have her boy," I mused. "She thinks it's awfully bad form that Nada only had one girl before having little David. Louise was asking me what this family was coming to if Nada only has to have one girl to get a boy."

Louis laughed at this nonsense.

"I'm afraid Georgie's not having a particularly easy time."

"Why? Because he married a strong woman? You did, and I don't think that people said that you had a hard time..." he squeezed my hand. "You're just being an indulgent father and Georgie's lazy. He was one of the most brilliant students at Dartmouth and the laziest. I hear that he has the potential to go, perhaps, as far as you did."

"Further," he replied quickly. "He won't have the handicaps I've had."

"You overcame all of them brilliantly."

"So's Georgie," he retorted. Defending his first born—and the boy that looks most like him, I thought. "He's served on the Vice-Admiral's staff and is a gunnery lieutenant. He's far more brilliant than I ever was, but yet he manages to get along much better with his fellow officers. He's just young, Victoria and newly married to a rather difficult young woman."

"Not so newly—Nada's just different. She's very continental, and she's very outspoken."

"Just your type..."

"Well, yes," I admitted. "I've always appreciated an outspoken person—as long as they appreciate that I will be equally so."

"That is usually harder to find, my dear."

I smiled.

"If Georgie can't handle a strong and unconventional young woman," I continued with the subject, "I won't believe that you two ever lived in the same house together."

"Yes, but dear, they're having problems with Tatiana, as you well know."

Little Tatiana, who was just three years old, was already exhibiting the mental problems that would dominate her life. It was eventually decided that she was severely mentally retarded and could never lead a normal life.

"Alice, too, had severe problems. You and I coped with them together."

"Yes, but Alice was, in every other aspect, normal. You're not making allowances, Victoria."

I sighed.

"Perhaps you're right." I took a bite of one of the sticky cakes. I thought a change of subject was in order. "Umm, try one of these cakes, Louis, they're delicious."

He smiled.

"Now if you want to talk about lazy, let's talk about Dickie," he said as he bit into one of the cakes. He made a face. Louis didn't like overly sweet things.

"Dickie's not lazy," I defended my little one. "He's just been through a war, and he's young. He wants to have a little fun, though I'm pleased he's going to Cambridge to do some courses."

"Yes, and in between courses, he seems to be falling in and out of love every day of the week."

"Yes, something like his father and uncles at that age," I smiled and Louis chuckled. "We've discussed that. He knows, as well as you and I do, the difference between infatuation and real abiding love. I don't think we need to worry about him. Also, you know, he isn't quite as brilliant as Georgie and your resignation hit him harder than any of the other children. He didn't like the humiliation for you."

"I know..." he sighed.

"My point in bringing that up again is just to tell you that I think that that and the competition with his brother is going to make him work all that much harder. Adversity and all that..."

"I'm sure you're right," he replied distractedly.

I knew that it was still tough for him to talk about what had happened to his family. When you thought about it, only Franzjos was a Prince of Battenberg now. The rest had died or changed their names. Franzjos and Anna never had any children—so that was it for the dashing Battenbergs.

"Oh, darling, so much has changed—for all of us," I said with a catch in my voice.

"Well, you know how I've always stood for progress, my dear. I've made it no secret in the navy that I wanted to bring her up to the twentieth century."

"...and you did, Louis, never think you didn't. If it weren't for you, I don't know where we would have been when war was declared."

"Winston was a factor, as well, even with all his weekends in the country."

Louis had always complained that the ministers were never available in emergencies because they insisted upon taking their weekends in the country no matter what befell the nation.

"You get letters every day, you know you do, lauding all you've done for the navy—they still haven't found anyone that can really replace you."

"I don't think I could do it now," he said, flexing his shoulder muscles and flinching. His joints ached in this weather just like my circulation gave me problems in the cold. I suppose we were getting on.

We were silent for a few moments and heard the call of the muezzin—'God is great', and I looked around and saw Fuad, his uncle and several of the other gentlemen getting out their prayer rugs and prostrating themselves on the floor. I sipped my cooling tea.

"Do you ever regret not marrying some great prince and being queen of a country?" he asked suddenly.

"I can't imagine you ever asking me a thing like that," I replied. I was puzzled—where had that come from? "Louis, you and I have been married thirty-seven years and I haven't regretted a day of it—even if I don't always say so. You know how Grandmama used to scold me about never being tender. I try so hard..."

He grinned.

"Why did you never do anything with the pink pearl?"

"You know perfectly well that the reason is that I don't want anyone else to see it. It belongs to me..."

"I wonder if the little pearl fisher didn't mean it to be shared. Maybe some of our marital happiness will rub off on a new owner."

"That's sweet of you, darling. But, I shall leave it to Louise, or else, I shall give it to one of my other children or grandchildren who I deem have half as happy a marriage as you and I have had."

"So I suppose that leaves out Alice and Andrew..."

My heart skipped a beat.

"I should never underestimate you, should I? You may not be in the thick of the domestic drama, but you don't seem to be missing much," I hesitated. "I don't know about Alice and Andrew, but, no, they don't seem to me to be the picture of connubial bliss these days. I've always felt it was because of their situation."

"You know that's nonsense."

"True, I suppose they were just too young."

"Now Georgie and Nada..."

"What about them?" I asked, ready to defend Nada.

"I suppose they're just a little unusual—and they have that father of hers constantly looking for money."

"Well, you can't say that Georgie has any of that," I chortled. I, too, was annoyed at the importunities of Miche-Miche. He seemed quite convinced that everyone in the world had money except him and that they were in some way holding out on him. Most disagreeable...

"No, Georgie and Dickie will have to make their way in this world."

"Just like you and your brothers did and I don't see that it warped your characters much, if anything..."

"No and besides, just like me, they'll have several indomitable women at their sides."

"I don't know what you mean."

"Well, I had Grandmama and Mama and they'll have you and Aunties Beatrice, Louise and Lenchen to keep them in line."

I groaned comically and then we both laughed.

"You've forgotten the unfortunate creatures also have two sisters...and not so sweet as your Marie!" I replied, thinking of Louis's sister, who had been living quietly as a widow all these years. She was a dear woman, devoted to her children and her brothers. "Anyhow, I think Georgie and Dickie could do a lot worse."

He leaned over and very uncharacteristic of him in those later years, kissed me. We sat thus for some time and then a voice intervened, "Some more mint tea?"

It was little Mahmoud, evidently done with his prayers. I blushed and we both laughed again.

"Shall we get back? I think Louise is going to need waking up—she looked much too grateful that I had taken on the sightseeing responsibilities this afternoon," Louis rose, and gave Mahmoud several piasters.

"Yes, let's. If necessary, I'll throw water on her. She isn't about to get out of going with us to Sir Herbert's this evening," and we laughed.

Louis had committed us to dinner with Sir Herbert that evening. After all, we had avoided most of the invitations, but Sir Herbert had been so good and so helpful, it didn't seem fair not to spend at least one evening with him.

I remembered that conversation we had in Fuad's uncle's café for many years afterward. The thought of Louis and me, in a little spot in Jerusalem, with our guides at prayer and the sound of camel bells in the air, reviewing our children and our lives never stopped tickling me. It seemed so right and so in character for both of us.

The peacefulness of those moments, however, was no reflection of the years to come. As always, with my numerous family there were many other tragedies and joys to come, to be experienced and to be endured. And in the face of the storms, I and my family were to continue to be buffeted by fate.

CHAPTER TWENTY-THREE

Osborne Bay, Isle of Wight, November, 1923

The sound of the waves breaking against the shore reminded me of the ovation. In fact, it was hard to distinguish between the two sounds. The crashing waves and the clapping of hands—I had never realized that they were so similar. It was freezing cold and my legs felt like blocks of ice. What I was doing watching the ocean at this time of year in this kind of weather, was a puzzle to me. But I sought solitude. It was windy enough that I hardly felt the tears on my face, but they did come. This time, I let them come unchecked—there was no one to see, no need to worry about doing my duty. So much had happened and there was no one here to see my grief.

In June of 1921, my Alice finally had her boy, Philip, born in the family villa at Mon Repos. Alice sent us an elated telegram and Louis and I were thrilled about this latest addition to our family. Boys, as I've said, were precious, though I loved Alice's girls. Alice had wanted this one very badly. Indeed, for a while, things in Alice's family seemed to go well. The children were overjoyed to be in Greece again, Alice had her boy and Andrew was where he so badly wanted to be. We made plans to see little Philip later that year, though things in Greece, as usual, were precarious. We read about the constant fighting with Turkey in the newspapers.

That ovation, though, and a sea of smiling faces, that's what sticks in my mind about that year of 1921. Louis was invited to be the Chair of the Royal Navy Club dinner given in London in July of that year. The dinners were given every year, it seems, to honor the victory of the English Navy over the Spanish Armada. The guest of honor was the current First Sea Lord, Arthur Lee.

Louis was excited about chairing this event. When the invitations went out, he told me happily that fifty or sixty fellow navy men ought to be attending. It was, he said, going to be very good to see them all again. It amazed me that the man had no bitterness towards his fellows in the navy nor it seems towards anyone. I found it just a little too saintly, but resentment wasn't in his personality.

That evening, instead of the fifty or sixty naval men that Louis mentioned, a wonderful thing occurred. In tribute to their beloved admiral, several hundred men attended. We were all amazed and gratified as they streamed into the room. Apparently, when they heard that Louis was the chair for the evening, they came from everywhere to give him honor and acknowledgment.

It was a gala affair full of uniforms and glitter. It was most gladdening to me to see a tremendous amount of retired admirals, officers and many who were still serving. After dinner, Admiral Lee rose, lifted his glass and offered a toast to the chair:

"To Lord Milford Haven—one of the most able men in the Royal Navy. A man, who, without rancor and acrimony, accepted the low blow that fate had in store for him at the beginning of the Great War—we must all now thank you for what you have done for the navy and the nation—how you prepared her for the war, and the desperate hours that ensued. It is with great pleasure that we wish you and your family well. It is incredible to me," he paused and looked around the room, "the number of men who have come to honor you, Admiral. It is a tribute to the beauty of your character and great accomplishments of your career. No one deserves three cheers more than you do, sir. Let us all stand and drink..."

And, when he finished these words, there were loud "hip, hip, hoorays," and a five minute ovation. The men would not stop cheering their admiral—and it was as though he had not been gone from them for the last seven years. I could see that Louis was pleased, nearly overcome and there were traces of moisture in his eyes as he got up to acknowledge the toast—but the men continued cheering. They would not let him speak. It was overwhelming. It took every bit of self-control I possessed not to dab my eyes with my handkerchief. However, I was not as noble as Louis and I was thinking that this was only what my dear husband deserved and they should bloody well give him an hour ovation.

It was, however, an excellent vindication and it didn't end there. Admiral Lee was immensely impressed by what had occurred the evening of the dinner. Afterwards, he wrote several letters urging Buckingham Palace to give Louis an accolade that would indeed be the supreme vindication. From all reports, George was thrilled to be able to do this for his cousin, whom he, among so many others, had thought so wronged in October of 1914.

In August of 1921, by a special Order-in-Council, Louis was raised to the rank of Admiral of the Fleet on the Retired List. He was only the second man in naval history to be so honored. This made Louis and me extremely happy and I was beginning to feel less angry about all that had occurred, though it had been a seven year sorrow. They seemed to want to make amends to their very excellent officer and I was glad to see that Louis was finally getting some of the appreciation that he deserved. I thank heaven they did.

The culmination of that unforgettable summer was an invitation, extended by Dickie and his commanding officers for a celebratory cruise on board the battle cruiser the *Repulse*. The thought of being on board one of the cruisers once again boosted Louis' morale considerably. He was sixty-seven years old now and I had seen a noticeable slowing down. The great anticipation of that cruise, sailing across the bounding main as it were, seemed to take thirty years off of his face and put a little spring back in his step.

They cruised along the northern waters of Scotland, which even in the summer must have been icy cold. Dickie, however, wrote to me that he and Louis were having a fine time with excellent weather. Papa, he told me, was supremely happy and in his element.

After the cruise, Louis returned to London. Louise and I, who were on our way to Scotland, met him there for a day. We were anxious to hear about his adventures with Dickie and I, I suppose, just wanted to see the happy, fulfilled look of old on his face once again. He was staying in the Naval and Military Club in Piccadilly and Louise and I took a hotel room nearby.

We met Louis at the club for tea. He was extremely excited and full of anecdotes of his cruise. However, we were both shocked at how flushed he looked. I mentioned this to him.

"I caught a chill on the cruise, Victoria, was in bed for a few days and that is all it is," he replied impatiently. Louis, as usual, hated to be fussed over, but Dickie had written me that he had run a temperature and that his lumbago had acted up. It was not, in my opinion, auspicious. I didn't like the way he looked, but said nothing further about it. I would insist on his seeing a doctor.

"Dickie was marvelous!" he continued, "he's quite a sailor now and so well-liked by his fellows. He's going to make an excellent officer."

Dickie was a little different than Louis in this respect. Louis had always been liked and admired by his men— they would have followed him anywhere. But to his fellow officers, he was a puzzle. Many loved him, but many couldn't understand his intellectual personality or his lack of interest in the usual male pursuits of drinking and carousing in various ports. Dickie, on the other hand, didn't cause this kind of enmity with certain of the officers. He seemed to be able to adapt to his various surroundings much better than Louis. He was a little more chameleon-like.

"Georgie is so looking forward to your going on the cruise with them," I said with a change of subject. Louis was planning to cruise the Mediterranean with our eldest boy.

"Yes, it will be good to get out in those warm waters once again."

I could understand that for more reasons than one.

Louis' flush left him and instead he seemed to get paler by the minute as we sipped our tea and Louise and I were able to prevail upon him to go straight to bed. Strangely enough, he listened to us. He said something about being tired. I called a doctor, who came round very quickly.

"There doesn't seem to be anything much wrong with

the Admiral, ma'am," he told me deferentially. "He just looks a bit tired. Let him have a night's rest and I'll look in on him some time tomorrow."

I nodded, but I wasn't pleased. He didn't look the least improved after his nap and I didn't like the idea that he was being so docile. Louise and I extended our stay several more days. Louis protested when I wouldn't let him get out of bed the following day and I was encouraged slightly by his stubbornness.

"You're still looking poorly, darling, isn't he, Louise?"

"Indeed you are, Papa," she agreed briskly. "I'm sure the doctor would agree that another day in bed is definitely in order."

We both plumped his pillows and tried to make him comfortable. Even though it was September, Louis's room was chilly, so I sent Louise for a hot water bottle.

"I'd prefer to get up," he began, but at my frown, he lay quietly. "All that nurses training does her credit," he murmured after Louise had left.

"It's a family failing, I'm afraid," I answered with a smile.

"I wish she'd settled down with someone," he said for the hundredth time.

"You have to admit the candidates weren't particularly promising," I remarked, thinking of Manoel.

"I think, besides the obvious," he grinned his old grin, "she didn't want to change her religion."

That sounded painfully familiar as I remember Alicky's dilemma.

"Possibly not, but I think Louise has enjoyed the traveling we've done and I believe she was happy to have been single during the war so that she could go to the Red Cross in France and nurse."

He nodded and coughed. I handed him a glass of water.

"I always thought that since Daisy died, the man that would suit Louise best is Gustav of Sweden."

"Gustav? Really?" I asked. That seemed to come out of the blue. "Why would you think that—I mean he's a dear boy and all that, but why Louise and Gustav?"

"Well, like Louise, he has a great interest in archeology, and history. He's also quite a progressive thinker from everything I've heard and so is Louise, especially after all her wartime experiences. Whenever we met before the war I found him well-informed and intelligent. He has a great variety of interests, he loves to garden, I would think that would please both of you."

"It isn't me he has to please," I muttered, not wanting to think about losing Louise. Selfishly, I was getting used to having her around and had the vague thought she would continue indefinitely as my companion. How like Grandmama that was.

"Who has to please whom?" Louise breezed back in. "Here, Papa is your very hot, hot water bottle. The doctor's downstairs, shall I have him come up?"

We both nodded, and out she went.

"Her personality is so much like yours, my dear," Louis remarked. "However, the world she lives in is much freer, so many less constraints on her. With her independent spirit and her experience, she can be tremendously useful—give herself free reign of expression."

Since when had Louis become so progressive?

"I shudder to think," I replied. I briefly wondered at Louis' attitude towards the New Woman and what I would have done to be young in this new world. No, then I wouldn't have had the same life and I wouldn't change it, tragedies and all.

The doctor entered to the both of us laughing about Louise and the idea of giving her "free reign."

"Ah, the patient is cheerful, that's always encouraging," he said, as though speaking from a prepared "doctor speech."

Louise rolled her eyes at me as we both left the room.

"Papa *does* seem more chipper this afternoon, even if the doctor does say so."

"I don't suppose he'd really lie."

"No, but it's not beneath him to try to make everyone feel better."

I thought that a strange remark and said nothing. One of the maids brought a tea tray up the stairs. We waited for the doctor's examination to end.

He eventually emerged and gave me a prescription to have filled.

"What's this?"

"Just something to perk the Admiral up," he answered vaguely. "I'll be back tomorrow to see him. He should be feeling better by then—he is resting comfortably."

Louise and I brought the tea tray into Louis' bedroom and we had tea together.

"Louise and I will go and get this prescription filled, there's a chemist on the corner—I don't think it will be too difficult," I smiled. I was thinking about how far I'd come if I was getting prescriptions filled instead of asking a servant to do so.

"I'll close my eyes and then, perhaps, I will be able to get up for supper."

"Don't push, Papa. Mama and I will have supper on trays up here. You won't have to go anywhere," Louise said soothingly.

I asked a maid to look in on Louis once or twice while we were gone and we both set out.

"I think Papa will be all right. He just seems extremely fatigued. It's time he slowed down. Perhaps instead of going on a cruise with Georgie, you and he can go somewhere warm, like the south of France."

"Maybe even Malta," I said, thinking of that beloved, *warm* place.

We made the trip to the chemist and back in under an hour, and were hanging up our coats and scarves when the maid and several staff members came up to us, very pale and trembling. It took the maid what seemed like a few minutes to get up the courage and then she said, "Ma'am, oh ma'am, I'm so sorry, but...oh, the Admiral is dead."

My mouth went dry—I didn't really understand what they were trying to tell me. There was silence.

"What has happened?" I croaked and cleared my throat. My hand groped its way into Louise's.

The maid looked at the head of the staff who nodded, and encouraged, the girl spoke.

"Well, ma'am," the maid began, tearfully. "I went into the Admiral's room after you left—I wanted to fetch the tea tray. There was no answer when I knocked so I figured he was sleeping. I looked at his face as I got the tray and something didn't seem right—he looked all peaceful like, but then..." she began to sob, "I realized, ma'am, he wasn't breathing..." and she dissolved into tears.

I said nothing. My heart began to pound as it always did in extreme distress and thousands of things started going through my brain, but I could think of nothing to say.

I had to see him.

I rushed up the stairs with Louise on my heels, and went into the room. He was lying there as we left him. They hadn't covered his face...his beautiful face—my keystone of beauty in the world. I sunk down next to him and took his still warm hand and began to weep. I heard Louise shut the door and she began the same thing, crying "Papa, Papa" in a way that tore at my heart. I stopped crying after a while, but sat there without moving as the room got darker.

"Mama," Louise said quietly, tears in her voice, "we must let the others know."

I got up slowly; my hand went to Louis' face. I stroked his beard and forehead. I sighed heavily, leaned over and kissed him and straightened up.

We went downstairs where everyone else was still standing around, as if waiting for orders. I began to issue instructions, getting telegrams sent, making phone calls and doing all those things that were necessary in order to make the arrangements. I began to watch myself doing these things, as I had done when I had heard about the deaths of Nicky and Alicky. I realized that I was again pushing aside my feelings in order to be strong for everyone else to be as Ella had been when Serge was blown up. I wondered if some time in the future, I would actually experience the feelings I was suppressing, but I couldn't think about it.

I arranged for Nona's brother, Admiral Kerr, a man quite devoted to Louis and later his biographer, to make the arrangements for the funeral itself and then proceeded to comfort everyone for several days. The children arrived within days, though, poor Alice, who raced across Europe to get here, wasn't able to reach England until after the funeral. Dickie and Louise couldn't seem to stop crying for their father and Georgie was silent. I was glad for that, because I wouldn't let myself cry either—and their sobs were about all I could bear.

Louis lay at the Private Chapel at Buckingham Palace for several days then, on the 19ᵗʰ of September, a procession was arranged. It was quite impressive and only what Louis was due—it started along The Mall, through Admiralty Arch and thence to Westminster Abbey for the service. Most of the royal family sent representatives because their obligations took them elsewhere, but I understood. I knew that they, at least, had never faltered when it came to Louis. They knew where his loyalties were and had always been.

We brought the body to St. Mildred's Chapel, Whippingham on the Isle of Wight, where Auntie Beatrice, in her capacity as Governor of the island, met us. The funeral took place there and then, along with Admiral Kerr, I traveled back to Fishponds at Netley, for Alice had finally arrived.

* * * * * * * * * *

The winds in the bay finally died down. I pulled my wool shawl close and took a few deep breaths. Why was I thinking about all of that today? No reason, I suppose, except that I thought about it often.

It had been a terribly hard fall and winter. Louis gone. I, at first, had no idea how I would get on without him. I was terribly lonely and forlorn and I believe my children worried for me. I sometimes saw Dickie and Georgie huddled up in corners whispering, I'm sure, about me. What shall we do with Mama? I could hear them saying. What will she do now? But, I found a solution—I began to practice a little deception. I decided to think that he was not dead, but just on one of his long voyages and that I would see him again in a couple of months. Little by little, this lessened the hurt, though he was never far from my thoughts—he is never far from my thoughts.

Dickie's year looked up considerably from then on—he met the Honorable Edwina Ashley, daughter of Sir Wilfred Ashley and granddaughter of Sir Ernest Cassel. Edwina was a beauty, one of the most sought after girls of her set—and she was one of the wealthiest girls in England. I know that Dickie did not marry her for her money however, I certainly knew that having no money worries was an extremely convenient thing; something that smoothed many a path. Edwina was a very strong and determined girl—and very independent. I always rather liked her—she had the sort of progressive ideas I admired and didn't think I was the least outrageous. Well, I wasn't, compared to her and her sister-in-law. She and Nada became good friends and eventually, got each other into a good deal of trouble. I, however, always got along well with both of them, and they both called me "Aunt Victoria".

The ceremony took place in the summer of 1922 at St. Margaret's, Westminster and it reminded me, somewhat, of one of our old royal gatherings. There was a strong royal presence, although, in comparison to the old days, it was severely depleted. David, the Prince of Wales, acted as Dickie's best man and Alice's girls were among the maids of honor. George and Mary were there as well as Cousin Minnie and Aunt Alix—it was good to see these two old royal dowagers, but they were looking entirely too venerable now and neither had too many years left. It was always curious to me that neither of them ever looked their age—I had heard a peculiar rumor that they put some sort of acid to strip the surface epidermis of their faces and then smoothed porcelain on the raw skin to make their faces look wrinkle-free. I couldn't imagine doing anything like that for vanity, but it was, as I said, a rumor.

A more extraordinary development began the following year. Of all things, Louise became engaged—and to the man that Louis had predicted would be the only right man for her—Gustav of Sweden. They had met at a party in London and met frequently at Georgie and Nadas' home. They were seen together at Ascot that year which was highly remarked upon. Beside the fact that pairings of royal persons are always highly remarked upon, my Louise's being spotted with anyone, at this point, was also big news.

She was reluctant at first. She didn't like the idea of leaving England at all. In addition, I believe that her single state suited her, she was so accustomed to it, but the plots around her thickened. It seemed that Alice's girls were in on the stratagems and were constantly contriving to leave them alone together. The more she would plead for them not to, the more they giggled and did so, earning Gustav's love and thanks. Eventually, she succumbed to his attentions—I believed he liked Louise very much for her intellect, her practicality, which would stand her in good stead when she took over being a step-mother of five children and her independent sense of fun.

"I won't be wearing white," she told me adamantly in the late summer of 1923, as we were talking about her wedding.

I eyed her suspiciously and she laughed.

"Oh, Mama, it's not because of that. It's just that, well— can you imagine me in white? It's too ludicrous. It's not as if I'm a young girl you know...can you just see me swanning down the aisle in yards of white satin and loads of taffeta? It's comical."

She laughed, but I didn't think it was so funny.

"What in heaven's name will you wear? It's hard to imagine a bride not in white."

"Pretend this is a second marriage, Mama. It is, at least for Gustav. I'll wear an elegant suit of some sort."

"Then they'll really think you're not royal."

The Swedish Government had needed some reassurances that Lady Louise Mountbatten was indeed a member of the Royal Family. Since she was no longer a princess, it was feared that she might actually be a commoner. We, none of us, cared about the designation, but Gustav wouldn't have been permitted to marry Louise if she were a commoner. The strange part was that if he were a king, he could have, but as a crown prince, he had no say in the matter.

"You know," I began, "your father predicted this...he said that the only man that would ever suit you was

Gustav and he did so want you to have a family of your own."

"Did he?" she smiled. "Fancy that—well, I'll certainly have plenty of family of my own now," she sighed. "Oh dear, I wish Papa was here, I know he would have liked to be. It would have done him good to see me settled."

I nodded. Louis had remarked upon that so many times. I knew that it was the truth—but I would most definitely miss my girl, my friend and my companion.

In the end, Louise did wear silvery white and had all of Alice's girls for her bridesmaids. I look at the pictures now and Louise looks as though she hasn't eaten in days—somewhat glum, though I know she was as happy as she could be—and the girls look like something out of an art deco print, with the headbands and the Grecian-style draped dresses. It was the same with Dickie and Edwina's wedding—the styles from the twenties seem so dated today.

*   *   *   *   *   *   *   *   *   *

I decided that I had had enough of the sea air. I rose and began walking back to Auntie's home on the island. I waved as I saw her walking towards me. We were both alone now. Her surviving son and daughter were married, as were mine and we were both widows—though dear Auntie had been a widow for nearly twenty years and would be so for nearly another twenty years. I used to sometimes wonder if she even remembered that she had been married. It was such a small part of her life.

I hoped that I had more courage than to lament that my life was over, but in a way, the life that I had been leading was, indeed, finished. I was no longer the head of a family, either of my siblings or my own—but now I was independent and would, for what time remained, be in the background. I was now living in Kensington Palace along with some of the other elderly or single royals—a sort of Royal Old Folks Homes. Without question, it was lovely being near Aunts Beatrice and Louise who had apartments there. That certainly assuaged my loneliness a little, and I was happy enough that as timed passed, I had plenty of visits from my children and grandchildren.

Besides all of that, there was nothing more charming than having Hyde Park as my garden. Sadly, it wasn't quite the same as the gardens on which I had worked so vigorously at Kent House. However, it certainly wasn't unappealing to get out of the eye of the storms, for storms there would no doubt be. For the moment, I liked retiring into the background, but it was a tame role of which I doubted I'd be contented for long.

"Victoria, what are you doing out here in this dreadful weather?"

Auntie reached me, concern in her face.

"Nothing, dear, I'm just coming in now."

I took her arm and we both walked quickly inside where tea was waiting. We ate without a word then both settled back with cigarettes.

"Remember when you gave me my first cigarette?"

"Ah, yes, that was at, I believe, dear Heiligenberg, about the time that Louis and I were getting married." She nodded as she blew out a stream of smoke. "You were just beginning to be the object of Liko's attentions...what a handsome rogue he was," I said, smiling.

"He wasn't a rogue," she answered primly, "but a fine young man."

"I suppose I was thinking of what a horrible beast he was as a child."

"Maybe, but I didn't know him then," she answered again, too primly. We caught each other's eye and began giggling.

"If our children could see us giggling," I said.

"It's always good to laugh at our age. Life has dealt us enough cruel blows without taking away our ability to see what's amusing."

"I completely agree." I thought that was extremely wise of her.

"So, what is the latest with Alice?" she asked.

Alice! Poor child, she had had several very difficult years, since Louis' death. Greece had, not surprisingly, proved extremely fickle, once again. They welcomed Tino back after poor Alexander died of poisoning from the monkey bite, but it seemed as though he, too, was virtually under house arrest. He was eventually deposed once again in 1922, and Alice and her family waited at Mon Repos for whatever would come next. And, what came next was the arrest of Andrew.

To make a complex story short, after a lot of pleading from his royal relatives all over Europe, Andrew was released, while fellow prisoners, including cabinet ministers, were shot. George was very decisive in making sure that nothing untoward happened to Andrew. I often wonder if this was done out of guilt—because he had failed to save Nicky and Alicky.

Andrew was given virtually no time to get out of the country. He was escorted by an Englishman, an emissary from George, and Alice, who quickly boarded a Royal Naval vessel and made for Corfu to gather up the four girls and little Philip. They went into exile once again and even this time, it wasn't for good. Alice and her family went to Paris where they settled in St. Cloud.

"Alice has decided to open a boutique," I told Auntie.

"Really, she's becoming a shopkeeper?" she said this more out of amazement than snobbery.

"Yes, she's decided to call the place *Hellas* and she's going to sell Greek souvenirs and embroidery and give the proceeds to charity—sounds rather fun."

"How nice. As ever, she wants to keep busy and help people."

"Yes, Auntie, I believe that this is good for her. She's been talking about Ella a great deal lately and I believe that if she were free, she would enter Ella's order."

"She's that interested?"

"Very much so." Again, it wasn't something I understood well, but it was, without a doubt, rampant in my family. "I'm a little uneasy about it, though, because she really needs to take care of her family. She's been under a great deal of strain since the Balkan Wars. Oh, for the last ten years or so and she's not feeling terribly well. I think, like poor Alicky, she's got some heart problems."

"Our children seem destined for problems, look at poor Ena, and all the difficulties she's had with the children."

Ena and Alphonso had a difficult time producing healthy children—several of her boys were born with hemophilia and another was a deaf mute. Only one boy was healthy. And as I mentioned, this did nothing to help their crumbling relationship. Auntie had her share of trials.

"Poor girl," I answered inadequately and Auntie sighed.

"So many are gone..." and we were on a familiar theme. I wasn't one to dwell on the losses, but I could understand her feelings. Aunt Lenchen, dear useful Aunt Lenchen, had died in June and the only brother Auntie had left was Uncle Arthur Connaught and the only sister she now had left was Aunt Louise and heaven knows they had had their differences in the past.

As usual, I didn't much listen to her monologue after that. I was too busy thinking of Alice and her children. Georgie and Dickie would be all right, but Alice was a continual worry to me. I felt that she wasn't, perhaps, living enough in this world and I worried for her children. As for Andrew, he grew away from her and they eventually separated. I was sorry for this, but not surprised. As long ago as 1917, I had seen this coming though I prayed that they could heal their rifts. '

As time went on, Alice did, indeed, go into the sanitarium in Switzerland; she was in fact, in and out of them through most of the twenties and thirties. Andrew seemed to abdicate responsibility for his children, thinking that they would be better off with their aunts, uncles and grandmother. Therefore, the girls and Philip, in particular, spent a lot of time with me, Georgie and Dickie. They were also quite close to Nada's sister Anastasia, or Zia and her husband Sir Harold Wernhers.

In the end, it was these three men who exerted a great deal of influence over Philip, though, he talked often, even recently, about how much his father meant to him. I, in the happy role of Grandmama, just took him to the cinema a lot.

CHAPTER TWENTY-FOUR

Kensington Palace, August, 1939

It's no good getting old. I find it most annoying, though humorists often exhort us to think of the alternative. Well, that particular alternative doesn't seem as frightening to me as it once did. I suppose the familiarity I have with that one option—all the friends and family who have perished—puts me in no mood of fear when contemplating my imminent demise.

My hope was that it would be a burden that would be lifted from my children soon enough. I had no wish to linger and no wish to be here more than was agreeable to my family. Luckily, I enjoyed the best of health even at my advanced age. Seventy-six is such a large number and, some would say, six years passed the biblical allotment. I don't see myself this way and if I'm not looking in a mirror, I don't bother to try.

It was a glorious August. The sun was beating down that afternoon and there was a blue, blue sky with some very fluffy white clouds. I could look out my windows and see the Londoners in Hyde Park—perambulating, sailing or simply enjoying the day. On the sofa in my sitting room, a tall, blond, handsome young man was lounging comfortably. Philip, who was at Dartmouth Naval College, was cooling his heels here, as we affectionately called it, at K.P. Philip had spent a good deal of his life here in England and I was thrilled that he used my apartments as his home base during holidays. It meant that I was very close to this grandson and had a strong hand in his upbringing.

Andrew, his father, occasionally visited Alice in Greece, but mostly spent his time on the Riviera, with a martini in one hand and a mistress in the other. Alice, I knew, was contented in another absorbing interest. It wasn't another man, but her deep spirituality that was finally given voice. I was sorry in this case, that Alice should so resemble her Aunt Ella. Ella, however, at least waited until she had no dependents and Alice, I fear, did not. With regard to Andrew, however, I was never one to criticize and say the foregoing with little malice since he really did take an intense interest in his boy. In turn, Philip loved his father dearly and always insisted that his father had a large role in raising him—even going so far as to resent that my Dickie and Georgie were thought to be more influential.

The girls all got married in the early thirties. Alice's youngest, Sophie, interestingly enough, was the first married to Christopher of Hesse, my cousin Mossy's son. Cri, as he was called, died during the war. It was said that he was an ardent Nazi, but according to Sophie, he had been murdered by them because he had, in fact, renounced Nazism. Cecilia married Ernie's son Don, so their children were my nephews as well as my great-grandchildren. No wonder Philip always said we were inbred. The other two also made German marriages. For some reason which I still don't really know, I didn't give any of them the pearl, though I believe their marriages were happy ones. Nevertheless, something told me to keep it—it was meant for someone else.

I spent a great deal of time in Germany in those years. I went to Darmstadt and stayed with Ernie at least once a year. The visit I remember, most pointedly, was in the year 1933. Hitler and the Nazis had come into power and the entire country seemed to be blanketed with those red banners with the black swastikas. I am now ashamed to admit that at the time, I, along with other members of my family liked and admired them. I thought any party that called itself National and Socialist had to be a good thing—ignorant creature that I was. I also thought it would be a good thing for Germany's pitiful economy. Believe me, I cringe when I think of that now.

We watched with great concern as Hitler revived the economy by rearming and, thereby, abrogating the

Versailles Treaty. I remember Cousin George once telling me how roundly he castigated a German minister, telling him that if Germany went on at her present rate, there was bound to be another war in ten years.

"What," he asked the minister, "is Germany asking for?"

The minister protested that they were only trying to protect themselves and that France, after all, had the Maginot line. Whereupon, George, honest and upright fellow that he was said, "The Maginot line and fortifications will be as useless now as they were in the last war."

So as the thirties continued, our concern grew to dismay and eventually to real consternation. If one read the newspaper thoroughly, from cover to cover, which I always did, one saw before long what these "socialists" really were—murderous fascist thugs, instilling nightmarish fear and wreaking violence on any of the peoples who were unlucky enough to be in disfavor.

Things for my family were quite unsettled, as well. Cousin George died in 1936, God rest his simple and trustworthy soul. David, who had, at that point, been ensnared by his inamorata, Wallis Simpson, was quite determined to marry her.

It was at one of our family gatherings at Balmoral that I was able to speak to David. He usually didn't attend the summer retreats, but after the death of Cousin George, he began to feel that he was head of the family. I was surprised at this since he didn't seem particularly interested in either the job of King or his position in the Royal Family. Perhaps, in reality, he was trying to feel out the members of his family. Perhaps he wanted their reactions to Wallis Simpson—what they thought of her; whether he should marry her, or keep her as a mistress, whether she should be Queen, or whether he should marry her morganatically.

He seemed particularly annoyed at me that I had called her thus.

"Aunt Victoria, you made a morganatic marriage—and everyone knows how well it turned out. I see nothing wrong with doing the same."

He had ambushed me as I stood in front of the fire in the drawing room. Everyone else was busy playing a particularly fierce game of charades, but I wasn't in the mood. It was an extremely cold September. I wasn't sure what I was doing there, but May had invited me and I suppose she wanted my support. I could see her across the room, watching my conversation with David.

"The difference is, my boy, that in my case, Uncle Louis never turned me away from doing my duty, nor did I him."

He winced slightly. I had hit a nerve. Certainly the stories about his excesses were true. I had heard about the cocktail glass rings on state papers. He simply didn't care about the job. However, I didn't think at that juncture, pointing it out would be politic.

"Do you think that Wallis strongly influences me in that way?"

"I really don't know, David. That is something that you should tell me."

He said nothing.

"I want, as one of your most loyal subjects, to think that you will place the importance of the throne, the matters of the country and the job you have to do first, never mind the family. Louis was so happy with your support back in 1914, it meant a great deal to him. He thought you the most excellent of men. He had every faith that when the time came, you would make a great king."

Louis hadn't expressed this to me quite this way, but I thought it might do some good if David really admired Louis.

"Did he really think that? I have always thought that this country did him a great wrong. He was one of the great naval minds of our time."

"Of course he thought it," I answered positively.

"I wish my own Papa had such confidence in me—I was afraid of him, did you know?"

I knew. I also knew what a cold father Cousin George had been. Obviously, the wrong kind of parent for David.

"He wasn't my father, so he didn't seem at all terrifying to me."

"He was of your generation," he murmured, as he began to poke the fire with an andiron. "I suppose I thought you might understand..."

"What?"

"Well, everything that's happened. You've done such a

good job with your sons, but they married rather unconventional women." That's just what Louis had said. "Nada, Edwina and Wallis are great friends and I thought, perhaps, since you're on such good terms with your daughters-in-law, you Lmight be well-disposed towards Wallis."

It was a logical assumption to make. I was on excellent terms with both women, but I didn't understand their friendship with Wallis. She was, to me, extremely mannish and unappealing. And, I had heard some very strange things about her. She certainly didn't seem to exert any kind of positive influence on David. Besides which, she had already been divorced twice and both of her ex-husbands were living. I had never been a religious woman in the style of Alicky or even Alice, but this was a little much for me. No, this was quite a different thing than my daughters-in-law and their unusual style of living.

"Don't you think you might help me make Mama understand?"

I was taken aback. He wanted me to intercede with May about Mrs. Simpson. I took a deep breath, "David, I can't do as you ask. Your mother believes that doing her duty is the most important thing in the world. It is the very foundation on which she bases her life. You can't ask her to take away those foundations—she could not live that way."

Didn't he realize that this was a woman that cheerfully

accepted the brother of her dead fiancé because she felt it was her duty to do so? Giving in to this would kill May and I wouldn't be the one to ask it of her.

"No, I suppose you, of all people, could not," he sighed, and put down the poker.

I never understood what he meant "of all people," unless it has something to do with my being part of that close knit family of Grandmama's. He didn't remember Grandmama, being so young when she died. He did understand the meaning of being part of that golden group—the "Royal Mob."

The unfortunate man abdicated at the end of the year. Some thought that spelled the end of the monarchy in England, but frankly, David's abdication seemed to be met with nothing more than slight disquiet or possibly, feeble interest. Taking his place, was George's second son, now George VI, whom we called Bertie, his charming wife, Elizabeth Bowes-Lyons and their two pretty young daughters, Elizabeth, whom we all called Lilibet and little Margaret. This family stepped easily, without much comment, into the shoes of Bertie's father. It was, in fact, so smooth and quiet, that after a while, few people remembered the months that David had spent on the throne. Dickie did since he was a great friend of David's and David had been in his wedding party. We all agreed, in the end, the whole sorry business turned out in the best possible way.

I was happy I saw a lot of Ernie during the early and

mid-thirties since he died in 1937. Poor Ernie...I always felt that Onor, good woman that she was, spent a lot of time shielding him from the harsh realities of life. He, wrapped, as it were, in cotton wool, continued the Hessian tradition of cultural and artistic activities and Onor continued with the nursing and social work that my Mama had started. Ernie, himself, was an avid artist and decorator, enjoying the Art Nouveau school as well as the Surrealist one—some of the drawings he did, even the doodles in the guest book at dear Wolfsgarten, reminded me very much of Salvador Dali. His death, in view of later events, was again, perhaps, for the best.

Ernie died a month before his second son, Lu, was to marry the Honorable Margaret Geddes, whom we called Peg. It was going to be a wonderful occasion. Onor and their eldest son, Don and his wife, my Alice's daughter, Cecilia and their two sons would fly over to England for the wedding. We were all tremendously excited about the match and Peg quickly became a family favorite.

Alice came, which was becoming a little unusual. She was slowly withdrawing from the world. The current Greek monarch, Tino's son George, had once again been restored in Greece and Alice took a small apartment in Athens. She eschewed grandeur now and would not live at the Royal Palace.

I remember that day in November, oh so well. Peg and Lu were anxiously awaiting the plane that was to bring over the entire Hessian Grand Ducal Family. It grew to be very late and the two of them began walking up and down the runway at Croyden field. As it became later and later, one of the airport officials stepped up to Lu and whispered something in his ear. He told Peg to wait there while he went inside.

He emerged, a few minutes later, completely ashen. The plane had crashed at Steen, Belgium, killing every single person on board. In one fell swoop, Lu lost his entire family. Peg told me later she didn't know where to look. She was so completely shocked she forgot to move and Lu had to nudge her with his arm to walk.

We were all informed and, as was usual for me, I approached the entire situation stoically. We met at Peg's father's estate at Kent and talked over the entire matter.

"They must be married right away," I said, in a voice that I recognized right away as my actor's voice. This was the voice I used during the months I mourned for Alicky and Ella.

"She's right," Sir Auckland, Peg's father, agreed. "It will be easier for you two to bear this if you bear it together."

Lu and Peg, whose faces continued ashen and colorless both nodded, as if they were both in the same bad dream.

That is exactly what we did. The following day at the Church of St. Peter, in Eaton Square, with Dickie as the best man instead of Don, who was, excruciating to think about it, dead, Peg and Lu were married. It was another one of our funereal weddings—I remember Orchie telling me about Mama and Papa's wedding and how sad everyone had been, crying and crying. We, however, were not Victorian mourners and we did not cry. Oh, I think we all cried when we were alone, I certainly did. I had to, I couldn't stop myself this time—but at least there was no one there to be shocked.

I went into my bedroom, took out my pearl, which now seemed blemished and wept for my family and my brother, my granddaughter and my nephews and, oh, God, everyone. It was enough, I thought. I didn't want any more slaughter. Nevertheless, I emerged from my agony, as I always did and went to the wedding, though the bride wore black, not the Hessian veil that had belonged to my Mama or the jewels, all lost in the crash, as well. I waved them goodbye as they went off to the scene of the crash and thence on to Darmstadt to take over the raising of Don and Cecelia's little girl, Johanna, who had been thought too young to come to the wedding. Poor Johanna, she was three years old when she died in 1939 of meningitis.

I was certain at that time, that the Hesse family had been cursed—that the stories of a monk putting a malediction on the family were true. If not, how could we have had such terrible bad luck? All the family slaughters by diphtheria, Bolsheviks, airplanes—well, there was no other explanation. Surely there was a vengeful angel out there, punishing us for our arrogance and our absolute certitude that we were above common people. Well, he could snigger now—for I frequently had the belief that I had far less purpose than most. That feeling had started with Louis' resignation in 1914. Without our positions and our titles, I had a strong suspicion that I and my family were of absolutely no value to anyone. It was a despair that Grandmama would not have tolerated. But could she have been quite so indomitable after quite so many tragedies? Then, of course, to her, losing Grandpapa was the worst possible nightmare imaginable, and nothing I experienced could bring me so much grief.

And so, I came upon my last birthday with hope of no more tragedy ahead. What else, I asked myself, could happen? I began to think of who was left. Irène seemed about as stout-hearted as I. She had lost Henry in 1927 and lived quietly, at Hemmelmark, without much excitement. That was very much like her life had always been, excepting that we could not visit as much as we would have liked. It was really too bad since we were all that each had left. The Battenbergs, Marie and Franzjos, were sadly gone by this time, though Anna still lived. Unfortunately, though she was close to my daughter, Alice, I didn't see nearly as much of her as I would have liked.

Wryly, I also remembered that Willy was still alive. He was happily remarried and chopping wood in Holland at a place called Doorn. Willy, who had done so much harm, whose lack of intellect and leadership had put Germany on its present course—the road to another, even more savage war. Willy, who had left his country cheerfully as an exile—he was still there, living into quiet old age. His life was the absolute personification of the saying that no one gets what they deserve. He certainly didn't and try as I did, I could only be faintly happy for poor Aunt Vicky's sake. He had even sent Cousin George and May congratulations on their Silver Jubilee in 1935. I believe when absolute impudence and nerve were invented— Willy was the illustration in the dictionary.

My Georgie had quit the navy in 1932. There was every indication that he would have gone as far as Louis and even further, but Georgie had a family to support and unlike Dickie, didn't have a rich wife. He took a job as the Director of Sperry Gyroscope Company. This was no honorary appointment with an illustrious name to put on their masthead. This company really wanted Georgie's expertise and inventiveness—both of which I believe he got from his father.

He was happy in the years that he worked there. If he regretted the navy, I never heard about it. He spent a lot of time with Philip and Philip and my other grandson David, became very good chums. Nada traveled a great deal with Edwina, so there were few times that we could all get together as a family. Nevertheless, those years were good ones for Georgie until, just a month or so after the tragedy at Steen, he broke his leg.

I remember him telling me afterward that he had just been walking normally and without warning, it was as though his leg snapped like a rubber band. What a terrible feeling and how frustrating when the leg refused to heal properly. We knew soon enough the reason for it—it was cancer of the bone and Georgie was given no hope.

Through that winter until the spring of 1938, all of us stayed by Georgie's side, trying our best to alleviate his tremendous suffering. This was the hardest of all the things that ever happened to me. When I was hurt, I knew that I could cope with it, but when my child hurt and there was nothing to do—this was agonizing. I don't think I had cried so much since I was a child, before Mama died. Poor Georgie, he was as cheerful a patient as could be imagined, bearing up with the tremendous pain that such cancers give. When he died in April of that year, I could not be stoic. I even believe that I shocked my children and grandchildren with the magnitude and the outward show of my grief. But I had not been prepared for this. I had not been prepared to lose a child—not a sickly one as Alice had been with her heart and lung complaints all these years—but a healthy vigorous man, who like a piece of ice in the sun, just melted away. Dear man, he was so like Louis, it was like losing my darling all over again.

Too much to bear.

* * * * * * * * * *

"I've got a surprise for you, Grandmama," Philip said from the sofa.

"What's that?" I coughed as I settled myself in my favorite spot in front of the fire. What I loved about August was that it was light for so much longer. More time to make more heat.

"There's a new Bette Davis movie at Leicester Square and I'm going to take you to see it."

I was quite the avid cinema go-er and Philip knew that the only thing I didn't like about the pictures was the same thing I didn't like about the wireless; I couldn't talk back to it. But, I loved Bette Davis. She was an actress whom I saw as having true determination and what the Americans call grit. She always played strong women characters, and that appealed to me.

"What is it this time?"

"It's called *The Old Maid*."

"Oh, yes," I coughed again. It was getting to the point with me that I coughed, talked and smoked all at the same time. I think it drove Dickie crazy, but Philip had the good manners to ignore it. "I've read about it—it's based on a story by Edith Wharton. I have always enjoyed her books." This film was based on one of a group of four novellas called *Old New York*, and was one of my favorites.

"And then after, how about supper at the Savoy?"

"What's the occasion?" I asked. "And can you afford it?"

"The occasion, dear Grandmama, is that I never celebrated your seventy-fifth birthday with you last year."

"None of us felt much like celebrating anything—not after Uncle Georgie..."

"Yes," he said quickly. "Well, that's why I want to celebrate today. I feel like celebrating today. Perhaps even giving you a twirl or two around the dance floor—who knows when we'll get another opportunity?"

I was never one for the *carpe diem* philosophy, but he did have a point. We were all reading the newspapers in that summer of 1939 and unless you were impaired mentally, you had to be aware of the purposes of the dictators in Europe. The storm clouds, as the newsreel commentators often said, were hanging low. There was Franco, using his people as cannon fodder and a proving ground for the weapons of destruction Hitler was manufacturing and there was of course Mussolini's cowardly invasion of Ethiopia—modern tanks against spear-chuckers in ceremonial outfits—it was pathetic—reprehensible.

I rang for Pye, whom Philip now took to calling "Pie-crust" and asked her to lay out one of my better black dresses. I was thinking about getting out of my chair, which at that point required some consideration, when Philip said, "Ask Pie-crust to wait a moment, I've been wanting to tell you something else, too, Grandmama, before we go on our outing."

I nodded, sat back and settled down once again. I took out my smoking kit and lit another cigarette.

"Oh, yes?" I asked in a tone that I hoped matched his confiding one. My eighteen-year-old grandson could only be telling me something about a girl.

"Well, Uncle Dickie and I were talking about—well..."

"What is it, Philip?" I coughed and blew out smoke.

He thought for a moment, as though he was determined to tell me something in the most tactful way.

"I've recently met up with Lilibet and Margaret."

I looked at his face—whatever was he talking about? It seemed to me he had met the girls before, certainly at Bertie's coronation several years ago.

"Yes?"

"Uncle Dickie has intimated, well—he seems to wish..."

"Spit it out," I snapped with my customary impatience.

"Sorry, Grandmama. Uncle Dickie is already toying with the idea of my marrying Lilibet."

Dickie—good grief, the man was, no startling surprise, ambitious.

"And what do you think of this?"

He twisted and turned around in his seat.

"It's a little awkward, isn't it? After all, she's just a little girl still."

She was thirteen, of course she was a little girl.

"And you're just a very young man starting a career, so what's really to think about?"

He breathed a sigh.

"That's just what I was thinking. It's seems awfully early to wonder who Lilibet will marry and it still seems early enough to me to wonder who I'll marry."

"Sensible boy—so what do you think of Lilibet?"

He smiled.

"You're as bad as Uncle Dickie," he laughed. "She and Margaret are quite pretty, but Lilibet is extremely shy."

"Really, what happened?"

He put his elbows on his knees and leaned forward, seriously.

"Cousins Bertie and Elizabeth came to Dartmouth last month with Uncle Dickie. They were cruising on the royal yacht."

I nodded. Dickie had probably arranged the entire episode, it was entirely in character.

"Most of the boys were pretty struck with Margaret, she's already quite a beauty, but I noticed Lilibet right away because she had this look on her face, as though she wanted so desperately to please everyone. It was a look that seemed strange for a girl her age—so serious and determined."

"That's her Grandmother May," I answered, thinking about May, the personification of duty. "And it's her position, unfortunately. One doesn't have the luxury of showing one's true feelings."

"Well, I was assigned to entertain the two girls and their governess, Miss Crawford. We had a snack and played some games, but I was at a loss. What does one do with a thirteen year old and a nine year old?"

I smiled. I remember Louis' knowing exactly what to do with one particular five year old...I could almost hear his gentle voice.

"Well, there wasn't much, so I decided to demonstrate

my high-jumping ability." I raised my eyebrows. "I took them out to the tennis courts and jumped over the nets."

I couldn't help it, I burst out laughing.

"That's the silliest thing I've ever heard."

He puffed himself up.

"I had no idea what to do with them," he repeated, "and well, they both liked it well enough."

And, so they did, I later learned from her mother Queen Elizabeth, who told me how very impressed Lilibet was with Philip. She was, she emphasized, extremely affected by his jumping.

"Well, I suppose Dickie is happy with you."

"Yes, but he's already talking about making me a naturalized citizen of Britain—I wish Uncle Georgie were here, Grandmama, he was a lot more quiet about things like this—he wasn't so conspicuous."

This was the first show of sensitivity I'd seen from Philip, so I concluded that this was all extremely distressing to him.

"Don't worry, Philip. It's hardly time for you to get married. Please, just sow as many wild oats as you like and ignore Uncle Dickie."

"If I can," he sighed.

"You can, just do it. Do you want me to talk to him?"

"No, no, thanks anyway, Grandmama. I have to stand up for myself," he said with determination. I thought I heard an unspoken "like I always do," in there, but, perhaps it was just my imagination, and my guilt, though why I needed to feel guilty...

He smiled at me again, and I marveled at what a handsome young man he had become. To me, he had inherited a lot of Alice's beauty.

"That's what I like about you Grandmama, you don't beat around the bush."

"Whatever for?" I asked, but smiled. "It's important that you remember that we, Hesses, have a wonderful tradition of marrying where we love. It started with your Great-Grandmama Alice and went through me and my sisters and I believe your sisters, too."

At that he looked at me skeptically.

"Well, if I had had a hand in them, you wouldn't look so skeptical."

"It's just harder and harder these days to love royalty, we do seem a bit inbred," he pointed out once again, as I had heard him before. "Besides, there just aren't that many eligible princesses around. We haven't got the great restrictions put on us that there were when you were young, we can meet anyone we please."

"That's true and I can see that it has its good and bad points. But Lilibet has to marry someone and she will be Queen Regnant. Perhaps Dickie is being old-fashioned—but he's definitely looking out for your better interests."

"Dickie's got me in the Royal Navy and to tell the truth, Grandmama, if it wasn't such a family tradition, I really would have preferred the RAF."

"Would you now?" I smiled back; it wasn't such a great revelation. Unlike most of my family, I wasn't so hide-bound in traditions that I couldn't see another point of view. "The most important thing is that you be happy."

"On that we agree," he grinned.

"What does your Papa think about you joining the British Navy instead of the Greek one?"

There had been some discussion about this; after all, Philip was a Prince of a country that currently did have a monarchy. His serving in a foreign navy might not appear very politic.

"Papa is all for me joining the British Navy. I think he's also interested in me following in Grandpapa's steps."

"Always a good idea," I concurred.

"I know that some wondered why I didn't join the Greek Navy, but Papa wouldn't have it."

I nodded, I had an idea why.

"He felt that it was all too uncertain. They had thrown us out so many times. What's to keep them from doing it again?"

"Absolutely nothing," I answered, remembering my talks with my Greek guide all those years ago. He had intimated that the family was there, as the Americans say, on a pass and he had been right. I knew most certainly that I didn't want my grandson to be a victim of Greek caprice and I was gratified that Andrew had evidently felt the same way.

"Anyhow," he sat back again. "It's all settled. I'm going to stay in the Royal Navy—I've always felt I belong more in England than anywhere else."

I nodded—Louis had felt that way as well.

Sometimes, when I'm in a strange and curious mood, I look back in my life. In my mind's eye, the time before 1914, before all the wars and assassinations and disappointments, is remembered as though it were all behind a pink gauze curtain—the people, all beautiful, in uniforms and elaborate fairy-like dresses, with servants about, seeming to be doing things just as instinctively as animals and as unconsciously. It's like one of those dreams where you watch what is going on, you're hovering above the company, but you're most definitely there. Everyone, however, ignores you. You move about the room trying to speak, trying to get someone to acknowledge you, but no one seems to hear anything you're saying. You're completely removed and that world seems no longer relevant.

Then, as always, my thoughts move to after the Great War and all the beauty seems to have vanished. It seems as though everyone is wearing black, taking cable cars—and getting drug prescriptions. It's obvious that we, my class and I, have less purpose than the street sweepers. But, that last I felt only when I was in a very lonely and glum mood. When I had my family about me, I felt essential. Perhaps it was because of all the tragedies, but I sensed deeply that my daughters, son and grandchildren needed me desperately if only for continuity—that I, perhaps only out of attrition, became the center of my family.

CHAPTER TWENTY-FIVE

I
Westminster Abbey, November 20, 1947

Stately—that is how I thought I looked that day; very subdued, with great dignity, but very stately. I had stood, rather shakily, before my full length mirror and admired myself—something that I didn't normally do in the course of my day. I had a dove-grey wool dress that fell in long, soft, folds to the floor. Very nice, I decided, with a black hat and gloves and, happily, not at all funereal. That was how all of us felt for the first time in a long time—happy. I was thrilled that I was finally attending a wedding that didn't have dark clouds hanging over it. This was an event that was free of any discord.

I remember so well that last day in 1939, before we plunged into war with Germany again. Philip and I had a lovely time going to the films and then to the Savoy. I remember waltzing around with him in a very calm and decorous fashion. We had talked about what we knew was to come and Philip, along with Dickie, Georgie's David and all the others had gone off—each of them fighting. It was a worrisome time, and I resisted leaving Kensington Palace, I always thought it was best to keep close to home in emergencies. However, eventually, with all the air raids, I was persuaded to go to Windsor with Bertie and Elizabeth. It was difficult for me to make the move, but everyone simply insisted. The one interesting part of it was that the princesses were put in charge of me. They had the job of taking me for walks, like a precious old dog and listening to me natter on about a dozen or so subjects. I thought they were very nice and extremely polite. As the war wore on, Lilibet became a Subaltern in the army and was given the job of fixing trucks. It was no publicity stunt; she did a very good job of it. It also gave her a break from me and my chattering.

Dickie and Edwina had sent their girls, Pamela and Patricia, away to America.

"Their great-grandfather was Jewish," Dickie explained to me, referring to Sir Ernest Cassel, Edwina's maternal grandfather. "If Hitler were to invade, which wouldn't happen in a million years, the girls would be off to the gas chambers."

I shivered. What a thought. Of course, at the time we had no idea how many millions had already been marched off. Dickie was even criticized for the move, people pointing out that Bertie and Elizabeth had not, indeed, would not send the princesses away. However, I could see his point.

For Britain, it was a long, hard, war. A terrific struggle, especially when we were alone against the Nazis from 1939 to nearly 1942. Bertie and Elizabeth proved to have a tremendous amount of mettle. There was much appreciative talk about Elizabeth, clad in her best flowery dresses, going to the devastated East End which had been bombed out in the blitz and visiting the people. They were extremely delighted to see her, highly attracted by her beaming countenance and she seemed to know how to say the right thing at the right time. When Buckingham Palace was hit by bombs, she smiled calmly and cheerfully said that since they had been bombed, she could now look the East End in the face.

We were lucky, I suppose, in that none of us really lost anyone in the war. Dickie, as well as Philip and David, managed to escape unscathed. I felt guilty in my relief. My granddaughter, Sophie, lost her husband in the war, but in 1946, married Prince Georg Wilhelm of Hanover, so I suppose she was well consoled.

I sighed. Since the war, so much of what happened seemed like a dream. I felt very disconnected from what was going on and wondered if it was because I was getting so old. After all, I was in my eighties and perhaps my brain was naturally detaching itself from the life that couldn't last much longer.

Even now, as I looked at myself in the mirror and put my dear pink pearl in my little handbag, I was thinking more about the past than the present. With my pearl, luminescent today, I would feel that my darling Louis was here too—that his spirit was present at the marriage of his grandson, Philip to Princess Elizabeth of Great Britain, the heir to the throne.

How excited he would have been, though, in a way, I think he would have felt it bittersweet since his granddaughters, Alice's surviving girls, were not invited. But, unfortunately, they lived in Germany and had lived out the war there—as had Irène. It was a tricky business at best and so they were not asked. Louis, however, would have looked at the entire thing in a positive light and would have seen no bitterness in any of it. It was a great thing for the Battenberg Family, he would say and then I would retort that it was a great thing for Grandmama's family.

I thought so much about Grandmama these days. I felt as though she were everywhere. Even when I was younger, not a day went by when I didn't think about her. How I still missed her.

As I sat in the Abbey, I thought about how many people were there and how many people were gone. It was a characteristic of old age I suppose that one was in as close touch with the departed as one was with the living.

It was to be an austere wedding, although, it couldn't have looked less so. Lilibet had a gorgeous dress of pearl satin, with clouds of tulle, seed pearls and crystal, with a long train. The material had all been bought with ration coupons. She wouldn't have had it any other way, though girls from all over England wanted to donate more coupons and materials. She received thousands of presents, which were all laid out at St. James Palace. Philip took me to see them and told me they'd had to hide Mahatma Ghandi's gift from May. It was some material he'd hand-spun, but she was evidently convinced that it was a loin cloth. It wasn't, but it was considered best to just put it away whenever she came round.

The entire country was excited about the wedding. It was something happy and exciting and England, in those difficult days after the war, and the world, desperately needed a distraction.

People were filing in slowly as the organ played. People were thrilled to have an August occasion for which to dress and therefore, had trotted out their best. I was seated with Marie Louise, who had also been escorted to her seat early, so we could see and criticize as many outfits as we wished. She and I had our canes at the ready—poor dear, she was even more arthritic than I.

"So many people not here," she muttered. She was fidgeting, trying to get comfortable on the pews. Even with cushions, the benches were hard.

"Yes, but so many are here, more's the pity," I said sharply looking at the groups and groups of people coming in: the King of Denmark, the King of Norway, the

King and Queen of Yugoslavia, the Count and Countess of Barcelona, Queen Helen of Roumania...I was protesting too much, I suppose, something like Grandmama when she complained about the "Royal Mob."

Marie Louise followed my gaze—taking in all the people.

"One person's not here and I'm extremely glad of it," she began, "Willy."

"Dear," my lips twitched at her vehement tone, though I couldn't have agreed more, "it would be hard, he's been dead since 1941."

"Awful man and he was a dreadful young man from what I remember."

"I don't disagree, he *was* a dreadful young man, always wanting his own way and insisting on reading the bible to us all the time," I replied, thinking of those odd walks Ella and I endured with Willy. I certainly did not worry about speaking ill of the dead, nor for that matter lowering my voice. There weren't really any Germans here to offend. Besides, at my age, I had the luxury of not worrying about offending people. It wasn't that I did it purposely, hardly that, but I had never been one to keep quiet. "That's one villain that didn't get what he deserved."

"Lived out his life in that place in Holland, the lap of luxury, I'm sure, chopping wood..."

"Doorn," I supplied.

"Yes, Doorn—marrying that silly Hermine of Reuss with all those incomprehensible Roman numerals."

I hadn't met Willy's second wife, so I had no idea whether she was silly or not. However, my youthful prejudices told me that anyone who tolerated Willy had some kind of emptiness in her upper story. I, like all the English members of the family, avoided him after the Great War. Cousin George said it best when he said that they just didn't understand the bitterness they had instilled in us.

"Roman numerals?" I asked, deciding whether I liked the Countess of Barcelona's gown. I was still not much for fashion, but it didn't stop me from criticizing bad gowns and this was a red-letter day for that.

"My lord, yes, Victoria, you know how the Reuss do it—they have their older and younger line—they start at the beginning of each century counting—I don't understand it. Why can't they just be consecutive like everyone else?"

I shook my head. Marie Louise's mentioning Willy reminded me of perhaps the one good thing I had heard about him. He said towards the end of his life that he was ashamed of Hitler's policies towards the Jews. It wasn't much after what he had been doing his entire life, but his crimes weren't quite as heinous as Hitler's—never that.

I hadn't gone back to Germany much after the disaster at Steen. With no Ernie and Onor or most of the family, things just seemed too sad at Wolfsgarten. I suppose that was wrong of me since Peg was such a darling, so loveable. She and Lu made their home at Wolfsgarten—the New Palace had been bombed out in the War and so their home was permanently there.

How I missed Hesse sometimes, but, in any case, it wasn't the same as it had been. There could never be the idyllic summers at Wolfsgarten or the Heiligenberg anymore and it hurt too much to see so many changes. I didn't want any more hurt.

"Too bad Auntie Beatrice isn't here," Marie Louise was saying. Auntie had died during the war and I missed her. We had shared so much through the years. Actually, there were none of Grandmama's children left.

"Ena is here," I said. Ena, indeed had walked in and was being seated near to us. She and Alphonso had been exiled years ago. They separated and Ena lived alone in Switzerland. Like Alice and Andrew, their marriage had not survived adversity.

"She still looks wonderful," Marie Louis commented. "She always had those blonde good looks. She's one of the few women that looks good in those marcelled hairstyles—not like Missy," she tittered.

Missy, too, was gone. Her son, King Carol II, was now in exile—an execrable young man who treated his mother and family abominably.

"Yes, Missy did, at times, look rather theatrical," I agreed, thinking fondly for a moment about my Malta chum. I tittered a little too, thinking of a picture I saw in the newspaper when Missy visited America in the early twenties. She was sitting with President Calvin Coolidge, who looked immensely uncomfortable and on her head was the most enormous Indian headdress anyone had ever seen. There she was smiling, toothily, as though it were everyday that she wore such things. She was, as the young say today, a game girl.

"I always thought she believed her own publicity too much—'sin like Elinor Glyn on a skin', indeed..." Marie Louise puffed out a bit.

"I don't think she actually commissioned La Glyn to write *Three Weeks*," I chuckled. Missy didn't have to commission anyone to write about her life—the style in which she lived just naturally attracted someone like Madame Glyn. She had written romances about the Russian Court, but her most famous opus had been about a mad and passionate affair between a Balkan Queen and a young man on a continental tour. This Queen, whom the young man worshipfully called "Queen," used to loll about seductively on tiger skins. This was all very obviously patterned on behavior Missy had exhibited.

"She certainly was flamboyant...and so pretty," Marie Louise said wistfully. She looked at me sternly. "You didn't read that book, did you?"

"You should know me better than that," I replied. "I read everything I can get my hands on—I always have—pulp fiction, books on philosophy.... Yes, I read it, and a sillier lot of nonsense I never read...."

"I don't think it was very close to Missy, do you?"

I smiled—she had read the scandalous tome as well.

"Not really—or perhaps just superficially. But there is no question that Missy was rather...er—exotic."

"Yes, but her memoirs were a treat. She really was quite a fine writer—better than Glyn," she laughed. "It was interesting to see what she thought of the old days—all she said and didn't say."

"That's exactly what I thought. We all had so much to hide though so much to reveal. I'm not sure I'd want universal publication of my memoirs or Louis'."

"Did you write memoirs?"

"Yes, but they'll be going into the archives at Broadlands," I said, referring to Dickie and Edwina's home. "I really am not sure that I want them for public consumption. I can't understand this need people have nowadays to reveal all to anyone unfortunate enough to be listening."

"Hmm," she said. She was silent for a moment then picked up a previous thread. "What I couldn't understand was that Missy was one of the few people that really loved Serge—if you don't mind my saying so—I could never understand dearest Ella's involvement with him."

The prerogative of old age I was just talking about. Marie Louise felt that she could say anything she wanted. But, who was I to disapprove?

"Serge was difficult to love," I said after a minute or two. "But, Ella did...and he was utterly devoted to her," which I like to believe was true.

"Well, I suppose there's someone for everyone, but that man made me extremely uncomfortable—there was something unwholesome about him. Ah, well, I don't suppose he deserved such a violent death."

We both sighed thinking of our family members who had met with such terrible brutality.

"Yes..." I agreed seeing my Louise with her husband seated near us. She grinned her grin and waggled her fingers at me. That got me out of my temporary dolor. With her was Alice, who had dressed with considerable care for the nuptials and retained some of her wonderful beauty.

"Alice is looking very well, don't you think?"

"Yes," I replied. "I believe she is feeling quite well."

"Is she a nun or isn't she?"

"She is and, she isn't," I answered, cryptically.

Alice had founded a Sisters of SS Martha and Mary Order in Athens, though she had never actually been received in holy orders. Nevertheless, she always dressed like a nun and throughout the war, she had remained in the city at great peril, nearly starving to death. She had hidden Jews in her apartment, which gratified me. I hoped that Ella, wherever she was, knew that and that it might in some way make up for Serge's oppression.

Yes, my daughter had, somewhat, followed in Ella's footsteps and had braved much danger to do so. I was very proud of her, but couldn't help but think, as I had so many times before, that this really was not what I had wanted for my daughter. She, however, was very happy. Andrew, on the other hand, was a sad and frustrated man in many ways. He died in Monte Carlo in 1944. I hope there was comfort nearby, but I cannot say.

"Your Dickie is back from India. He is, I understand, doing an excellent job there."

I nodded. I didn't like Dickie's assignment as the last Viceroy of India. I felt very strongly that if anything went wrong they would look to him to place the blame—who better? Dickie protested that it wasn't like that at all, but I was, I felt, understandably skeptical. How I longed to visit him there, to go to the places that Louis had told me about all those years ago. How wonderful it would have been to see the incredible palaces, the rajahs, the exotic animals—but I don't think it is today anything like Louis told me. Things had changed so much—had to—after all that was over sixty years ago. Even if I could have persuaded Dickie to take me, I don't think I could make the trip now and that, perhaps, was the thing that bothered me most about old age.

I watched his two girls, Pammy and Patricia walk down the aisle of the church. They were bridesmaids that day. Winston and Clementine walked to their seats just before Lilibet was scheduled to walk down the aisle.

"That man!" Marie Louise hissed. "He always wants attention."

"I don't suppose you can blame him. After all, he was voted out right after the victory. He may have felt a little underappreciated, dear."

Philip appeared and looked exceedingly handsome in his naval uniform. Before the engagement was announced in July, he had become a naturalized citizen. Curiously, he took the surname Mountbatten, though that was certainly not his father's name—nor when I think about it, was it his mother's. Alice had been a Battenberg until she married Andrew. Nevertheless, Philip became plain Lieutenant Philip Mountbatten, RN. Bertie created him Duke of Edinburgh and a host of other titles just before the wedding. I was quite warmed by the Edinburgh title...after all, Uncle Affie had had a very strong hand in deciding Louis' career. It was nice that the Dukedom, which had become extinct after Uncle Affie's death, was inherited, in a way, by Louis' grandson. I liked the tidiness of it all.

"Philip looks very fine," Marie Louise whispered. "One can certainly see what Lilibet sees in him."

"I won't disagree," I smiled. He had put his hand on the hilt of his sword and was waiting for his bride. "That was Louis' sword," I told her and without warning, tears came to my eyes. Marie Louise took my hand and we waited for the bride...dear Marie Louise, she had always been a comfort. She was one of the finest women I knew.

Lilibet looked absolutely marvelous in her gown. She had an excellent figure and I knew that she was quite the sportswoman.

"Can she smile any more broadly," Marie Louise tittered again.

"She does look awfully pleased with herself. It's always a treat to see a royal bride that's happy—and so rare."

"That's not the case with you," she answered, and I realized I'd blundered. But Aribert of Anhalt was so long ago—surly that didn't hurt her anymore.

"No, I was always happy with Louis—never anything else."

"Lilibet's a good girl, with a wonderful sense of the history of her family. She's always interested in any stories I can tell her about anyone in the family."

I knew Lilibet was a fine, serious young woman who, at the moment, was joyously happy and I hoped that Philip was too. My worry was that he was such a private person—and as the eventual consort of the Queen of England, he would be in the spotlight whether he liked it or not. I hadn't any idea how well that would sit with him. He had made a snide remark to me about the service being broadcast over the wireless. It was obvious he was uncomfortable being on display. Like Alicky...

The service went by in a blur. I usually didn't pay much attention to such things—there is a point where they all seem the same. We all went into the study to sign the marriage certificate: Nada, Edwina, Dickie, Louise, Alice, Patricia Ramsay, who had been Princess Patricia of Connaught and I.

As strange as it sounds, when I signed, I felt like someone was pressing my hand, so the signature looks wobbly on the certificate. I believe that Louis was signing with me. When I stupidly told my children about this afterward, they all pooh-poohed the notion. I could hear their minds clicking: "Mama is imagining things," "Mama is eighty-four years old and losing her grip." But I knew what I felt and I knew he was there and was glad of it.

When the service concluded, Lilibet and Philip bowed and curtsied to her parents and May. Philip looked directly at me and I smiled and Marie Louise again took my hand as tears brimmed my eyes.

It wasn't fair. Louis should have been here to see this. His grandson would be the husband of the Queen and no one could make remarks about our family or his ancestry anymore.

Life isn't fair, Grandmama would certainly have said to me. She wouldn't let me get all soppy and tear-drenched. That would have been a prerogative she would have reserved for herself, for as long as she wanted.

"Grandmama would have loved all of this—the ceremony the splendor and all the royalties attending," Marie Louise said with great satisfaction.

"Yes," I agreed, as we both slowly, very slowly, stood up. An equerry came with Marie Louise's wheelchair. "Grandmama would have loved it all."

I smiled broadly.

II
Buckingham Palace, December, 1948

I dressed very carefully this morning. I didn't want my great-grandson Charles to be ashamed of his great-Grandmama at his christening. I put on the gray dress I had worn for the wedding, and put on my usual black gloves and shoes. I had Pye comb my hair and brush it back the way I always do, but oh, I wish Ella had been there to do it; she always did such a good job. She made my hair look truly lovely. I sighed.

My life was mostly like this now. Although I don't think it was self-deception to think that I was as sharp as ever—after all, I could always see an Agatha Christie red herring without any problem—but I did tend to sprinkle my day with memories from the distant past. I sometimes believed that this was due to so much of the suppressed pain I hadn't allowed myself to experience. I had read enough psychology books to know that it seeps out eventually, like lethal gasses. I was glad though, that my particular dementia was only living somewhat in the past, with all my benign ghosts about me. It was almost as if I had one foot each in two worlds.

There was always my family and I, taking sepia brownie pictures of one another, sailing on large yachts, walking through the countryside of Germany or Russia, attending Grandmama for tea, sneaking cigarettes, showing ourselves at some ceremony or another, looking regal, but always complaining and gossiping about one another.

And then there was the much less colorful world of today. The world where my son Louis was back, much to my great satisfaction, in the Royal Navy. He had done a first rate job in India—nothing about which anyone could complain. Through his skill and diligence, we were able to somewhat smoothly hand India back to the Indian people. Oh, there would be problems ahead, as there always were for countries who found themselves independent, but I believe that Louis did Britain proud. He would be First Sea Lord someday, I was sure of it. His daughters were also doing well, Patricia was happily married and I expected Pammy would be in time, as well.

Louise thrived in Stockholm—she adored her Swedish family and they loved her, calling her Aunt Louise. Her only heartbreak was that her little daughter, born soon after her marriage, was still-born and no other babies came. She continued her social work as Crown Princess, and had already made a place for herself in the hearts of the Swedes.

Alice would be there today. She continued to live in Athens, doing the work she loved and so was, I believe, content, as were her daughters. I didn't see much of my granddaughters anymore. They still weren't welcome at family celebrations in England. Philip, though, was happy as could be and Lilibet was thoroughly enjoying being a navy wife. It was her chance, for a while, to be an ordinary wife.

It was a shivery cold December morning and I so felt the cold—even more than I used to which is saying something. I would wake up in the morning and gaze around my bedroom and say, usually out loud, "What? Still here?"

But this morning I did not. I was extremely glad to be here this day. It was another red-letter day, as the wedding had been. Today, we would christen little Charles Philip Arthur George, Philip and Lilibet's first born—I imagine my happiness would have been complete if they had given him "Louis" as one of his names, but, never mind. It would have to be enough just to have the satisfaction that he would be king someday.

The christening took place at the Music Room at Buckingham Palace and much of the family was in attendance. Charles was a lusty looking child of about a month and was wrapped up in the christening robe that my Grandmama had used for her children.

I took Philip aside briefly. I dug into my purse—not only had I brought the pearl in its original box, but I had written a long letter, that had taken me several days, to tell its story, as Louis had told me on our wedding night. Thank heavens, my memory was sharp and I seemed, in almost exact recall, to recollect the entire evening. Of course, there were some parts that were not to be in the letter, but the beautiful story about the Rajah who had never found true love and the faithful little pearl fisher, would be given, now to Philip and whichever of his children he determined would be most worthy—though that, I think, is perhaps a silly way of putting it.

"I want you to have this Philip. You and Lilibet can decide what to do with it later, but it is now time for me to pass it on."

He looked at me for a moment and though he had been in motion, greeting everyone and in general looking the proud Papa, now, for a moment, he was still.

"What is it, Grandmama?" he asked with uncharacteristic gentleness.

"It would take too long to explain about it now, dear, but I have written a letter that you and Lilibet can peruse at your leisure. It should tell you everything. Suffice it to say that this is the most precious thing that I have ever owned."

I looked at him and I could see after a moment that my hard-boiled grandson had just a trace of tears in his eyes. I handed him the box and letter and felt, just for a heartbeat, empty.

"Thank you, Grandmama, for whatever it is."

"I entrust you to decide who should have it, but Philip, dear, choose well. It's very important that you choose well."

He patted my hand and put the box with the pearl and the letter in his jacket pocket. He leaned over and kissed me.

"Thank you," he said softly and walked away and I felt happy, and bereft at the same time.

The service, itself, took little time, but, as with the wedding, I had been to so many of these, I rather wandered in my mind as this one progressed. Alice had to nearly shake me awake when it was over, though my eyes weren't closed.

"Mama, you're not paying attention," she told me sternly.

"What for?" I asked with a little smile. "It always happens the same way."

Louise, who was also sitting with me, giggled and the company looked at us. It was always the same, I was making a scene and one daughter was embarrassed while the other laughed with me.

We posed for pictures, I being one of the Godparents, along with Bertie, Elizabeth, Olav of Norway, Prince George of Greece, Dickie's Patricia, and Lilibet's Uncle David Bowes-Lyon. The photographer was seating us, I on one end and Elizabeth on the other end, and we all looked into the flash.

It was wonderful not to have to wait minutes for the exposures. Our faces never appeared as glum as they used to in the old days. As the flash exploded I was back for a millisecond at the Heiligenberg. I had snuck away from Aunt Lenchen, Papa and the company and saw Ella coming to me with her arms held out, wide.

"Dearest Vicky, you got away," she said gently, smiling. "I told you that story about it being cold was too silly, but you're here now and, look, there is Serge," and sure enough, loitering by the fountain, there he was, tall, austere and ram-rod straight, waiting for us.

We walked over to him, and he took both of our arms.

"Serge," Ella said quietly, happily, "here we are."

We walked arm in arm to that little glade, just on the hill, that had such a wide view of the house. There was Liko, smiling and looking handsome in one of his uniforms, planning some mischief. There was a decidedly teasing look on his face. Next to him and, as always, watching him intently was his younger brother Franzjos. Thora and Marie Louise were talking with Alicky and Irène and, as usual, were pointing at Ella and me and giggling. Bothersome little girls. Ella and I looked at each other and smiled.

She looked over my head, saw something, and waved, "Here we are Louis," she cried, and I turned—now we were all together.

There he was, walking towards us in his naval uniform, looking as handsome and distinguished as a lieutenant. There was a smile on his tanned face and his brown eyes were laughing and squinting as the sun got into them.

I broke away from Serge and ran up to him, ignoring the titters from the younger girls. I had something important to tell him. When I reached him, I took both of his hands in mine, and looked up at him.

"Victoria, you're all out of breath, have you and Liko been chasing each other again?"

"As if I would, Louis, I'm way too old for that and I'm not such a tom-boy."

"You are, but I wouldn't want it any other way," he grinned.

"Louis, I have something wonderful to tell you," I looked up at his dear face, and my heart pounded at his nearness. "Our great-grandson is going to be the King of England."

He smiled, elated, pulled me close and said whispered softly, "Does it really matter?"

I laughed for a moment with jubilation and then whispered back, breathlessly, finally, "No."

Printed in the United States
121251LV00003B/6/P